BOTH KNEW
WOULD PAY IF

But it was impossible to deny the attraction, the inexplicable bond that seemed to exist between them. Slowly, Duncan lowered his head, and with a sense of approbation Grayson rose up on tiptoe to meet his kiss. His eagerness appeased some faint lingering doubt deep inside her, and she gave herself without reserve, trusting that he found her the most desirable of women, trusting that now he was as helplessly beguiled as she.

She twined her arms around his back, opened her mouth to the probe of his tongue. The flick of it against her own was a revelation, and she went dizzy and soft in response. She had never felt this before; she had never known that in an instant two lives could touch so powerfully, so poignantly. . . .

MIDNIGHT LACE

A stunning novel of dark, undeniable passion
by the national bestselling author, Elizabeth Kary

PRAISE FOR
LOVE, HONOR & BETRAY:

"A great story, charged with emotion. . . . These two lovers will not soon be forgotten."
—*Johanna Lindsey*

"Thrilling and evocative . . . a page turner!"
—*Roberta Gellis*

Also by Elizabeth Kary

LOVE, HONOR AND BETRAY
LET NO MAN DIVIDE
FROM THIS DAY ONWARD

MIDNIGHT LACE

ELIZABETH KARY

J

JOVE BOOKS, NEW YORK

MIDNIGHT LACE

A Jove Book / published by arrangement with
the author

PRINTING HISTORY
Jove edition / October 1990

ISBN: 0-515-10420-5

Jove Books are published by The Berkley Publishing Group,
200 Madison Avenue, New York, New York 10016.
The name "JOVE" and the "J" logo
are trademarks belonging to Jove Publications, Inc.

PRINTED IN THE UNITED STATES OF AMERICA

10 9 8 7 6 5 4 3 2 1

TO MY FAMILY:
Mom, Ken, Keith and Renée,
and baby Courtney Lynn.
You asked for it.

Acknowledgments

Writing *Midnight Lace* provided me with an exciting new challenge. As I learned, rewrote, and struggled with the story and the research, a number of people were on hand to offer me help and encouragement.

In the area of research, I could not have done without the assistance of Charles Brown at the St. Louis Mercantile Library Association and the friendly, caring staff of the Webster Groves Public Library.

I also drew invaluable information from my friend, the ultimate Anglophile, Marian Horton. Your patience and generosity in offering me your books and expertise were wonderful resources for which I am truly grateful.

Midnight Lace was not the easiest project I've ever undertaken, but I had wonderful friends, from both inside and outside the writing community, who were there for me with cheers and pom-poms. They are Norma Beishir, Kim Bush, Debbie Dirckx-Norris, Christie Boyle, Jill Marie Landis, Linda Madl, and Libby Beach. I would never have made it to the very last page without your help and support.

I would also like to thank my wonderful husband, Tom, who understood when the house was a mess, when there was no dinner on the table, and when we ran a little short of necessities of life like diet Coke and toilet tissue. Without you, Tom, there would be no romance in my life.

I would also like to offer special thanks to Eileen Dreyer who single-handedly taught me the intricacies of writing mystery and suspense. You never lost patience, not even when making me understand was like trying to teach a fifteen-year-old linebacker to tango.

And in closing, a special word for Murphy, who, in an odd way, came very close to being a collaborator on this book. You certainly made things interesting.

London
April 1844

Prologue

THE LAST WHORLS OF NIGHT MIST LAY THICK AND CLOSE TO THE ground as the old lamplighter made his early morning rounds. He moved slowly, his joints aching with the damp as he extinguished the pale hovering glow of the hissing gas lamps. He had walked this route for more than twenty years, knew every house and every tree, every family that claimed Mayfair as its home. Yet as he moved between the dark familiar landmarks, passing from one wavering puddle of lamplight to the next, an inexplicable chill traced a pathway up his spine.

All at once there was something unsettling about the streets he knew so well, something ominous about the sound of his footsteps sounding on the cobblestones, something ghostly and sinister about the shifting banks of fog. The garden walls loomed high at the edges of the sidewalk; the morning air seemed dank and stale, as if breathed from a freshly opened tomb. The stillness swelled around him with a presence of its own, as menacing as a specter in the dark, as disturbing as a half-remembered nightmare.

Even as he turned to glance behind him, he knew there was no reason for the tension that had suddenly clustered between his shoulderblades, for the knot of numbing dread that seemed to tighten in his chest. He had spent the larger part of his life in this half-world between night and day; never had he known this kind of apprehension.

His senses strained to probe the dimness. Had he heard the rustle of movement down the lane to his left? Was there someone lying in wait for him in the bushes just ahead? He moved forward with faltering footsteps, feeling his heart beating high in his throat, with his hands clenched tight to still their trembling.

The clang of a church bell tolled the hour, and from somewhere near at hand came the deep, hollow baying of a hound. A shudder burst along his nerves. Sweat beaded on his brow as he succumbed to a dread he could not name.

In response he quickened his pace, intent on finishing up his work and seeking out his bed. His daughter Jenny would be awake when he got home. She would make a steaming cup of strong dark tea to calm his fears and warm his bones. He had but a little way to go, and the lamps would all be dark.

But as he reached the gas lamp on the corner of South Audley Street, he came upon a bundle lying shrouded in the shadows. At first it seemed nothing more than a clutter of old rags. Yet as he neared it, he could see it was the figure of a woman, huddled cold and still before him.

He halted for a moment staring down at her. What was a woman doing here at such an hour? Was she sleeping? Had she had too much to drink? In other parts of London public drunkenness was a way of life, but in Mayfair such behavior was never seen, never tolerated. He nudged the woman with his foot, and when she did not stir, he set his ladder and equipment aside.

"Miss?" he muttered gruffly, bending over her. "Here now, miss, you can't sleep here."

The woman gave no answer. The quiet that hung around them seemed to grow even more oppressive and menacing.

"Are you all right, miss?" he asked with growing solicitude. "Are you ill?"

The lamplighter's hands shook as he reached for the woman's shoulder. He gently rolled her onto her back. She came limply, bonelessly, her face contorted and pale.

She was dead. The realization came to him in a rush. His heart leaped hard against his ribs. A jolt of panic sent shivers down his arms. A swell of sickness made him gag.

Reflexively he recoiled from her, staring in horror at his discovery. Then, as if in recompense, he fell to his knees beside her and gathered the woman in his arms. She was young, about Jenny's age, seventeen or eighteen at the most. From her sturdy build and plain dark clothes, he guessed she was a maid in service at one of the houses in the neighborhood.

Perhaps it was her youth, or that she reminded him of his own daughter home safe in her bed, that made him pull the woman closer. As he did, her head lolled against his arm, exposing the length of her alabaster throat. With her head hanging back, he could see that the buttons of her bodice were ripped from their holes, that long deep scratches marred the flesh beneath her chin. It came to him all at once that the girl had not died a natural death. The life had been wrung from her lithe young body; her neck had been broken clean.

Another shudder eddied through him, and he swung around, fearing her assailant might still be near. But the streets around them were silent and empty. With the high garden walls crowding to the edge of the sidewalks, with the faint graying of the light, there was no place for a man to hide. And though the old lamplighter listened, there was no sound of footfalls, of breathing, of imminent peril.

Convinced that there was no one about, the lamplighter turned his thoughts to what he should do. Should he raise an alarm? Should he shout for help? It seemed wrong to raise a hue and cry, as if it might unintentionally disturb her.

Would it be best to leave the woman alone in the shadows and seek out the police? he wondered as he rocked the pale still figure in his arms. Should he remain beside her until someone came?

It was cold and dark on the deserted street, and though the woman was far from caring, the old man could not bring himself to abandon her. Soon the costermongers who sold their wares to the mansions surrounding them would be making their rounds, or perhaps the constable himself might come upon them. The lamplighter elected to stay with the woman a little longer, thinking that someone would find them soon. Through the trees he could see the sky was brightening. It was almost dawn.

One

IT WAS ALMOST DAWN, THE BLEAKEST AND LONELIEST TIME OF DAY. As Grayson Ware stared out her window, she was one with the pale and dismal morn. She felt as frail as the filmy light that sifted through the glass, as fragile as the mist that wafted across the garden. Watching the approach of a fine new day, she knew she was as incapable of changing the cycle of daylight and dark as she was of changing the course her birth had fated her to follow.

Last night she had been made irrevocably aware that her life was not her own, that what she felt or wanted mattered not at all. She had been betrothed against her will to Harry Torkington, the Duke of Stinton, a man she could not abide. That her guardian could care so little for her feelings angered and appalled her, and Gray knew she would never forgive her uncle Warren for seeking this blatantly cold-blooded alliance with the Stinton lands and riches.

To be fair, she had to admit that when she made her debut three years before, her uncle had been more than willing to let her make her choice from among the dozens of eligible bachelors who were dancing in attendance. But none of them had pleased her, and her refusals were only partially based in the suspicion that it was her own vast fortune and not her charming self that they were after. If truth be told, she had no aspirations to be the simpering silent wife of an influential man. Gray had a calling of her own that could never be expressed within the confines of a conventional society marriage. And now, with her wedding to the duke set for two months hence, she had no hope of achieving the dream she had jealously harbored since childhood. For someone of her station that dream might well be unattainable, but that made it no less vital to her well-being, made its loss no less painful and devastating.

Her feelings of regret made the reality of her engagement all the more difficult to endure, and Grayson stirred from the chair where she had passed most of the night, alternately weeping and cursing her fate. It seemed now that her misery could no longer be contained within the walls of her bedroom, within the halls of her guardian's home. The room was too close, too confining, like the future her guardian had planned for her, like the life she had been forced to live since the day she had been orphaned nearly eighteen years before. With escape on her mind, she donned her velvet slippers and a ruffled satin wrapper.

Noiselessly Gray tiptoed from her bedchamber, through the tall marble columns, and down the staircase to the elegant reception hall. The long picture gallery at the back of the house was on her left, and she crossed the expanse of polished marble to a pair of tall French doors that led to the terrace and garden beyond.

The filmy mists of morning swiftly penetrated the layers of delicate satin and lace, but she welcomed the chill. The freshness seemed to clear her head, to remind her that there were worlds beyond the one that had ensnared her in its web of propriety and convention. Grayson breathed deep, letting the cool air fill her lungs, letting it carry away her anger and confusion.

The sky was just beginning to lighten, turning powdery blue and apricot with the hint of the rising sun. She paused for a moment beside the graceful stone balustrade and looked out across the garden's manicured boxwood hedges, the three-tiered fountain, and the precise arcs of her aunt Julo's rose garden, laid out across the lawn. Toward the center of the yard was a folly in the shape of a circular Greek temple. It had been built at the end of the last century when pseudo-Classical buildings were such popular affectations. Through the drifting mist, it looked isolated and inviting. Descending the terrace stairs, Gray made her way across the grass toward the tiny limestone structure.

As she walked, the silvery dew-wet lawn whispered beneath her slippers and dampened the hem of her nightgown and wrapper. But Gray hardly noticed. She needed time alone, time to think, time to make peace with the future that lay before her and the dissolution of her most cherished dreams. Perhaps it was a futile hope that a few solitary moments at the beginning of a new day could help her reconcile her feelings, but Grayson knew she had to find a way to live with what was to come.

Her feet crunched on the pebble walk as she made her way to the steps of the rotunda, but when she reached the top, she could see that the structure was already occupied. A man had taken up residence.

All Gray had wanted was to find a modicum of peace in the deserted garden, and without so much as a by-your-leave, someone had usurped her only refuge.

The man lay sprawled on one of the stone benches in the center of the pavilion, stretched full length and covered by his cloak. A tall beaver hat was set on the floor by his head, and beside it a dark silk neckcloth lay pooled on the well-worn stone. A scuffed pair of Hessian boots had collapsed sideways and lay toe to toe at the opposite end of the bench, and the man's stockinged feet protruded from beneath the hem of his makeshift blanket.

Gray skulked closer to get a better look at the intruder. His clothes indicated that he was a gentleman, and she wondered if he had been one of the guests at her betrothal party the night before. It was more than possible that he had crept off into the garden to sleep off the effects of the whiskey punch. But as she peered down into his sleeping face, she was sure she did not recognize him.

Still, there was something infinitely compelling in the rugged cut of his features: his broad, intelligent brow; the angular width of his cheekbones; the square of his chin and jaw, shaded faintly gray with the night's dark growth of whiskers. His nose was narrow, high-bridged, aristocratic. His mouth was wide, well-defined, and slightly curled, as if it had been molded for arrogance—or was it pleasure?

Even in sleep, there was a ruddy flush of health and vitality to his skin, and she could see a faint whiteness at the corners of his eyes, as if he had spent long hours squinting into the sun. His hair was thick as thatch, unfashionably long, the shiny brown of chestnuts. It fell back from his face in heavy strands that flared against the wadded-up frock coat he was using for a pillow. Although he had not spoken a word, something about this stranger intrigued and captivated Grayson, and suddenly it seemed imperative that she learn who he was and why he had selected her uncle's folly as his bedchamber.

Though she was loath to disturb his sleep, she reached out to touch his shoulder. But as she did, his fingers lanced out to close around her wrist. As he tightened his hand, he yanked her toward him, dragging her down onto the bench. In an instant she was on her back with him sprawled above her, his eyes flashing dangerously, and his face hardened with suspicion.

He had moved with such speed that Grayson was not quite sure how he had managed to reverse their positions. Though she struggled to break free, he easily subdued her. He held her roughly, his fingers clamped around her wrists in a merciless grip. Yet in spite of the slight pain, her skin tingled at his touch.

Then all at once Grayson's senses were flooded with impressions: of his considerable weight pinning her to the bench, of his chest crushing her unbound breasts, of the firmness of his thighs against her legs. Her muscles coiled warm and tight in response. His alluring scent of wine and brandy and bay rum swirled around her, and in the roaring silence, his breathing was every bit as fast and as unsteady as her own. She was aware of the slide of satin against rough wool as he shifted to more effectively subdue her, was aware of his seemingly limitless strength lying poised above her.

Helplessly she raised her gaze to his and found she could not look away. His eyes were a clear, translucent blue, the color of sunlight through seawater and every bit as dazzling. Gray drew breath to ask for explanations, but the air seemed trapped in her chest, and she went dizzy with the effort.

"Who are you?" she finally managed to gasp. "What are you doing sleeping in my garden?"

His hold on her seemed to slacken, but though she tried, he would not let her twist away.

"I might as well ask you who you are and why you are disturbing me." His voice was low and cool, his speech faintly upper class but diluted somehow by an accent she couldn't quite place.

As he held her pinioned with his weight to the unyielding stone, Grayson realized that the man was taking a thorough inventory of her person, and that knowledge did nothing to calm her misgivings. She was suddenly aware of how early it was, of how far the folly was from the house, and of how isolated they seemed to be. If he was not a gentleman or chose to behave in a reprehensible manner, could she make herself heard at the stables in the mews at the back of the garden or draw the attention of the servants in the mansion? Panic flooded along her nerves, and she could feel her quickening pulse bound against his thumbs.

Then all at once the stranger let her up, moving with an unconscious lazy grace. In their tussle her wrapper had become untied, baring the translucent lawn nightgown beneath, and her skirts had ridden high, showing a good deal of her calves and thighs. Mortified by the display, Grayson hurried to restore her clothes to some semblance of modesty, while the man took exaggeratedly careful note of everything she was doing. Under his bold, faintly contemptuous gaze her fingers stumbled at their task, and the intensity of his observation did strange, inexplicable things to the rhythm of her heart.

When she had satisfactorily repaired her disarray, Grayson squared her shoulders and pinned the man with her most imperious stare. "Well, then, who are you? And why are you sleeping in the garden?"

The censure of her usually effective stare seemed lost on the intruder. Instead of being intimidated by it, he merely bobbed his head in greeting. "Captain Duncan Palmer of the good ship *Citation* at your service, madam. And to whom do I have the pleasure of addressing myself?"

His formal, almost pompous words seemed ridiculous in this situation, and an uncomfortable flush rose in Grayson's face. Still, she glared down her nose at him and replied in equally stilted tones, "I'm Lady Grayson Ware, the Duke of Fennel's ward."

"Well, well, a real English lady, are you?" A hint of amusement laced his tone. "And may I ask why your ladyship is prowling around the garden at this ungodly hour of the day?"

Grayson drew a breath that added two inches to her height. "I have every right to be anywhere on these grounds I choose," she sputtered, angry both at herself for answering his question and at Palmer for forcing the explanation from her. "Why is it you are here?"

"I wasn't feeling well last night and let myself in through the gate to take refuge from those who might have done me mischief on the street."

"But the garden gate is always locked," Gray protested.

"Only to those lacking certain illicit skills."

Grayson was stunned by his response. She had expected some far less blatant admission of his misconduct.

"You were too drunk to find your way home," she accused,

having heard from reputable sources that sailors spent their time in port searching for comfort and companionship at the bottom of a bottle.

"I hate to shatter your illusions," the man confessed with a rise of his impressive wedge-shaped brows, "but that simply wasn't the case."

His mood changed with his denial. It was as if something warm had gone suddenly cold, as if something lighthearted had become inexplicably serious. While Grayson pondered the change, Palmer pulled on his boots and rose to stand over her.

Lying beneath him and sitting beside him, she'd had no idea he was so tall. Or so well built. He filled out his clothes most admirably. His shoulders seemed to block out the rising sun, and they tapered to a wide chest, a flat stomach, narrow hips, and long sturdy legs encased in ink-black trousers.

Sitting while he stood seemed to put her at a distinct disadvantage, so Grayson came to her feet, though even her considerable height was not a match for his. It put the top of her head on a level with the collar of his shirt, and she could see the same ruddy tan that tinted his face ran down beyond the opening. Indeed, she found herself wondering if he was the same warm honey color all over.

The indecency of the thought kindled a new fire in her cheeks. No man had ever made her wonder such a thing before. Appalled by her own curiosity, Grayson looked away.

"Grayson?"

In spite of the fact that his manner of address took unacceptable liberties, there was something very pleasant about the sound of her name on his lips. And though she wished she could, she found it impossible to deny him her attention.

As she raised her head, her gaze locked with his. His eyes were the most extraordinary color, pale cerulean blue, as if brilliantly lit from within. As they strayed over her, they warmed, darkened. A soft, slow smile drew the corners of his mouth. Gray felt his gaze drop to her lips, and a tingling response that began at her toes swept upward through her body. She became intensely aware of Duncan Palmer beside her, of the heat of him reflected across her breasts and hips, his warmth a teasing promise along the fronts of her thighs. The faint spicy scent of bay rum prickled her nostrils and rose in her head in dizzying whorls.

With slow deliberation he raised his hand, his long fingers

probing the hair at the nape of her neck, his callused thumb testing the skin along her throat. A shiver of something glittery and bright sifted through her, as if her blood had turned to French champagne. She was filled with a strange breathless fluttering that was tempered by a sense of fierce and imminent peril. Grayson willed herself to pull away, but the hypnotic stroke of Duncan's thumb against her skin held her helplessly immobile.

As if he knew he had overcome her reticence, Palmer's smile widened, deepened, bowed.

In response Gray wet her lips. As he lowered his head, she drew a long uneven breath, anticipating and dreading what was to come.

But nothing happened. Duncan's lashes drooped, and when they rose again, the glow in his eyes was gone. It had been replaced by a certain reserve, a certain cold disdain that was more unsettling than even his frank perusal had been.

Grayson stared up at him feeling stunned, cheated, bereft. In a larger sense it was not an unfamiliar feeling. Weren't her expectations often left unfulfilled?

Then he was dropping his hand, stepping away. "I thank you for the hospitality of your garden, my lady," he began. "I hope my using it as a refuge has done it no real harm."

Without waiting for a response, Palmer bent and gathered up his cloak and frock coat, his top hat and cravat. He was leaving, and Grayson had no idea why she felt so reluctant to see him go.

"Captain Palmer?"

He turned to her with a half-smile on his lips, with the early morning sun glinting in his hair. "Yes?"

She hesitated, not knowing what it was she wanted of him.

"Will—will you be in England long?"

He regarded her curiously before he gave her his reply. "Only until my ship's repaired. It's in dry dock down in Portsmouth."

"Ah, well, I hope you'll have a safe voyage home."

"Thank you for your good wishes. I'll be glad to get back to New York."

He was an American, she realized. That explained his subtle arrogance, the strange cadence to his words.

"But I'll remember meeting you, Lady Grayson," he continued as he strode toward the stairs, "as one of the most pleasurable parts of my stay in England."

With the slightest of bows he took his leave, crossing the garden at a comfortable lope, his long shadow preceding him to the wooden gate. As Grayson watched, he fiddled with the lock and then, without a parting glance, closed the wooden panel behind him.

She stood staring after him for a few moments more, feeling confused and abandoned, shaken and unsure. With Palmer's departure, the questions and concerns that had brought Grayson to the garden returned with devastating force. Duncan Palmer's presence had provided a momentary diversion, but now she had to acknowledge her problems again.

She sank to the wide stone bench once more, overwhelmed by all her encounter with the American had made her forget: her detestable betrothal, her feelings of betrayal and entrapment, the precious dreams that would be forfeit to the future her uncle had planned. The bench was cold and rough beneath her, and the comforting warmth he had briefly imparted to the stone, like Duncan Palmer, was gone.

Once out on the street, Captain Duncan Palmer secured the high garden gate behind him and glanced around. On the nearest corner at South Audley Street a group of people had gathered, and something about their demeanor spoke of confusion and alarm. From where he stood, Duncan could see the gleam of satin livery among the shabbily dressed street vendors, and a sprinkling of fine, dark broadcloth frock coats was evident in the crowd, as if even some of the neighborhood gentlemen had come by to discover what this disturbance was all about. Towering above their heads was the tall black hat of the local constable. It was an intriguing scene, and in other circumstances, Duncan might well have indulged his curiosity. But this morning he was far too intent on returning to the town house on Berkeley Square to let himself be waylaid.

That had been his destination the night before when the headache had come upon him, forcing him to take refuge where he could. The migraines had been with him most of his life, and though he tried to exert a modicum of control, they still struck him unrelentingly. This was not the first time one had overcome him before he had been able to reach home and his medicine, but it was the first time anything even vaguely pleasant had come as a result.

As he moved briskly up the street, thoughts of the crowd faded from Palmer's mind in favor of the memory of the glorious young woman who had awakened him. None of the fashionable ladies at the levee his cousin had coerced him into attending the night before could have held a candle to her beauty. Gazing at Grayson Ware this morning had been like staring into the sun. Perhaps it was the vibrancy of her coloring that had made such an indelible impression: the blazing green of her eyes, the rich deep red of her hair. In contrast her skin had been luminous, parchment pale, and he knew from a single touch along her throat that it was as delicate and sweet-scented as gardenia petals.

A smile tugged at the corners of Duncan's mouth at the memory of awakening to find Lady Grayson hovering over him. With her free-flowing hair a glowing nimbus around her shoulders, with curiosity alive in her face, she had been utterly enchanting. That she was comely and well formed had made it his very definite pleasure to get to know her more intimately.

The tweak at the edges of his lips became a full-blown grin.

Nevertheless, Grayson had proved herself every inch the lady by managing, in even so compromising a circumstance, to retain her cool and imperious demeanor. When another woman would have squalled for help, Grayson had simply glared at him and demanded to know what he was doing in her garden.

Duncan chuckled as he remembered.

Once she had escaped the press of his body and righted her clothes, Lady Gray had greeted him as if they had met on the edge of a dance floor with a full retinue of chaperons looking on, treated him as if by merely conversing with him she was giving him a privilege granted to only a chosen few. But in spite of her aristocratic arrogance, it had been no lie when he had told Grayson that meeting her was the highlight of his stay in England. But then, a single, even marginally pleasant occurrence in this cursed country of his birth was something to be remarked upon.

Palmer was so caught up in his thoughts of Grayson Ware that he reached Berkeley Square with surprising alacrity. As he passed beneath the iron arch that guarded the door to the town house, he noted that the white limestone steps had been thoroughly scrubbed and the hanging lamp that was left burning during the night had already been extinguished. It was a testimony to the care with which his cousin had trained the servants in Duncan's long absence, and he was pleased once more by the evidence of Quentin Palmer's diligence on his behalf.

As he let himself into the town house, Forbes, the butler,

materialized to greet him. Without a word of reproof the man took his cape and hat. His uncle Farleigh's American butler, Duncan reflected, would never have practiced such restraint.

"Have Barnes attend me as soon as he is up," Duncan ordered as he made his way toward the stairs. "I have need of bathwater, a shave, and a change of clothes before I go on about my business."

"I believe Mr. Barnes is already in your lordship's rooms," the man informed him in dulcet tones. "And I will have a footman bring up bathwater as soon as it is ready."

As he headed toward the master suite on the second floor, Duncan was reminded of how beautiful this town house really was. Designed by Robert Adam himself, it was graceful and perfectly proportioned, with an elegance that seemed evident in every detail. As the early morning sun peered into the central stairwell, the steps shone with the rich honeyed warmth of polished marble, and the classical swags and medallions gleamed white and pristine against the saffron-colored walls. The curve of the steps flowed sinuously upward, so that the columns at the landing formed a dramatic entry to the forum of public rooms that occupied the first floor of the house. With an uncomfortable clutch of nostalgia Duncan remembered how often he had seen his parents standing here, greeting the ranks of bejeweled ladies and dandified gentlemen who had attended his mother's levees. But that had been long ago, at a time when the house was filled with fascinating people, with laughter, with his mother's warmth and vivacity. But for all its impeccable beauty the house stood silent and empty now, and Duncan regretted the change for more reasons than he cared to contemplate.

Struck by the discord of the memories with the advent of a fine new day, Palmer frowned and continued to his chambers on the floor above. It was just such unguarded moments that seemed destined to blight his stay in London. Being here stirred too many of the regrets, too many of the griefs he had fought for years to overcome. If he'd had his way, he would never again have set foot on English soil. He didn't want to confront the ghosts of the past, and he didn't want to stir up memories best left undisturbed. He could hardly wait for the repairs to the *Citation* to be completed so he could escape the curse of his English identity.

When Duncan reached them, Ryan Barnes was indeed in the suite of rooms at the front of the house, brushing imaginary lint from one of Palmer's impeccably tailored jackets. Barnes seemed not at all concerned that his master had elected to stay away all night, though there was something about his demeanor that made Duncan feel he must explain. Perhaps it was their long association or the fact that it was Ryan who had accompanied him to America when he was a confused and frightened lad that made Palmer feel he owed the valet some kind of accounting for his absence. Ryan had been his only link to England when Duncan was sent to live with his uncle in New York, and that had left them with a somewhat different relationship than a peer and his manservant usually shared.

"I'll wager you're wondering where I've been," Duncan began, removing his coat.

"Where you spend your nights, my lord, is none of my concern," the smaller man answered carefully, continuing his brushing. "My only thought is for your comfort and how I best can serve you."

Duncan frowned at the reply. Since their enforced return to England, Ryan's manner toward him had subtly altered. He was suddenly saying "my lord" in the place of "captain," a mark of cool reserve on Ryan's part that seemed to point up the disparity of their roles as master and servant. Palmer did not like the change, and for the second time in as many minutes, he found himself fervently wishing that the *Citation* had never foundered in the storm or put in to Portsmouth for repairs.

"Since you're bound to see to my every whim," the taller man began irritably, "I want a bath and a bite of breakfast before I set out to meet with my uncle's partner."

"You won't be waiting to breakfast with Master Quentin in the dining room?" Barnes's lips were drawn together above the wisp of pointed beard, and his round, ruddy face registered surprise and disapproval of his master's ungentlemanly ways. After his humble beginnings as a common laborer on the family estate in Dorset, Barnes had embraced the role of gentleman's gentleman with a vengeancc as fearful as it was benign. It was he who had been responsible for much of Duncan's upbringing, for Duncan's attitudes, for Duncan's strict adherence to the proprieties that marked him, even after the years as a common sailor, as a member of the aristocracy.

"I'll warrant that after a night of revels, Quentin won't be up until ten or eleven o'clock," Duncan observed. "No, I'll have a tray in my room. I've had concerns about the losses the English branch of Uncle Farleigh's company has been experiencing, and while we're stranded here, I intend to have a look at the records. I have an appointment with his partner, Samuel Walford, set for nine o'clock."

With a nod and an expressive sniff, Barnes hung the well-brushed jacket in the armoire and turned to do his master's bidding. "I'll go see about your breakfast immediately."

While Barnes was gone, Duncan stripped off his clothes and donned a brand-new dressing gown. It was among the items he had bought as additions to his wardrobe, necessitated by his unscheduled stop in England and his foray into polite society.

Whenever he accompanied Quentin to the social gatherings his cousin seemed determined to foist upon him, Duncan found he had little patience with the other members of his class. What he'd seen at the various parties and balls had underlined his general intolerance for the life he had been born to live. He couldn't understand why men took such pleasure in gambling long into the night, losing incalculable fortunes on the turn of a card. Nor did he relish the senseless flirtations with other men's wives or the way the swains fawned over those same men's vapid daughters. The life of the English aristocracy seemed meaningless to him now, and he vastly preferred the Americans' pride in their "crass" accomplishments.

Was it only the experiences of these last years that had convinced him the move to America had been in his best interest, regardless of the cause? Would he have felt as trapped and joyless as the men and women he encountered at the constant revels and balls if he had remained? But then, the thought intruded, he had not encountered Lady Grayson Ware during his stay in London. Perhaps the entertainments would not have seemed so meaningless with the solace of her company.

More than a little unsettled by the idea that Lady Grayson might be able to alter his perceptions of life here in England, Duncan tried to put her from his mind. But the memory staunchly refused to go. Although he had spent only a short time with her, he could remember everything about her, from the patrician cut of her features to the glitter in her eyes. It was no surprise that he had responded to her as he had, responded as any man would to the intimate press of a beautiful woman's flesh against his own. A heady warmth had spun through his veins, igniting a sharp, purely masculine response that had made it imperative that he move away or reveal the evidence of his sudden desire. He had wanted to act on what he felt, had nearly given in to the overwhelming urge to kiss her. But the realization of who she was and what she stood for had prevented that. Grayson Ware might well have glowed with life, intelligence, and energy; she might well have been one of the most gloriously vital women he had ever met; but she was part of a life he had been forced to deny. And somehow, even in those few minutes in the garden, she had become too strong a link with a past he could never accept.

Ryan Barnes's return to the room cut short Duncan's musings. Several footmen accompanied him, and as they settled the copper tub before the fire and filled it with steaming water from the kitchen, Duncan took note of Barnes's expression.

"You look as if something's on your mind," Duncan observed after the footmen had departed and he was soaking in the tub. "Is there something bothering you?"

The smaller man hesitated for a moment, pulling thoughtfully on his beard. "Indeed, my lord," he admitted reluctantly. "I was wondering if last night you were stricken with one of your headaches."

Duncan's eyes narrowed above the facecloth he was using to lather his chin. "I was, yes," he answered. "Why do you ask?"

"Oh, it's nothing, sir. Nothing." In spite of his denial, Barnes's face had taken on a look of even greater concern.

"Speak up, man. What is it?"

Ryan hesitated and lowered his gaze.

"For God's sake, Barnes, speak up!"

The valet drew in his breath. "There's been a real flurry of excitement belowstairs," he began. "It seems a young housemaid was found murdered this morning, over near Hyde Park. One of our men happened by as he was bringing in the supplies from the country estate. He says the girl was strangled, her neck broke clean."

That must have been the reason for the crowd he had seen gathered on the corner near South Audley Street, Palmer realized with a shudder.

"Strangled, you say? Wasn't a flower girl strangled over near Green Park just last week?"

"Yes, my lord." The valet nodded reluctantly. "It happened the night you were down with one of your headaches."

Duncan hadn't pegged the date so precisely, but as he considered what Ryan had said, he realized the man was right.

"Did they say if there are any suspects in the crime? Or have there been any arrests in that case last week? Two murders so close together might well be more than chance."

The valet shrugged and busied himself laying out Duncan's clothes.

"I suppose the evening papers will have more information," Barnes added after a moment, "though I don't recall reading anything about an arrest in the other case."

"It's odd, you know," Palmer observed, as he rinsed the soap from his chest and shoulders, "to have two murders in this part of the city. If it had happened down by the docks or over near the Empire Theater where the whores ply their trade, it wouldn't be quite so unusual."

His valet nodded in agreement as Duncan rose from the tub and accepted a towel.

"Well, it certainly makes you wonder," Palmer murmured as if in conclusion of the matter.

"Yes, sir," Barnes agreed, sending a sidelong glance in his master's direction. "It certainly does."

With the towel wrapped tight around his hips, Duncan made his way to the ornate shaving stand and stroked his bone-handled razor along the strop. There was no question that this sudden spate of violence would cause an outcry. Such things didn't happen in the rarefied world of London's West End. Murder was an affliction of the lower classes who had not yet learned to rein in the more strident expressions of their passions. It was an unwelcome intruder here where the trappings of property and privilege should have sheltered one from the grim realities of life. It was a belief he should have come to reconcile early, Duncan reflected bitterly, but even then he had understood the basic fallacy in the claim.

As he slathered soap along his chin, Duncan Palmer resolutely put the murders from his mind and turned his thoughts instead to the business of the day, to the discrepancies he hoped to find in Samuel Walford's ledgers.

When Grayson entered the dining room, her guardian, Warren Worthington, and his wife were already seated at the table.

"Good morning, Grayson," her uncle intoned. "I trust you slept well after the festivities last night."

"Oh, yes, dear," her aunt gushed. "It was a lovely party, wasn't it?"

Without answering, Gray took her seat on the near side of the long mahogany table, glancing once at each of its occupants. Her "uncle" sat at the head, a broad, bluff man with a thick shock of graying hair that had crept down in front of his ears to flank the curve of his cheeks. Between the sweep of whiskers his features were widely set: dark penetrating eyes, a fleshy nose, and a mobile mouth that clearly showed Grayson she was the cause of this morning's displeasure. Her "aunt" had long ago accepted the subordinate place to her husband's left and seemed frail and small beside him. Her frilled lace cap and demure expression made her seem younger than her years, and there was a sweetness in the turn of her lips that was an antidote to her husband's demeanor.

"You did enjoy yourself last night, Grayson, didn't you?" Her aunt's pale gray eyes held a hopeful light.

"Just about as well as a condemned man enjoys his execution."

Her aunt's face puckered with a worried frown. "I was so hoping, Grayson, that once your betrothal was a fact, you would feel differently about your marriage."

"It doesn't matter how she feels, madam," Warren Worthington boomed. "In two months' time she'll wed Harry Torkington. It's not a course that's open to discussion."

"Yes, and I'm sure I'll enjoy the wedding even more than I did the betrothal party," Grayson observed with virulent sarcasm.

"Here, here, girl, you listen to me," her uncle went on in a lecturing tone. "Once you are the Duchess of Stinton, you'll see this was the wisest choice I could have made. You'll have lands and a fortune twice the size of what you've got now, and I'm sure that will make you more than happy with your lot."

"Will it, Uncle Warren? You'll give me leave to doubt that, won't you?"

"I'll give you no leave at all, my girl. I say you'll marry Harry Torkington, and that will be the end of it."

"Well, dear," her aunt consoled, "Harry's happy with the match."

"Ah, yes, and when I become his wife, Harry's happiness should be my only concern."

The tiny woman on the far side of the table looked actively

distressed. "A husband's happiness should always be a wife's first concern," she counseled sagely.

That philosophy had certainly governed her aunt's marriage to Warren Worthington, Grayson reflected sullenly. Julo Worthington had given up life in her beloved countryside in accordance with her husband's political ambitions, and though Grayson knew she was not always happy as one of London's most influential hostesses, Julo was unfailingly gracious to the myriad of visitors who paraded through Worthington Hall. How her aunt had found the fortitude to meet the demands of her position when neither her constitution nor her interests were up to the role, Grayson did not know. But then, Julo and Warren's had been a love match from the start, and even in the case of a couple with such disparate interests, perhaps love made all things possible.

Feeling regret that she had spoken to her aunt in such a manner, Grayson reflected that perhaps she should take a leaf from her aunt's notebook and school herself to accept the marriage her uncle had made for her. But then, she could not imagine that Julo Worthington had ever wanted a life of her own as passionately as Grayson did.

Juliet Louise Stuart Markham Worthington, known as Julo since childhood because she had always seemed too slight for such a grand and imposing name, was a warm and gentle woman. She was unfailingly kind, unerringly gracious, unquestionably the very personification of the lady she had been born to be. She gave of herself unstintingly, seeing to the welfare of Warren's constituents, opening her home to the flocks of people who came to see her husband at all hours of the day and night, taking in the orphaned daughter of Warren's best friend after Grayson's parents were killed in a boating accident on the Channel. Julo was a rare woman, with a wondrous loving calm deep within her nature. But she had never known the kind of ambition that burned in Grayson's breast, had never had a desire to be anything more than Warren's wife and helpmate.

It wasn't that Harry Torkington was a homely and miserable specimen. He was years older than Grayson, to be sure, but girls who had come out in society the same year Grayson made her debut had married men far older than Harry and considered themselves fortunate indeed. But then, those girls had aspired to little more than attracting a fortune, a title, or preferably both. And the Duke of Stinton was not only well turned out and well connected; he was rich, frightfully rich. He was rich enough to give Grayson the magnificent sapphire betrothal ring that weighted the third finger of her left hand, rich enough to regard the diamond and ruby necklace and earbobs he had presented to her the previous evening as nothing more than baubles. But to Grayson, Harry embodied all of the worst things about English society. He loved gambling and horses and indolence, and he was sunk deep in the life of a truly frivolous man. He had no substance, no heart. There was nothing about him to complement Grayson's own passionate delight in living. He would never be more than a shadow to her rich reality, and his blatant indifference to life was an offense Grayson could not forgive.

But even Harry's unsuitability was not what distressed her most about the match. It was that marriage would force her to irrevocably forfeit her own most passionate ambition. She wanted with all her heart and soul to be an actress. It was an ambition that had been with Grayson since childhood, since before Grayson had understood that what she aspired to was totally beyond her.

Grayson could remember the exact moment when she had learned that truth. It had been during her second year at Ellison's Finishing School when the headmistress had caught her reciting from *Tartuffe* for a dormitory room full of delighted classmates. The woman had torn the playbook from Grayson's hands and burned it in the fireplace, then dragged her off to the kitchen where she had sprinkled pepper on Grayson's tongue, as if it could burn away Molière's blasphemous words. The woman had made it clear that Gray was never to recite again, never to read plays, never to step before an audience. After that, Grayson had been denied the chance to read aloud in class, to sing in the spring recital, to be singled out for recognition. But instead of the headmistress's censure dimming Gray's ambition, it had made it glow more fiercely until having the chance to tread the boards was all that Grayson cared about. Though logic and her station made finding a place for herself as an actress an impossibility, she could not give up the hope of one day using the talents even her worst detractors could not deny. She could not give up the only thing she had ever wanted, and she certainly couldn't give it up for a man, especially a man like Harry Torkington.

"Yes, Mortimer, what is it?"

Her uncle's deep voice broke into Gray's rebellious thoughts, and she glanced up to find the butler standing over them.

"There is a matter of some importance I would discuss with you, your grace," the man responded with a meaningful glance at the women.

"Need we speak of this now?" Worthington asked, clearly unwilling to leave his breakfast to go cold while he conferred with one of the servants.

"I believe you would think me remiss if I did not bring it to your attention," the steward answered softly.

"Very well," the duke conceded. "I will join you in the library."

Both Grayson and her aunt watched as Warren made his way to the door, and they waited with marked impatience until he returned to the dining room some minutes later. Their curiosity was not appeased by the decidedly grim set to his imposing features, and before he had settled himself in his chair, both women were deluging him with questions.

Though he did his best to fend them off, Worthington was no match for their persistence.

"I suppose you will learn of this soon enough, anyway," he conceded with a weary sigh. "There has been a woman murdered just up the street, a maid from one of the houses on Park Lane. It seems the lamplighter found her just after dawn, and there is every possibility that the police will be by to question some of our servants."

"Good heavens, Warren! A murder! However did it happen?" Julo asked after the women had a chance to digest the news. "Surely they don't think any of our people are involved?"

"I should think the questions the police will want answered have more to do with something our servants may have seen, with some stranger who might have been about, than with their guilt or innocence."

Gray immediately thought of the man she had found sleeping in the garden, and an ominous chill of apprehension trickled down her spine. She remembered his determination and his strength, the feel of his fingers against her skin. But as soon as the thought was fully formed, she dismissed it as preposterous. The man she had encountered was a sea captain, a gentleman. And besides there had been nothing sinister in his presence for all that she had found it unsettling.

"What happened to the victim, Uncle Warren?" Grayson

demanded. "Was she strangled, like the other woman found last week over near Green Park?"

Her uncle turned to her with new concern in his face. "She was found strangled," he admitted. "And I'd forgotten there was another woman murdered in the area so recently."

"I read about it in the *Times*. They said her neck was broken."

"Good God, Grayson!" Worthington exclaimed. "This is hardly something for a young woman like you to be reading about."

Julo shuddered and rubbed her hands together. "I can't understand why a reputable paper like the *Times* prints such grisly news as that. This new murder will have half the women in London cowering in their beds before the day is through."

"But if this is the second killing of this kind, it might be more than a coincidence," Gray mused, thinking aloud.

"I'll not have you saying that kind of thing, Grayson," he warned, "especially where the servants might hear you. They'll draw their own conclusions soon enough, and we don't want to do anything to worry them. We're safe enough here with the walled courtyard and garden to protect us, and the police will surely make an arrest as soon as they have a chance to learn the facts."

"Still, it seems very odd—"

"Enough, I say," her uncle ordered, turning on her. "I'll not have you speculating about things you can't possibly know. Still, I'd rather you paid no calls until this thing is settled."

He rose and tossed his napkin down beside his half-eaten breakfast. Warren Worthington was obviously worried by the news of violence here in Mayfair, and both of the women found that once he had left the dining room, they had no appetite for breakfast either.

Two

"I CAN'T THINK OF ANY REASON WHY YOU SHOULD WANT TO REVIEW the ledgers." Samuel Walford spoke with what seemed to be a mixture of reproach and genuine confusion as he led Duncan to a tall bookkeeper's desk in a tiny Spartan room that overlooked the St. Katharine Dock. "I send your uncle copies of all the invoices that pass through this office, and he surely has kept records of his own."

Duncan nodded as if in perfect accord with Walford's words. "I just thought that while I'm stranded here in London, I would take advantage of the situation. This is only a formality, but I'm sure you understand that it's just good business to double-check the records of a company as complex and diversified as ours."

A V-shaped crease appeared between Walford's eyes, adding one more crevasse to the deeply etched tracks that furrowed his brow. Walford's sixty-odd years had left his face heavily lined and jowly, collapsed in upon itself and sliding toward his chest. They had left his eyes sunk deep in fleshy pockets, so that only a faint predatory gleam showed beneath his drooping lids. His body had fared no better over the years, and either good living or persistent laxity had left him with a paunch of formidable proportions. Not even the expensive clothes he wore could hide the evidence of excess. But then, there were many men of Walford's years who had borne aging no more gracefully.

"It will be several weeks before the repairs to the *Citation* are completed," Duncan continued in an effort to put the older man at ease, "and I can't spend every waking moment trekking from one party to another in my cousin Quentin's wake. I'm used to working for my keep, and since my uncle's half of the business will someday come to me, I think it's in everyone's best interest if I have a thorough understanding of what you do on this side of the Atlantic."

Once Duncan made it clear that he was not going to back down on his request, the other man seemed to acquiesce. "I suppose it is necessary for you to know all the facets of our operation," Walford conceded grudgingly. "Mr. Haversham is my head bookkeeper. If you have any difficulties with what you see, take your questions directly to him."

And no doubt Haversham is as deep in this deception as you, Duncan thought as he nodded in reply. Still, at this juncture of his investigation it was not wise to seem too suspicious of Walford or of the records he had kept.

"I'll do that, Mr. Walford. Indeed I will. And thank you for your cooperation."

The door closed as Walford left the small glass-fronted office, and Duncan made himself as comfortable as possible on the high wooden stool. Before him were the ledgers that covered the last year's transactions. As he opened the first one, he considered what he knew of the man who was his uncle's partner.

As Farleigh Wicker had explained it, both he and Samuel Walford were younger sons who had been seated side by side as schoolmates at Eton. With the position they had shared in their respective families, they had become friends and had faced the usual choices open to them when they graduated: They could marry an heiress, sign on with the East India Company, enter the clergy, or serve in the army. Since England had been at war with Napoleon then, both had chosen the latter course. They had served with Wellington during the Peninsular Campaign and later at Waterloo. But when peace was finally secured, they had the same problem many of the less well connected soldiers faced: They needed a way to support themselves.

Pooling the resources they had managed to amass during the war years, they had scandalized both their families by "going into trade" and founding the shipping concern of Wicker and Walford Ltd. Farleigh had made the choice to leave England behind and volunteered to oversee the American branch of the company. It was a decision he had never once regretted. In spite of the prejudices that had existed against Englishmen so soon after the

United States' Second War for Independence, Farleigh had flourished in New York, and the company had flourished with him.

The English side of the concern had grown more slowly, but eventually Wicker and Walford had become a force to be reckoned with in international trade. It was the unexplained reversals the English branch of the company had been experiencing these five years past that Duncan was so eager to investigate. Granted, there had been considerable social unrest in Great Britain, and the economy had been shaky as a result of it. But those factors did not explain the sharp drop in revenues the London office had been experiencing. His uncle Farleigh patently denied that his old friend could be diverting the company's profits, but now that he had met Samuel Walford at last, Duncan's suspicions were not assuaged.

There was something about the man that made Duncan mistrust his stewardship. Walford was a little too evasive in his appraisal of the business problems, a little too condescending toward Duncan. It was possible that his condescension was based in the fact that Walford had been instrumental in sending Duncan to America when he was a boy, but it did nothing to explain Walford's reticence in opening the records of the company to Palmer's perusal now.

Yet on the surface there seemed to be nothing amiss. His uncle's partner behaved appropriately for a man of his station. He lived in a fine new house in Belgravia that for all its beautiful decor and prestigious address was not beyond his means. He seemed to have no more vices than many wealthy men pursued, and he was known for his continuing support of several prominent charities. Samuel Walford also seemed to be a pillar of the London business community, and he was well known and well respected by acquaintances and colleagues alike.

In spite of how it looked, there was a nagging inconsistency in Walford's life that Duncan could not identify. There was about Walford the manner of a man who was living on the edge, a man with a secret that could do him irreparable harm if it should be discovered. And for an instant, when Duncan had first suggested that he review the company papers, Walford's murky dark eyes had shown a glint of furious frustration.

Shrugging away the thought, Duncan turned his attention to the page of figures before him, not knowing just what it was he hoped to find. For hours he pored over the minute notations, the columns of tiny figures as he reviewed the ledgers from the years 1843 and 1844. And though he worked with concentration and diligence, Palmer found nothing that led him to believe there was anything amiss. The pages were clean, the profits and losses of the company carefully set down in black and white. There were no obvious changes or deletions, no unexplained expenditures. But then, Duncan had sensed from the beginning that he was dealing with a devious and clever man who would carefully cover his tracks.

It was well past noon when he finally stirred. His back was stiff and his muscles cramped from bending over the high, uncomfortable desk. He was not looking forward to the rest of the day when he would press on to examine the figures from the preceding years. But for the moment he was content to escape the confines of the office, to stretch his legs and get some air. Whistling under his breath, he snatched his coat and hat from the peg by the door and headed for the harbor.

The short walk and the cool crisp breeze quickly revived Duncan, and as he watched the activity along the docks, he felt his spirits rise. It was here that he was his most effective, here where his bartering skills were at their best. He was his own man when he was meeting with other traders, his own man when he was in command on the rolling deck of his own ship. He had no aptitude for the drawing room, for all that he had been born to the skill. He felt stifled in cheerless, airless offices like the one where he was damned to spend the day. It was the life of a sailor that he loved, and he yearned for the time when he could put the coast of England far behind him and be on his own again.

But for the moment he was marginally content. He had the puzzle of the company's losses to tease his brain and keep less pleasant thoughts at bay. He had the diversion of the repairs to the *Citation* to give him an excuse to escape London and the round of social obligations he had already begun to abhor. He embraced the diversions for what they were, when there was so much about this stay in England he did not want to contemplate. It was only a matter of weeks before he could leave, and he would stay busy until then.

It was the first flutter of rain moving in across the water that forced Duncan to gobble the last of the meat pasty he had bought at a dockside pub and down his mug of ale. As he reluctantly turned his feet back toward the office and the pile of ledgers still awaiting his perusal, he noticed Samuel Walford standing silhouetted in the window overlooking the docks. Across the space their gazes met, and at the naked animosity in Walford's glare, Duncan felt a potent thrill of fear.

Three

Quentin Palmer was a man who met his obligations only for the gain he could see in them. For nearly twenty years he and his father before him had overseen the Palmer lands and fortunes because in doing so they could enjoy the benefits Duncan Palmer seemed more than willing to renounce. But now, with the heir to those vast riches once again in England, Quentin felt the sting of bitterness and envy, the sense of fear and desperation. They were feelings he did his best to hide, and as he sat across the breakfast table from his cousin, Quentin tried to give the impression that he was delighted by Duncan's unexpected return.

He had made a point of including Duncan in the round of parties and balls that proliferated in London at the height of the Season, and he had seen the way his cousin was welcomed by all the most important hostesses. Whether it was Duncan's fortune, his connections to some of the most prestigious families in England, or the man himself that attracted such attention, Quentin could not say. There was an aura about his cousin that made people notice him in even the most crowded rooms, an air of certainty and confidence that he wore like a mantle of command. It did not hurt that Duncan was handsome, heir not only to the Antire lands and title but to the best of the Palmer features. Nor did it detract from his mystique that there was a scandal in his past. All people found a scandal fascinating, and no group of people more so than the English aristocracy. And in spite of his less than affectionate feelings for his cousin, Quentin meant to make the most of it.

Duncan was breakfasting unusually late this morning because he had returned after midnight from several days in Portsmouth overseeing the repairs to his ship. Quentin's own exploits the previous evening had not been quite so productive, but when he joined his cousin in the dining room, they had exchanged the usual pleasantries. Now Duncan was poring over the *Morning Chronicle* as he sipped coffee from a delicate Sèvres cup.

"I see the police have made no progress in finding the man who strangled those two women," Duncan observed, glancing up from the newspaper.

"None at all, I hear," his cousin answered, "but I do wish they would get on with it. The panic those murders is causing could prove an inconvenient impediment to the rest of the social season. A killing off in the East End somewhere is nothing to be concerned about, but both these crimes have taken place in the fashionable part of town. That has some of the ladies worried. A few showed up at the ball last night with a retinue of burly footmen, and some of the women refused to come out at all and chance violence on the streets."

"Neither of the victims was from such an exalted group as yours," Duncan said with a wry twist to his mouth. "The first was a flower seller, wasn't she? And the second was someone's upstairs maid."

"It still has all the women in a terrible state. I'll be glad when they catch the fellow."

Duncan took another sip from his steaming cup of coffee and wondered at his own preoccupation with the murders. In his travels he had seen things far more gruesome and grisly than these crimes appeared to be, and yet they seemed to fascinate him as much as they appalled him.

"The murderer's a powerful man, to be sure," Quentin continued. "Both the women's necks were broken clean."

Duncan shuddered at his cousin's words, then turned to the next page of the paper, eager to search out news without such dire implications.

For a time the two men sat in silence, Duncan scanning the sheets of newsprint and Quentin crumbling his breakfast roll while he battled his aching head and roiling stomach. He should have known better than to mix wine and brandy, he chided himself; it was a mistake he'd made often enough in the past to be aware of all the less pleasurable consequences. And he never played hazard quite so skillfully when he'd drunk too much. It was an indulgence he could ill afford.

"I say," Quentin mumbled after a time, "are you planning to attend Lady Monmouth's musical soirée with me this evening? We could see who's in attendance and go on to Crockford's from there."

Duncan's mouth thinned, though he didn't look up from the paper. "You know I don't much enjoy being dragged along to your social functions."

"But Lady Monmouth will be so disappointed if you don't put in an appearance."

As much as he resented Duncan's intrusion in his life, it had made Quentin the object of a great deal of solicitude. Hostesses knew he could ensure his rich and fascinating cousin's attendance at this affair or that, and the number and prestigiousness of his invitations had increased geometrically since "Captain" Palmer had been in town.

"Please, Duncan. We'll only stay for a little while," he coaxed, both eager for his cousin's company for the good it could do him and irritated that he himself could not generate the kind of attention Duncan did.

Since sitting at home or seeking out his own amusements held little fascination for Duncan Palmer, he decided to acquiesce. He would only be in England a little while, he told himself, and he might as well bide his time enjoying the amusements London had to offer. It did no good at all to hover over the shipwrights in Portsmouth who were attending to the *Citation*'s repairs, nor had he found the evidence of misappropriation he was looking for in Wicker and Walford's ledgers. It bothered him no small bit that his investigation had come to naught, and he was at a loss as to how to proceed.

Palmer turned to the back page of the paper and let his eyes skim down the narrow columns. He supposed he could not give all his time to business while he was here in England, and while the diversions Quentin offered were pleasant enough, they were nothing more than that. At least no one at any of the parties he'd attended thus far had been so insensitive as to mention his parents' deaths, and he could not help but hope the scandal that surrounded his family had long since been forgotten.

With a sigh of resignation he agreed to his cousin's request. "Very well, Quentin, I'll attend Lady Monmouth's party with you. But no matter how grand or gay it is, don't expect me to enjoy myself."

* * *

The quality of Mercy is not strained,
It droppeth as the gentle rain from heaven
Upon the place beneath: it is twice blessed;
It blesseth him that gives and him that takes:
'Tis mightiest in the mightiest; it becomes
The thronèd monarch better than his crown . . .

The glorious titian-haired woman stood tall and regal at the front of the room as Shakespeare's words rang through the air. She spoke in a voice so rich and deep, so charged with the emotion of her plea that not a soul of the assembly stirred. It was as if their breathing was suspended, their every thought attuned to the sentiments the woman was uttering. There were tears in her viewers' eyes, the strain of empathy around their mouths. Even as he took a place at the rear of the chamber Duncan Palmer felt her command of the audience, fell under the spell she was weaving around them all. The hair on the back of his neck stirred, and a flurry of shivers ran down his arms in response to her power and her majesty. The woman's performance was riveting as she gave vibrant life to the Bard's own truths.

As she continued, her voice rose and fell, the scope of her magic so strong and all-encompassing that there was no way for the crowd to deny her their most rapt attention. Her gestures were controlled but underlined the meaning of the elegant phrases, her bearing so straight and proud that she truly became the passionate Portia pleading her case before the bar. Her audience became the judges to whom she pled, and her eloquence made it impossible for them to reject her arguments.

With the last, fading, husky words a profound silence filled the hall. Whether it was a score of seconds or a lifetime before her listeners stirred, Duncan could not tell, but at last the hall was filled with applause, thunderous in even so grand an enclosure, echoing from the mirrored walls and high medallioned ceiling. It was a fitting tribute to the actress's skill, for the way she had so ensnared the crowd, an outpouring of the feelings she had stirred in all who had witnessed her performance.

At first she seemed surprised by their presence before her, stunned by their adulation. Then, as if remembering where she was, she bowed and smiled in response to the swelling accolades, and abruptly Duncan recognized the woman at the front of the hall. It was Grayson Ware.

It took a moment for him to reconcile the accomplished actress with the imperious young woman who had awakened him in the garden nearly a week before. She had said she was ward to the owner of the house where he had taken refuge, a lady of the realm, an aristocrat. Now he saw her as someone with a gift for drama, a woman with an incomparable ability to breathe life into a poet's moving phrases. It took a moment for Duncan to accept the transformation, and he was not sure which of the two illusions he preferred. All he knew was that he suddenly needed to renew his acquaintance, to be presented to her properly.

Duncan leaned closer to his cousin. "Who is that woman?" he asked, his gaze still fixed on Grayson.

Quentin turned and saw the object of his cousin's query, took note of the light in Palmer's eyes. "She's Lady Grayson Ware, the Duke of Fennel's ward."

"She's not an actress, then?" Duncan asked incredulously. "Where did she learn such wondrous technique? She's as good as Sarah Siddons in her prime, as good as Fanny Kemble."

Duncan was well aware of the role theatrical entertainers played in polite society. They were sometimes acceptable in a salon, but only if their wit was equal to their talent on the stage. In the last century David Garrick, who managed the Drury Lane theater, was considered an amusing acquaintance, and Sarah Siddons, the famed actress, claimed admirers of her own in the upper reaches of society. But it was clear Grayson Ware was not one of the theatrical throng, and her talent was a fluke, not something she had studied to affect. Even as he recognized Lady Grayson's brilliance, he knew there was no way she could be both an actress and a member of the ton; society would not allow her such an unlikely dichotomy. Yet there was no denying the power of her talent, the magic she had been able to weave around them all.

"Oh, Lady Grayson has some skill at recitation," Quentin acknowledged with a shrug, "though it's hardly an acceptable skill for someone who is about to become a duchess."

"A duchess?"

"She's the Duke of Stinton's fiancée."

That the woman he had met in the garden was betrothed suddenly seemed to Duncan a terrible misfortune. Without any knowledge of her intended, he knew her fiancé could not be worthy of her, worthy of either her beauty or her cleverness, her intelligence or her talent. With the thought, Palmer's need for an introduction grew until he found himself extricating Quentin from his conversation with a dowager dressed in flowing purple silk and steering him toward where Grayson stood in a clump of fawning admirers.

By then she had removed the long black robe that had been her only concession to theatrical costume, and the illusion of her majesty was gone, replaced by the cool semblance of a society beauty. She looked every inch the part in a fashionable gown of ribboned silk and lace, cut low across the shoulders. It was in a delicate shade of sea-foam green that highlighted the luminous glow of her skin. Her features were strong and clear, just as he remembered, and with her rich red hair dressed high and the flush of pleasure tinting her cheeks, she was truly a delight to behold. He had forgotten her vivacity, how her beauty had warmed and stirred him, and though he knew the attraction was dangerous and forbidden, Duncan was not disappointed to rediscover his response to her.

He and Quentin waited a little way apart until the last compliments had been spoken and acknowledged, until the press of men and women around Grayson Ware had begun to thin. Finally she turned to where the two men stood. Her smile for Quentin was sweet and warm, and then, as she looked up at Duncan, recognition lit at the back of her eyes.

"Lady Grayson," Quentin began, "may I introduce my cousin, Duncan Palmer, the Marquis of Antire. He has been most eager for me to present him. Duncan, this is Lady Grayson Ware, the late Earl of Loughborough's daughter."

Duncan made a graceful bow, taking Grayson's hand in his own and brushing the backs of her fingers with his lips. "It is my pleasure to make your acquaintance, Lady Grayson."

Duncan had had a moment to prepare for the meeting, but his presence and his title took Grayson by surprise. Nor did the response she felt at the touch of his lips against her flesh help her gather her scattered wits. Without the fabric of her gloves to protect her, his mouth was as soft as a stroke of satin, as hot as a spark landing on her unprotected skin. At the contact a ribbon of scintillating sensation slid up her arm, and she felt the betraying warmth of a blush kindle in her cheeks. When they had met in the garden, Duncan Palmer had pronounced himself an American sea captain, and the shock of finding him a welcome guest of one of London's most popular hostesses, the shock of discovering that he was a man of position and wealth, with a title of his own, left Grayson feeling more than a little compromised.

Still, she was glad to see him, glad to find that the things she had felt that first morning in the garden were more than an illusion. In the days since their encounter, she had thought of Palmer more often than she would have liked. Perhaps her attraction to him lay in the fact that he seemed so different from most of the men she knew, or that he had made her forget, for a little while at least, the tangle she had made of her life. At any rate, this was not the time to ponder the effect Duncan Palmer seemed to have on her.

Propriety and her innate poise made it possible for her to acknowledge Quentin Palmer's words. "My lord," she said, with a nod of her head, "it seems you wear a different guise each time I encounter you."

"Alas, my lady," he replied with a grin, "I have no more guises than you. But I believe you've now seen my full array of masquerades, though I doubt very much that I can say the same."

Grayson opened her mouth as if to answer tartly in response to the challenge in Duncan's voice. But before the words were out, another man joined the group. He was tall and of a build that could well be described as portly.

Quentin turned at his arrival and made the necessary introductions. "Your grace, may I present my cousin, Duncan Palmer, the Marquis of Antire, who has been living in America. Duncan, this is Lady Grayson's fiancé, His Grace Harry Torkington, the Duke of Stinton."

The possessive way Torkington claimed Grayson's hand and the relationship revealed in Quentin's introduction made Duncan take more careful note of the newcomer. Stinton must be well nigh to his fiftieth year, Palmer surmised, with hair that was more gray than brown. The duke's full, flushed face gave evidence of his excesses and his hedonistic life. That he was a man who greatly enjoyed his pleasures, and had little care for anyone except himself was immediately obvious, in his clothes, in his bearing, in his blatant condescension toward the woman who stood beside him. Stinton was the embodiment of all Duncan found least appealing about the English aristocracy. The duke was also a man who was born to be a cuckold.

Even as Duncan recognized the trend of his own thoughts, he was dishonored by it. It was not his way to envy another man his fiancée, not his way to be so attracted to a woman from the first moment they met. That he had been more than a little intrigued by

Grayson Ware the morning of their first encounter, more than a little caught up in those memories in the days since then, challenged Palmer's perceptions of himself, the distance he was determined to maintain between himself and his past. Now that he had seen Lady Grayson in another light, he found his affinity for her growing.

To reverse the uncomfortable direction in which his thoughts seemed to be taking him, Duncan acknowledged the introduction. "You must be very proud of your fiancée's accomplishments, your grace," he continued. "I've seen very few professional actresses who could render Portia's words so eloquently."

The duke glanced down at the woman beside him. "Yes, Grayson has a penchant for the dramatic, I'll admit. But once we're married, recitation is an interest she'll have to forgo."

"Well said, your grace," Quentin murmured, cutting off any answer Gray might have been preparing to make. "Recitation is a talent there's no call for in a wife."

Duncan watched the effect the interchange had on the beauteous redhead. He saw a mutinous expression tighten her mouth, saw a flicker of panic light her eyes. That "recitation" meant the world to her was obvious, and he wondered if Lady Grayson was truly willing to forfeit the pleasure she took in acting for the sake of Stinton's dukedom.

But then the duke was making their farewells and leading Grayson away. "Ah, my dear," Duncan heard him murmur as they turned to go. "I believe the orchestra has begun to play, and a group of my friends awaits us in the ballroom."

Duncan and Quentin watched as the couple passed through the gilded double doors that led into the hall.

"I wonder what she sees in him," Duncan muttered, almost to himself.

Quentin turned to look at the man beside him, surprised and intrigued by the contempt in Duncan's tone. It struck him all at once that his cousin was attracted to the Duke of Fennel's ward, and that made for a pretty pass, a pretty pass indeed.

"She sees what all these women see when they look at him," Quentin answered. "She sees three country estates, a town house in Portland Place, a fortune in family jewels, and thirty thousand pounds a year."

That his cousin could list the duke's assets so succinctly surprised Duncan, as did the hint of bitterness in his tone. Why did

Quentin feel such obvious envy of the duke, of his station and his riches? Neither fortune nor position could shield a man from tragedy, from guilt, from intimate disaster. A fortune did not protect a man from the tricks fate chose to play on him. Duncan knew that truth firsthand, and he pitied Quentin his ignorance.

Then Quentin was also turning toward the door, his face devoid of the jealous expression that Duncan had seen in it only a moment before.

"Let's go on to Crockford's, then," he proposed, "since you didn't want to come here anyway."

Duncan considered the suggestion for a moment, then surprised himself by saying no.

"And then he said, 'Well, sir, this is the best damned jumper I ever rode, and I don't care if your wife was the dam.' So Smithfield bought the roan, though I don't know if he bred it."

Grayson tried to maintain some pretense of interest in the story her fiancé was telling. It did not help that she had heard the tale more than a dozen times in the weeks Harry had been courting her, and as she stole a peek at the blank faces of those around them, she suspected that his friends had heard it nearly as often as she. That Harry Torkington was not a brilliant conversationalist was another mark against him in the tally she was keeping, and Gray wondered how often she could hear him regale his companions with these same stories before she began to shriek with boredom. But then, she suspected that Harry did not have either the intelligence for wit or the ingenuity for inventiveness. He knew horses and hunting and cards, and anything that fell outside that domain was totally lost on him.

Her inattention to her intended was not helped by the fact that Duncan Palmer was lounging against a pillar on the far side of the ballroom and had been watching her openly since the dancing had begun. She was surprised that he had remained in the hall when most of the unattached gentlemen had already adjourned to the gaming tables set up in another of Lady Monmouth's opulent salons. Grayson suspected that was where Quentin Palmer had gone, and she chided herself for not having made the connection between the two men that morning in the garden. But then, Palmer was a common name, and Duncan had introduced himself as an American seaman. How could she have known that he was the mysterious Marquis of Antire of whom so many tales were told?

As she stared at him from behind the blind of her fiancé's shoulder, she tried again to recall what she had heard of him. Someone had mentioned once that Palmer had lived in the United States for a number of years and that his cousin Quentin had been overseeing his extensive holdings while he was out of the country. He must be very rich indeed, with the vast Antire property and investments that would have come to him with his majority. She also knew there was something scandalous in his past, something that made people speak of him in voices hushed and low. What that scandal was, Grayson could not guess, but as soon as the opportunity presented itself, she meant to ask her aunt. Julo Worthington was not herself a gossip, but that did not prevent her from keeping up to date on what seemed like half the families in England.

Grayson sneaked another look at the man who so intrigued her and found that, instead of leaning negligently against the column, he was threading his way across the dance floor. As he passed, people turned to stare at him. In the men's faces she could read curiosity or disdain, while the women watched with unfeigned interest or open admiration. Duncan Palmer was the kind of man who would never be anonymous in a crowd. His carriage was too proud, his air of command too evident, his handsomeness too pronounced. With his thick chestnut hair and bright blue eyes, with the aristocratic cut of his features and his imposing height, he was not someone who could be easily ignored. And as he passed the center of the ballroom, Grayson suddenly realized that he was about to make her conspicuous, too.

She ducked behind her fiancée's bulk, wanting to deny that Duncan Palmer was coming for her, wanting to deny that she had hoped all evening he would do exactly this. Beside her, Harry was oblivious to what was about to happen, though it seemed impossible that he could not hear the pounding of her heart, impossible that he could not sense her silent pleas to save her from herself. Inside her fine kid gloves, her hands were clammy, as she tried to think how she should respond when Palmer appeared at her side. Her mind raced to the proprieties of the situation, seeking the strength to refuse his request for a dance from prohibitions outside herself. But she found no escape in the strictures of proper etiquette. It was unusual, though not impossible, for a woman to dance with another man when her fiancé was in attendance.

Though it would have been wiser to refuse Duncan's invitation, Grayson doubted she had the fortitude to do so.

Then the decision was upon her as Duncan reached the tight-knit group at the edge of the dance floor. He gave her only the slightest of nods before he addressed himself to Stinton.

"Would you mind, your grace, if I took a turn with Lady Grayson? She's the loveliest woman in the hall, and I fear I can no longer deny myself her company."

Grayson felt a blush rising in her cheeks at the boldness of his blandishments, but Harry seemed to take no offense.

"Antire, isn't it?" he asked, turning to where Duncan stood. "Well, I suppose I can allow Grayson one dance with you, since I've been remiss in asking her myself."

It was true that Torkington had not danced with his fiancée all evening, and Grayson had been content to stand at the side of the hall, if only to save her feet from being crushed by Harry's expensively shod feet.

"Lady Grayson?" Palmer offered his arm. "Would you grant me the pleasure of a dance?"

It was the moment Grayson had been dreading, the moment when she should refuse him. She hesitated, searching for the strength to make her excuses and leave the ballroom, but she was woefully inadequate to the task.

Her voice was strained as she gave her answer. "Since you have requested it so gallantly, my lord, how could I deny you my company?"

Harry was deep in conversation with his cronies before they had moved a yard away, scarcely aware that she was gone. But, for herself, Grayson had the sense that she was escaping from a web of boredom and inactivity, from lies about fidelity and propriety which had grown tedious in the telling.

What Palmer offered her was the opposite side of that coin. He was offering temporary tenancy in another world, one of attention and admiration, of danger and excitement. It was a heady temptation, one she had no strength or desire to resist. For an instant Grayson didn't care that there were probably matrons whispering behind their fans, matrons probably condemning her for dancing with someone other than her fiancé. All Gray knew was that she was about to have a few minutes alone with someone whose presence stirred her senses, someone whose attentions soothed and flattered her.

As Duncan took her in his arms, the orchestra, perched high on the balcony, began to play. How Palmer had known this dance was to be a waltz, Grayson could not guess, but though she was wary of his nearness, she found she welcomed the unexpected intimacy.

As Duncan led her skillfully through the first turns, she was surprised by how wondrously right it felt to be held in his arms. It was a rightness she knew she had no business feeling, a rightness that was unsettling in its intensity. Yet she could not deny that they fit together with an amazing compatibility. Her height was well matched to his, and the hard planes of his body found a complement in the gentle curves of her own. She was unaccountably aware of the breadth of his shoulder beneath her hand and the pressure of his fingers at her waist, gently turning and guiding her. She felt her flounced skirts brush his legs as they moved across the floor, felt his hand tighten around her own as if he were as aware of the contact as she. There was the sharp scent of bay rum clinging to his clothes and skin, ruddy color in his cheeks, a warm insistent glow in the depths of his sky-blue eyes. That glow made her feel precious, revered, extravagantly special. The feeling, she suddenly realized, was one she had been seeking all her life.

Grayson was so attuned to Palmer's physical presence, so aware of her own contentment and gratitude, that when he spoke at last, the sound of his deep voice startled her.

"I meant to tell you before," he began, "that you're a most accomplished actress."

"I'm glad you had a chance to see me at my best. Acting means a great deal to me."

"That was evident from the moment you began to recite, the way you made everyone in the room feel your passion, your emotion. There aren't many who have your talent."

His compliment was like a gift, freely offered, totally unexpected, exceedingly precious. But because she knew flattery was often insincere, Grayson was not sure how to respond to him. She did not want to probe his praise too deeply for fear of finding it devoid of sincerity. Yet she needed to bask in its radiance, draw encouragement and comfort from his words when her most closely held dreams were in the gravest jeopardy.

There was something about this man that made her feel he might understand what happened to her when she began to perform, the renewed sense of self, her conviction in her performance, the myriad of things she had never before wanted to or tried to verbalize. Palmer seemed to approve of what she'd done, seemed to find her abilities not scandalous but admirable. For Grayson, who had spent her life defending her unlikely interest in the theater, Duncan's was a very liberating attitude.

"Sometimes when I'm called on to recite," she began, "it's very much like magic. I can't explain how it happens, but the character seems to take hold of me somehow, to dwell inside my skin. I lose track of where I am, of what I'm doing, of who is watching me. I forget everything but what that character sees and feels, how the character's words are filtered through me to the audience."

He was silent for a moment as he digested what she'd said. "I think your listeners sense that," he agreed at last, "though not in any tangible way."

"And when it goes well, as it did tonight, some kind of energy seems to come upon me."

"Energy?" Duncan asked, smiling as he drew her out. "What kind of energy?"

Grayson shook her head as she struggled to explain. "When I recite, a feeling seems to well up from the people in the crowd, a kind of charge that somehow both calms and invigorates me. It runs like lightning up my arms; it ignites something inside me that builds and glows."

"Is that good?"

"It makes me feel—stronger, surer, somehow. It makes me feel as if I'm more myself, even when I'm pretending to be someone else."

Duncan was silent for a moment, then spoke abstractedly, seeming to understand far more than she had said. "That energy is the ultimate approval, isn't it?"

His offhand observation made her hesitate before answering, made her feel both warmed and invaded by his perceptiveness.

"Approval? Yes, I guess it could be approval, or perhaps it's their empathy I feel." Then abruptly she denied the wondrous power of the thing she had been describing. "But what the audience feels is sympathy for the character I am playing, for the person I've created before their eyes. Their approval is not for me."

Though Grayson neither suspected nor understood how much she had revealed about herself, Duncan saw the insights that were eluding her. He saw her more clearly in that moment than he had ever seen anyone in his life. He saw her foibles and her strengths, her liabilities and her dreams. He saw her loneliness, her ambition, her vulnerability. He knew that there were things deep inside this woman that lived within him, too. A knot of recognition and empathy tightened in his chest.

In the last lilting measures of the waltz, in the few brief moments left to them, he felt compelled to offer her what encouragement he could. "You are a wonderful actress, Grayson, better than many I've seen on the American stage. You have a gift for expressing emotion, an unusual grace and eloquence."

She was surprised by his assertion, by the sudden bond she sensed between them. It was as if they had touched in a more than usual way, shared something fragile and infinitely precious. Yet even as she felt the need to prolong the moment, to seek reassurance in his words, she dared risk no further closeness. She dared ask no more than this from a man who was a virtual stranger.

"I thank you for your praise," she answered almost bitterly. "But I fear you've just witnessed my last performance—my debut in society and my final farewell."

"Does that mean Stinton feels such talents as yours are a liability in a duchess?"

She gave him a long, hard look before responding. "I fear it's a point of view all England shares."

"Then you should take your talents to America where we are not so staid and narrow-minded."

"Take my talents to America?" Her voice was breathy as she echoed his words, soft and weak in comparison to the pounding of her heart. Hearing his casual comment was like receiving the answer to a prayer she had been praying all her life. Without considering the consequences, she clutched his suggestion to her heart. Leaving England to seek expression for her talents was not a course she had thought about. But now that Palmer had planted the idea in her mind, she could nurture it, tend it, and watch it grow. At the very least, Duncan was offering her encouragement when she had given up hope, was suggesting possibilities when all she had been able to see was a trap of inevitabilities.

Without intending to, she smiled up into Palmer's eyes, and what she saw shining in their depths was a wealth of understanding and unexpected tenderness. The strength of his emotions took her breath; they made her feel giddy and terrified and marvelous. Then abruptly his arm tightened around her waist, and before she realized what he meant to do, he was sweeping her toward the ballroom doors, toward the dark beckoning terrace just beyond them.

The night air was cold against her skin, fresh and astringent after the cloying closeness of the ballroom, crisp and sharp after the scent of beeswax candles and expensive perfume. The light from the open doors to their right and left cast long, pale rectangles onto the face of the wide, smooth stone, but the darkness between the doors was soft and deep, anonymous and welcoming. Duncan stopped just short of the second opening and drew Gray hard against his body. She felt the crush of her gown and petticoats against his legs, the press of his chest against her bodice. She felt Duncan's hand tighten at her waist, as the other skimmed slowly past her shoulder.

Heat blazed in her cheeks, a flush of eagerness and exquisite anticipation. Above her Duncan's face was cast in shadows, but she could see the gleam in his eyes, the faint bowing of his mouth. She sensed the tenor of his mood, his wariness, the inevitability of what was to come. His fingers brushed the curls beside her cheek, and she felt the roughness of his callused palms as they came to rest against her skin. It was the moment when she should move away, but as Duncan turned her face to his, she wanted nothing but his tenderness.

His mouth moved over hers, tentative and bittersweet. His lips brushed hers, once, twice, three times, before he retreated, still cupping her face between his hands. Time seemed suspended as they stared into each other's eyes, as his breath pooled against her skin, as they contemplated the scope of their nascent recklessness. Both knew the danger, the price they would pay if they succumbed to the temptations taunting them. But it was impossible to deny the attraction, the inexplicable bond that seemed to exist between them.

Slowly, Duncan lowered his head, and with a sense of approbation Grayson rose on tiptoe to meet his kiss. As he took possession of her mouth, her lips molded to the contours of his, budding beneath the slow, insistent pressure, softening to accommodate the urgency she sensed in him. His eagerness appeased some faint lingering doubt deep inside her, and she gave herself without reserve, trusting that he found her the most desirable of women, trusting that now he was as helplessly beguiled as she.

As they kissed, the flick of his tongue moistened the silky inner surface of her lips, explored the tender corners, the extravagant fullness at the bow. He courted her response with a spate of deepening kisses, and Grayson gave it freely, leaning into his embrace. As she did, his arms curled around her shoulders, and with the increasing ardor of his caress, she felt more sheltered and secure than ever in her life. It was as if for this moment she was the center of Duncan Palmer's world, infinitely valuable and precious. But beyond the importance his unqualified attentions seemed to grant her were the unexpected sensations that streamed along her nerves.

There was a flush melting hot against her skin, tingling awareness where her body was pressed to his. A tightness bound her chest, and her heart volleyed thunderously in the confines. She seemed at once to be straining for closer contact and swooning with delicious lassitude, tensed with an unnamed wanting and succumbing to the satisfaction she found in his arms. Grayson gave herself to Duncan's embrace, opening, surrendering, letting him introduce her to her first sweet stirrings of passion.

She murmured helplessly deep in her throat, sounds of inexplicable delight, sounds of incipient provocation. She twined her arms around his back, opened her mouth to the probe of his tongue. The flick of it against her own was a revelation, and she went dizzy and soft in response. She had never known such pleasure, such gentleness, such complete communion. She had never known that in an instant two lives could touch so powerfully, so poignantly. Delight swelled through her veins; sweetness curled in her chest and belly. She had never felt like this before; she had never felt like this when Harry kissed her.

Harry—the thought streaked across her consciousness like a comet in the darkened sky.

Harry! Oh, God, Harry!

Duncan seemed to sense the change in her and raised his head.

She stared up into his eyes, her own blank with disappointment, dark with dawning conscience.

"Harry," she whispered.

"Harry," he replied, understanding everything.

Grayson was not sure her legs would hold her when Duncan stepped away, but he seemed to regain control of his faculties far more quickly than she. Or perhaps he had not been as lost in their passion as she thought.

While she stood trying to regain her breath, Duncan's hands moved over her, smoothing the wrinkles from the front of her gown, tying one of the bows down the center of her bodice that had inexplicably come undone, tucking away a tendril of hair that had drooped against her shoulder.

As he worked over her, the world around Grayson reasserted itself. She felt the breeze against her skin and shivered, heard the staccato notes of a polka drifting from the ballroom. How long had they been here, alone on the terrace? How many people had taken note of their absence? Fear clutched her heart when she considered the repercussions they might face. If Harry realized what they'd been doing, he might challenge Duncan. And though dueling was technically illegal, her uncle might be placed in a position where he would be expected to do the same. At the very least her reputation would be in ruins, and with her unacceptable aspirations to the theater fresh in their minds, people might well consider her as much of a trollop as the actress she had pretended to be.

"Courage," Duncan whispered, reading the concern in her face. "We'll stop by the punch bowl before we seek out your fiancé. I'll wager half my worth he hardly knows you've been gone."

Duncan made no further attempt to reassure her. He must know, too, that there were certain proper matrons who took careful note of such behavior. But Duncan was probably right, Grayson was forced to admit. Harry would not have missed her.

They entered the adjoining room from another set of doors farther down the balcony and procured a cup of sticky pink punch to cover the unusual length of their absence.

When they returned to the ballroom, Harry was still with his cronies, engaged in a heated debate about whose hounds were the best in all the Midlands. He acknowledged Grayson's return with a nod of his head, only half listening to her disjointed explanations.

After graciously thanking her for her company Duncan bowed and turned away, leaving Grayson feeling lost and shaken, helplessly staring after him.

Four

"THERE'S BEEN ANOTHER MURDER," RYAN BARNES REPORTED AS he settled a tray of coffee and freshly baked rolls on the table at Duncan Palmer's bedside.

Palmer rolled over and cast a jaundiced look in the valet's direction. He had been stricken with one of his headaches the previous night and had dosed himself with laudanum before seeking out his bed. The drug always left him feeling logy and unfocused, so that he was totally unprepared for either Ryan's presence or his news.

Duncan buried his face in the pillow, still courting sleep, but his curiosity was aroused. "Where was the victim found?" he finally mumbled.

"Over on Maddox Street, near St. George's Church, or so the papers say. She was a Bond Street shop girl making her way home last evening. And her neck was broke clean, just like both the others."

Palmer moaned both in response to Barnes's grim words and with the effort it took to sit up.

The smaller man hovered over his master, a frown of concern on his bearded face. "You told me to wake you at seven, my lord, but perhaps you'd prefer to go back to bed."

"I had another headache last night," Duncan responded by way of explanation.

Barnes retreated half a step, his face gone strangely pale. "Another headache, sir?"

Duncan nodded. "It seems they've come more often since we've been in London." The admission was slow, difficult.

There was a long pause before Barnes replied. "Perhaps it's the air," he offered hopefully, "though it's not particularly foul this time of year."

"Maybe it's being back in England."

An uncomfortable silence fell between the two men. They rarely talked about the incidents that had sent them fleeing the country more than fifteen years before. The reality was too difficult, the grief too deeply buried in each of them. What Duncan could not remember, or what he chose to forget, had not been spoken of between them for many years. It was as if they had made a tacit agreement that silence could change the past, as if pretending could somehow alter the tragedies that marked them both. There had been a time, years before, when Ryan would have been able to offer consolation, when Duncan could have accepted it, but their roles of master and servant were now too firmly set. It was as if the gulf between what they had been and what they had become made intimate communication impossible.

Instead of responding to his master's words, Barnes resorted to a more practical suggestion. "Why don't you get a bit more sleep, my lord? Master Quentin never rises before ten, and you can breakfast with him then."

But before he could give way to the temptation, Duncan was levering himself off the bed. "No, I want to go back to Walford's offices and have another look at the ledgers. I know there's something wrong with them, though I can't seem to put my finger on it."

With a worried frown and a lingering glance at his master, Barnes turned toward the door. "Then I'll go see about your bath."

When the valet was gone, Duncan moved to the window and looked down into Berkeley Square. The sun was still low in the sky, and its shimmering apricot rays skimmed just above the housetops to gild the uppermost leaves of the trees in the mall. It was going to be another glorious day, Duncan thought and leaned out the open window. Spring had come to London without preamble this year, with bright sunshine, gentle breezes, and wondrous warmth that lingered into twilight. Quentin said the weather was most unusual, and Duncan cursed his fate at foundering in the last hard winter storm that had blown in across the Channel. If only they had waited another week to brave the passage. If only the winds and rain had not taken such a toll on the *Citation*, he would not be trapped in England now. He would not be trapped with his past, his regrets, and his steadily worsening headaches.

The migraines had been with him since adolescence, since shortly after his parents died. They had come upon him suddenly, unexpectedly, but with the same pattern and intensity that persisted to this day. Nor was there anything he could do to prevent the attacks once the first symptoms had begun to appear. The headaches always began with a pinprick of heat deep inside his brain, a heightened sense of smell, an awareness of the sounds around him, as if they were echoing in his head. His vision would begin to blur, and then the pain would come, so intense he could not think, so all-encompassing it forced everything else from his mind. When that happened, the best he could hope for was oblivion, either the blackness that overwhelmed him in response to the pain or the drug-induced stupor that was his only hope of relief.

He leaned farther out the window and breathed deep, hoping the soft spring air would sweep the cobwebs from his brain, the memories from his mind. But in spite of the early morning freshness, the dark thoughts continued to plague him.

Why were the headaches coming so often now? Was being back in England really making them worse? Were the headaches tied to the events he could not remember, the things he had tried half his life to deny? Was he being punished anew for what he'd done all those years before?

Duncan did not know the answers to those questions, and for the sake of the new life he had built on the ashes of the last, for all he hoped to accomplish in the years to come, he refused to dwell on such dire possibilities. He had determinedly built his future on thin air in a land that was not his own, and it was as if all he had struggled to achieve in life could be destroyed by the acknowledgment of the reason for his exile.

He would remain in England, he vowed, only until his ship was repaired, only until he found proof of Walford's malfeasance, only until he had seen Grayson Ware once more. The thought intruded, surprising him. Though her beauty and vitality intrigued him, Duncan knew he should stay away from Grayson, too. She was a part of all he was seeking to escape, part of the country and the culture he was trying to put behind him.

He must be prepared to leave when the *Citation* was finally ready to go. And when the day of leave-taking came, he prayed he could escape, once and for all, the pain, the doubt, the grief, the dark specter of his past.

The shabby inn that lay between Covent Garden and the river in St. Giles was not, to Quentin Palmer's mind, the ideal meeting place. The mere sight of its crumbling walls and rotting wood spoke of poverty and wasted lives, of sloth and hopelessness. As he climbed the narrow stairs that led to the room John Leaphorn kept on the second floor, he could smell the sour stench that drifted up from the courtyard, could taste it on the back of his tongue. He could see the filth collected on the walls, could sense the malaise that afflicted this part of London. It was not an area a gentleman would frequent, and Quentin would not have come here had he not felt an overwhelming need to see his business partner.

Palmer knocked on a scarred wooden door at the top of the stairs and waited for it to be opened, feeling vulnerable and conspicuous in his fashionable clothes. Just being here was risking robbery or worse, though the danger was not so acute at this hour of the morning. Most of the footpads would still be home in bed, sleeping off a night of debauchery. In truth, Quentin wished he was doing the same.

The door came open with a jerk, and even with the morning sunlight sifting through the grime on the windows, the room beyond was as dark and forbidding as a cave. The man who had granted him admittance was no more welcoming. He was tall and gaunt, almost cadaverous, dressed in rough, ill-fitting clothes.

"I want you to put an end to this," Quentin Palmer hissed even before his host had closed the door behind him.

The man gave no reply but crossed the room instead and poured wine into two murky mismatched glasses.

Quentin was too eager for a drink to take much note of the sticky smudges on the receptacle, and he downed the wine in a single draft, grimacing at the taste.

His companion filled the glass again, and fortified by the second helping of ruby liquid, Quentin once again turned his thoughts to the reason for his visit. "I want you to stop this now, immediately. This is foolish and dangerous. It could be the death of us all."

"And what would you 'ave me do instead? It's your cousin's return that 'as brought us to this pretty pass."

"But what if Duncan should find out—"

" 'E won't."

"But if he should, he'll surely go to the magistrates."

Leaphorn took a turn around the chamber, his menacing stance and manner the antithesis of Quentin's own. "Then we'll 'ave to make sure 'e can't."

Leaphorn's words made Quentin's belly crawl. He had been worried about the younger Palmer's presence in the country from the moment his cousin had set foot on English soil. And that was before Duncan had expressed his interest in Wicker and Walford's affairs, before he had begun asking probing, pointed questions about the management of his holdings here in Britain. With that, Quentin's concern had turned to naked fear. But as frightened as Quentin was by what Duncan might discover, as terrified as he was by the consequences of what might somehow be revealed, he was even more horrified by the plan Leaphorn had set into motion the day of Duncan's arrival.

"I just don't think this is right," Palmer muttered shakily, extending his glass for another serving of wine.

In response to Quentin's words, Leaphorn smiled, showing stubby teeth as dingy and unkempt as his hair and beard. "Right, partner? Right? 'Ang right. Just remember you ain't done nothing right since you fell in with us eight years ago."

It was the truth, but Quentin was loath to be reminded of all he had become a party to during the intervening years. Where had he gone wrong? he wondered desperately. When had he become the kind of man Leaphorn was, a man without honor, a man without scruples? His father had reaped the benefits of overseeing the Antire holdings without compromising himself in any way. Why hadn't Quentin been able to do the same?

What Leaphorn had planned for Duncan was the most dangerous thing Quentin had been a party to yet. Still, he was honest enough with himself to admit his inability to deal with his cousin's questions, with Duncan's unexpected return to England.

"If only we could buy him off," Quentin murmured almost to himself. "But what would Duncan want with a few pounds more? He's richer than Midas already."

"And why should you care what 'appens to 'im?" Leaphorn argued. "You'd be a-rolling in gold if 'e was out of the way. We've a sweet thing 'ere, and we don't want your cousin mucking it up."

"No, that's right. We don't." With the admission Quentin could feel the sweat bead up along his brow. As much as he was appalled by what Leaphorn was doing, he wanted the ruffian to resolve the problem of Duncan Palmer for him.

" 'Ere now," Leaphorn murmured as he ushered Quentin toward the door, "put all this out of your 'ead. I'll do all that needs to be done as long as you play your part. You just see to the things we've talked about, and your cousin will rue the day 'e ever returned to England."

Duncan sat back and rubbed a hand across his eyes. He had spent another morning fruitlessly poring over Wicker and Walford's records. The longer and more diligently he looked for some kind of discrepancy among the columns of tiny figures, the more frustrated he became. Still, he was sure the answers to his questions about Wicker and Walford's losses were in the ledgers somewhere.

It was clear Samuel Walford had hoped Palmer would lose interest in the project, would be caught up in London's social whirl and diverted from his quest. But Samuel Walford had no way of knowing how determined and single-minded Duncan could be. Nor did the other man realize that the inquiry into the company's records had become a way for Duncan to distance himself from the many things in England he did not want to confront. The search for the discrepancies made Palmer feel useful in a situation over which he had no control, made him feel he was accomplishing something important. In exploring Walford's records, he could divert himself from the painful recollections of his parents' death, from his increasingly frequent thoughts of Grayson Ware. By taking refuge in his diligence, Duncan could occupy himself when there was nothing he could do to speed his departure from the land of his birth.

With a sigh, Duncan consulted his pocket watch, then eased himself off the high wooden stool. It was nearly half-past twelve, and he had a one o'clock appointment at an inn in the financial quarter. Even on such a lovely day, it would take him time to make the walk.

Palmer took his hat and coat from the peg by the door and left the small glass-fronted office.

"Will we be seeing you this afternoon, my lord?" Haversham,

the head bookkeeper, asked as Duncan crossed the larger room outside. "Or shall we put the ledgers away?"

Haversham, like Walford, had become more sullen and less cooperative every time Duncan had returned to the office. The fiction that Palmer was merely familiarizing himself with the English side of Wicker and Walford's operation was wearing thin, and hostility was taking the place of grudging acquiescence. Haversham and Walford must surely suspect that Duncan was looking for something in the ledgers, and they must also know that in spite of the hours he had worked and his single-minded diligence, he had not found it—yet.

"Oh, yes," Duncan answered the bookkeeper with a nod. "I should be returning shortly. I'm just getting a bite to eat." As he left the crowded, dusty office, he could feel the heat of Haversham's stare burn against his back.

Once out on the street, Palmer put Haversham's hostility from his mind and stretched his long legs in a ground-eating lope, making his way north and west along the perimeter of the Tower. Against the clear sky, the dun-gray turrets and battlements of the ancient fortress seemed to give mute evidence of its long unhappy history. It was here that the two young princes, sons of Edward IV, in all probability had been murdered by their uncle; here that Lady Jane Grey and several of Henry VIII's wives had lost their heads; here where countless men and women who displeased the Crown had been imprisoned.

Duncan shuddered in the warm spring sunshine and quickened his pace, moving into London proper, into the dark narrow caverns of the crowded streets. It was here where the city had truly begun, here where the Bank of England and the Royal Exchange truly held sway over London's prosperity. The people along the walks on either side of the busy thoroughfare seemed to represent every faction of the city's populace. There were well-dressed men with portfolios under their arms, probably on their way to one of the popular coffee houses; tradesmen whose clothes clearly professed their skills; costermongers crying their wares, selling fruits, vegetables, and fish from their dilapidated carts. There were patterers on every corner extolling the virtues of their nostrums, while others shouted news of the latest crimes and scandals in the hope of selling tracts to the people passing by. The fellow killing women in London's streets had been dubbed the

West End Strangler, and the atrocities he was committing were prime fodder for such as these.

Carriages, omnibuses, and drays of every description passed hub to hub along the road. Advertising vans with enormous placards rolled past, followed by shiny carbriolets and lumbering coal wagons pulled by teams of husky horses. In the wake of a crossing sweeper, Duncan turned into Gracechurch and then Lombard Street, moving past St. Edmund's with its tall square tower of Portland stone. The eatery he was seeking was in Castle Court, a tavern with the unprepossessing name of the George and Vulture Inn.

When he reached the place he was looking for, Duncan was reluctant to relinquish the freshness of the day for the gloom of the crowded taproom. The smell of ripe cheese, stale beer, and cooking onions assaulted him as he went inside, and he spent a moment peering through the smoky haze in search of the man he had come to meet.

The fellow recognized Palmer first and motioned him into the opposite side of the high-backed booth near the back of the narrow hall. They ordered their meal from the menu the barmaid recited, then settled back as each took the measure of the other.

As Duncan studied the man across the table, he realized that Hannibal Frasier had deliberately adopted the semblance of an everyman, in his dress, in his manner, in his precise unhurried movements. It was as if he had learned long ago that a score of truths could be read in a man's demeanor and had no intention of revealing much of himself to the world at large. Yet there were things Frasier could not hide. He was not a big man, but he was burly and strong, and in his broad, world-weary face there was evidence of vast experience. A grizzled, rough-cut beard hugged the square of his jaw, and his nose had been mashed flat as if in a brawl he'd fought long ago. Frasier gave no hint of great intelligence, but beneath his gray, unruly brows his eyes shone with disconcerting intensity. Palmer could well believe that Frasier was an expert at ferreting out people's most closely guarded secrets, at finding out the things no man would want the world to know. It was just the talent Duncan was looking for, the one he was fully prepared to employ.

The silence between them was filled with the clink of dishes and silverware, the resonant murmur of masculine voices, the clap of pewter tankards. But Palmer held his peace until the other man broke off his equally frank perusal.

"Well, then, what do you want of me, my lord?" Frasier's question was direct, and his mode of address surprising in that Duncan had set up the meeting in his guise as an American sea captain.

Duncan acknowledged both the other man's question and his thick Scottish brogue with a lift of one dark brow. "I see you've learned a bit about me already," he observed. It was testimony to Frasier's powers of inquiry that he had so quickly discovered Duncan's other identity.

"It always pays to know from the start who it is you're dealing with. And I admit, yours is a curious history."

Duncan felt an uncomfortable warmth swell along his cheekbones. "It's not my history you are here to look into," he said with more heat than he'd intended. "And it has no bearing at all on what I want you to do."

"And what's that, gov'nor? Your note didn't give so much as a clue."

Duncan hesitated for a moment, wondering suddenly if asking for Frasier's help would prove more a mistake than an advantage. But then, he was hardly in a position to seek out the kind of information he needed. He had no contacts here in London, little knowledge of the city and its people.

Duncan drew a long breath and decided to plunge ahead. "There's a man I want investigated, a man in business here in London, Mr. Samuel Walford."

"Mr. Walford, is it? Your uncle Farleigh's partner?"

It shouldn't have been so disconcerting to find that this man, who had seemingly unearthed all the secrets of Duncan's past, knew so much about his business. It reinforced the reports Palmer had heard of Frasier already: that he was privy to the affairs of high and low alike, that as an investigator he was canny and effective. Still, the extent of the man's knowledge surprised him. How much had the other man learned in the few hours since Palmer had contacted him? What more would he learn in the weeks to come? Frasier was just the kind of man Duncan needed to look into Samuel Walford's business practices, but as he stared across the table, Palmer felt mixed confidence and concern at having this man in his employ. With difficulty he pushed his misgivings aside.

"That's right. I want you to investigate Mr. Samuel Walford, my uncle's partner."

"You think he's skimming profits from Wicker and Walford?"

Duncan was prepared for Frasier this time and nodded sagely. "Well, then, Mr. Frasier, you're as shrewd as they say."

A smile puckered the corners of the other man's mouth.

"Can you tell me what I want to know today," Duncan continued, "or will you need some time to ruminate?"

Frasier laughed outright at the question. "I'm good, Captain Palmer. I'm very good at what I do, but even I will need a bit of time to look into Mr. Walford's affairs."

Something inside Duncan responded to the dry humor in the other man's boast. "And what's your extensive expertise going to cost me?"

"A hundred quid, more or less," Frasier answered coolly.

When Palmer seemed ready to balk at the amount, Frasier continued. "For a swell like you, I doubt even that amount would be a hardship, but to a man like me, it would be as good as picking the winner in the Derby. Besides, you wouldn't have me looking into Walford's affairs if there weren't more than that involved."

There was truth in what Frasier said. Duncan had no idea how much Walford had embezzled, but it surely ran into thousands and thousands of pounds. In that light, the price the man was asking was certainly more than reasonable. Besides, Duncan was forced to admit, for all his diligence he had not been able to find even one small inconsistency in Wicker and Walford's records. Without the figures to back him up, without some knowledge of Walford's private life, any allegations he might make would be ineffective, groundless. If Palmer could find out where the money was going, if he could determine Walford's vices, it might be easier to find the documentation to prove his suspicions correct.

"Very well," he conceded with a shrug. "I'll pay you what you ask, but you'd better turn up something that will help me prove my case."

Frasier's eyes narrowed as he considered the man across the table. "I'm not in the business of manufacturing proof that isn't there," he warned. "There's some who will do that, though a man like you, your lordship, wouldn't much enjoy dealing with most of 'em."

Palmer's face went hard at the contempt in Frasier's tone. "I want the truth, Mr. Frasier, nothing more. For my uncle's sake, I hope the reverses Wicker and Walford has suffered in England are nothing more than what Walford claims. It's my own reservations I bring to this matter, not my uncle's. I'm seeking nothing more than what's really there."

Their conversation was interrupted by the arrival of their meal, and as they applied themselves to their plates of mutton, potatoes, and boiled cabbage, Frasier continued questioning Duncan.

"Just how long has Wicker and Walford been losing money?"

"That's just it," Palmer replied, taking a sip of his ale. "We're continuing to make money, but not nearly as much as we were making some years ago."

"And you're begrudging Walford what profits he can skim?"

"I think a man plays fair, no matter what his game. Walford is entitled to his share; I'm just not willing to see my uncle subsidize his underhandedness."

Seeming satisfied by Palmer's answer, Frasier continued. "And how long has this been going on?"

"The reverses began about five years ago. I was out of the country most of that time on Wicker and Walford ships. It was only while I was waiting for my new ship to be completed that I spent any time in the New York office. When I saw our profits were down here in England, I wanted to understand the reason for the decline and reviewed our copies of the ledgers. The losses began in 1839. From March on, profits began to drop. They're down thirty-seven percent in five years' time. If our concerns in America had not done as well as they have, the company would be in very serious trouble indeed."

"And it's not possible that the business here is just not as lucrative as it is on the other side of the Atlantic?"

"That's what I want to determine. While my ship is in dry dock down in Portsmouth, I plan to go over all Walford's records. There must be something there that will help me either prove my suspicions or put them to rest."

Frasier pushed his empty plate away. "You didn't come here to look into this, then?"

"I'm taking advantage of a disadvantageous situation," Palmer answered levelly. "I would never have returned to England on my own."

The other man nodded as if in perfect accord and asked no more. He seemed to need no further clarification of either Palmer's motives or his methods.

"How long will it take you to get the information I'm after?"

Frasier took a toothpick from the shot glass on the table and tucked it between his teeth. "It took you five years to decide to look into your company's losses, so I hardly think a week or two is long to make you wait."

"And how will I know when you've discovered something?"

"I'll contact you, your lordship. Have no fear of that. Now before you leave, I'll have half my fee, and the rest when I tell you what I've learned."

Duncan dug deep into his pocket, paying Frasier in crisp new ten pound notes. He also withdrew money to cover the price of the meal, but the older man pushed the coins back across the table.

"I pay my own way in the world. I don't owe anyone, and no one owes me."

Duncan nodded and rose to go. "I wish you luck in your search, Mr. Frasier."

The man grinned around his toothpick. "And you in yours, your lordship. And you in yours."

The sunlight was warm and mellow as Grayson made her way between the precise arcs of rosebushes that grew at the head of the garden. From the center of the concentric circles of plantings came the tinkle of water as it tumbled over the graduated tiers of the ornate marble fountain, and she could hear the lazy swish of the newly leafed trees that grew at the foot of the yard. The same spring wind that stirred the trees caught at her free-flowing hair, capriciously lifting glittering silken strands and letting them fall against the wide white collar that encircled her shoulders. As she walked, Grayson spared a glance at the marble folly farther up the path, and with the memories the building evoked she quickened her pace, intent on finding her aunt hidden somewhere in the maze of rosebushes.

All around her the new growth was thick and verdant, and she knew that in a matter of weeks the bushes would be hung with blossoms of every conceivable color: pale white, brilliant crimson, delicate pink, and dusty mauve. The roses were her aunt Julo's pride and joy, and Grayson knew that on such an afternoon her aunt would be among them somewhere, digging in the dirt and whispering encouragement to her darlings.

It had been Gray's intention for several days to get her aunt alone and pose the questions that had been plaguing her. But

Harry Torkington had been inordinately attentive, and Grayson had had little time for other concerns.

Just ahead of her she saw the crown of her aunt's thickly veiled hat and made her way in that direction. Dressed in a yellow, dirt-stained duster, Julo was doing just what Grayson had supposed. As she approached, her aunt looked up, obviously pleased by the prospect of her company.

"It's going to be a wonderful year for roses," she remarked, gesturing with the trowel she held in one smudged hand. "This nice warm weather is going to set them blooming weeks earlier than they usually do."

Grinning at her aunt's enthusiasm, Grayson spread her pale blue-gray skirts and settled on the grass beside her. "Don't you think there will be any more cold weather? The mornings have been downright chilly all this week."

"Cool mornings won't hurt my roses, and when the sun shines as brightly as it is today, you can almost hear them growing."

Grayson was silent for a moment, aware of the flicker of the wind through the leaves, aware of the fecund smell of the earth around them. In that instant she was sure her aunt was right.

"What's that you're burying there at the roots?" she asked, noting her aunt's continued activity. "It looks for all the world like chicken bones."

"Shush! It's my secret. It's what makes my roses grow," she answered conspiratorially. "I have the servants save the bones for me, though I'm sure they think me quite mad for wanting them."

"And we've eaten a great deal of chicken in the last few weeks, haven't we?" Grayson teased.

"Only so each rosebush will get its proper nourishment!"

Gray and her aunt laughed softly together, but there was more on the younger woman's mind than sharing gardening secrets. She had come to seek out Julo this afternoon with a specific purpose in mind, and she was eager to learn what she hoped her aunt would freely tell her.

As soon as their laughter had drifted away, she broached the subject she had come to discuss, the subject of Duncan Palmer.

"Aunt Julo," she began warily, "I have something I've been wanting to ask you, something that's been on my mind since the other night."

Julo sat back on the worn velvet pillow she used to pad her

knees and eyed her niece as if sensing the import of what Grayson was about to say.

"Then ask away, dear girl. You know I'll answer you as best I can."

Now that the moment was upon her, Grayson felt suddenly reluctant. In questioning her aunt about Duncan Palmer, she would be exposing her interest in the man, making the older woman aware of an unseemly curiosity about someone who was not her betrothed. The questions she harbored about Duncan were highly inappropriate for a young woman on the eve of her wedding. But Gray needed to learn more about the man who so warmed and intrigued her, the man who seemed to know things about her she did not know herself, the man who kissed her with a passion and abandon that sent fire through her veins.

Heat mounted to her cheeks at the memory of what had transpired the night of Lady Monmouth's soirée. She recalled how she had responded to Duncan's glance across the crowded ballroom, to the pleasure of being in his arms, to the fervor of his kisses. She remembered how the light filtering out onto the balcony had skimmed the angles of his features; how the sharp, bright scent of his bay rum cologne had set her nostrils tingling; how the hair that grew long at the nape of his neck had felt so vital and full beneath her hands. Her thoughts turned to the words he had spoken as they waltzed. They had been rich and tender with understanding, filled with praise and encouragement. It was as if with a dance, a single conversation, and a few tender kisses he had given her back a part of herself she did not know she had lost.

Hers was not an innocent quest, but Gray desperately needed to satisfy her curiosity. She felt compelled to learn who Duncan Palmer really was, to discover what made him capable of recognizing and assuaging her pain. The dichotomy of what she felt for him intrigued her. The sensations Duncan evoked intrigued her. The man himself intrigued her.

Because of her interest in Duncan Palmer, Grayson was reaching out in a way she had never done before, struggling for an understanding of character she had never dared to seek except in the context of the roles she hoped to play. But she needed to know why people whispered so accusingly about his past, needed to discover what scandal his return to England had resurrected. By questioning her aunt, Gray was risking the censure of those she had always sought to please. Yet somehow in her need to probe the complexities of Duncan Palmer's personality, Julo and Warren Worthington's approval didn't seem to matter.

Still, it took courage to form the words, the questions she wanted to ask. Julo would not press her unduly about Duncan, and perhaps if she was clever, Gray could get the answers she was seeking without revealing more than she wanted her aunt to know.

"I met a strange man at Lady Monmouth's the other evening," Gray began.

"A strange man, my dear? Surely you know every man in London society by now, the sane ones and the strange ones both."

Instead of smiling at Julo's gentle humor, Grayson plucked several blades of grass from the edge of the rose bed and turned them between her fingers. "He's from America and was attending Lady Monmouth's soirée with his cousin."

There was a gleam of recognition in Julo Worthington's gray eyes, but she let Grayson continue.

"His name is Duncan Palmer, and he was introduced to me as the Marquis of Antire."

Julo nodded once, as if her suspicions had been confirmed. "And just what is it you want to know about him, dear?"

Gray wrung the blades of grass as she tried to find appropriate words in which to frame the question. "There seems to have been some kind of scandal in his past . . ."

"And you want to know what it is?"

Grayson nodded. "I suppose I do."

Julo set her trowel aside, giving her adopted niece her full attention. "The story is rather a distressing one, I'm afraid. Are you sure you want to hear it?"

Gray lowered her head in silent assent. Somehow she had known that Duncan's secret was something horrible.

"It happened—oh, fifteen or twenty years ago, when Duncan was hardly more than a boy. I only know the particulars because the Palmers, especially Duncan's uncle Farleigh Wicker, were friendly with Warren's family."

"What happened?" Grayson prodded, wanting to hear the worst of it before her determination deserted her.

Julo drew a long, slow breath before she spoke. "Duncan Palmer killed his father."

The meaning of her aunt's softly spoken words took several moments to penetrate, moments when the sunny springtime world seemed to spin and wheel around her. Cold burst through her body; something in her chest seemed to flutter and constrict. She clutched the grass between her fingers until the blades began to fray.

That can't be true, Gray reasoned a moment later when the capacity for rational thought returned. Duncan couldn't possibly have committed such a heinous crime.

"What happened?" she demanded, her voice gone thin with disbelief.

"It was really very tragic," Julo went on. "It seems that Duncan's parents, Johanna and Jeremy, had a most passionate and volatile relationship. Though theirs was an arranged marriage, it was said they loved each other deeply. But there were times, many times according to the gossip, when their arguments fairly shook the walls. It was also said that Jeremy beat his wife, though I never myself saw any sign of it. When they were together in society, they behaved in a more than seemly manner. And she loved to entertain. Her parties at the Berkeley Square town house were a highlight of the Season.

"At any rate, according to what we heard, they were alone at Antire Manor one evening when a terrible argument erupted. No one knows what it was about, though there was some unsavory speculation afterward. To save from being overheard, they went into the marquis's study to have it out, and somehow, in the passion of the moment, Jeremy strangled his wife."

Grayson held her breath, waiting for her aunt to continue, waiting to hear of Duncan's part in the domestic debacle that was unfolding before her eyes.

"According to the stories, it was then that Duncan came upon them. To save his mother's life, he took one of the marquis's dueling pistols and shot his father, but the attempt to save Johanna came too late. The servants found them all in the study a few minutes later: Johanna strangled, the marquis dead of a gunshot wound through the heart, and the boy, Duncan, with the gun still warm in his hand, unconscious on the floor."

Tears rose in Grayson's eyes and spilled helplessly down her cheeks. The truth of Duncan Palmer's past was even worse than she had imagined. The scene spun out before her eyes so clear that she might have been a witness. She could almost see Duncan bursting into the room to find his father with his hands around his mother's throat. She could almost hear the boy's harsh cry of shock, of disbelief, or anguish. She could sense his desperation as he snatched up the gun, feel the smoothness of the pistol stock clamped tight in his young hand. It must have wavered with the weight and his own reluctance as he raised his arm to point the gun. Had the marquis tried to wrestle the pistol away from his son, or had he taken the bullet willingly as retribution for what he'd done? The sound of the shot seemed to echo in her ears. She could smell the acrid stench of powder burning the back of her throat, and then—

"How horrible," she whispered, gone white to the lips. "Oh, how horrible."

Julo reached across to take Grayson's cold fingers in her own warm grip.

"What a blight it must be on Duncan's life, to have to live with what he's done." Gray's voice was thick with compassion.

"They say Duncan Palmer has no recollection of what happened that night, no memory of the killing at all."

"But surely that's a blessing," Grayson murmured, seeking reassurance in her aunt's pale eyes.

"A blessing is sometimes a curse in disguise," she answered sagely. "It is a blessing that he can't relive those terrible moments, a blessing that they don't haunt him as they might otherwise have done. But it must also be a curse, to know he took his father's life and to be robbed of his only chance to justify the crime of patricide, even to himself."

Grayson nodded in response, her thoughts on the man she was only beginning to know. Had he realized what he was doing? Had he known his mother was dead? Had his father threatened him as well? She could not reconcile a father's murder with the child Duncan must have been. It seemed impossible, inexplicable. Palmer seemed too sensitive and gentle a man to have taken another's life, too solid and reliable to have lived through such a tragedy. Or perhaps Duncan had been irrevocably changed by his parents' deaths, tempered by what had happened.

"He wasn't tried for the killing, was he?" Grayson breathed after a moment.

"No. Good gracious, no," Julo hastened to reassure her. "The whole incident was handled with the utmost secrecy and discretion. Duncan was sent to live with his uncle in America, but word of what happened got out, and there was a horrible scandal. It was only then that Jeremy's abuse of his wife came to light, and that seemed to explain the circumstances. Still, there were those who thought Duncan Palmer should be tried for murder."

"But surely Duncan was only trying to save his mother's life, perhaps save himself as well!" Grayson cried, appalled that anyone should want a mere boy to answer for such a tragedy.

"I agree with you, Grayson, but to this day there are many who think that exile was not punishment enough for what he did. They're whispering about it even now. Frankly, I'm surprised that Duncan Palmer would even consider returning to England."

"He doesn't want to be here." Gray jumped to Duncan's defense without considering the consequences. "He's only in London now because his ship was damaged in a storm."

Julo Worthington eyed her adopted niece with sudden concern. "Just how well do you know Duncan Palmer?"

In response to her aunt's question, Gray drew back her hand and dashed the tears from her cheeks. "I only met him the other night, but he seems a man worthy of my sympathy. We danced a single dance, and he complimented me on my recitation. There was nothing more to it than that."

"But, Grayson dear . . ."

Without giving Julo time to say more, Gray staggered to her feet. "I believe there are some things I must attend to back at the house," she murmured as she turned to go.

"Grayson, wait," Julo called after her, but Gray was eager to escape her aunt's perceptive questions, eager to escape the things she had learned about the man she liked and respected. But even as she hurried between the rows of rosebushes toward the stairs at the edge of the lawn, she knew the truth of Duncan Palmer's past would haunt her for days and nights to come.

Five

"THAT'S DUNCAN PALMER," THE MATRON IN DEEP ROSE SATIN murmured conspiratorially as she adjusted the shaft of the frilled silk parasol that rested against her shoulder, "the Marquis of Antire. He's the one I was telling you about, the one who murdered his father."

The woman beside her craned her neck to see the man her companion had indicated. "The fellow over by the fountain?"

"No, no." The other woman shook her head. "The handsome, chestnut-haired one talking to Baron Brimley."

Grayson, who had paused a few paces behind the two gossiping dowagers, followed their gaze to where Duncan stood in the garden of Mrs. de Rothschild's country estate. Dressed in a frock coat of midnight-blue superfine, narrow buff-colored trousers, and a matching blue and buff striped vest, Palmer towered over his companion with whom he seemed deep in conversation. Gray had been wondering if Duncan had been invited to the breakfast at the beautiful de Rothschild home, but with several hundred guests circulating through the mansion and grounds, she had been heretofore unable to locate him. She had noticed Duncan's cousin Quentin in the grand salon where two Italian divas were giving a recital, though she had seen no sign of Duncan himself until just now.

But before she could turn her thoughts to her reasons for seeking him out, the two women continued their sotto voce conversation.

"When the former marquis died, oh, fifteen or twenty years ago, they circulated the story that Antire shot his father to save his mother from his father's abuse. I suppose there might be some truth in what was said, since Johanna, the marchioness, was killed in the same incident. But the way they hustled young Antire off to America so soon after the tragedy made everyone suspect there was more to the story than what came out."

"The marquis can't be more than thirty," the other woman observed. "How old was he when all this happened?"

"No more than twelve or thirteen, I should think. It's his return to England that is causing such a flap. The incident caused a scandal then, and it is even more of a scandal now that he's returned. Wouldn't you think he'd have the good grace to stay in America rather than returning to London where everyone knows what he did?"

Grayson had heard as much as she cared to hear about Duncan's past. Though she knew it would be wiser to guard her tongue, she could not resist the opportunity to set the record straight.

"Duncan Palmer is here because his ship was damaged in a storm. He never meant to return to England. And with such slandermongers as you reviving interest in his parents' death, I hardly blame him for his reticence."

Grayson spoke softly from directly behind the two dowagers, and with her words they turned, obviously curious about anyone who would champion Antire's cause. That they recognized Grayson was immediately apparent, but before either of the women could gather her wits to respond, Gray turned toward the terrace steps that led down into the garden.

Her defense of Duncan was a mistake, Grayson knew, and she was sure that once the two women recovered themselves they would put their heads together and speculate about Lady Grayson Ware's unlikely interest in the Marquis of Antire, especially in the light of her recent betrothal to the Duke of Stinton. But for the moment, Gray did not care what the two women thought. Their gossiping had made her angry, and she could not help the impulse that made it imperative she set the record straight.

In spite of what her aunt had told her about Palmer's past, she felt Duncan did not deserve such treatment. It offended her sense of fairness that he should be held accountable for something that had happened half a lifetime ago, something that couldn't have been his fault. In a way he had been as much a victim of the tragedy as his parents had been. He had been robbed of his homeland and his birthright. And though he still retained the title and the income from the family holdings, he had been robbed of the life he had been born to live.

However foolish her defense of Duncan was, Grayson was not so naive as to approach him directly. Instead she made a circuit of the garden filled with women in sumptuous gowns, fluttering across the lawn like a flock of bright spring butterflies. Beside them were men whose more somber dress played a subtle counterpoint to the brilliant hues the women wore. As she moved through the throng, past clots of people who were laughing and talking, past the impeccably liveried servants serving punch and wine and canapés, Gray was careful not to cast so much as a glance in Duncan Palmer's direction. Instead she paused to speak to a group of her uncle's associates, touched Harry's arm as he stood talking horses with his own cadre of fellow huntsmen, made a place for herself with some friends of her own. Still, she never lost sight of Duncan. She had been mulling over some of the things he had said the night of Lady Monmouth's soirée, and she was most eager to talk to him.

In time, Duncan took his leave of Baron Brimley and headed toward the lake down the hill from the enormous gray stone mansion. With marked impatience she watched him go, wondering what had sent him seeking solitude in the midst of one of the Season's gayest parties. After concluding her conversation, Grayson excused herself and discreetly followed after him.

The lake itself was lovely, like a blue and silver mirror glistening in the sun. Floating on its shimmering surface among the budding water lilies were several punts filled with laughing maidens and dashing swains, making the scene before her every bit as picturesque and idyllic as the garden's planners had intended. Along the northern perimeter of the lake the gravel path that wound through the grounds of the estate swept beneath some willow trees. Knowing that Duncan had disappeared beneath their swaying canopy some minutes before, Grayson moved purposefully in the direction he had taken.

It was cool and breezy in the shade of the trees, and the fresh, rich smell of the English countryside brought visions of her uncle Warren's country home. As much as she loved the bustle and excitement of London, she missed the beauty of the countryside where the delicate primroses of early spring would long since have given way to carpets of bluebells, clusters of wood anemones, and early orchids. Now at her feet, clinging to the edge of the lake, were creamy water violets, yellow-centered fleabane, and clumps of water mint. But though she appreciated the elaborate display, she took no time to revel in it. She had come this way in search of Duncan Palmer, and in the few minutes she could spare, she had to find and convince him to help her.

Grayson hurried on through the manicured woodland glade and caught up to her quarry a few minutes later where he stood in the cool dim shadows, staring back across the lake toward the vista of garden and mansion.

"Duncan," she called out in greeting.

As he turned, she could see the surprise that flickered across his face transformed by a smile of pure pleasure.

"Grayson! I didn't know you were here today."

There was something so compelling about Duncan when he smiled, something that set off shimmers of pleasure down deep inside of Gray. It was not just that he was a handsome man; Grayson knew men far more handsome than he. It was the welcome in his face that made his smile so deliciously warm and intimate, that told her his greeting was meant exclusively for her.

"I should have realized you would be at such a grand affair as this."

"I came with Harry, actually," she admitted as she stopped beside him at the edge of the shade. "There's hardly a party all season long he isn't invited to attend."

Abruptly Duncan sobered. "And how is dear Harry?"

"Tolerably well, I suppose. His health isn't something we discuss."

"And what do you find to discuss with your intended?"

"Very little, I'm afraid." She answered with the truth, though it would have been wiser to lie.

Duncan turned back toward the lake as if his attention had been diverted by the laughter drifting across the water from the people in the punts. "And just what is it you have come to discuss with me?"

Grayson flushed a little with the transparency of her ploy. She had not intended that her pursuit of him be so obvious, either to anyone watching or to Duncan himself. Still, she was determined not to let this opportunity pass. She had risked too much to have these few minutes alone with him.

"I have been thinking a great deal about something you said to me at Lady Monmouth's party."

"And what did I say that has been bothering you?"

The possibilities were endless, Duncan knew, for he had said and done far more that night than was either prudent or proper. Grayson's unexpected appearance on this side of the lake had awakened echoes of that evening in him, too: of their shared confidences, of the way their bodies moved together when they danced, of the lingering kisses they had shared on Lady Monmouth's terrace. Those memories were reinforced by Grayson's nearness, by the soft, sweet scent of gardenias that wafted toward him, by the white-gloved hand she had laid against his sleeve. Though he knew it was a mistake to succumb, a delicious heady warmth stirred through him, filling him with a reckless need to renew and revel in what they'd shared.

"You said the night of Lady Monmouth's party," Grayson went on, "that I might find acceptance of my acting abilities in America, on the American stage."

Apparently her memories of that evening, Duncan thought, were substantially different from his own.

"Yes, I suppose I did."

As he spoke, Gray saw the light go out of Duncan's eyes, though she couldn't fathom a reason for the change in him. Palmer seemed suddenly so remote, so uninvolved, when only a few moments before he had been genuinely glad to see her.

Perhaps he had been insincere in his praise of her the night of Lady Monmouth's soirée and was worried he would be called upon to elaborate, she reasoned with a stir of apprehension. Perhaps she had misinterpreted what he'd said or had been mistaken about the possibility of making him her ally. She was suddenly not at all sure she was prepared to voice the proposal she had come here to make. Still, she had no choice but to persist, knowing this might be her only chance to enlist Duncan's aid.

She drew a shaky breath and plunged ahead. "Once your ship is repaired, I want to book passage with you to New York. I want to do as you suggested. I want to try my talents on the American stage."

For a heartbeat Duncan simply stared at her.

"You want to *what*?"

Of all the damning things he had said and done that evening nearly a fortnight before, this was the very last one Palmer had expected to be called upon to answer for.

"You know the match with Harry Torkington is not exactly the answer to a maiden's prayer," Gray continued in a rush, "and once I've become Harry's wife I must forfeit any hopes I have for a career on the stage. Until you mentioned the possibility of going to America, I had never considered what advantages such a move might offer me.

"The audiences in the States seem to have a fascination with British performers, and in the past any English acting company that has braved the Atlantic has been warmly welcomed and generously rewarded for—"

"Grayson! For God's sake! What you're talking about doing is preposterous!" Duncan burst out, finding his voice at last.

He had indeed suggested that she might find acceptance on the American stage, but he had never dreamed she would take him seriously. Nor was he pleased that she had decided to make him her accomplice in this scheme to reach New York.

Storming the American stage was unthinkable for a woman like her. She was not some pretty girl with a bent for the dramatic; she was a lady of the realm. She was not a common actress; she was about to become a duchess. Taking passage to New York would mean giving up her life in England. Undertaking a career on the stage would mean forfeiting every advantage she'd been born to.

Yet from the determined expression on Grayson's face, Duncan could tell that she was fully committed to what she'd just proposed. Though it seemed ludicrous he should be called upon to champion the values of a society he had rejected long ago, it was up to him to save her from certain disaster.

"My God, Grayson! Consider what you'd be giving up if you followed this mad course."

Gray's face hardened. "And what would I be giving up, Duncan? What would I be forfeiting by going to America?"

"Well, you'd lose your chance to be a duchess," he began, scrambling for a footing from which to launch his defense.

"But I've no aspirations in that regard."

"You'd forfeit your place in society."

"And what advantage can that place afford me in the life I want to live?"

"You'd lose control of your fortune, which must be formidable indeed if Stinton is so hot to marry you."

"If I marry Harry, I lose control of the money anyway."

His arguments were the ones Grayson would have expected her uncle to voice. They were the obvious ones, the ones anyone in her circle of friends would have seen as the most important.

Hearing the words from Duncan's lips was an unexpected betrayal.

"As things stand now," she spat, "I'm past twenty-one and the fortune's mine to do with as I please."

"But you'll be giving up all hope of security, Grayson, if you run away to America."

The security was the hardest thing to sacrifice, and though their time together had been brief, Duncan must have understood enough about her to realize that the need for security was her greatest vulnerability. Yet in the days since she had seen him last she'd had a great deal of time to think—about her future and her past. She'd thought about the familial approval she'd never really achieved, the ambitions she'd been forced to hide. She'd thought about what life with Harry would be, and the way acting made her feel. She *had* thought about what she'd be giving up, but she'd also thought about what she stood to gain.

"The theater is a shaky business at the best of times," Duncan went on, obviously pressing his advantage, "and all alone in America, you would be prey to all kinds of unscrupulous scoundrels."

"I'm not nearly as naive as you think," Grayson challenged him.

"Nor are you as worldly-wise as you yourself believe," he assured her. "Do you know how hard it would be to make a place for yourself on the stage, where your respectability would be suspect, where your independence might be an invitation to be exploited? Would you know how to evade the bounders who will be attracted by your beauty? Do you know the dangers you would face?"

As he spoke, his fingers closed around her arm, and he gave her a desperate little shake, as if to awaken her to the truth in what he was telling her.

"If you were part of an acting company the risks in leaving England wouldn't be quite so overwhelming. But alone in America, Grayson, what kind of a chance do you think you'd have?"

Gray was well aware that her prospects of succeeding in New York would be better if she were part of a touring company come from England. But Grayson had no time or opportunity to make an alliance with such a troupe before heading across the Atlantic. If she wanted to escape her marriage to Harry Torkington, if she wanted the chance to prove herself as an actress, she had to do it now. In a month it would be too late.

There was the strain of desperation in her voice as she continued. "Please, Duncan. I know the risks I'd be taking. I know how difficult it may be for a woman with no experience on the boards to convince an American theater manager to hire her. But I'm as good as many actresses performing today; you said so yourself—"

He threw up his hands in exasperation and turned away. "I didn't expect you to take me literally when I suggested you try acting in America."

"Then why did you encourage me?"

Duncan cursed under his breath, feeling trapped between the well-deserved words of praise and the unexpected consequences of expressing them.

"Good God, Grayson!" he continued. "You know why I told you that. You obviously needed someone to tell you how good you were the night of Lady Monmouth's soirée."

"So you lied to me to spare my feelings? You encouraged me with empty praise?"

There was acid in her question, accusation and self-doubt.

"Damn it, Grayson. You *were* good, better than good. I had never heard Portia's speech rendered with greater feeling . . ."

Duncan saw the pain, the disillusionment that lay like a veil across her features. He admired Grayson's courage, her single-minded pursuit of what she wanted. If he hadn't understood her feelings, refusing her passage would have been a damn sight easier.

"Please, Duncan, I trust you—"

"Perhaps you shouldn't."

"I know you'll see me safely to New York."

"You don't know anything about me, Grayson."

But she did. She had given a great deal of thought to just why Duncan Palmer was the man to help her achieve her goals. In spite of the things her aunt had told her about Duncan's past, she trusted him. She trusted him far more than any man she had ever met. The night of Lady Monmouth's party she had touched emotions deep inside him. They were wondrous, strong, common to them both, and she had to make him acknowledge the things that bound them together.

"Please, Duncan, I know you understand. It's your achievements that have made you the man you are. In going to America I'm pursuing something I've wanted all my life. Can you deny me the chance to reach the goals I've set for myself? Would you refuse me the opportunities you have had?"

As he shook his head, she hurried on. "Please, Duncan, I'm a full-grown woman, not some child you need to protect. Once I've landed in New York, you need have no further contact with me."

This was not an argument that would help her win her way, though Grayson had no way of knowing it. It wasn't the responsibility once they reached New York that Duncan was trying to avoid.

There was one more card in Grayson's hand, a card she had hoped she would not have to play. It was her trump card, the one she believed would win his acquiescence.

"If you won't take me to America when you leave"—her voice went cold—"I'll book passage on another ship."

Duncan's eyes narrowed and his mouth went grim. His hand tightened on her arm once more.

"Don't do this, Grayson," he warned. "Don't try to force me to take you to America. I won't do it. I swear I won't."

"Please, Duncan, please," she repeated in a whisper.

"No." Their eyes clashed and his fingers bit deeper. "No."

The word lay between them, flat and unadorned, unyielding as ancient stone. She saw the absolute resolve in him, the unshakable belief that he was protecting her from herself. There was no possibility that he might reconsider, no uncertainty in him at all.

Then suddenly she crumpled, realizing her defiance was incomplete. No matter how much she needed to follow her dream, her courage was finite. Until that moment she had not realized that booking passage on another ship was something she wasn't prepared to do.

Duncan saw the light die in her eyes, saw the purpose seep out of her face. He knew that he had won, but there was no joy in his victory, no pleasure in knowing that by his refusal he had sealed her fate. He realized suddenly that this was the responsibility he had been trying desperately to avoid. This was the inevitability he had been loath to force upon her. In spite of the conviction that he was right, he could not bear the thought that he, Duncan Palmer, was the one who had condemned her, condemned lovely vibrant Grayson Ware, to a life with Harry Torkington.

That knowledge stirred a morass of emotions. They gathered in his chest, making his heart lumber painfully inside his ribs, making breathing impossible. Regret clogged his throat. Yet there was nothing he could do. His decision was right, iron-clad, irrevocable. It was the consequences of that decision that gnawed at his insides.

He slid his free hand up her arm to curl around her shoulder, meaning for the gesture to calm and reassure Grayson. If he could convince her that fate was not as cruel as she supposed, perhaps he could also convince himself.

He drew her into the curve of his body, resting his cheek against her face. Her skin was satin smooth, warm, and damp where a few telling tears had marred the ivory surface. They were tears he had put in her eyes and on her cheeks. That responsibility, too, weighed heavily on his conscience. Duncan would have drawn her closer still, would have succumbed to the need to hold her and kiss her tears away, except that there was the crunch of cinders on the path behind them.

Before they could step apart, Warren Worthington emerged from beneath the fluttering drape of willow branches. What he thought at finding his ward in the arms of a stranger was immediately apparent in his face.

"Harry's been looking for you everywhere, girl," Worthington announced through narrowed lips, his jaw clenched with proprietary anger. "And you've no business wandering so far from the house. Everyone's been asking for you. Run along now and assure Harry and Julo you haven't fallen in the lake."

"Why, Uncle Warren," Gray exclaimed, turning out of Duncan's embrace. "Captain Palmer had just suggested we return to the house to get some punch. You haven't met Captain Palmer, have you, Uncle Warren? He's your old friend Farleigh Wicker's nephew."

Worthington's gaze flickered over the younger man. It was patently obvious he knew just who Duncan was. "So you're Farleigh Wicker's nephew. I must say I'm surprised at your return to England."

Duncan acknowledged the comment with a lift of his chin. "I would not be here now, your grace, but that my ship was forced into Portsmouth for repairs."

There was a moment of tense silence before Grayson jumped into the breach. "And you know, Uncle Warren, I had just invited Captain Palmer to tea. I thought you might want to hear how your old friend Mr. Wicker is faring in America. It must be years since you've had word of him."

There was a pause before Worthington answered.

"It has been years," he agreed, though it was obvious he was as aware of Grayson's ploy as Duncan was.

"You would like that, wouldn't you, Uncle Warren? You would enjoy an opportunity to visit with Captain Palmer."

Worthington met her question with silence as he renewed his appraisal of the younger man.

"I thought a week from Thursday would be good," she hastened to add. "That is, if you've no political meetings to attend."

The older man eyed both his ward and Duncan Palmer for a long moment, wondering if he had somehow misjudged the situation. He would have sworn that Palmer and his ward were in the midst of a passionate embrace when he came upon them, but now he was not so sure. There was something more than passion here, something he didn't understand. Like the good politician he was, Worthington decided to study the matter more closely before deciding on a definitive course of action where his ward and the captain were concerned.

"Thursday would be fine," he conceded. "And now, Grayson my girl, it's time to bid Captain Palmer good-bye. Harry's been scouring the grounds of the estate for nearly half an hour."

As Duncan's hand dropped away from Grayson's waist, she turned and took her uncle's arm.

"It's settled, then," she offered with a sigh of relief. "You'll come to tea a week from Thursday, Captain Palmer?"

Though Duncan nodded, his eyes were kindling with bright blue sparks. "Until then, Lady Grayson. I'll be counting the hours, to be sure."

Gray ignored his blatant sarcasm. "Why don't you come by Worthington Hall about four o'clock?"

"Whatever you say, Lady Grayson. Four o'clock."

As Warren Worthington escorted her back through the fringe of willows, Grayson could feel the heat of Palmer's gaze burning between her shoulderblades. She had not been able to persuade him to take her to America, but she had done the next best thing. She had ensured another meeting, another chance to win him to her way.

She had lost this round of the argument, but Grayson was an optimist. There must be a way to persuade Duncan to take her to

America, and between now and a week from Thursday, she could muster some brand-new arguments. Grayson smiled to herself as she began to make her plans. Until the moment Palmer's ship left the wharf at Portsmouth absolutely anything was possible.

Six

DAMN GRAYSON WARE. DAMN HER BLAZING GREEN EYES, HER glorious red hair, her alabaster skin, and the soft, sweet scent of gardenias that seemed to envelop a man when he stood beside her. Damn her beauty. Damn her näiveté. Damn her for wanting him to take her to America.

Duncan Palmer stared down at the ledgers on the desk before him, unable to see the columns of tiny figures for the vivid apparition that seemed to hover between them and his need for concentration. Instead of the bookkeeper's careful notations, Grayson stood before him as she had looked the day before at Mrs. de Rothschild's party. Dressed in a gown of watered silk just the color of purple hyacinths, she had been as appealing as the warm spring day. With a fichu of filmy ribboned lace gathered close around her throat, with an ancient cameo to hold it in place, with matching ribbons plaited through her hair, Gray had looked fragile and enchanting. That her white-gloved hands had been knotted together at her waist was her only concession to the nervousness she must have felt at approaching him with her request for passage, and as her face had filled with a mixture of entreaty and hope, it had been nearly impossible for him to refuse her.

Duncan shook his head in disgust at the thought of what she wanted to do. Leaving her life in England for the uncertainties of the American stage was a preposterous notion—made all the more ridiculous because he had suggested it to her himself.

He could remember each and every word they'd spoken the evening of Lady Monmouth's soirée and knew exactly where he'd gone wrong. Grayson's distress at having to give up acting in favor of a life with Harry Torkington and her need for encouragement had stirred Palmer's protective instincts. While it was true that she was as good as many of the actresses performing in America, his had been a passing comment, nothing more. How could he have known that Gray would take him seriously? How could he have known that she would have the temerity to expect his help in reaching New York?

He supposed his empathy for her situation had come from the belief that no matter what the world thought of the life a man chose to live, he had an obligation to do his best. His years in America had taught him the power of accomplishment, introduced him to the strong, impenetrable shield of self-respect. Those beliefs made him the man he was. Yet weren't accomplishments a masculine domain? Surely a woman didn't need to achieve the same degree of success when she could bask in the reflected glory of the man she loved.

But even as the arguments formed in his head, Duncan knew them to be faulty, biased. They went against all he knew of human nature, all he believed about human dignity. It was Grayson's need for accomplishment and acceptance that was driving her to seek a career on the stage, and he applauded her courage. But if she failed to make a place for herself in the theater, what kind of a future would be left to her then? She would never be able to return to England, never be able to resume the only life she'd ever known.

He cared about Grayson Ware, Duncan admitted grudgingly, and he could not bear to see her hurt. Despite the contempt he felt for Harry Torkington, and though he recognized that Harry and Gray were a hopelessly mismatched couple, he felt that such a marriage was preferable to the uncertainties of life on the stage. And since Palmer was relatively certain Gray had not confided her plans to anyone else, he believed it was his responsibility to save her from herself.

When Grayson had announced to her uncle the previous day that Duncan had accepted an invitation to tea at Worthington Hall, he had been furious, but now he realized it was the perfect opportunity to convince Gray that what she wanted to do was courting disaster. There in the midst of all the creature comforts, in the midst of all she held dear, he would be able to make her see the wisdom of remaining in England.

If the truth were told, there were other reasons for him to accept the invitation as well. Warren Worthington was one of the men who had backed Wicker and Walford's trading ventures from the start, and once his anger at being manipulated cooled, Duncan realized there was something to be gained by having the chance to talk to him. What Worthington might reveal, Palmer was not sure, but at this point in his investigation, there was no telling what information might prove useful to him.

Though he tried to explain away his reasons for accepting the invitation to tea, Duncan was also grudgingly aware that he wanted to see Grayson again. She aroused feelings in him that were as compelling as they were unwelcome, as exciting as they were unsettling. That he was attracted to her was understandable; Gray was a very beautiful woman. But after the tragedy of his parents' marriage, he was uneasy with the emotions Grayson stirred.

She seemed linked to his darker nature, to the most confusing, complex things inside himself. She threatened to tap a part of him that he had long denied, threatened to loosen the tight rein he had always held on his emotions. When he was with her, unexpected feelings came to the fore: empathy, tenderness, desire, anxiety, pain. He did not want to acknowledge the delight Grayson could loose in him, or the anger she could stir. He did not want to accept her ability to make him feel, her ability to make him vulnerable. It frightened him to want to lose himself in the joy of making love to her when by that act he would have to reveal the parts of himself he had always struggled to suppress.

Yet a full day after their encounter on Mrs. de Rothschild's estate, he could still feel the pull of Grayson's innocent magnetism. He could feel the tingling in his palms that made him want to touch her, could feel the warmth down deep in his loins at the thought of kissing her. When she had appeared through the drape of willow branches, he had wanted to take up where they had left off that night on Lady Monmouth's terrace. He had wanted to claim her mouth with his, let this fingers graze her silken skin. Hell, he had wanted to strip away her clothes and make love to her there in the grass.

Duncan went dizzy with the thought of how it might have been: of how she would melt against him in response to his kisses, of how she would gasp with the first sweet stirrings of passion. As his tongue darted into her mouth, he would loosen the fasteners at the back of her gown, exposing the slope of her alabaster shoulders, the curve of her back. He would slide the slippery fabric away and nibble the swell of her breasts as his hand crept up along her thigh beneath the tangle of frilly petticoats. She would moan and breathe his name as he reached the cleft between her legs. She would arch against him, succumbing to his passion, his expertise. She would writhe against him, moaning, twisting, wanting more. He would stroke her, kiss her until she was moist and wild with desire. Then, after stripping away her clothes and his own, he would press her down onto the sweet green grass, smelling the fecund warmth of spring and of their uninhibited mating—

"Captain Palmer?" The voice intruded on his fantasy, the one that had nothing at all to do with dissuading Grayson Ware from going to America.

"Captain Palmer?"

With difficulty Duncan returned from his daydreams of making love to Grayson to the confines of the office overlooking the St. Katharine Dock. Cursing his own preoccupation, he turned his attention to Haversham, the bookkeeper, who was standing in the doorway.

"Yes?" Duncan answered in a breathless tone. He felt hot and weak and supremely disoriented.

"These are the ledgers you wanted to see, the ones from 1837 and 1838."

"Yes. Right. Just put them here on the desk. I'll get to them in a minute."

"As you say, sir," the man answered, doing as he had been told, then leaving the office.

With trembling hands Duncan reached for the first ledger, consigning the fantasy of making love to Grayson Ware to the farthest reaches of his mind. But his body was not so easily subdued and throbbed with the pain of thwarted pleasure.

"Damn you, Grayson," he muttered under his breath. "I don't have the time or the inclination to fool with you."

But as much as he tried to convince himself otherwise, he knew it was not Grayson's fault that he was so distracted.

It took a full five minutes before Duncan was able to turn his thoughts to the newest sets of ledgers. He had asked for them in frustration when delving into the accounts for the past five years had proved an exercise in futility. Before he was willing to concede that there was nothing wrong with Wicker and Walford's books, he had to try to find a break in the pattern of entries that would somehow coincide with the company's gradual loss of revenue.

Diligently he pored over the narrow columns of figures, realizing that, once more, the notations in the books were everything they should have been. It was well past noon when he finished with the records from 1837, and instead of stopping for dinner, he pressed on to the following year's ledgers.

He quickly saw that 1838 had been a banner year for the company. In spite of the social unrest that had been brewing in London, there had been a cautious optimism in response to the new queen's reign. Late in 1838, several new companies were added to the list of those Wicker and Walford did business with. Seeing that substantial payments had been made to each of them in return for manufactured goods, Duncan made note of their names.

When at the end of the day Palmer had a total of five companies on his list, he slipped the paper into his pocket with the intention of visiting each of them. It would be an interesting exercise at the very least, and perhaps he would find some link between Walford and the manufacturing concerns that would give him the proof of misappropriation he had been seeking these last weeks.

It was the only course left to him now. The ledgers had divulged every scrap of information, and there was nothing left for him to do but admit that he had failed. If this last effort proved as fruitless as everything else he'd tried, Duncan would apologize to Walford for the suspicions he had entertained. But if he was right, if in investigating the companies on his list he found the proof of Walford's embezzlement, that would be a different matter entirely.

As Duncan hailed a hackney cab outside Wicker and Walford's offices, Samuel Walford stood in the window watching him, a frown curling his heavy mouth. From the moment Palmer had presented himself at the firm nearly a month before, Walford had known he would bring trouble. Despite his explanations, despite his guilelessness and charm, Walford knew exactly why Duncan Palmer had come. He had come to poke his nose into things that were none of his concern, to demand explanations for things that were beyond his comprehension.

The younger man was too much like his uncle Farleigh, too much like his father before him. Duncan was honorable, honest, noble, and intolerable. Palmer played the game by a given set of rules, saw the world in black and white when there were only shades of gray. It was impossible to expect compromises from a man like that, Walford thought, impossible to expect him to compromise his principles or integrity. That inflexibility on moral and ethical grounds, that inability to see anything but right and wrong, would bring Duncan Palmer a world of grief, involve him in a kind of retribution he had escaped more than a decade before.

"Mr. Walford?"

Samuel turned away from the window to where his head bookkeeper stood hovering in the doorway.

"Yes, Haversham, what is it?"

The man slid inside the office and closed the door behind him, coming to a halt on the far side of Walford's massive desk.

"You told me to let you know if Captain Palmer showed any particular interest in the companies we do business with."

Walford placed his hands on the inlaid leather surface and leaned across the desk toward the bookkeeper. "Yes, and has he?"

The bookkeeper cleared his throat. His voice was soft, an octave higher than it should have been; it matched his personality perfectly. "Well, sir, to tell you the truth he has. I saw him copying names out of the ledger onto a separate piece of paper."

Walford took a moment to consider this bit of information. "And from which of the ledgers did he copy the names?"

"I believe it was from the one that deals with the latter part of 1838."

"And was Enterprise Manufacturing one of the names he copied?"

The bookkeeper shook his head convulsively. "I can't be sure," he answered, "but it certainly looked as though it might have been on the list with three or four other companies."

"What did he do with the paper, Haversham?"

"Why, he put it in his pocket."

Walford's face congealed into a menacing scowl. "Damn," he muttered as he turned back toward the window. "Damn!"

Seven

IT'S DUNCAN PALMER'S FAULT THAT I AM HERE. HE'S THE ONE WHO forced me into this. Grayson glared at the doors of the Varieties Theatre and fervently wished she was still home in bed. It was Duncan's encouragement, compounded by his refusal to take her to America, that had brought her to the theater district this morning. She had seen a notice in the previous day's edition of the *Morning Chronicle* that a company of actors was forming to tour the United States and realized it was a bit of serendipity she dared not ignore. If Duncan continued to refuse her passage, Gray might be forced to make arrangements of her own to reach New York.

As she stood on the walk before the theater, pretending to study the faded posters beneath the marquee, the London Grayson knew and loved lay all around her. Carriages and drays passed behind her; costermongers cried out the virtues of their wares. People brushed past her, busy with errands of their own. Outside this theater was the world as she had always known it. Inside the theater lay the dream that had sustained her all her life, if only she had the courage to test her abilities, if only she had the fortitude to accept the challenge of a real audition. Was she as good an actress as she thought? Was she brave enough to risk her dreams by reading for a theater manager? Was she prepared to change her life for the sake of her own ambition?

Fear lay like a cold empty bubble inside her chest. Self-doubt clutched at the back of her throat. She reached one hand toward the door handle and snatched it away. Did she really want to go inside and risk all she'd ever cared about?

Gray had long dreamed about what life as an actress would be. More times than she could count she had imagined herself stepping onto a stage costumed in an elegant gown, her face masked with skillfully applied makeup, her lines and her understanding of a character etched into her mind. She would look out across a sea of intent faces of people who had come to the theater to be moved and entertained. As she began to speak, she would forge the sacred bond of trust that linked an entertainer and her audience, weave her own wondrous magic as she disappeared into her role. She could imagine the intensity that would swell toward her as she performed, could feel the crowd's approval and their awe. At the end of the play the people beyond the footlights would rise and applaud, touched by what she'd said and done, fascinated by her ability to make them laugh and cry. Their adulation would rush toward her in a wave—warm, nurturing, fulfilling.

Then, with her heart hammering hard in her chest, Gray would turn to where her aunt and uncle were seated in a box toward the front of the hall. She would peer across the footlights, trying to gauge their reaction to seeing her perform. Her hands would grow damp as she studied their faces. Her stomach would flutter and dip with anticipation and unease. She would see Julo's eyes glowing with love and approval, but even in a moment of triumph, it would be her uncle's verdict Gray would truly want. He had been her harshest critic all her life, and she had been seeking his acceptance and respect for as long as she could remember. Finally he would rise to salute her with all the rest, joining in the round of thunderous applause, smiling with pride in her accomplishments.

Fortified by a vision of a future she longed to embrace, by Duncan's faith in her abilities, by the determination to make her aunt and uncle proud of her, Grayson reached for the handle, pulled the door open, and stepped inside the theater.

The half-light of the building swallowed her up, and as she waited for her eyes to adjust to the gloom, she was aware of the musty smell of the place, the penetrating silence. They were things that were usually masked by the press of perfumed bodies and the chatter of the crowd. The familiar space now seemed incalculably strange, and fear chilled Gray again.

The entrance to the stalls was directly ahead, and as she crossed the few scant yards of threadbare carpet, her shoe soles dragged like lead. Then somehow she was standing at the back of the pit. She had never seen the stage from here before; she had always watched plays from the more expensive boxes at the sides of the hall. This was what the common people saw; from these benches came an actor's harshest judgments. The view seemed intimidating somehow.

"You, you there at the back of the house," a man's voice called out from somewhere near the stage. "What is it you are doing there?"

It took all of Grayson's courage to answer him. "I came for an audition."

"Don't you know that you should have come to the stage door and given your name to the manager?"

Grayson hesitated and the man heaved a heavy sigh, a whisper of sound that must have reached her through some trick of the acoustics.

"No, I suppose you didn't," he went on, "or you'd not have come that way. Well, no matter. Come down here. I'll put your name on the list myself."

Mortified by a blunder that marked her as an amateur, Grayson fought the urge to flee. Instead, she forced herself to walk down the aisle to where the man was standing at the end of a row of seats. He had a handsome mobile face, a straight theatrical bearing. That he was used to being in the limelight was apparent in his broad but graceful movements.

"Your name?" he asked, taking a foolscap tablet from the fellow who sat beside him.

"Anna Arthur," Gray responded. She had decided on her stage name on the way over in the cab.

He nodded once and wrote it on a list with half a dozen others. "Take a seat just over there. We'll get to you by and by."

Grayson did as she was told, noticing only then that there were several others waiting: two men, one young, one old; a mature woman; and three other actresses of Gray's approximate years. She smiled a greeting, but they ignored her. As Gray settled herself on the uncomfortable bench, she began to understand the restlessness that was so often evident in the pit. The seating was just short of intolerable.

With the intention of determining what would be expected of her when she read, Grayson turned her attention to the stage. The woman standing there had been interrupted by Gray's arrival and was evidently quite put out. Still, she resumed her recitation with consummate skill. She was rendering one of Elmire's speeches from the last act of *Tartuffe*.

Gray felt the color rise in her cheeks. For her the play had unpleasant associations, and she wished that while she was feeling so frightened and unsure she had not been reminded of the incident at Ellison's Finishing School. It did not raise Grayson's confidence that the woman was very good. Her voice was rich and fruity, and the inflection she gave to Elmire's words was exactly right for the role. When she had finished, the two men seated in the audience had her sing to the accompaniment of a fellow who played a pianoforte set down in the orchestra pit. Though the actress lacked much in the way of range, her tone was clear and true.

After stopping to confer with the men for whom she was auditioning, the woman flounced up the aisle, breaking stride only long enough to give Gray a cold, hard look for having the temerity to interrupt her.

One by one the people on the list had their turns at reading, and from the gossip that hissed around her, Gray learned the two auditioners' identities. One was John Howard, the actor-manager of the troupe that would be touring in America. The other was William Grady, the backer for the enterprise. As she watched, she began to note that Grady was far more interested in the actresses than the actors, and with the echo of Duncan's warnings in her ears, Grayson realized that getting a place in the troupe might depend on far more than her talent.

Howard, on the other hand, was single-minded and demanding. He seemed to weigh each gesture, each inflection, each word spoken by the person on the stage. This made sense to Grayson somehow, for while Grady might have a say in the people selected for the troupe, it was Howard who would meld them into a cohesive ensemble for the tour of the United States.

Both the older man and the younger man who read were experienced and competent, as was the older woman who took to the stage just after them. Two of the younger actresses were more than adequate, too, but the last was hopelessly affected, though by far the prettiest of the three. A whispered conference took place between the manager and the backer when she had finished the first part of the audition. But then she was dismissed without being given a chance to sing. Grady followed her out when she was through and returned from the lobby afterward looking smug and self-congratulatory.

Then it was Grayson's turn to read, though when they called for Anna Arthur, it took her a moment to respond. With terror wringing her heart she hurried toward the stage. Her knees were all but knocking as she made her way up the stairs. She felt faint, light-headed, clammy—until she passed beyond the footlights. Then, as if by magic, Gray's fears dropped away. Being on a stage as an actress was everything she had dreamed it would be.

"Anna," Howard called over the footlights to her, "have you had any acting experience, dear?"

Grayson wondered if she should lie, then shrugged the thought away. "I've done a few readings for groups informally," she answered, "and been in one or two amateur theatricals."

It was the truth as far as it went. She had read plays to her schoolmates at Ellison's late at night, and she had done scenes once or twice in the drawing room with her friends. Then of course there was the recitation at Lady Monmouth's. That recitation and Duncan's praise had brought her here today.

"Very well, Anna," Howard continued with greatly diminished enthusiasm. "What are you going to perform for us?"

"I'd like to do Portia's scene from *The Merchant of Venice*."

Grayson drew a breath to muster her reserves, then stepped toward the apron of the stage.

"'The quality of mercy is not strained,'" she began. "'It droppeth as the gentle rain from heaven upon the place beneath.'"

As she spoke, she could feel the power of the words come over her, the power of the character Shakespeare had so clearly drawn. With every part of herself, she reached out to the men seated in the empty theater. But instead of seeing only their blank, weary faces, she imagined a receptive crowd filling the hall, people who would respond to her passion, her eloquence. She moved gracefully, her gestures and inflections those that Portia might have used; she employed the full range of her voice, varying the volume and intonation to highlight the importance of certain passages. Outside of herself she was aware of her own technique, of the game she played to heighten the illusion she was trying to create. But inside she was completely the heroine she had come to play.

As the last lines rang through the hall, Grayson felt oddly drained, strangely spent. She had put all of herself into the recitation.

Without a role to cloak her identity, her nervousness returned, and Gray could hardly catch her breath as she waited for John Howard's verdict.

"You do Shakespeare quite well, Anna," he began, though she

could hear the reservations in his tone. "But on the tour we are planning, we will be doing several recent plays, melodramas mostly. Have you ever tried anything like that?"

Grayson had seen one or two performed but had never read a melodrama herself. "No, Mr. Howard. I can't say that I have."

Coming around the row of seats and making his way through the orchestra pit, he handed a playbook up to her. "Would you read the section that is marked. It is a soliloquy spoken by a mother whose child is to be taken from her in the morning because of her own immoral acts."

Knowing nothing more about the character than the sketch Howard had given her, Grayson was not sure she could do the reading justice. Was the woman distraught by the prospect of losing her child? Did she blame herself for what was happening? If the child was taken away, what would happen to the mother? Gray wished she had a better understanding of the context of the scene. Still, she had no choice but to play the role as best she could.

"Shall I start here, on the top of page thirty-eight?"

Howard nodded, and Gray drew a long uneven breath.

" 'Oh, see how he lies sleeping in his tiny bed, his cheeks round and rosy, his skin as pale as cream. He looks so like a cherub lying thus. How in the morning should I give this cherub up? He is a part of my love and my body, my only hope of retribution for the dastardly sins of my past. How can I allow others to take my hope away? How shall I live if all my hope is gone?' "

"That's fine, Anna," Howard interrupted her. "Now let's hear you sing."

Had she done well or badly with the melodrama? Gray wondered. Had Howard stopped her because she had rendered the soliloquy unacceptably or because he had heard enough? Still, he hadn't dismissed her. He had asked her to sing.

"I—I didn't bring any music," she explained.

"I'm sure George knows far more songs than you do. What do you want him to play?"

Gray couldn't think of anything to request. It was as if singing were a totally new concept her brain was struggling to comprehend.

" 'Greensleeves,' " she finally said. The old melody was one she had always liked, though it was not the easiest song to sing.

The piano began its accompaniment and Grayson sang. She had

a more than acceptable voice in normal circumstances, but now her throat was tight. She couldn't seem to suck enough air into her lungs to make her voice carry beyond the first rows of theater seats.

They let her finish anyway, and as she made her way down the steps at the side of the stage, Howard rose.

"I would like to have a word with you, Anna Arthur, if I may. Perhaps I could walk you to the door?"

As Grayson gathered up her things, she was reminded of the "word" Grady had had with one of the other actresses. Was she about to receive an illicit proposal from the manager of the troupe? What would she say if he suggested that by showing him certain favors, she would win the role she needed so desperately? It was exactly what Duncan had warned her might happen, and she had been so naive as to think him wrong.

Howard said nothing to her until they had made their way up the aisle and into the lobby. In the privacy of the deserted foyer, Howard caught her arm.

Gray fought the urge to twist away.

"Who are you really, my dear?" he asked her kindly, his smile both curious and conciliatory. "For if you are just plain Anna Arthur, then I must surely be the Prince of Wales."

His question took Grayson by surprise, since she had been expecting something else entirely.

"I don't know what you mean," she managed to reply.

"Oh, please, Anna. I've seen hundreds of actresses come and go. You don't belong here with a broken-down troupe of performers any more than a golden nugget belongs in the depths of a coal bin. You're by far the most beautiful woman it has ever been my pleasure to audition, and the way you dress and carry yourself tells me what you really are. Everything about you speaks of money and privilege."

Grayson felt faintly affronted. She had dressed and behaved as she thought an actress should. She had worn her very plainest gown, a demure gray twill with a high lace collar and matching cuffs, and a low-crowned black straw hat that matched the jet buttons on the front of her gown. She had left Harry's ring at home, and the only bit of jewelry she had allowed herself was a pair of onyx earbobs.

"You're a woman of quality; that's quite clear. So why are you seeking a position with us rather than marrying an earl or a duke?"

That he had come so close to the mark made Grayson profoundly uncomfortable. Her reply, when she finally gave one, was far sharper than she had intended.

"Is that all a woman of quality is capable of?" Grayson demanded. "Is she only fit to marry a title and bear her husband's heirs? Does a privileged background prevent a woman from having dreams and ambitions of her own?"

"Are you telling me your ambition is to be an actress, even though that is not an aspiration of which your people could approve?"

"That's exactly what I'm telling you. And perhaps it's the approval of others I am seeking when the approval of 'my people' has never been enough." It was a conclusion Duncan's observations had led her to accept, one that rang undeniably true to her.

"Becoming an actress is not the wisest choice you could have made," Howard warned her.

"It's not wisdom I am seeking here. It's a chance to be on the stage."

"And you're determined that this is what you want?"

"Does that mean you think me good enough to go with you to America?"

"Oh, you're good enough," Howard conceded. "You're far better than most of the actresses who have read for me today."

Gray glowed with satisfaction, and hope rose in her breast.

"You have the natural abilities of a truly gifted thespian," Howard went on. "Your presence on the stage is most impressive, and you seem able to imbue your roles with real character and life. Your voice is pleasant and has tremendous dramatic range. And, when you are not so nervous, I suspect you sing quite well. But no, I won't take you with us to America, nor would anyone else I know."

After his praise of her abilities, the refusal was as sharp and stunning as a slap. "Why?" Grayson managed to gasp.

Howard touched her hand lightly, and there was genuine compassion in his eyes. "Oh, Anna, there are a hundred reasons, starting and ending with who and what you are. You're a lady through and through. If you came with us to America, you would hate the accommodations and the company you'd be forced to keep. You would hate the provincialism of the crowds and the attentions of the men who would doubtless dog your every move.

You would be giving up everything you know for something that would never make you happy."

When Grayson would have protested, Howard silenced her with a gesture.

"And I have to think of the company, too. On a tour such as the one we are planning, there has to be a certain camaraderie, a certain alchemy within the troupe. Personalities have to mesh; people need to complement each other. Through no fault of your own, you'd be a constant source of irritation. The women wouldn't like you at all, and the men would like you far too much."

"Then I can have no hope of making a place for myself in the theater?" There was desolation in her tone.

The man beside her sighed. "I didn't say that. There's no doubt you have the skill and magnetism to become a wonderful leading lady. But for a woman of your station, the possibilities of ever achieving that goal are impossibly slim. I wish I could tell you there was hope, but you need to know the truth."

Disappointment swamped her as she stared at him. Making a place for herself in the theater was all she'd ever wanted, all she'd ever cared about. Now that she had been assured that her abilities were up to the challenge, her background was proving an impediment. It was standing in the way of everything she'd ever hoped to achieve. While others might have aspired to all she had, Grayson cursed the circumstances that made her who and what she was.

"Find a man from your own class who loves you," Howard counseled. "Give him fine strong children as his heirs. It's the life you were born to live. Accept the things you cannot change."

With those words, Howard dropped her hand and turned to go. "I hope you find what you are seeking, Anna dear. All I can do is counsel prudence and wish you luck in whatever it is you decide to do."

Then Grayson was alone in the theater lobby, listening to the sound of Howard's retreating footsteps as he moved in the direction of the stage she would never tread. Her disillusionment went too deep for tears, was too complex for simple pain. It sliced at the heart of the person she had grown to be, at the ambitions that had sustained her for as long as she could remember. Duncan Palmer's encouragement had given her the courage to come to this theater today, but it had not enabled her to overcome this theater manager's prejudices. Yet John Howard had wished her luck. But had he wished her luck in achieving her goals, Gray wondered, or in living with her compromises?

As she made her way out onto the street, Gray knew she needed more than luck. She needed a miracle to gain acceptance as an actress, to win a chance to tread the boards in America. It was a miracle she wanted with all her heart. As she stood alone and desolate on the busy London street, she knew the miracle she wanted was one only Duncan Palmer could provide.

Eight

THE NIGHT WAS DARK AND CLEAR, THOUGH THERE WAS NO MOON to illuminate the ship that was riding just beyond the breakers. Still, Quentin knew it was there, a short-masted brigantine, broad, graceless, riding low in the water. He had been at Antire Manor since the day before yesterday, awaiting the brig's arrival.

From down below on the beach he could hear the faint ring of voices above the ceaseless swish of waves, the grinding of the longboats against the stones as they were drawn up along the beach. The smugglers were about their work, relieving the brig of its illicit burdens: the casks of fine French brandy, the trunks loaded with bolts of silken cloth, the crates of silver brought from Holland. There was not the profit in smuggling that there had been a decade or two before, when relations with the Continent had been less cordial, when import duties had been sky-high. But still there was money to be made in fleecing the tax men of their fees, and Quentin wondered how he would have managed over the years if it had not been for the alliance with Leaphorn and his men.

He liked the luxuries that would have been well beyond his means without this illegal income, the nights of revelry, the dandified clothes, the opportunity to play hazard until dawn with men whose fortunes dwarfed the money he could steal. Even if he had been bold enough or clever enough to appropriate funds from the vast reserves of Palmer wealth, he could not have taken enough to make the life he loved feasible. His use of the Antire property gave him the setting he required to fob himself off as a gentleman, but the large sums of cold hard cash could not have come from Duncan's trust.

But then, if Leaphorn's plans for his cousin came to fruition, Quentin would have far more than he needed to embrace the life he longed to live. It was only that the risk was so great; the danger of something going awry now that the cards had all been dealt worried him. His hands went cold and slick and his heart throbbed in his chest every time he thought about what they had committed themselves to do. Quentin drew a shaky breath and tried to push Leaphorn's plans to the back of his mind. It was too late in the hand to withdraw—not that Leaphorn would ever allow him to do so.

"'Ell of a lookout you are!"

The voice made Quentin jump, both from its suddenness and from the malice in its tone. From out of the darkness came an inky shadow, moving noiselessly across the wind-blasted grass at the edge of the cliff.

"I have been keeping watch," Quentin hastened to defend himself. "But I was looking for magistrates from the land, not for scoundrels from the sea."

Leaphorn laughed as he came to stand beside the other man, looking out across the Channel. "I'll warrant the troops would be upon us before you could warn us of their approach."

"If I'm so useless as a guard, why did you insist that I come down from London?"

"It seems necessary these days to remind you that you are as deep in this as we are. You've everything to gain, and yet you balk at carrying out the plans."

"I'm in league with you," Quentin gulped. "Haven't I been doing my part?"

"Aye, you 'ave. But not so willingly as I'd like. You just remember, you 'ave as much to lose as we do if your cousin isn't 'andled properly."

"I'll remember," Quentin vowed. "You can count on me."

There was a pause, as if the other man were weighing Palmer's assurances.

In the silence Quentin glanced at his companion. Leaphorn was as scurvy a character as there was, though Palmer had not realized it when he first fell in with the smugglers. Then the man had seemed supremely able, incalculably clever. Quentin had been totally taken in and had seen the unauthorized use of the Antire house and grounds as an opportunity to better his lot. But now he knew Leaphorn for what he was—ruthless, crude, violent, someone with whom a true gentleman would never associate. When this was over, Quentin promised himself, he would find a way to sever his connection to Leaphorn. He'd do it as soon as this was over, as soon as he was rich.

Abruptly Leaphorn nodded in the direction of the brigantine. "Well, then, since the merchandise is safely stored away in the cave, you'd best get back to London. You know what it is you 'ave to do. Don't waste our time. Get on with it."

"I will," Quentin murmured as he turned to go, eager to put some distance between himself and Leaphorn's threats. The man was a bully, truth and all, and Quentin hated knowing that, for the moment at least, he was under Leaphorn's control. Still, there was the promise of riches at the end, the promise of having all he'd ever coveted. But even as he flung himself onto the horse waiting in the thicket a dozen yards away, he shuddered with the knowledge of what more he had to do to accomplish the task assigned to him.

As the horse cab made its way up Ratcliffe Highway toward Limehouse, Duncan Palmer watched the rows of dilapidated buildings that moved past the smudgy window. They stood toe to toe with the edge of the road, shoulder to shoulder with each other, some leaning to the left or right as if nudging at their neighbors for support. Here and there a long dark alley would slice between them, giving a fleeting glimpse of a rubbish-littered court. Around these courts stood houses that were little more than hovels, with a common privy and a common pump, common maladies and common despair. The people on the streets seemed one with their surroundings. They were bowed and bent by poverty, drink, and indolence. Their hopelessness was malodorous, heavy and oppressive, thick and all-encompassing. Though there was poverty and degradation in the cities in America, Duncan could never remember seeing quite this kind of squalor. But then, the conditions here in London had had centuries to fester and ferment; by comparison American cities were fresh and new.

Shuddering, Duncan turned away from the window, glad he'd had the forethought to take a cab instead of the family's crested coach. It would have stood out in this part of town like a new-minted guinea in a fistful of copper pennies, would have been blatant provocation to the unfortunate people on the streets. It would also have drawn unwanted attention to the errands he had undertaken in his quest to prove Samuel Walford a liar and a thief.

The address he was searching for should be a little way ahead on Ratcliffe Highway, just beyond Butcher's Row. It was the fourth business on the list of new accounts that had appeared in Wicker and Walford's ledgers in the winter of 1838, shortly before the drop in the company's profits had so suspiciously begun. Duncan had already visited three of the five manufacturing concerns on his list, and though he had been appalled by the conditions in the factories where dirty children and whey-faced women were busy with their labors, the companies whose names had appeared in Walford's records seemed to be everything they should have been. If the remaining two proved to be as legitimate as the rest, Palmer knew he would be forced to drop his inquiry into Wicker and Walford's affairs, forced to admit defeat.

Accepting defeat was totally foreign to Duncan's nature. Since his exile to America, he had accomplished everything he had set out to do. He had graduated first in his class in the schools his uncle had sent him to, had won his master's papers in fewer years than it took most men to do so. He had been captain of his own ship by the time he was twenty-five, and had turned a handsome profit with each of the voyages he had undertaken.

But since being back in England, he had been thwarted at every turn. He had not been able to locate the discrepancy in Wicker and Walford's books. He had not been able to speed repairs to the *Citation*. He was unwillingly attracted to a woman who was betrothed to someone else. He had made no headway in facing the consequences of his parents' death. If he failed to find a connection between the companies listed in the ledgers and the losses his uncle's company was experiencing, he would be forced to leave the country of his birth without a single success in hand.

The carriage rolled to a stop just as black melancholy was threatening, and Duncan was glad to turn his thoughts to something other than his failures. Leaping out of the hack, he left word with the driver to wait. He would never find another carriage for hire in such a neighborhood as this.

After checking to be sure the address on the paper matched the one on the building before him, Duncan made his way along the side of the factory toward a door halfway down the alley. Fashioned of weathered brick, this building had never been a highlight of London architecture. It was long and low and unremarkable, its walls stark and unrelieved. The sign painted just above the door was all but weathered away, though from the smudges of flaking paint, he could just barely make out the name of the firm he was looking for: Enterprise Manufacturing.

Duncan stepped toward the door and turned the handle, but the wood was swollen and tight in its frame. When he pushed against it with his shoulder, the panel opened with a groan that echoed through the interior of the building. At this time of day a factory should be humming with activity, but there wasn't a soul around. The room inside was long and dim, lit only by the slivers of sunlight that managed to lance between the ribbons of grime that striped the building's skylights. The floor was made of uneven rough-sawn planks that gave it the texture of wide-wale corduroy. The walls were barren, scarred, and encrusted with dirt. There was about the place a certain dusty rankness that spoke of years of disuse.

Still, at intervals, there were signs of habitation: piles of dirty blankets, broken bottles, crumbled bits of molding food. And rats, a dozen of them eyeing him as if they resented his intrusion. When he stepped farther into the room, they scurried across the floor in an unwilling but orderly retreat. The scent of urine and unwashed bodies made Duncan wrinkle his nose. The hovering, waiting silence of the place made something else inside him roil. His first impulse was to whirl and leave. But he had come here for a purpose, and he meant to make sure of what he'd found.

In spite of the meanness of his surroundings, excitement crowded in his veins, forcing the uneasiness aside. His footsteps echoed on the planks as he moved across the floor; his heartbeat thundered as the suspicions he had fostered turned to unmitigated certainty. There were no desks, no machines, no raw materials to be used in manufacturing. There were no goods piled off to one side waiting to be sold. There was nothing here at all that spoke of recent industry. He made a circuit of the room, kicking at a cluster of blankets, trying a door at the far end of the room, which opened onto another alleyway.

This was exactly what he had been hoping to find when he undertook his investigation: an uninhabited factory, a bogus company where a portion of Wicker and Walford's profits could be cleverly but illegally hidden. He had discovered Walford's game. Once he had made sure of the man's association with Enterprise Manufacturing, he could confront his uncle's partner and force his hand.

With the certainty of his discovery, the uneasiness returned. His instinct for danger, honed sharp after years of exploring some of the most unsavory parts of the world, was potently aroused. There was malevolence here, and it seemed wise to take the knowledge of his success somewhere else to gloat.

The main door creaked with the same mournful tone when he opened it to leave, but outside, sweeping the stoop of the building across the alley, was a boy of perhaps sixteen years.

At Palmer's appearance, the fellow paused, looking up with both fright and curiosity in his eyes. As Duncan approached, the lad retreated, holding his broom before him as if he meant to use it as a weapon.

"What do you know about the property there?" Duncan asked, indicating the building at his back. "I'm thinking of renting the space, and I want to know a little about its history."

The boy's stance seemed to loosen at Duncan's words, as he recognized the man before him was a gentleman. He lowered his broom to a more seemly angle and smiled. "It's been empty as long as I can remember," he began. "For two years and more."

"What about the company on the sign? How long have they been gone?"

"Never were there, as far as I know. Nor has my master ever mentioned them."

Duncan took in the information, his curiosity not yet appeased. "What's the building been used for, then? There is evidence that people have been inside."

"Aye, they have," the lad explained. "And you're lucky the place was empty when you arrived or I'd not be talking to you now. There's wastrels that live in there. A scurvy lot. Sailors too far gone in drink to get a berth, footpads so far down on their luck that they'd as soon cut your throat for a penny as a pound. You'd not have gotten out alive if they'd been inside. They're most likely at some tavern at this time in the afternoon, drinking blue ruin and waiting for night to fall. Luck was with you, all in all."

Duncan suppressed a shudder at the boy's words of warning. His instincts, as usual, had been correct.

"Hope you do take the space," the apprentice continued. "Clean out the rat hole and put an honest business there. Everyone in the area would be glad to see those fellows gone."

Duncan nodded noncommittally. He had discovered what he had come here to learn. What he needed to determine now was who owned the vacant building, who the president of Enterprise

Manufacturing was, and how the company was connected to Samuel Walford.

He took a coin from his pocket and flipped it in the apprentice's direction. "Thanks for your information. You've done me more of a service than you know."

With rising spirits Duncan headed for the street, but when he reached Ratcliffe Highway, his cab was nowhere in sight. With narrowed eyes he scanned the area, thinking the cabby might have pulled up to a nearby tavern to get a drink. But there was no sign of either the cab or its driver, and the disappearance bothered him. He still owed the cabby his fare.

Muttering under his breath, Duncan turned west, back toward the center of town. Even on such a warm spring day, this neighborhood was hardly conducive to an afternoon stroll. The street was narrow, clogged with mud from the previous night's rain, and filled with trash. The inhabitants of Limehouse seemed no more concerned about the filth and grime than a brood of pigs might have been. This was one of the meanest areas of London, inhabited by drunkards, whores, and footpads. He was glad it was no later in the day, or a man dressed as he was would be inviting robbery or worse. It was not that he was afraid to be here alone and on foot. In his travels Duncan had visited far more dangerous places than this. But on those occasions he had been part of the milling crowd, not an intruder who had stumbled into the area unaware of its reputation and undesirability.

As he moved in the direction of St. George's Church, whose bell tower was visible over the housetops, the strange uneasiness he'd experienced in the factory came over him again. It made the hair stand up on the back of his neck, made his shoulders clench. His eyes swept from side to side as he strode along, his senses sharpening with every step he took. He did not hurry, but lengthened his strides, intent on covering the ground between Limehouse and the more respectable parts of London as quickly as he could.

The hand that yanked him into the shadowy space between two buildings was not totally unexpected, and Duncan reacted with lightning speed to fend off the ensuing blow. Still, the momentum of it sent Palmer staggering. By the time he recovered his feet, two men loomed in the narrow space between him and the relative safety of the street.

Jockeying for position, Duncan assessed his situation. It was not at all promising. He was cut off from the street by the two burly men, both carrying weapons. The taller one clasped a black leather sap that swung loosely from one meaty fist. The other wielded his long narrow knife as if it were an extension of his arm. Fear rose in the back of Palmer's throat. Sweat beaded along his brow. A cry for help would go unheeded in such a neighborhood. He was completely on his own in facing his attackers.

It took only an instant for Duncan to realize his purse was not their goal, but he deliberately thrust his fingers deep into his pocket and extracted a handful of chinking coins.

"Here, here, take what you want and leave me alone."

As Duncan spoke he shifted his stance, trying to put some distance between himself and his two assailants. Warily he stepped around a mound of trash. The ground was soft and treacherous underfoot.

As he maneuvered for advantage, the two men stalked his every move, countered his every feint. He could hear the sticky earth sucking at their feet. He could see the feral light glinting in their eyes. Their breathing was repressed with the strain of waiting to attack. His own breath shuddered loudly in his ears, reverberating off the narrow canyon of crumbling brick and stone.

Duncan dodged to the right and left, hoping to provoke some unguarded movement. But the men stayed with him. The tall man's sap rocked like a lethal pendulum. The knife blade gleamed in the half-light with a malice of its own. These two had played this game before, stalking a cornered quarry.

As he retreated, a cold slimy wall came hard against Duncan's back. His heart galloped inside his chest, thudding with wild frustration. He was trapped, cut off. There was nowhere for him to go.

Satisfaction flared in his assailants' eyes, narrowed the corners of their lips. Their muscles bunched as they prepared to take him. In the split second before they sprang, Duncan flung the handful of glittering coins into their faces as hard as he could.

The man on the right flinched as the money pelted his forehead and chin. The one on the left gave ground to avoid the hail of coins. His half-step backward gave Duncan space enough to make a desperate sprint for the street. As Palmer made his move, the taller man's sap came down in an arching swing that sent pain lancing down Duncan's arm. With the momentum of the blow, the footpad slipped. But as Duncan darted past, the man hooked Palmer's ankle in his elbow.

Duncan fell full length, battering his shoulder and knee, driving the air from his lungs. His breath rasped in his throat as he fought to twist away, but the grip on his foot was unrelenting. He raised his opposite knee and brought his boot down hard, driving the heel into his assailant's face. He heard a crunch of bone, a grunt of pain, and the man went limp beside him.

But before Palmer could scramble to his feet, the second man loomed over him. His knife was raised, ready to strike. Duncan scuttled backward, twisting away from the lethal thrust. The blade bit into his outer thigh, buried hilt-deep in muscle. White-edged pain seared from his knee to his groin as Palmer tangled his hands in his assailant's clothes. With a livid curse, a ragged moan, he jerked the man down across his body.

Duncan threw himself on top of his assailant as they scuffled for control of the knife. With both their hands clutching at the hilt that protruded from Duncan's thigh, the knife blade barked and squirmed against the bone. Agony tore through Palmer's senses, set off lights behind his eyes. He tried to twist the knife away, but the man beneath him maintained his grip.

With sweat pouring down his face, Palmer clenched the muscles in his leg to hold the knife in place. As he did, he lunged forward to grab his attacker's throat. It was thick and rough beneath his hands. His thumbs bit deep into the base of the man's Adam's apple, and the high-arched column of cartilage beneath them gave.

Deprived of air, the man thrashed wildly, relinquishing his hold on the knife for a crushing one on Duncan's throat. His fingers gripped and squeezed. His muscles bunched and swelled.

Palmer strained against the pressure, jerked back in a futile attempt to escape. The air was cut off to his lungs. They spasmed inside his chest. A red fog swirled before his eyes. Panic spun through his brain.

The muscles knotted in Duncan's arms. His wrists arched. His fingers clenched tighter, beginning to tremble. Could he outlast the other man? Was he going to die?

In desperation Palmer yanked the fellow toward him, thrusting with his thumbs. A grinding snap echoed in his ears. The vibration was telegraphed through his hands, quivered up his arms. The man beneath him went limp. He drooped against the earth, and his grasping hands fell away.

Duncan heaved back on his haunches, gasping for breath. It rasped through his battered throat, filled his burning lungs. The swirling red mist in his head began to recede.

The man between his splayed knees was utterly still. No breath lifted the wall of his chest; no light shone from his staring eyes. Grabbing his lapels, Duncan pulled the man toward him. The fellow's head lolled helplessly. He fell back with a thump when Palmer let go, lay motionless as Duncan reached for the pulse at the base of his throat. There was no thud beneath his searching fingers, no appreciable sign of life.

Oh, God, I've killed the man!

Duncan's head spun with the realization. Gorge rose in his throat. Weakness wept down his arms like icy rain.

He hadn't meant to kill him. He'd only meant to defend himself.

Slowly, very slowly, the alley came into focus around him. Somewhere close at hand there was another man to be reckoned with. Groaning, Palmer struggled to his feet and limped to where the other assailant lay. He was still sprawled unconscious in the mud, but there were definite signs of life in him.

Panting, Palmer sagged against the slimy wall, shaking with reaction and relief. He might have stood there indefinitely if the piercing pain in his leg had not forced him to stir. The knife was still deep in his thigh, and with a grunt of effort, he pulled it free. New agony hit him in a strong dark wave. He went tingly and cold with the intensity. Blackness swooped through his head as blood surged out of the open wound. It was hot against his icy flesh, thick and bright and fresh. Duncan stared at the huge red stain on his pant leg, unable to believe all that blood was his.

Dropping the knife, he pulled a handkerchief from his pocket and quickly bound his thigh. The bandage was ineffectual at stopping the flow, but Palmer had no time for more effective measures. He knew he had to get out of there.

With a lurch he struggled to stand and went dizzy all over again. Bracing himself against the wall, he blinked the vertigo away. He just could not lose consciousness here, not in the alley where he'd done murder.

Determinedly he staggered toward the spear of light that marked the street and burst out into the blaze of sunlight. He was dazzled and disoriented by the brightness, dazed by the loss of blood, stunned by the viciousness of the attack in the alleyway. But desperation drove him on.

Duncan put several blocks behind him before he slowed his pace, before he was able to think. The shock of what he'd done rushed over him again, making his stomach heave, making his head go light. Shivers washed through him, and he tried to block out what had happened in the alley. He had not meant to kill the man. He had broken his neck accidentally, in self-defense. It was clear his attackers had meant to do him in. But was this a chance encounter or something more?

Fighting to clear his mind, Duncan tried to concentrate on what he must do. He had to make his way back to the town house, disassociate himself from the bodies in the alleyway. He needed a cab, medical attention, and rest before he could confront what had transpired this afternoon. Absently he tried to rearrange his clothes, tried to make himself more presentable. Few cabbies would take him as he looked now, though in truth there was little he could do to improve his appearance.

It was a testimony to how inured the people of Limehouse were to violence that a man, beaten, limping, and covered with blood, could walk the streets in broad daylight without anyone taking note of it. It confirmed that violence was a way of life here, convinced Duncan that the two men he had left lying in the shadows would be treated with indifference even when the constable came to investigate.

That he had murdered one man and seriously disabled another would trouble Palmer no small bit in the months and years to come. But here, where life was cheap, no one else would take more than a passing note of it. Nor did the people on the street pay him any mind when Duncan chose to walk the distance into central London in the very middle of the thoroughfare.

Nine

WORTHINGTON HALL WAS MAGNIFICENT, OPULENT, STATELY, grand. It bespoke great wealth, superb taste, a long and distinguished family history. The high stone wall and ornate iron gate, the elegant arcades at the front of the subsidiary buildings to the left and right, the pattern of paving stones in the drive, all drew the visitor's eye toward the elegant bisque-colored cut-stone house at the apex of the courtyard. At its center was the doorway, flanked by gleaming columns and an ornate medallioned lintel of deep gray Purbeck marble. High above rose three tall tiers of windows, each bracketed by a brace of wide pilasters. Duncan Palmer drew his breath in appreciation as his carriage pulled up before the door. A porter in gold and green livery came forward to help him alight, and before they had reached the entrance, a footman was in the doorway to greet him.

Once inside, the fellow took Duncan's hat, gloves, and walking stick. The butler ushered him through the receiving room with its cane-seated benches for the tradesman who came to sell their goods, up the enormous stairway of creamy marble that rose through the center of the house, under the colonnade of Corinthian columns, and across an expanse of polished stone tiles to a pair of high mahogany doors.

Preceding Duncan into the drawing room, the butler announced him. "Your grace, Lady Grayson, the Marquis of Antire has arrived."

As he moved past the butler, Duncan's attention was immediately drawn to his hostess, who was seated by the fire on an amber velvet couch. The deep gold color was the perfect foil for Grayson's dress of blue watered silk, for her ivory skin and deep red hair. The slope-shouldered, long-waisted design of the gown accented her womanly curves while the deeply ruffled collar of filmy lace heightened the pale creamy glow of her skin. With her hair piled high in a coronet of braids, with her grace and her aristocratic bearing, she was a woman who would have been any room's centerpiece, its most precious and exquisite accessory.

As she rose from where she sat, her face changed. Her eyes brightened; her cheeks warmed with a becoming blush. Her mouth curled into a smile of pure welcome.

Her greeting awakened an equal gladness in Duncan, though he tried diligently to repress the feelings this woman seemed able to stir in him. But in spite of his best efforts, he found himself striding across the sea of blue and gold Turkish carpets to take her hands in his.

"Grayson, how good it is to see you!" His smile was wide, as dazzling as the sunny day.

"I'm so pleased you could come to tea. But, Duncan, you're limping. Have you hurt yourself somehow?"

"I had a small accident—down at the shipyard, but I'm fine now," he assured her. "And it's my pleasure to accept your invitation. I'm glad to have another chance to see you before we sail for America."

"You wouldn't leave without letting me know, would you?" Grayson asked. "You wouldn't leave without giving me a chance to wish you well?"

"Perhaps it would be wiser if I did," he muttered under his breath.

By her carefully chosen words, Gray had made it clear that she was still intent on going with him to New York. That guaranteed an argument between them before the day was through, and Duncan did not welcome the prospect.

Then, as if to remind the two younger people of his presence in the drawing room, Warren Worthington rose from the high-backed chair that had all but hidden him from Duncan's view.

"Welcome to Worthington Hall, Antire," he said. "We have visitors from America far less frequently than I would like."

Whether the duke's was a personal or political comment, Duncan could not say. After what had transpired at Mrs. de Rothschild's estate, Duncan was not sure just how eager Worthington was to have him here.

"I'm flattered that you could spare me some of your time, your grace. With Parliament in session surely every minute is at a premium."

"It is at that," the Duke of Fennel conceded. "But please, Antire, take a seat. Let's make the most of the moments we have."

Grayson motioned Duncan to a place beside her on the settee. "I was just telling my uncle about the storm that forced your ship into Portsmouth for repairs."

"An unfortunate incident, to be sure," Palmer noted.

"Yes, I understand the Channel can be quite treacherous this time of year. Wouldn't a more seasoned master have waited a few weeks longer to brave the crossing?"

Color lit Duncan's cheeks at the faint accusation in the other man's tone.

"Wicker and Walford has made its name in international trade on daring, your grace," he countered, "not on reticence. Since I've been captain of my own ship these five years past, this is the only mishap we have suffered."

"And your uncle has complete faith in you as one of his captains, does he?" Fennel inquired with a lift of his brows. "How is old Farleigh, anyway?"

Torn between the desire to further protest his competence and answer Fennel's question about his uncle's health, Duncan decided on the latter course as the one a gentleman would choose.

"My uncle is very well indeed. The years in America have agreed with him."

"I remember when he and Samuel Walford decided to start the business," Fennel mused. "Not everyone was sympathetic with their reasons for going into trade. They were two younger sons and might well have found a place for themselves in society or in politics. But after the years with Wellington, I think they were both too restless to accept such passive roles."

"It seems *you* understood their motives, your grace."

Worthington nodded. "Indeed I did. I was with Wellington, too, and that experience changed us all in one way or another."

The duke paused as if remembering other days. "I was one of Wicker and Walford's first investors, and my faith in their abilities has paid off very handsomely over the years."

This was the opening Duncan had hoped for when he was invited here to tea, but he wasn't sure how direct he could be in asking about his uncle's partner.

"I met Samuel Walford for the first time only a few short weeks ago," Duncan ventured. "He seems very staid and settled to me, a pillar of the community."

"Ah, well, we've all changed a bit since the wars, Samuel as much as anyone."

Palmer struggled to contain his curiosity. "Oh?"

"Back then Samuel was like all of us, I suppose. While we were with Wellington, we lived life to the fullest, as men do when each day might be their last. Once they experience it, most men need to taste a bit of danger now and then. But the danger changed Samuel, I think, changed him in ways young men really shouldn't change. He must have felt that nothing in England could compare with the life he was leaving behind once the wars were over." He continued with a shrug. "I know that's how I felt until I became involved in politics. I suppose that, for your Uncle Farleigh, going to America to make his fortune had that same appeal. It was daring, challenging, and stimulating."

"From what Uncle Farleigh has told me, those must have been exciting days: returning victorious from the wars, trying to get a business going, lining up investors like you."

"He and Samuel were quite a persuasive pair," the duke volunteered before he looked away. "And they had amassed a fair amount of capital on their own.

"But that was years ago, and what I want now is for you to tell me how my old friend Farleigh is faring. I've only a few more minutes before I must be on about my business, and I'm most eager to hear the tales of his exploits in America."

For a time Duncan talked about Farleigh Wicker and the life he had made for himself. He spoke about the difficulties his uncle had faced as an Englishman establishing a business in the States so soon after America's Second War for Independence, about the gambles he and Samuel Walford had taken in being one of the first shipping concerns to stop in Singapore after the establishment of the British colony. Wicker and Walford had always been a progressive company, one of the first to commission clipper ships, one of the first to see the possibilities of steam and screw propeller vessels. It had led them to prominence in international trade, and Palmer was very proud of it.

Fennel laughed at some of the stories Duncan told and seemed delighted to hear about his old friend's exploits and successes. Before he left to pursue more pressing matters, he gave Duncan a letter and his good wishes to pass on to Farleigh Wicker.

Once her guardian had said his good-byes, Grayson rang for refreshments, and several minutes later the butler and two footmen appeared laden with silver trays. Gray waited quietly as they fussed over her, drawing a tea table up to her knees, spreading a fine Irish linen cloth, settling an oblong tray upon it, arranging a mahogany cake stand just to her left.

Grayson waited until the servants had departed, leaving the door to the library carefully ajar. A tall young footman was stationed just outside the room, for propriety's sake, and Grayson suddenly appreciated why burly footmen were paid at such a premium.

Pushing the observation aside, she unlocked the old walnut tea caddy and mixed several scallop shells full of leaves in the crystal bowl at the center of the box.

"I prefer mostly Darjeeling with a hint of Formosa oolong," she confided as she placed the mixture in the round pot and added water from the kettle. Setting it aside to steep, Gray offered Duncan a black Wedgwood tea plate and a lace-trimmed napkin, then removed the heat-clouded dome of the muffin dish. Inside were fat west country scones, deliciously brown and steaming hot. Palmer took two, a healthy dollop of clotted cream, and some strawberry preserves from the jam dish.

"I don't remember that afternoon tea was such an occasion when last I was in England," he observed.

"Oh, no, it wouldn't have been," she agreed. "We have the Duchess of Bedford to thank for making afternoon tea an institution." Her eyes began to twinkle and her voice deepened conspiratorially as she went on. "You see, her grace would get downright peevish somewhere between luncheon and late dinner."

"Would she, now?" Duncan asked, encouraging her.

"Oh, but she would," Gray confirmed, raising one arched brow. "So to avoid her grace's tantrums the servants began to take her tea and a few good things to eat 'round about four o'clock. Just to avoid a row, you know."

"And did having tea and a bite to eat improve the duchess's disposition?" he inquired with a grin.

"Ah, yes it did. And the duchess, never one to overlook an opportunity to entertain, began inviting a few of her friends to partake of her secret bounty. To make a long story short, the idea spread like wildfire, and soon everyone who was anyone stopped what they were doing at four o'clock for a cup of tea and plate of goodies."

"And do you mean to tell me we owe all this to her grace's bad temper?"

"We do, Captain Palmer, indeed we do."

Humor twinkled in Duncan's eyes. "Is that the strictest truth, Lady Grayson?"

She looked back as if stricken, her eyes gone wide. "But would you doubt me, Captain Palmer?"

He laughed outright at her expression. "No, Lady Grayson, no. Perish the thought."

She paused to add more water from the kettle and took a cup and saucer from the table to her left. Setting a silver tea strainer over the mouth of the cup, she poured out a stream of rich brown liquid.

"Will you have sugar and cream with your tea, Captain Palmer?"

"A little of each should do quite nicely."

Grayson smiled prettily, enjoying her role, and handed him the mixture he had requested. She fixed a cup of the brew for herself and settled back on the settee.

For a few minutes they munched in silence, anointing each bite of the feather-light scones with clotted cream and a dollop of jam, licking the crumbs from their fingers like two children in the schoolroom.

"Oh, these are marvelous," Duncan mumbled around the very last bite. "When I was a boy, we had an old Cornish cook who used to make scones like these. She said they had to be patted and rolled with the tenderness a woman showed her lover, though I can't say I knew much about that then. I'd sit on a high stool in the kitchen and watch her work, eating the scones as fast as she took them out of the oven. My mother always said Gertrude's scones were as light as clouds and—"

Duncan stopped abruptly, the light going out of his face.

In an instant Gray saw him transformed from a laughing, lighthearted companion to a silent, moody stranger.

She laid a hand against his arm. "Duncan? What is it? What's the matter?"

He turned to her, his eyes empty and remote. "I don't talk about my parents."

Though she knew the answer to the question, some instinct made her press for a reply. "But, Duncan, why?"

"You know," he murmured so softly she could barely hear him. "All of England knows why I don't talk about them."

Her fingers curled around his sleeve. "I've heard the stories," she admitted, "but having known you even these few short weeks, I find I can't quite believe them."

Duncan shivered as if unaware of the sunlight streaming in the windows, of the warmth radiating from the fire a few feet away.

"The stories are quite true," he said at last. "I killed my father in the hope of saving my mother from his abuse. I'm sure it happened just as they say."

Grayson's heart went out to Duncan just as it had that day in the rose garden when her aunt had told her the tale for the very first time. Yet in spite of his words of confirmation, she could not imagine how a man of Duncan Palmer's strength and sensitivity could have done such a horrid and violent thing.

"I can't remember anything about it," he went on, "strange as it seems. I remember the day before. My parents and I went on a picnic up on the bluffs behind Antire Manor, and everything seemed just the way it should have been. My mother was laughing at the attempts my father and I were making to get my kite aloft. My father was running along the cliffs, acting like a boy himself. But from that day on, my mind's a blank. It's as if I fell asleep the night of the picnic and didn't wake up until after I reached my uncle in America."

Grayson pursed her lips, undecided about whether to press Duncan further. But just when she had decided to find some way to divert him, he continued.

"My valet, my father's valet, told me what happened: how they had found me in my father's study with the gun still warm in my hand, how I had shot my father to save my mother from his brutality. But I don't remember any of it—not finding them together, not trying to save my mother, not pulling the trigger of the gun . . ."

His pain was evident in the set of his jaw, the turmoil in his eyes. Gray ached with concern for this man who had laid claim to her emotions, with sympathy for his pain, with compassion for his confusion.

"Oh, Duncan. I'm so sorry."

Some of the glassiness left his eyes, and he turned to her again.

"It's all right, Grayson. I've known from the moment I returned to England that I wouldn't be able to deny what happened here."

As he spoke she noticed how pale he had become, how the usually ruddy color had abruptly drained out of his face. Against the saucer he held in his hand, the teacup rattled like a window in a gale.

Rising, Grayson went to the decanter of claret on a table by the wall, and filled a cut-glass goblet.

Duncan downed the wine in a single draft. Then, as he watched her cross the room to provide him with a refill, he wondered why he'd told Grayson what he had. It was years since he had spoken of the incident, years since he had let himself dwell on what had happened that night at Antire Manor. His parents' death was something he never discussed with anyone, not with his uncle, not with Ryan Barnes. Why had he suddenly chosen Grayson Ware as his confidante? Had he sensed he would receive no censure from her? Had he realized that beneath her womanly trappings there was some quiet, steady strength that he was desperate to absorb? There was honest compassion in Gray, a kind of understanding that somehow made the deed he'd done less horrible, less damning. Was that why he had spoken of it now when it would have been so much wiser to hold his peace?

He took the goblet of wine from her, realizing suddenly how cold and unsteady his hands had become.

"It seems to be your misfortune to see me at my worst," he observed as he sipped from the glass.

"Your worst is not so terrible, then," she offered quietly.

He frowned, toying with the stem of the goblet, watching the way the rug's ornate floral pattern sent shimmers of gold and blue through the ruby-colored liquid.

"You're very kind," he demurred, turning as Gray resumed her seat beside him.

There was something brittle about him, something so tense and strained that it made Grayson want to break off the conversation. Yet there were more important things than comfort that she could offer him. Though it took a great deal of courage to put her instincts into words, Grayson continued.

"Don't you ever talk about your parents or what happened?"

"Never."

"Don't you think talking about it might help?"

"No."

"Duncan." She drew a long breath, wondering why it seemed imperative that she demand responses when he was so very, very vulnerable. "Duncan, it has been a long time since your parents died. You need to talk about your feelings, express your grief. Have you been back to Antire Manor during your time in England?"

"No! Of course not. Why would I want to go there?"

"It might help you remember exactly what happened that night. It might help you find some way to understand the tragedy, find some way to forgive yourself."

"Can you tell me how you forgive yourself for killing the man who fathered you?"

"But, Duncan, you didn't set out to hurt him. You were only trying to protect your mother. And surely you loved your father in spite of what he did to her."

His eyes were stark, their pale cerulean depths swirling with emotions that were powerful and destructive.

"Oh, God, Grayson! I suppose I loved them both. But they used to fight as if they hated each other, as if they hated me. When they began to argue, I'd run away. I'd go out onto the cliffs until I couldn't hear the shouting, until all I could hear was the wind and waves.

"I suppose I ran away that night. I can't remember. But if I'd stayed—if I'd stayed at the house instead of running away, perhaps I would have been there to save my mother. Perhaps I would have been able to intervene . . ."

Grayson fought the impulse to take Duncan in her arms. She wanted to hold him, comfort him, use her strength to banish the taint of tragedy that clung to him. But words were the only solace she could give.

"You can't second-guess what happened, Duncan, not without remembering more than you do. You need to go to the house and face your past," she insisted quietly. "You need to accept what happened there as something you can never change. Even I can see what the grief and guilt are doing to you. You can't carry this around with you forever."

In the recesses of his mind, Duncan recognized that what Grayson said was true. Though he had schooled himself to deny his life in England, his parents' death was never out of his mind. Returning to the country had only brought the memories to the fore, made him more aware of his failures and regrets. But confronting his past would entail things he might never be ready to do. It would demand that he return to Antire Manor, that he remember all that had happened the night his parents died. That was simply too much to ask when there was no guarantee that going to Antire Manor would free him from the memories. That was too much to ask when he was desperately afraid he might discover even more reason to hate himself.

"I put my past behind me when I went to America," he insisted stubbornly. "I started my life again. I haven't done too badly at making a place for myself in the world, in spite of everything that happened before."

Gray saw his defense for what it was, a mask for his fear, his anger, his guilt, and his pain. There was nothing she could do to make him acknowledge those emotions, nothing she could do to make him accept what he had done. Yet it was wrong to let him live with his delusions, wrong to let him believe that he had escaped the past unscathed when even she could see it was patently untrue.

"How can you say that you've started your life again when there is still so much that's haunting you?" she demanded almost angrily. "Aren't the questions there every morning when you open your eyes? Doesn't what happened temper everything you do? Duncan, be honest with yourself. You'll never find any happiness until you put all this behind you."

"No, no!" Duncan shook his head and downed the last of the claret. "None of it matters, Gray. None of it. Not now, not when in three weeks' time I'll be on my way to America. Once I leave for New York, I'll never have to think about this again. I'll never think about it again, and I'll never return to England."

There was no question that the subject of his parents' death was closed to her. Duncan had said all he was going to say on the matter, had balked at doing the only thing that would ever bring him peace. She was sorry that she could not persuade him to return to Antire Manor, sorry that there was nothing she could do to end his torment. But she had long since crossed the boundaries of friendship and concern, long since passed beyond the strictures of what was proper. Society did not endorse the kind of intimacy she and Duncan had already shared, and it would never approve of trespassing into areas that were so private, so intensely personal.

She withdrew her hand from where it had lain against his sleeve, poured more tea into their cups. She added sugar and cream and tried to turn her thoughts to her primary reason for inviting him here. It seemed inappropriate somehow for her to turn the conversation to her own ends, yet she knew this might be the only opportunity she would have to persuade him to help her reach America.

"When you do leave for New York, Duncan," she said, broaching the subject directly, "I still want you to take me with you."

The spoon in his hand stilled as he raised his gaze from the tea swirling in his cup. She could see the weariness in his eyes, his reluctance to argue with her.

"For the love of God, Grayson," he answered on a sigh. "Can't you simply give this up?"

"Give up what, Duncan?" Her tone was almost pleading. "Shall I give up the most important thing in my life? The opportunity to make something of myself on my own terms? Don't you know that acting means the world to me?"

She could see the lines deepen around his mouth, see his lips thin as he sought to muster his resolve.

"By insisting that I grant you passage to New York, you are asking me to sanction something I believe is a mistake," he began. "If you leave with me now, you'll be forfeiting everything you have. And for what, Grayson? The chance to tread the boards? The opportunity to stare across the footlights at an unappreciative crowd? The certainty of being exploited? No, I won't take you to New York, and it's for friendship's sake that I'm refusing you."

His answer lit sparks of fire in her eyes. "How dare you pretend to know what is best for me? How dare you try to dissuade me from what I'm determined to do?"

His anger rose to answer hers. "Yet you are more than prepared to counsel me on my life, aren't you, Grayson? You are more than willing to tell me, for friendship's sake, what to do to 'escape my past.' As a friend, I would be remiss in letting you court disaster by going to America. As a friend, I would be remiss in aiding you."

Hectic color rose in her cheeks, and the revealing words were on her lips before she could even try to censor them. "Are we friends, Duncan?" she demanded. "Is that really what we are?"

Her challenge lay between, forcing both of them to acknowledge feelings neither was prepared to name, making both of them aware of what had been growing between them since that morning in the garden.

"Yes, I think we're friends," he finally answered her. "I believe that's what we are."

Satisfaction flickered in the depths of her eyes. "As my friend, Duncan, you told me I had the talent to be an actress. As a friend you gave me the courage to pursue the only future I've ever wanted. Now be a friend and help me to achieve the dream I've harbored all my life."

Duncan was moved by the passion of her arguments, by the desperation he saw in her. That she would be forced to marry Harry Torkington if she stayed in England weighed heavily on his conscience. Yet the union with Torkington was a something Gray would have been forced to accept if she and Duncan had never met. That a single meeting and a few unguarded words could change so much bothered Palmer. It was as if he had tampered with the future, thwarted something that was fated, preordained.

"I can't take you to America, Grayson," he finally said. "As a friend, as someone who cares about your future, I'm doing what is right for you."

Desolation moved through her, tightening her chest, bringing tears to her eyes. That he was implacable was painfully clear. Duncan was not going to change his mind.

Grayson sighed and tried to think what else she could do. She had tried to make a place for herself with a troupe of actors and been refused. She had prayed for a miracle to happen, and her prayers had gone unanswered.

Duncan reached out as if to take her hand, but Grayson snatched it away.

"Oh, Grayson, I'm so sorry," he whispered. "More sorry than you know."

To her his apology was nothing but empty words that matched the emptiness inside her. Was he sorry he had raised her hopes with a few glib compliments? Was he sorry to be refusing her? The words seemed to trip so easily off his tongue that it was impossible to believe in their sincerity.

What else was there for her to do but accept the future that was planned for her unless she had the courage to go on alone from here? Was she brave enough to book passage with another captain? Might she somehow make an alliance with another troupe of actors bound for America? Could she stow away on Duncan's ship?

Grayson caught her breath. Stowing away on Duncan's ship offered some interesting possibilities, ones she had never considered before. Could she get aboard without Duncan knowing? Was it possible that she could hide effectively enough to avoid discovery? Once they had cleared the English shore, Palmer could not force her to return. He could only bring her back himself, something Duncan would never do.

But in order to stow away, Grayson would need to know the exact day and hour of his departure. She would need to maintain her contact with him. Her mind worked furiously, searching for a way to do that, searching for a reason to see him again. And with a surge of inspiration, she knew just what she wanted to do.

Drawing on her abilities at make-believe, Gray slanted a measuring look at Duncan from beneath her lashes. "Then, if you won't take me to America," she drawled with the slightest of smiles, "will you take me to Evans's Song and Supper Room?"

"What?"

"I want to go to Evans's Song and Supper Room. Surely you've heard of it. It's down in Covent Garden."

Palmer's mouth thinned. "Instead of taking you to New York, you want me to take you to a song and supper club?"

Grayson nodded.

"Why?"

"I have heard so much about Evans's from Harry and his cronies," Gray explained, "that I'd like to see the place and hear the entertainment for myself."

That Grayson had switched priorities and emotions with such facility made Duncan wary. How much of the actress was coming to the fore? What plot was forming behind the mischievous glint in her deep green eyes?

"But women aren't allowed in song and supper rooms," he pointed out.

A look of pure devilment flickered over her face. "Then I'll simply go dressed as a young man."

"Grayson!"

"I'm very good at disguises, Duncan," she told him with a laugh. "You'll never be able to tell it's me."

"I very much doubt that, Grayson. I'm sure I'd know you as a woman if I were struck suddenly blind."

She hurried on, obviously trying to convince him, obviously trying to prevent him from puzzling out the reason behind her request.

"Please, Duncan. Once Harry has made me his duchess, I'll have to be eternally staid and proper. You could give me my last taste of freedom, and this just might be fun."

"Fun!" he echoed. "Fun?"

"Harry would never do this for me, but you could. You're unconventional enough to see that there's really no harm in letting me have an evening at Evans's."

"Grayson, I don't think—"

"Duncan, please," she cajoled. "You've already denied me so much. This is really the simplest request."

Duncan felt guilty, suspicious, unsure.

"When would you want to go?"

"There's a singer named Jones at Evans's all this week. They say he's very good, and he's only booked there through Saturday night."

It was mad to agree to take her to the popular song and supper room, Duncan knew, but somehow the idea of thumbing his nose at conventions here in England held a strange appeal. At least she hadn't asked to go to the Coal Hole on the Strand, or the Cyder Cellars where the acts were decidedly blue. What she was proposing was preposterous, but in comparison to what Grayson had wanted a few minutes before, her request seemed sane and reasonable. And that worried him.

Her reputation would be in jeopardy should her identity be discovered, but if properly disguised, Gray would be safe enough with him. After what he'd been forced to deny her, Duncan found he was willing to offer concessions. And in spite of himself, Duncan wanted to see Grayson again, just once more before he left England forever.

Palmer was still trying to come to terms with that discovery when the first faint spark of pain kindled deep within his brain. He tried to blink the sensation away, tried to deny the warning of the headache to come. But even as he sought to extinguish the glow by dint of will, it flared higher, glittering, glimmering, deep inside his skull. Shimmering tendrils of heat crept slowly outward from the spot, slithering incandescent ribbons, writhing, curling, glowing brands. A swirl of vertigo moved through him; his stomach quivered in response.

"May we go tomorrow night, Duncan? Will you take me to Evans's then?"

His fingers had gone tingly and cold, and there seemed to be a faint undulating curtain of light between him and the world around him.

"Tomorrow night?" he echoed, suddenly unbearably aware of the high sweet scent of her perfume, the essence of gardenias. "I suppose that would be all right."

He only half heard his own response, was hardly aware of what he'd agreed to do.

Delight colored Grayson's tone. "Oh, thank you, Duncan! You won't be sorry. We'll have a wonderful time."

Palmer nodded absently, aware of a rushing in his ears. Her exclamations of pleasure seemed to eddy and echo around him.

With the slight nod of his head, the pain flared to full bray behind his left eye, pulsing, glowing, flickering in time with the beating of his heart. The heat inside his head was becoming a conflagration, and he was sure Grayson could see the veins throbbing in his left temple.

He was not sure if it was a moment or a century before she sensed the change in him.

"Duncan?" She reached out to touch his hand. "Duncan, are you all right?"

She became suddenly aware that there was perspiration on his brow, on his upper lip. His eyes had lost their clarity, their attentiveness, and now seemed hazy and impenetrable.

"Duncan?" Her voice was soft, filled with concern.

He seemed to come to her from far away. "I think I should take my leave of you, Grayson. I'm feeling rather indisposed."

That was easy enough for her to believe; his face had gone strangely gray. Without waiting for further explanations, Grayson rang for Duncan's carriage, and when it came, she walked him as far as the door. He seemed dazed, withdrawn, distant. His sudden transformation frightened her.

"Will you be all right?" she asked as he turned to go.

With an evident effort he answered her. "I'll be fine. It's only a headache."

She watched him clamber into the carriage, saw his eyes close and his head fall back against the squabs as the door to the coach swung shut.

"Only a headache," she repeated to herself as the coach pulled away. "Only a headache or hell on earth?"

Ten

ANOTHER HEADACHE. ANOTHER MORNING OF AWAKENING WITH the vague unsettled feeling that always plagued him after taking laudanum. For a moment Duncan slumped on the side of the bed wondering, for what might well have been the dozenth time, why the headaches had been so much worse since he arrived in England. They never bothered him while he was on a voyage, never came with such frequency in New York. Why were they so much worse now? What in God's name was wrong with him?

This headache had come upon him yesterday while he was with Grayson Ware, and he hated that she had seen him at less than his best. Yet there had been nothing but concern in her eyes as she rang for his coach, only solicitude in her touch as she walked him to the door.

Had talking about his parents brought on the violent headache? Had delving into the events at Antire Manor triggered the pain? Yet somehow Duncan felt relieved at being able to confide in Gray, at being able to air parts of his life he never discussed with anyone. Grayson knew what had happened in his father's study all those years ago, and yet it seemed to have no bearing on how she viewed him as a man. Hers was a most liberating attitude.

With Gray's quiet understanding, her unquestioning acceptance of his past, Duncan found his feelings for her were intensifying, growing beyond the bounds he had set for himself. This wasn't the wisest thing that could have happened, but he didn't seem able to govern his emotions where Grayson was concerned. Still, he could not bring himself to disavow what he felt, and he staunchly refused to deny himself her company.

A wry smile drew up the corners of Duncan's mouth as he thought about the plans they had made for the evening ahead.

What devilment made Grayson want to see the inside of Evans's Song and Supper Room, invade the very heart of London's masculine domain? What was she up to? Was it her love of anything theatrical that was driving her, or was it something more? He supposed he would not have fancied being barred from someplace he wanted to go, either, and with Gray's willingness to flout society's prohibitions, the evening might prove interesting indeed. He could hardly wait to see what disguise she concocted to pass herself off as a young man. For someone as soft and womanly as she, the transformation would be a worthy test of her acting abilities.

With a rolling stretch, Duncan came to his feet and padded into the adjoining dressing room. Before he could give himself over to the revelry of the night to come, he had several things to accomplish. He meant to find out just who owned Enterprise Manufacturing and make an effort to see the company's president.

Reaching for the bell pull, he signaled for his bath, and while he waited for Barnes and the footmen to appear, he rummaged through the clothes he had left draped over a chair the evening before. Systematically he emptied the pockets of his waistcoat, jacket, and trousers, placing the contents on the dresser. What he found was the usual array of objects that made their way into any gentleman's pockets: his father's heavy watch and fob, two dark cheroots, a silver match-safe with *Citation* engraved on the cover, a handful of coins, and his wallet well filled with ten pound notes. There was a monogrammed handkerchief, the old Spanish doubloon he always carried for luck, and a bit of folded paper. Without paying particular attention, he flicked it open to see what it was, then stared down at the narrow rectangle of reddish stock. It was an advertising card with the name of a drinking establishment, the Crown Inn, and a crude illustration of a patron raising his glass.

Staring at the paper, Palmer wondered where he could have picked it up. He turned the advertising piece over twice, carefully looking for some notation he might have made on the back. There was nothing written on either side. His eyes narrowed, and the corners of his mouth tipped down. How had this found its way into his pocket?

Just then he heard Ryan enter the room beyond and tossed the advertising card on the dresser beside his other belongings.

"The water is heating for your bath, my lord," Ryan announced as Duncan entered the bedroom. "It should be ready shortly. I thought you might want your breakfast while you're waiting, since I know you've had nothing to eat since teatime yesterday."

"Very good, Ryan," Duncan answered with a nod. "Set the tray on the table by the window. I confess I'm more than a little hungry."

The valet did as he had been directed and poured his master coffee from the silver pot. He also parted the folds of the napkin on the serving plate to reveal several freshly baked rolls and a large dollop of yellow butter.

Drawn by the smell of the coffee and the prospect of good things to eat, Duncan took his place at the table and applied himself to the meal. The rolls, spread generously with butter, were soft and delicious, and he thoroughly enjoyed the light repast. As he dawdled over his coffee, waiting for his bathwater to arrive, he picked up the morning newspaper, lying folded at the edge of the tray. He opened it with a snap, and his eyes fell immediately on the headline that blared from the top of the page: "West End Strangler Strikes Again—Woman Found Dead on Silver Street."

Duncan peered out the window of the cab and checked the address of the house before him against the one he had copied from *The London Economic Directory*. The time he spent in the Archer Library this morning had been most productive, and by noon he had a list of Enterprise Manufacturing's officers. That Samuel Walford's name was not in evidence had disappointed Palmer initially, but he knew it was possible for someone to hold a controlling interest in a company without being on its roster. Now it was up to Duncan to find a way to persuade Enterprise Manufacturing's president, Sidney Layton, to give him a complete list of the firm's stockholders. Duncan was willing to wager half his worth that if he was able to do that, Walford's name would appear somewhere in that document, probably near the top. With the proof of Walford's complicity in hand, he would finally be able to confront his uncle's partner and demand concessions.

After paying the cabby, Duncan approached the stone-fronted town house in one of Bloomsbury's more prosperous streets. He moved through the heavy wrought-iron gate, past the tiny garden, alive with wildly blooming daffodils and hyacinths. The steps that led to the tall double doors were wide and neatly swept, bracketed with flowerpots filled with frilly red geraniums. The glinting brass knocker was warm in his hand, heated by the steady midday sun, and he had been waiting less than a minute when the door was opened by a footman.

"I've come to see Mr. Sidney Layton," Duncan told him.

"Mr. Layton, sir?" the man intoned. "May I ask your business?"

"It's a personal matter of some importance," Duncan replied.

The man hesitated, looking Duncan up and down with the cold, fishy stare that English servants seemed to have raised to a high art. He must have passed inspection, Palmer realized a moment later, when he was admitted into the hall.

"May I say who is calling, sir?"

"Tell Mr. Layton it is the Marquis of Antire," Duncan replied. There was no sense in giving Layton an opportunity to connect him to Wicker and Walford's affairs, as the Palmer name might have done. There were times when a title and all it implied were a distinct advantage to an unexpected visitor. Besides, Duncan wanted the element of surprise on his side in this transaction, and he saw no point in forfeiting it for the sake of an imperious servant.

"Very well, my lord. Perhaps you would prefer to wait in the parlor."

With a flourish the man opened pocket doors to the left of the hall and ushered Duncan into a vast high-ceilinged room. The parlor was larger and far more lavishly furnished than he would have expected. It gave the impression that the Laytons were people with a fondness for opulence, people who liked to entertain.

Bright spring sunlight shimmered through a wide window that faced the street, and though the glare was softened and muted by a heavy velvet swag, the filmy lace curtains beneath cast a faint flowery pattern on the rug. On a table in the center of the window alcove was a large, rather tasteless bronze, obviously based on Poussin's *Rape of the Sabine Women*. There were other statues of scantily clad men and women placed strategically around the room, and several enormous gilt-framed mirrors reflected Layton's riches. Maroon velvet couches and chairs that matched the muted tones in the marbelized wallpaper were clustered here and there across the floor. Tables with papier-mâché tops were set nearby, bearing decanters and glasses on enameled trays. In one corner of the room stood an inlaid grand piano with a thick sheaf of music on the music rack.

Duncan took a seat on one of the chairs near the fireplace and sat turning his hat in his hands. It was only when he began to glance around impatiently that he took note of the indelicacy of the carvings on the limestone mantelpiece. The uprights were two nude maidens, enticingly twined with garlands of flowers and fruit, and on the lintel, nymphs and satyrs cavorted in a most lascivious manner. But before he could do more than register his surprise at finding such a scene on a domestic mantelpiece, the pocket doors swept open to admit a tall, dark-haired woman in a loose-fitting gown of ivory lace.

Duncan stared at her a moment, then came to his feet with a jerk. "I'm sorry to disturb you, ma'am. I was looking for Sidney Layton."

The woman glided toward him, a gust of expensive perfume preceding her.

"I'm Sidney Layton," the woman breathed, gazing up at him with sultry eyes. "What exactly do you want with me?"

Duncan caught his breath in surprise and disbelief. It had never even occurred to him that a woman might be the president of Enterprise Manufacturing.

When Duncan did not respond immediately, Sidney Layton continued. "My very dear marquis, won't you have a seat on the couch here by me? May I offer you my hospitality and a brandy while you tell me why you've come?"

As she settled herself on one of the velvet settees, the skirt of her filmy lace gown parted to give him a glimpse of shapely silk-stockinged leg and a rosette garter of palest blue.

For an instant Duncan simply gawked. Didn't this woman know how much of herself she was revealing to him? Wasn't she aware of the effect such a glimpse of leg might have on a man?

As he stood over her, she reached up to catch his hand, and with gentle, unhurried motions brought it to her lips. Before he could gather his wits to pull away, she traced a delicate wavery pattern across his palm with the warm, moist tip of her tongue, sending a burst of delicious sensation slithering up Duncan's arm.

His heart slammed against his ribs as he jerked away, reacting to her blatant seduction and to what he'd abruptly realized. Suddenly it all made sense: the opulent parlor, the lewd scene on the mantelpiece, the predominance of mirrors in the decor. He almost laughed aloud at his own stupidity. This was a very expensive brothel, and Sidney Layton was a very expensive jade.

Catching his hand again, Sidney Layton drew him down beside her on the settee. "Why don't you tell me," she purred, "exactly what it is you want of me?"

"Apparently not what you seem to think," Duncan murmured on a gust of laughter.

"No?" she queried prettily.

"No," he assured her.

"A pity, then. I would have very much enjoyed spending this afternoon with a pretty man like you." Her dark eyes slid appraisingly over his neck and shoulders, across his chest and ribs, and down to the bulge between his thighs, clearly revealed by the narrow cut of his trousers. "Are you sure you won't change your mind? I can see you're not completely immune to my charms."

In another circumstance, Duncan might well have welcomed this woman's interest, responded to her blatant seduction. She was beautiful, to be sure, with her jet black hair and porcelain skin, with her soft, lush body temptingly revealed beneath the drape of the flowing lace. But today there were other matters on his mind, things that were far more important than an afternoon of bartered pleasure.

"I'm quite sure," Duncan asserted, though he wasn't entirely certain that the woman would take him at his word. Her hands were continuing to wander over him. "I came here to talk to you about another of your businesses entirely, Enterprise Manufacturing."

"Enterprise Manufacturing?"

Duncan drew a sharp breath as one of Sidney's hands slid along the inside of his thigh, while the other was busy undoing the buttons on his waistcoat.

"You are its president, aren't you?"

The woman lowered her eyes. "Its president? Who told you that?"

"It's a matter of public record. I looked it up in a business directory just this morning."

Delicately she shrugged. "An investment my solicitor suggested, no doubt. Are you sure you wouldn't like a glass of brandy while we talk?"

"No, thank you." Duncan tried unsuccessfully to disentangle himself from the woman at his side. This was hardly a situation that encouraged the discussion of her other business interests. "I want a list of the stockholders in the company."

"How businesslike you are," she complained in a throaty whisper.

"Surely no more than you."

"I suppose it depends what business we're discussing."

"Indeed it does, madam. Indeed it does."

Her hands retreated from the inventory she was taking of his person, though she remained cuddled close at his side. "And you're determined to talk to me about this manufacturing firm when there is a much more pleasurable transaction we could discuss?"

"I'm afraid that's what I'm here for."

"A shame. A terrible shame."

"To be sure," Duncan answered amiably.

"Well, then. What is the name of this manufacturing company again?"

"Enterprise Manufacturing."

"I don't believe I've ever heard of it. What is it they make?"

"That's exactly what I am trying to determine. There's a factory down in Limehouse."

"A most disagreeable neighborhood."

"Yes."

"And dangerous, too. I noticed you are favoring your right leg, my lord. You weren't hurt in a scuffle down in Limehouse, were you?"

Duncan's eyes narrowed with suspicion. "Something like that."

"Well, since you've been to the factory, why don't you tell me what kind of business this company does?" she proposed.

"The building is deserted. It seems to have been empty for quite some time, unless you count the rats and the vagrants who have made the place their home."

The woman wrinkled her pretty nose. "Why do you want to know about Enterprise Manufacturing?"

It seemed to Duncan that there might be as much to be gained by forthrightness as by deception.

"My uncle's company has been paying substantial sums of money to Enterprise Manufacturing for five years and more; and there's no evidence that we've ever received anything in return. Enterprise Manufacturing doesn't seem to have any employees, any inventory, any way to manufacture the goods our company has been paying them for. There doesn't seem to *be* any Enterprise Manufacturing—except on paper, of course."

Duncan waited for the woman to respond, and when she didn't, Palmer continued.

"I had hoped that you would give me a list of Enterprise Manufacturing's stockholders."

"I can hardly give you what I haven't got. And as I told you, my dear marquis, I have never heard of Enterprise Manufacturing," she assured him.

"Then why is your name on the records as its president?"

The woman shrugged again. "I'm sure I don't know."

Duncan's frustration began to rise. "And I don't suppose you've ever heard of a man named Samuel Walford, have you?"

There was a flicker of something in the woman's dark eyes. "No, I can't say that I have."

"Then I suppose you can't tell me why Samuel Walford has done such a brisk business with a company that doesn't exist. I suppose you can't tell me how he's connected with Enterprise Manufacturing."

"I have no idea," the woman answered, then went on. "Perhaps the president of the company is another Sidney Layton. It's a common enough name."

Duncan waited, hoping the silence would encourage the woman to say more.

Instead she shrugged in what seemed to be a characteristic gesture of evasion and slowly rose to stand over him. It was clear that as far as she was concerned, the interview was over.

"Then if we've no really interesting business to discuss, my lord, may I suggest you allow me to return to more profitable pursuits?"

Duncan doubted he would learn more from Sidney Layton today, though he was convinced she knew far more than she was saying. She had heard Samuel Walford's name. Of that Duncan was very sure. In the hope that she might somehow be persuaded to enlighten him at some later date, Duncan took a calling card from the inside pocket of his frock coat.

"If you should recall any more about Enterprise Manufacturing, I trust you'll contact me at this address."

The woman shook her head. "My memory is notoriously short."

"An asset in some businesses, I understand."

The woman nodded and smiled as if pleased by his observation.

Gesturing to the card in her hand, Duncan went on. "Perhaps I could arrange for some incentive that might help clarify your thoughts."

He did not expect her to take the bait directly, but she did look long and hard at the address handwritten on the heavy gold-edged paper.

"And this is where I can find you, at this house on Berkeley Square?"

"Only for a few weeks more," he answered without elaborating. It would not hurt for her to know his offer was conditional.

"I'll see if there's anything I can recall."

Bowing, Duncan took his leave. But he did notice that Sidney Layton was peering intently around the edge of the lace curtain as he moved up the street.

Saloons the world over smelled the same. Whether it was in Halifax, Constantinople, or Baltimore, a ripeness enveloped a patron as he pushed through a barroom door, an aura that was both vaguely offensive and profoundly welcoming. It was a yeasty smell, mellow and rich, diluted by the accumulated smoke of a thousand cigars, spiced with the tang of sweat and honest work. It proclaimed the establishment a masculine domain, a place of rough talk and hard liquor, of sharp expletives and bitter reality.

The Crown Inn was as familiar to Duncan as his own name, as beckoning as a friendly smile, as comfortable as home, though he had never set foot inside the place before. He stood in the doorway for a moment, taking in the clumps of scarred tables flanked by a shotgun pattern of chairs, the long sweep of polished countertop, and the round-faced barman who stood drying glasses at the very center. A painting of a horse and jockey hung on the wall behind the man; dark bottles of brandy, whiskey, and rum were lined up along the shelf beneath it, jars of pickled eggs like bulbous sentries standing guard at either end. The occupants of the room were what Duncan had expected, men in wrinkled work shirts, leather vests, and jackets cut from common cloth. They were bowed over pewter mugs clamped tight in work-worn hands, sitting in groups of two or three, talking quietly among themselves, or sunk deep in their own dark reveries.

As he moved in the direction of the bar, a few of the men raised their eyes to watch him pass, but most were too deep in conversation or too far gone in perpetual weariness to take notice of a stranger. Reaching his destination, Duncan propped one boot on the polished foot rail and leaned his elbows against the bar. It was a pose that fit like a well-worn glove. He ordered a pint of the tavern's best ale and sipped silently from his tankard. The taste was strong and harsh, but the bite of it quenched his thirst.

It had been a long frustrating day, and his meeting with Sidney Layton had been far from satisfactory. He had no sense of having accomplished what he'd set out to do, felt no closer to unraveling the mystery of Samuel Walford's connection to Enterprise Manufacturing. And his time in London was growing short. In two weeks, or three at the most, the *Citation* would be ready to sail, and he was no closer to proving Samuel Walford's complicity in the embezzlement than he had been when he arrived in England more than a month ago. His suspicions had been confirmed; Walford was involved in some kind of scurvy business. But Duncan had no hard evidence to support his claims, and he was loath to leave England without exposing the man's chicanery.

Duncan drained his glass of ale and signaled the barman for another. Perhaps Hannibal Frasier had found some indication of what was going on or had uncovered some more tangible connection between his uncle's partner and Wicker and Walford's losses. Duncan would be willing to bet Walford was behind the empty factory, the men who'd tried to kill him. Perhaps Walford was even involved with Sidney Layton and her establishment in Bloomsbury, but he had no earthly way to prove it. In the time he had left to him, Duncan had to unravel Walford's skein of deceit, answer the questions that grew more compelling and complex with every passing day. First thing in the morning, he would contact Hannibal Frasier, he told himself. He would see if the Scotsman had earned his hundred pounds by unearthing the kind of intrigues that would confirm Walford's crimes.

With the decision about his next step in the investigation made, Duncan turned his thoughts to the advertising card he had found in his pocket earlier in the day. That card was the reason he had selected this particular tavern in which to quench his thirst. The curiosity he had aroused by looking into Samuel Walford's affairs seemed to have spilled over into his own life as well. It bothered him that he could not remember having picked up the advertising card, and that wrinkle in the fabric of his life seemed to have taken on an exaggerated importance. Not being able to remember where he had gotten it unsettled him, and at this moment, when he wanted to be most certain of his perceptions, they were inexplicably dark and skewed. Here in England, where he was more vulnerable than he had been since he was a boy, Palmer's usually sharp wits seemed to have deserted him.

It was undoubtedly the commonality of taverns across the world that had made him feel immediately at home here, Duncan told himself. Though it was not all that far from Mayfair, he was sure he would have known if he had savored the Crown Inn's hospitality before this afternoon.

As the barman set the mug of foaming ale before him, Duncan looked into the man's face. There was no recognition in his eyes, no sense that the man had ever served him before. Still, Duncan stopped the barkeep before he turned away.

"Is this your advertising card?" he asked, withdrawing the bit of pale reddish stock from the depths of his waistcoat pocket.

The man hesitated and looked down at the crumpled paper, at the rows of smudged type and the crude illustration of a patron raising his glass in a drunken toast.

"It is," the man confirmed. "Didn't want to have them printed up at first. Thought it was a blasted waste of money. Me partner insisted, though. Said it might bring swells like you in for a pint or two of ale."

Duncan took a sip from his tankard. "And has it worked?"

The barman shrugged, picking up another glass and turning his towel laconically inside it. "A few come in from the better parts of town. The majority of the fellows we see are our steady customers, workingmen mostly, perhaps a stable hand or coachman now and then."

"Do you recall if I've been into the tavern before?" Duncan asked, trying to make the question seem more casual than it was. "I was having a drink with some friends last night, and they brought me to a tavern in this neighborhood somewhere. While we were out, I lost a silver penknife my father gave me, and I was hoping that by retracing my steps, I might be able to track it down."

"No one mentioned a penknife," he answered, "though I wouldn't count on getting it back. Folks here 'bouts would likely keep it for themselves if they was lucky enough to find a silver one."

"But you don't remember seeing me."

"I can't say one way or the other if you was here. And it's not as if I ain't been asked about who was in the tavern last night, either. Worked from midday till closing yesterday, I did, but me partner was working, too. Like as not he took care of you."

Duncan digested the barkeep's words in silence. "Is your partner here today? I'd just like to be sure that this is where we came."

The barkeep shook his head. "Won't be in till Wednesday next. He's taken his wife and young'uns down to Surrey to visit her kin."

Duncan shrugged, at a loss as to how to proceed. This man didn't remember seeing him in the tavern, but that didn't put his mind to rest. If he'd never been here before, how had he come by the bit of advertising? He drank down an inch or two of his ale and searched his mind for a logical explanation. Perhaps someone had given him the advertising card on the street, and he'd tucked it in his pocket without even realizing what he'd done. He'd been preoccupied lately, that was sure, and he could have picked it up somewhere absentmindedly.

" 'Course with the excitement last night," the barkeep went on as he put a final polish to the glass, "it would have been easy enough for me to miss you."

Duncan raised his head, turning his gaze from the card he held balanced between his fingers. "Excitement? What kind of excitement?"

"Was just before closing, you know, when the fellow wandered in. Shaking like a leaf, he was, and yelling for the constable."

"What was the matter with him?" Duncan asked, a twitch of something foul skittering down his back.

"Why, he'd found the Strangler's latest victim, that Simington girl. A seamstress she was, on her way home from the shop where she worked. And from what the fellow said, her neck was busted clean. Not a pretty sight, I'll warrant, not a pretty sight at all."

The breath Duncan drew was like ice in his lungs, and apprehension crept through him like a fog.

"She was killed near here, was she?" he finally managed to ask.

"Not half a block away. A beauty she was, too, though not by the time our Strangler was through with her, I suppose."

The barkeep's words whirred in Duncan's head, sparking images he did not want to see: of a woman whose dark hair was spattered across a field of fog-slicked stones, of a comely form lying twisted and still in a rubbish-littered alley, of a face distorted and dark in the last terrible throes of strangulation. Were the images from the story he had read in the morning paper, from something he had seen nearly a score of years before, from his own imagination? They were vivid enough to send spangles of cold spilling down his arms, to fill him with a terrible sick dread that curled deep down in his vitals.

With trembling hands Duncan fumbled some coins onto the counter in payment for the ale and the barkeep's information. But it was not the description of the Strangler's victim that so desperately upset him, not the image of the woman's broken body that the barman's words had given form. Lately there had been too many inexplicable incidents hovering at the edges of his life for him to continue to ignore them, too many brushes with the Strangler who was terrorizing London for him to be able to keep from noticing the pattern. It was the uncertainty those coincidences stirred that sent him stumbling toward the door. It was the coincidences and the horrible creeping suspicion that was slowly taking root in the recesses of his mind.

Eleven

West End Strangler Strikes Again

WOMAN FOUND DEAD ON SILVER STREET

In a dark, dank alley just off Silver Street, Lily Simington, Bond Street shop girl, met her end, the fourth victim of the man who has come to be known as the West End Strangler. Her body was found just after midnight by Joshua Little, who described the scene as follows: "I was just on my way home from a neighborhood tavern when I stopped to heed the call of nature. As I stepped into the alley, I all but stumbled over her. She was laid out on the paving stones, neat as you please. But she was dead. I could tell right off. Her face was all twisted and dark, and her head was bent to one side at a most peculiar angle."

Police Inspector George Lawrence, who is in charge of the murder investigation, confirmed that Miss Simington's neck was broken, as was the case with the three other women who have been found murdered in various parts of the West End in recent weeks.

Shaking his head, Duncan lowered the newspaper he had bought on the way back to the town house. After the story he'd heard from the barkeep at the Crown Inn, he had wanted more information about the killing. Now he was sorry he had been so curious.

The story spread across the front page of the *Morning Chronicle* brought memories of another body in another alleyway. No mention of that murder had appeared in the newspapers, but that made the incident no less abhorrent, the memories no less damning. As he sat alone at the table in his bedchamber, Duncan could almost feel the roughness of his assailant's skin beneath his palms, feel the way the man had struggled as Duncan's fingers closed around his throat, cutting off his air. Palmer's own throat worked as if his attacker's hands were wrapped around it. It was hard to breathe, and the brassy taste of fear rose on the back of his tongue. His hands knotted on the edges of the newspaper as the give of crushing cartilage, the grinding snap of vertebrae, the sudden stillness of the man's body beneath him, returned to haunt him. An icy shiver spilled down Duncan's spine, though his clothes were soaked with sweat.

Had the women the Strangler killed fought as desperately for their lives? Had they struck at their assailant's face and hands? Had they known what was about to happen to them?

A new shudder eddied through Duncan, and his stomach heaved spasmodically.

Palmer knew what it meant to kill the way the Strangler did. He knew the strength it took, the determination, the ruthlessness. He knew the suddenness with which life flew away, the terrible remorse that followed the act of killing another person. Without the threat of imminent peril, how could anyone kill in such a manner? How could anyone voluntarily take a life with his bare hands? How could anyone murder another human being deliberately?

The memory of his father's death skittered across his mind, but he forced the thought away. There was no deliberation in what he'd done. For all that he could not remember, Duncan was sure of that.

Though he resisted, Palmer was compelled to read on.

> Lawrence, a veteran of fifteen years on the Metropolitan Police Force, says that in response to the hue and cry from some of the most influential people in the metropolis, the police are stepping up their investigation of the West End Strangler's crimes. More officers are being assigned.
>
> "There is no need for the panic that has been sweeping the city," Lawrence assured this reporter. "We are on the Strangler's trail, and we have received information that shortly before her death, Miss Simington was seen in the company of a man who dressed and carried himself like a gentleman."
>
> Does this mean that the Strangler is from the highest reaches of society? this reporter asked.

"Not necessarily," Lawrence answered. "But we are not ruling out the possibility that the Strangler may be from among the privileged classes."

Miss Simington, an employee of Ferguson's Millinery, worked until the shop closed at ten last night and was apparently on her way home to her rooms in . . .

Duncan tossed the paper aside, but Lawrence's phrases seemed to shimmer before his eyes: "We are on the Strangler's trail . . . Miss Simington was seen in the company of a man who dressed and carried himself like a gentleman . . . We are not ruling out the possibility that the Strangler may be from among the privileged classes."

This afternoon when the barkeep at the Crown Inn had told him that the West End Strangler's fourth victim had been found less than a block from the tavern, Duncan had gone sick with dread. Impressions of the crime had floated before his eyes; images he could not explain seemed to flicker inside his head. It was as if he had seen the woman die, as if he had been to the alley where her body was found. But he hadn't; he had been home in bed when this murder occurred, drugged with laudanum and insensible.

In spite of the fact that the advertising card had led Duncan to the tavern, to a place not a hundred yards from where the Strangler had struck the shop girl down, it seemed impossible that there could be a connection between the card's appearance and the crime. Though, when he took time to think about it, this was not his first brush with one of the Strangler's victims. The second murder, the one on South Audley Street, had taken place just outside Grayson Ware's garden gate on the night he'd taken refuge in her uncle's folly. He had seen the crowd gathered around the body when he left the yard the following morning. The realization chilled him anew.

That each of the crimes seemed to have taken place on a night when he had been incapacitated with a headache was something else Duncan could not explain. Was it mere chance that the headaches and the murders seemed to coincide? What other explanation was there?

From the start, Duncan was forced to admit, he'd had a grisly fascination with the murders occurring in London's West End. He had followed the stories in the newspapers, had listened to the servants' gossip, had entered into speculations about the Strangler's identity during several of the dinner parties he'd attended in these last weeks. Had his prurient interest in the affair linked him to the murders in some voyeuristic way? It seemed impossible, and yet . . .

Perhaps it *was* only coincidence that his path had crossed the Strangler's again. Perhaps it *was* mere coincidence that each of the murders had taken place on a night when Palmer had been stricken with one of his headaches. He was letting a series of unexplained events turn him wild and fanciful, he told himself. He was an extremely logical man, and there was no basis in fact for any of the doubts running rampant through his mind.

Though his hands shook as he reached for the newspaper again, he ripped the story from the front page and tucked it and the advertising piece into a box at the bottom of one of the drawers in the dressing room. They would be safe enough hidden there, and if there should be other murders, he might want to look at the article again. There was nothing more than curiosity behind his actions, Duncan told himself with more conviction than he felt. There was no other reason to save the card and the bit of newsprint.

Once he had put the box away, Duncan went to his desk and drew a sheet of heavy vellum toward him. He needed to send a note immediately. He picked up a pen and began to write.

Dearest Lady Grayson,

Pressing business prevents me from accompanying you to the entertainments we had planned for this evening. I am very sorry that this has occurred, but the circumstances are quite beyond my control. I hope you will understand and forgive me for disappointing you.

If I do not see you again before I leave for New York, may I say that I have thoroughly enjoyed making your acquaintance. I shall always remember meeting you as the most pleasant part of my stay in England.

Very truly yours,
Captain Duncan Palmer

Duncan looked down at the words scrawled on the creamy sheet of paper with satisfaction and regret. He wondered what Grayson would think when she received the note. She would be disappointed, to be sure. He was aware of how much she had been looking forward to their illicit visit to Evans's Song and Supper Room. If he was honest with himself, he would have to admit that he had been looking forward to it, too. He had wanted to see what masquerade Gray would adopt to hide her identity, wanted to watch her reaction to the sights and sounds of the music hall, wanted to share her enjoyment of the evening. She would have been at her best in this kind of situation: irrepressible, gay, brimming with curiosity. One of the things Duncan liked best about her company was that she made him embrace life with the delicious abandon she did herself.

Being with Grayson always made the world seem more real, more compelling than it was from his solitary view. Apart from her desirability as a woman, Grayson warmed him with the irresistible lure of her vitality. He was all diligence, determination, and control; she was all passion, emotion, and delight. Being with her lit a glow inside him, brought to the fore a part of himself that he had never allowed to flourish. It was a part of himself that made him uncomfortable, a part that both intrigued and appalled him. It harked back to the way he had been as a boy, before his parents' death, before his exile to America. It was a part that had no place in the life he was living now. But for all that he found it unsettling, he liked what Grayson made him feel, liked the man he was when he was with her.

Yet it was just as well that circumstances had prevented him from spending tonight with Gray. She was coming to mean more to him than she should. She was becoming too important, and a tie with a woman like Grayson was something he could not afford. Besides she was betrothed to Harry Torkington, and in a few weeks Duncan would be leaving for America. There was nothing to be gained by continuing their acquaintance. It was best that he sever the relationship now.

Duncan melted a bit of wax onto the seam of the paper, took the carnelian quartz seal he wore as a watch fob, and pressed his sign into the congealing wax. The Palmer coat of arms was instantly recognizable: crossed swords and scallop shells emblazoned across the fold. Having sealed the note to his satisfaction, Duncan rang for a servant to deliver it.

As he gave instructions to the footman, Duncan tried to quell his own disappointment. There was no question that this was the most prudent course for him to follow. It was for her own good that he was refusing to take Grayson to Evans's this evening. Not only would the visit compromise Gray's reputation should her presence at the gentlemen's preserve be discovered, but there was something else afoot—something Duncan did not understand.

There was something going on here in London that filled him with a slow seeping dread. He was afraid deep down inside, afraid in a way he had not been afraid since the months after his parents' death. Then it was his loss of memory and the necessity of acknowledging what he'd done that had triggered the fear. Now it was something else that made him feel hollow and alone.

At any rate, he was doing the right thing in canceling his engagement with Grayson. By doing so he was preserving her reputation, ensuring her safety. He was doing what every gentleman was sworn to do, protecting a lady's virtue. But that knowledge was cold comfort when what he wanted most was to bask in Grayson's verve and vitality just once more before he left England forever.

"'Pressing business' indeed! 'Very sorry' my foot!"

Grayson ranged back and forth across the drawing room, the missive Duncan Palmer had sent her crumpled in one fist.

"I thought a sea captain who had the courage to make a winter crossing of the North Atlantic would be brave enough to escort one lone woman to a music hall," she raved. "I thought an American would be unconventional enough to realize there is nothing wrong with a lady visiting a popular eatery and hearing a few bawdy ballads."

Palmer was stunned to silence by Gray's unexpected arrival at the town house, and she was pleased that he was too surprised to argue with her.

Instead he stood transfixed just inside the drawing room door, even when Gray hurled the wadded piece of paper at his feet. As she moved toward him, he seemed unaware of the fury in her eyes. He was clearly far too busy taking in what she was wearing.

Gray had dressed tonight, as she always did, in the very height of fashion. But tonight the fashion she had adopted as her own was that of a dandified young man. Preening before him with all the reticence of a bantam rooster, Gray smoothed her hands along the lapels of the gray broadcloth frock coat she'd had specially made for just such an occasion. The coat was cut in the prevailing slope-shouldered, narrow-waisted masculine style, and with her breasts bound tight, the fullness of her velvet-collared waistcoat and the ruffled shirt beneath presented a good approximation of the current masculine silhouette. Her dark pin-striped trousers sported fullness at the waist and tapered toward the ankle just as Duncan's blue ones did. She had also made very sure that the skirt of the frock coat was cut full in the back and fell just to her knees to obscure the telling contours of her rounded derriere. With the close-cropped wig and cinnamon-colored mustache she had affected to complete her transformation, Gray was sure she seemed as likely a companion as Palmer could want for an evening of masculine carousing.

"Grayson, wait," Duncan murmured at last, caught halfway between an admonition and a laugh. "If you'll only let me explain—"

"Explain?" she scoffed, feeling the hot blood rise in her cheeks again. "Explain, Duncan? Do you want to explain that you haven't the stomach for this adventure? That you prefer to sit home instead, secure in the opinion that by denying me a single evening in a music hall you are playing guardian to my virtue?"

Palmer watched her as she whirled away. He would not have given quite that face to this ludicrous situation. He would have preferred to remind her of her position as a lady of the ton, as the Duke of Stinton's betrothed. He would rather have pointed out that she had all but coerced him into agreeing to her plans. But in essence, she had stolen the best of his arguments with a few well-chosen words. Or at least she had stolen all the arguments he could safely reveal to her.

He crossed the room to get a drink, hoping that in the few moments it would take him to pour a brandy, he could find some way to convince Grayson of her folly. But even as he searched, there was an imp of mischief stirring inside him, an imp that tempted him to grant her exactly what she asked.

"Brandy?" he inquired, turning to where she stood.

"Of course," she answered gruffly. "If it's what you yourself are having."

As she watched, Duncan poured three fingers of the amber liquid into the tumblers on the table, then strode across the room to offer her the glass. There was humor in his eyes that hinted that he might eventually acquiesce to what she wanted: an evening alone with him and the chance to see the inside of Evans's establishment.

"So you think you are prepared to spend the evening in masculine revelry, do you?" he challenged her.

Grayson was not quite sure what he meant by "masculine revelry" and restated her position instead. "I want to go to Evans's Song and Supper Room and hear the entertainers there. If that is your idea of 'masculine revelry,' then I'm more than prepared to enjoy it."

"You have no desire to see the inside of Crockford's or a brothel?"

Gray blinked twice in shock before she answered him. "I want to see what goes on inside a music hall, just as I've always managed to find my way to the burlettas and melodramas being given at some of the less respectable theaters here in London. All I care about is seeing this form of musical theater, and I think it's totally ridiculous that women aren't allowed to attend."

"If we do go to Evans's you'll hear words no lady should be acquainted with," Duncan warned.

"I've spent enough time in the stables and around my uncle's estate to know cursing when I hear it."

"And there will likely be some jokes no lady could approve of."

"I'll try very hard not to blush."

"The songs they sing may well be bawdy."

"Bawdier than the Bard's own plays? More scandalous than *Tartuffe*?"

Grayson could see Duncan's resolve eroding, sensed that whatever good intentions had led him to write the note earlier in the evening were crumbling beneath her more than able assault. She felt a surge of satisfaction. She wanted to spend the evening with Duncan in any case, but an entrée to Evans's would add spice to the experience.

"It would be a shame for such a fine disguise to go to waste," she cajoled. "Don't I make a convincing youth, perhaps one who's just down from Oxford to see the town?"

Oddly enough, she did, Duncan conceded. She made a far more believable lad than he had ever expected. And in spite of himself, he found Grayson was very much in danger of winning her way. Even his own uneasiness in the matter of the Strangler, his own sense of something in his life being hopelessly amiss, was swiftly being overcome by her determined arguments. Nor did it help his resolve that he had been looking forward to sharing a very unusual evening with her.

Grayson continued to press her case. "If you're not willing to accompany me to Evans's tonight, I may just go alone. No one will penetrate this disguise, and I'm sure I will be safe enough on the streets if I come and go in a covered carriage."

Her blithe, offhanded threat sent a ripple of uneasiness through Duncan. Whatever happened, he did not want Grayson wandering around London on her own. She might look the part of a young man in her frock coat and trousers, her wig and mustache, but there was danger on the streets for any man who looked as inexperienced as she.

His own concerns in the matter of the Strangler again came to the fore. The odd connection he felt to the Strangler's crimes was the reason he had refused to take her to Evans's in the first place, but he could not let her brave the London streets alone. She might think she was safe enough dressed as she was, but if the Strangler stalking lone women recognized that Gray was not a man . . .

The thought of what could happen to her turned him cold.

"If I agree to take you to Evans's it will be against my better judgment," Duncan warned halfheartedly.

She instantly sensed that he was close to giving in.

"Oh, Duncan, if you agree to take me to the music hall, I promise to behave. I won't be rowdy. I won't draw attention to myself in any way. All I want is a chance to see the show. As soon as it is over, you may take me home and go on about your business."

Palmer still looked skeptical. "And I suppose your uncle Warren is fully aware of your plans, that he approves of how you want to spend the evening."

Grayson tossed her head. "Of course he has no idea what I'm about. He'd have apoplexy if he knew. I left the party we were attending on the pretext of having a headache. I dismissed my maid and told her I did not want to be disturbed. No one will know I've even left the house. You must trust me in this."

"Are you certain, Grayson? Really sure? I have absolutely no desire to answer to the Duke of Fennel for leading his ward astray."

Gray's impatience began to grow. The more they talked about it, the more she wanted to go with him to Evans's.

"I promise you, Duncan, no one will know I'm gone. I've even brought the key to the garden gate so I can slip back onto the property unobserved."

"I don't know, Grayson. You're taking a terrible risk."

"But aren't the risks we take in life half of what we're living for?" There were sparkles of excitement in her eyes, sparkles that were only partially based in the danger of being discovered. "Haven't you taken risks, Duncan, as you've sailed the seas? Haven't the risks you took made living a far sweeter thing indeed? What's one risk more or less?"

What she said was true, yet Duncan had the feeling that to agree would be a terrible mistake. But then, it would not be the first mistake he'd made in his life. Or probably the last.

"Well, then," he conceded with a frown, "be sure your disguise is securely in place. That mustache is tacked on firmly, isn't it? And, Grayson, please try to act like a man. No mincing, no clasping your hands to your breast, no—"

Grayson swelled with indignation. "Once I'm in character, Duncan, I swear you'll never have any doubt that I'm a boy. Didn't you say I was one of the best actresses you've ever seen? Didn't I play Portia most convincingly?"

He gave a nod of grudging acknowledgment. "I don't know, Grayson. No matter how convincingly you comport yourself, I won't be able to forget that you're no man."

Then, shaking his head as if to put the concerns from his mind, Duncan rang for a footman and requested his walking stick and hat.

Once the man had gone to do his bidding, Palmer turned to Grayson again.

"Have you a name, my good man? Something I should call you this evening?"

Grayson grinned at his words, at his apparent ability to play his own part. "Herbert," she replied after a moment's deliberation. "I shall be the Honorable Herbert Fortescue."

Duncan choked back a laugh. "Then Herbert it is. And may I say, my dear Herbert, that I look forward to the evening being a most unusual and diverting one?" With his words as a toast he tossed back the contents of his glass.

Without thinking of the consequences, Grayson did the same, swigging down the brandy in a single draft. The stuff was like fire on her tongue and raked along the back of her throat. It burned all the way down, and tears rose in her eyes.

"I believe this is an evening I'll remember all my life," she replied in a raspy voice, "for its interesting companions and the adventures we're bound to have."

Duncan had no chance to respond to her words, because just then there was a knock on the door. A small bearded servant entered.

"Are you going out, my lord?" the man inquired quietly.

"I've had an invitation, Barnes, that I find I can't refuse."

Conscious that Ryan was eyeing his companion, Duncan made hurried introductions. "Herbert Fortescue, may I present my valet, Ryan Barnes. Barnes has been with me since I was a boy."

Even as he spoke the words, Duncan knew it was highly improper to present a servant to one's friends, but he meant the introduction as a test. He needed to be sure that Barnes was taken in by Grayson's new persona.

In response to the introduction, Grayson inclined her head with just the right attitude of acknowledgment and reserve.

"It's my pleasure to meet you, Mr. Fortescue," the valet answered with what seemed like no undue curiosity.

"Mr. Barnes," Grayson responded to the valet as she pulled on her immaculate dove-gray gloves.

Barnes turned to offer Duncan his cane, gloves, and high silk hat. "Will you be out late this evening, my lord? Do you want me to wait up for you?"

Satisfied that Barnes had seen no more in Grayson than what she appeared, Duncan gave a sigh of relief and placed the top hat on his head. "I don't know what time I will be returning to the house. Feel free to spend the evening however you choose."

As they turned toward the door, it was with great difficulty that Duncan stifled the urge to offer his arm to Grayson, and he realized all at once that the single greatest impediments to her disguise might well be his own unspoken attitude.

"Let's be off, then, shall we, Herbert?" he murmured to cover the moment of awkwardness, motioning for Grayson to precede him out the door.

Twelve

EVANS'S. GRAYSON WAS ACTUALLY GOING TO EVANS'S, INVADING London's most notorious male preserve. As she and Duncan strode up King Street from New Row and St. Martin's Lane, excitement fluttered in her throat and bubbled in her veins. Still, Gray schooled her face to nonchalance as her role as a young-man-on-the-town demanded. She squared her shoulders and thumped her cane against the cobblestones, adjusted her top hat to a more rakish angle and lengthened her strides to match Duncan's long-legged lope. She felt secure in her portrayal of Herbert Fortescue, totally comfortable with her debut in a breeches role.

Duncan was playing his part in the deception with consummate skill, letting her jump down from the horse cab unassisted, giving her the opportunity to pay and dismiss their driver. Now as they approached the western end of Covent Garden, she could see Evans's just ahead. The music hall was an elegant building that dated back to the reign of Charles II. Since then it had been a fashionable private residence, public offices, and most recently a hotel. Made of dark red brick, it sported a graceful pillared entrance and four tall white stone pilasters that ran the full height of the building. A matching balustrade marked the perimeter of the roof, and just behind it loomed a high arched dormer that crowned the whole, giving mute evidence of the building's long, distinguished history and undeniable importance.

Though it was just before eleven o'clock, there were still men milling around the entrance of the building beneath the glow of the gas lamps that illuminated the square. Grayson and Duncan shouldered their way through the crowd in the hope of getting a good table from which to watch the evening's entertainments.

Though Duncan had been in England just slightly more than a

month, the majordomo instantly recognized him as the Marquis of Antire and led them ceremoniously through the vestibule. It was a long, narrow passage with dark mahogany wainscoting and rich blue damask walls on which portraits of famous actors and actresses were hung. Grayson lagged behind to get a better look, dreaming of the day when her portrait would hang there, too.

Beyond the vestibule lay an elegant hall that had been recently added to the rear of the building in response to Evans's growing popularity. The room was all of seventy feet long and thirty feet wide, with a raised platform and small proscenium at the far end. Along the sides were tall Corinthian columns, crowned by arches that rose toward the high medallioned ceiling two stories above. Beneath the rows of gleaming chandeliers, tables were arranged to run the length of the room. Offering a bow and flourish befitting Duncan's rank, the fawning majordomo gave them places midway down the hall.

As they nodded greetings to the men seated to their left and right, Grayson suddenly felt conspicuous. It was ridiculous to think she would draw undue attention in a room rapidly filling with distinguished men, that someone would notice that she didn't belong. But in spite of her faith in the effectiveness of her disguise, Gray's palms began to sweat and her stomach quivered with unexpected nervousness.

Once they were settled in their chairs, Duncan leaned forward and touched her arm. "Is this everything you hoped?" he whispered.

Grayson nodded once in answer. "It's everything I'd hoped and more."

Before they could continue their conversation, a waiter came to take their supper order. They requested the pork chops for which Evans's was justly famous, a glass of wine for Grayson, and for Duncan a tankard of ale.

As they waited for their meal to be served and for the entertainment to begin, Grayson watched the people who were taking places at the tables across the hall. Evans's was a gathering places for the elite of literary, artistic, theatrical, and political London, and as they moved toward their tables she pointed out some of the celebrities: Benjamen Disraeli whose society and political novels were enjoying wide popularity; George Cruikshank, whose satirical drawings and cartoons regularly lampooned the most sacred bastions of London society; and Douglas Jerrold, who wrote for the scandalous new London magazine, *Punch*. Among the jostling, well-dressed throng, Gray also noticed several of her uncle's cronies from Parliament and a suitor whose offer of marriage she had repeatedly refused. She chose not to draw Duncan's attention to these men, fearing that their presence might unnerve him. It had certainly unnerved her.

Somehow it had not occurred to Grayson that there would be people here from her social milieu, and she worried that while her disguise might fool a roomful of strangers, there were others who knew her well enough to see beyond the masquerade. In response to her concern, Gray shrank back against the wall, surreptitiously checking the glue on her mustache and hoping that Duncan would not sense her sudden urge to bolt.

No one would penetrate her disguise, she tried to tell herself. But until the room began to fill, she had not realized what a gamble she had taken by asking Duncan to bring her here. When their food arrived, Grayson applied herself to the chops and potatoes, the cabbage and wine, trying to push thoughts of discovery to the farthest reaches of her mind.

At last the lights in the chandeliers began to dim, and a hush fell over the crowd. The piano and harmonium struck up a familiar tune as the first singer stepped through the tier of curtains that hung in the arched proscenium. The card to the right of the stage identified him as S. A. Jones, and once he had acknowledged the applause, his powerful bass voice filled the hall. His song was rich and melancholy, and Grayson was immediately swept up in her enjoyment of the evening's entertainment.

Beside her, Duncan watched not the performer on the stage but his own companion. He saw how Grayson's eyes shone with appreciation of this artist's skill, saw how her face glowed with the excitement of her illicit evening on the town. He noted that her lips were parted in awe, that her cheeks were tinted a rosy hue. It seemed impossible that others would not see through her disguise when to him she appeared so soft and womanly.

As Jones sang, she turned to Duncan with a dazzling smile. Thank you for giving me this, she seemed to say. Thank you so much for tonight.

Something warm and fluttery seemed to soar through his insides. A deep contentment settled over him with the knowledge that by bringing Grayson here he had made her happy. He reached across to touch her hand, then hurriedly snatched his own away.

The mustache glued firmly in place beneath Grayson's nose had suddenly reminded him of the roles the two of them were playing. It would not be seemly for men to touch in the way Duncan had intended, and he subsided into his chair, vowing to keep his actions under an even firmer control.

Though there had been no speculation about Grayson's sex from the men seated at the tables around them, Duncan found his basic uneasiness was not assuaged. It was foolish to worry about someone discovering her identity, Duncan tried to tell himself. Her disguise was really quite effective. He was anticipating problems that would never arise. Yet in spite of Duncan's apprehension about bringing her here, Grayson's delight in the performance seemed to make the risks worth taking.

When Mr. Jones had concluded his part in the entertainment, Grayson turned to Duncan again. "He was wonderful, wasn't he?" she asked.

"Simply wonderful," he agreed.

"His voice was so strong, so resonant."

"Aw, he was not as good as all that," the tall fellow to her right broke in. "Sounded like some damned bullfrog croaking, if you ask me."

Irritated by the comment and that the man would break into a private conversation, Grayson turned and glared at him. But before the fellow could respond, before Grayson could say anything more, a comedian began to sing.

This man, known to his admirers as Jackie Sharp, sang songs in a much more lighthearted vein. They were satirical, amusing comments on the politics of the day. A chorus of male glee singers performed next, the blending of their voices sending shivers of appreciation spilling down Grayson's spine.

She looked across at Duncan as they sang, and she could see that he was enjoying them, too. His lips were moving slightly, as he mouthed the words of the sentimental song. His eyes were soft and shining, his gaze riveted on the stage. Tenderness stole through Grayson as she watched him in the dimly lit room, and in that moment Palmer's allure for her had never been more encompassing.

There were deep feelings in Duncan Palmer, honest emotions, strengths, and fears. There was a fathomless understanding in his heart, a kindness, and a genuine concern for her that Gray had never experienced. He was by far the nicest man she'd ever met, by far the most considerate. He was the kind of man a woman could come to love, the kind of man a woman could build a life with.

For the first time since she was a girl, Grayson saw the attraction in something she'd always shunned. For her, marriage, a family, a home had seemed to be a trap, an impediment to what she really wanted. Marriage to Harry, she knew, would be all of that and more. He would demand things from her that she was unwilling to give. He would confine her, stifle her, crush her spirit. But with a man like Duncan Palmer, the things that Harry would demand were things Grayson would want to provide.

It was a stunning realization.

All Grayson had ever wanted was to be an actress. It was the only dream she'd ever had. She had decided years before that if following her ambitions meant giving up the things most women seemed to crave, she was willing to make the sacrifice. She'd dedicated herself to making a life on the stage, and it bothered her no small bit that Duncan Palmer's intrusion in her world was making her examine her own priorities.

Yet even with a man like him, Grayson could see the rending compromises a woman would be forced to make. There would be the responsibilities of a home to drain away her energies, the chance of pregnancies to interrupt any career she hoped to have. Children would make demands on her time, and how could a woman find a way to reconcile such strong and compelling loyalties?

Would she be willing to change her life for a man like Duncan Palmer? Grayson wondered. Would she be willing to set aside the ambitions she had cherished for a chance at another kind of happiness? The prospect of giving up her most treasured dreams frightened her; the possibility of looking to another kind of future turned her cold. Would life with a man like Duncan be worth all it would cost her in terms of thwarted hopes? Could she, could any woman, be happy with a man who could offer her more than she'd ever wanted but less than she'd hoped to achieve?

Just as the glee singers concluded their set, Grayson's attention was diverted by a disturbance at the door. She glanced over her shoulder to level a quelling frown at these inconsiderate newcomers, and her stomach lurched toward her shoes.

Harry Torkington was in the doorway, the ringleader of the noisy, jostling group.

"What's he doing here?" Duncan hissed in her ear a moment later.

"How on earth should I know?" Grayson whispered back. "He was supposed to be at his estate in the country until at least next Thursday."

She drew several shaky breaths, wondering what she should do. If Harry discovered her here in Duncan's company, she hated to think of the consequences.

"Do you want to leave?" Palmer went on, gripping the back of her chair.

Gray shook her head emphatically. There was nothing to be gained by a hasty retreat. In a room with three or four hundred others, there was no reason for Harry to notice her.

Please don't let him see me! she prayed for good measure. Please don't let Harry recognize me and cause a scene!

When she dared glance over her shoulder a few minutes later, Harry and his friends were gathered around a table at the back of the room, close enough to the door to make an inconspicuous exit impossible.

Grayson had a hard time keeping her mind on the entertainment after that, though the acts were skillfully performed and of the very highest quality. There was a fine tenor named Binge, a man who yodeled most impressively, and an improviser by the name of Charles Sloman, who made rhymes and songs on topics suggested by the audience.

As Sloman proceeded with his act, the man at Grayson's right, by now far gone in drink, began to shout improprieties for the rhymer to use in his ditties.

"'Harlot,'" he shouted above the murmur of voices. "Make a rhyme on 'harlot.' 'By-blow.' Use 'by-blow' in a rhyme."

After several unsuccessful attempts at ignoring the man, the comedian on the platform stepped to the apron of the stage and shaded his eyes to more effectively see his tormentor in the audience. As he did, heads all over the room were turned in Gray's direction.

Please don't let anyone recognize me, she prayed again as she slunk lower in her chair, trying to become invisible beside the drunken heckler.

When Sloman had sighted the man, he gave a wry grin and the slightest of nods. Then he began to recite:

Once there was a by-blow
Who sat in the midst of the hall.
I'd gladly come give him the heave-ho
If only he weren't so tall.

The room erupted in laughter at the expense of the drunken heckler, and a flicker of applause could be heard from the tables near at hand.

The man beside Grayson seemed to be far better at handing out abuse than taking it, and he rose menacingly from his chair with some kind of retribution obviously on his mind. Those around him reached out to catch his arms, and after a slight scuffle, he staggered back, nearly missing the seat of his chair. Turning, he glared at Gray, as if something more than his own momentum had made the chair skitter out from under him.

Grayson looked back at him wide-eyed, trying to convey her total innocence. But as the man turned away, she became aware that beside her Duncan was tensed and ready to defend her if the need to do so arose. The moment passed, however, and Grayson once more turned her attention to the performer who now claimed center stage.

The card to the right gave his name as W. G. Ross, and she knew him by reputation as one of the foremost dramatic singers of his day. He usually performed at the Cyder Cellars, a few blocks away in Maiden Lane. But tonight he was here at Evans's, and she could hardly believe her good fortune. Surely he was about to sing his famed "Sam Hall," a scena about a thief condemned to die on the gallows for murder.

Grayson caught her breath as Ross began to pace the stage, the piano and harmonium playing a low accompaniment. The man's darting eyes and restless movements conveyed the stark terror of a murderer about to face his doom. His hunched shoulders and the faint trembling in his hands as he removed a short clay pipe from his pocket silenced the room. Then, as he lit the pipe and drew on it, his stance straightened, and he moved with brittle bravado to face the audience:

My name it is Sam Hall, I'm a thief.
My name it is Sam Hall, I'm a thief.
My name it is Sam Hall.
I've robbed both great and small,

but they makes me pay for all,
Damn their eyes.

The last line was echoed over and over at the end of each stanza, sung with varying degrees of fury and bitterness as the chimney sweep recounted the events of his misspent life. He made no attempt to enlist the sympathy of his listeners or excuse the macabre nature of his deeds, but that made the singer's words and characterization all the more poignant, all the more tragic.

Grayson felt Ross's magic enfold her, felt her throat tighten, felt tears sting the back of her eyes in response to the lyric of his song. She and "Sam Hall" might well have been the only ones in the vast silent room for all the awareness she had of those around her. It was theater at its very best with all the magnetism and power that could be generated by a truly gifted actor. It was the very essence of what she had come to see, and Gray was overcome with awe. Ross's portrayal was a revelation, and Grayson marveled at the audience's spellbound response to him. It was one of the strongest and most compelling performances she had ever seen.

She glanced at Duncan to gauge his reaction to the man. It was clear by the compression of his lips and the stiffness along his jaw that he was as moved by the performance as she was. Fresh tears rose in her eyes, and she blinked them away, feeling as bound to Duncan by the emotions in his face as she was to the man on the stage.

When Ross was finished, the people in the room erupted with applause. There were enthusiastic shouts of praise for what was clearly Ross's masterwork. Men at the tables around them were on their feet cheering, wiping self-consciously at their eyes, giving this extraordinary performer his due. Grayson and Duncan were on their feet with all the rest, and the tall man to Grayson's right hauled himself up unsteadily.

"Damned sentimental slop," he muttered as he stumbled into Grayson.

In self-defense she jostled him back, nearly knocking him off his feet.

But instead of ignoring what had happened, he turned on her.

"I've had enough of you," he muttered, "you damned aristocratic twit. Pull my chair out from under me, nearly push me down . . ."

Before either Duncan or Grayson could react, the drunkard

balled his fist and swung at her. The man's reflexes were impaired by the amount of alcohol he'd consumed, and his punch glanced off Grayson's shoulder. But there was enough force behind the blow to knock her into the wall.

Suddenly furious, Grayson regained her feet and raised her own clenched fists in the classic Marquis of Queensberry pose. She'd take the fellow down a peg if it was the last thing she ever did.

The drunkard sneered and raised his hands in response, obviously pleased that he'd managed to pick a fight with his tormentor, and an opponent so much smaller than he was, at that.

There was the stutter of feet around them, the scrape of chairs on the polished wooden floor. A wave of anticipation swept through the room, as every man turned to watch the scuffle, hoping that this might prove to be the most unexpected and exciting part of the evening's entertainment.

But before a full-blown brawl could break out between Grayson and the drunkard—a brawl she could hardly hope to win—Duncan grabbed Gray's arm and dragged her toward the exit. All eyes watched their progress toward the rear of the hall as speculation buzzed around them. There seemed to be approval in its tone, admiration for a fellow as slight as this one who was game enough to challenge a larger opponent.

As much as Grayson hated being conspicuous, she reveled in the sound of the crowd's approval. She was proud she'd stood up to the drunkard, after what he'd tried to do to her. She was pleased that the other men had taken note of her bravery, though it also drew unwelcome attention to their retreat.

But as Duncan stood in the doorway settling their account with Skinner, the cashier, Grayson had reason to curse her impetuousness. As she waited, she risked a glance at where Harry sat near the doorway at a table with a group of his friends. From the way that he was staring, totally stunned and open-mouthed, it was obvious he had recognized her.

"Couldn't you have picked a fight with someone who wasn't twice as big as you are?" Duncan teased gently as he and Grayson made their way down South Street from where they had dismissed their carriage at Park Lane. Gray had been pale and utterly silent since they made their hasty exit from Evans's nearly an hour before, and Palmer felt both clumsy and helpless in trying to lighten her mood.

"It's not that I don't think you could have handled the fellow," he went on. "Your fighting form looked most effective, and the man was clearly a drunken sot."

Grayson summoned up a twist of a smile, touched by Duncan's attempts to put a different face on what had happened. Still, there was no question that the evening had ended in disaster. She should have listened when Palmer tried to dissuade her from going to Evans's; she should have accepted his counsel. But she had been too headstrong, too driven by feelings she could not explain, to acknowledge that his might have been a more prudent view.

With the approach of her wedding day, Gray seemed to have been seized by a frantic need to rebel, to defy convention. It was as if she was compelled to see things and do things she would never have another chance to see and do. With incipient panic as a goad, she had proposed the visit to Evans's, demanded that Duncan take her there. Now she would pay the price for her foolishness, her recklessness. When Harry came to break their engagement, as he undoubtedly would, the whole story would come out, and she was afraid that in the ensuing scandal her aunt's and her uncle's reputations would be damaged along with her own.

As she and Duncan approached the rear of Worthington Hall, Grayson dug deep into the pocket of her trousers for the key to the garden gate, and turned it in the lock. But before she could open the wooden panel or step inside, Palmer caught her arm.

"Grayson, this isn't quite the tragedy you seem to think. Fights break out at places like Evans's and the Coal Hole almost every night. The crowds don't feel they've gotten their money's worth if everything is peaceable. You really didn't do anything so terribly wrong."

"Everyone noticed me," she lamented softly.

"And what does it matter as long as all they saw was a youth and a drunkard scuffling?"

"But, Duncan—"

"Hush," he whispered resting his forefinger against her lips. "Hush. Everything will be fine in the morning, believe me."

His touch was tender, soothing, infinitely gentle. Still, Grayson couldn't believe that things would be fine in the morning. She knew, in fact, they wouldn't be. But as they stood together in the shadowy street, what the morrow would bring really didn't matter. What mattered was that Duncan was here with her, consoling her when he might have been angry, treating her with care and courtesy. It was more than she deserved when her actions might have imperiled them both.

Before they parted, Grayson knew she had to thank Duncan for standing by her tonight, had to apologize for involving him in her irresponsible schemes. And in spite of her reticence to do so, she knew she should bid him good-bye. Once the scandal broke she would be sent away to her uncle's country estate, and that would destroy any hope she might have had of stowing away on Duncan's ship. A clot of emotion constricted her throat, but the feeling was less regret for having forfeited her chance for passage than sorrow at having to part from a man who had become so unexpectedly dear to her.

Duncan must have felt some of that reticence, too, for as they stood caught in the cocoon of silence, in the web of the warm spring night, his finger moved against her mouth. It changed the gesture he had made from one of silent admonition to something else entirely.

With the same deliberation he might have used in mapping a course across the world, with the same focused concentration he might have used in committing a passage of poetry to memory, he charted the contours of her mouth. He traced the lush deep curve of her upper lip, the pillowy fullness of the lower one. Her lips warmed and tingled at his touch, seemed to bud and flare under the pressure of his fingertip.

Around the two of them was the rich smell of the dark garden: the cool damp earth, the hint of lilacs on the wind. The verdant leaves rustled overhead; there was the chime from a distant clock tower. It struck two long, slow peals, and when the sound had echoed away, all was quiet. It was a resonant silence, like heavy sleep, profound, vast, fathomless.

Moving as if caught in that slow, sensual world of dreams, Duncan slid his finger to the point of Grayson's chin and nudged it upward. He gazed into her eyes, and she suspected that he could read both her sadness at their parting and the scope of her regret.

In the dimness she could see the subtle changes in his expression, the softening of his features, the droop of his heavy lashes, the bowing of his mouth. His lips came down to hers, brushing lightly, tenderly. Her mouth moved against his in response, flickering, fluttering. Their tongues touched; their breath merged.

The contact was tentative, faint, and feathery. It was delicate, exquisite, enticing.

Gray's heart began to thud against the wall of her chest as they hovered on the brink of deeper contact, and she could sense that Duncan was as entranced by the moment as she. They wavered, still standing a hairbreadth apart, and when the waiting became intolerable, the kiss became lush, full-blown and heady. Their mouths opened, crushing and clinging. Their tongues reached, probing sinuously and deep. Gray opened her lips to him, pulling, drawing on his mouth. He answered her invitation, savoring, nibbling, feasting on her sweetness.

Delight melted through her as his arms curled around her shoulders. A moan quivered in her throat as his hands splayed against her back. His touch was compelling, reassuring, oddly and comfortably possessive.

Grayson nestled into the curve of Duncan's body, homing to his strength, the potent power of his masculinity. The protection of his arms around her was like a bastion against the world, against a kind of trouble from which her cleverness and bravado could offer no deliverance. But Grayson found more than solace and reassurance in Duncan's embrace. She found a rightness she had never known, a sweetness and acceptance she had only dreamed existed. A sob gathered in her chest, a soundless protest at losing all he had come to mean to her. The salt of unshed tears stung her eyes, and she clasped her arms more tightly around him.

As she did, her fingers skimmed beneath his frock coat, over the silky material of his vest to where his shirt had bunched up at the back of his waist. She slid her hands beneath the wrinkles in the fine linen fabric, stroked the smoothness of his flesh, the broad hollow of his spine. There was a delicious intimacy in touching the warmth of a man's skin beneath his clothes, a delicious intimacy that sent delight shimmering through her in shivery waves. As she clung to Duncan, the sensation grew, setting off a sinking, pulsing ache down deep inside her, an ache that was as insidious as it was compelling, as sweet as it was frightening.

Grayson began to sense the infinite possibilities in Duncan's embrace, and as their kisses went on and on, sweet and moist, sleek and warm, pure intemperate joy rose in her heart. She realized suddenly what Duncan could be to her, knew what she could be to him. There was a world of emotions they could share, if only they had the time, if only they had the opportunity to explore the scope of their emerging feelings. But fate had given them nothing but this, these last moments to be together.

Gray arched against him, determined to make the most of the time they had. She wanted to cling to Duncan for as long as she could, take refuge in his strength. In these moments she wanted to open herself to him, offering him her tenderness, her femininity, her heart.

Her mouth moved under his, nibbling at the curve of his lower lip, laving the upper one with the enticing flick of her tongue, exploring the corners of his mouth. She let her kisses stray along the angle of his cheek, across his cheekbone to the corner of his eye. His lashes lowered and she brushed his eyelids with her lips.

His breath shuddered as he bound her closer still. With a moan he claimed her mouth once more, drawing her into his kiss. He drank deep of her, sipping, tasting, savoring, taking her mouth in longer and longer drafts. She turned viscous in his embrace. Weakness melted down her arms and legs.

"Oh, Duncan," she whispered into his mouth. "Oh, Duncan."

They kissed and touched and kissed again. They curled together as if they could not bear the leave-taking that was bound to come. They plumbed the magnitude of the delicious physical sensations, the devastating enchantment that both drew and bound them together. And when Duncan finally raised his mouth from hers, they were both breathless and intoxicated.

It was a full minute before either of them could speak, before either of them had need of words. But though the lingering contact continued, he moved a step away.

"One side of your mustache has become unglued," he told her, and there was amusement in his tone.

"Small wonder," she returned and attempted to press the fringe of crepe hair back in place.

"To tell the truth, I like you better without that," he admitted as he caught the corner of her sagging mustache and carefully peeled the thing away. "I'm not used to kissing someone with more hair on her face than I have."

Grayson chuckled at his words. "You know, Duncan, had someone chanced to come upon us just now, they might well have thought you quite a different kind of man than the one I know you to be."

Her observation startled him. Surely she couldn't mean what he thought she did. How would a woman as gently reared as Gray know of pederasty?

"And just where did you learn about some men's baser appetites?" he wanted to know. "Such things are hardly appropriate knowledge for someone like you."

"Why, I read about them in Christopher Marlowe's plays," she answered. "Do you know his work?"

Palmer was stunned by her matter-of-fact acceptance of things that would send most women into a swoon.

"I do know Marlowe's work. But I wonder, Gray, should you? Some of the things he wrote are scandalous. I sometimes think your uncle might as well have left you illiterate for all the indecent knowledge you seem to have come across. It's left you with some very strange ideas."

"Strange ideas?" she echoed.

"Well, for a woman, you've some very peculiar notions about ambition."

As he looked down into her luminous eyes, it struck him again that Gray was a woman of vivid contrasts: of innocence and worldly wisdom, of idealistic beliefs and the ability to counterfeit emotions. She was guileless, inquisitive, and shrewd, passionate, elusive, and reticent. She confused him, enticed him, enthralled him. Every encounter, every conversation with Grayson opened new worlds to him, engaged his intellect, stirred his senses, and trespassed into the uncharted lands of his own emotions. He was undeniably drawn to her, but the passions she could stir were new to him, unequivocally terrifying. They seemed too much like the passions that had governed his parents' lives, too much like the passions that had made his parents' marriage a living hell.

"All right, then, Duncan," Grayson was saying. "Just what are these peculiar notions I have about ambition?"

To avoid discussing her need to succeed as an actress and the uncomfortable trend of his own thoughts, Palmer lowered his mouth to hers. He wanted to return to the way things had been only moments before when there had been nothing between them but the delight of physical contact, a need that had been uncomplicated, pure. The kiss he pressed upon her mouth was deliberately demanding, purposefully seductive. He used it to close off the question of his own irresolute emotions, his regrets about her imminent marriage, his thoughts of his impending departure. He let her high, sweet gardenia scent enfold him, let her taste fill his mouth. Grayson stirred him in a way no other female ever had, and he wanted nothing more than to revel in the delight that she alone could give. He wanted for the few brief moments left to them in the deep, dark night to hold her, simply hold her for what might well be the very last time in his life.

As his mouth moved over hers, the magic between them came stronger than before, more intense, less controlled. It was a sorcery so deep, so fundamental that neither could hope to withdraw from the vital sphere of enchantment that surrounded them. It was more potent than a charm, longer-lasting than a spell. It came from the depths of what they were, of who they hoped one day to be. It touched the essence of themselves, the eternal truth in both of them.

Each gave wholly to the other, in a thrill of deep communion, with the rush of nascent ecstasy. The kisses became more than the brush of lips and tongues, the embraces more than the contact of bodies bound heart to heart. They became the surrogate for all that time and circumstances would not allow them to say. They became the only truly acceptable expression of the bond that had grown between them.

With a moan, Duncan pressed Grayson back against the garden gate, crushing her soft, lush curves between him and the scarred wooden panel. The contact was inflaming, unaccountably right, and as Duncan thrust his hips against the V of her legs, the gate swung open behind them.

As they stumbled into the yard, a glare invaded the dark, a blaze of lanterns chasing away the protection and anonymity of the night. Blinking, they raised their heads. Beyond the wall of light were two figures, unrecognizable in the brightness. For an instant Gray and Duncan stood frozen in their embrace, dazzled and disoriented.

Then a voice boomed from just beyond the arc of lantern light. "Grayson! Good Lord, Grayson! What in God's name is the meaning of this?"

Duncan felt Grayson stiffen as she recognized the fury in her uncle's tone, and she abruptly wrenched free of his encircling arms.

"Uncle Warren?" she gasped. "Uncle Warren, what are you doing in the garden at such an hour?"

The lanterns swung away, and Duncan could see Warren Worthington, dressed in his nightclothes, glaring at them.

From beside him one of the grooms spoke. "You see, your grace, I did hear voices from over this way."

Worthington ignored the comment, focusing a scowl on his ward. "I could ask you the same question, Grayson, though I believe I can predict your answer. Just what do you think you're doing, sneaking out of the house dressed like that? Coming home at such an hour? Letting someone handle you in such a—"

Worthington turned away with a snort of disgust. "Come into the house, Grayson, where we can discuss this with a modicum of privacy. And you, Antire, you come, too. It appears you're as deep in this as she is."

With his stomach sinking toward his boots, Duncan followed Gray and her guardian across the lawn. A walk to the gallows would have been more cheerful than this one was.

They entered the house through the portrait gallery at the back and crossed the entry hall to the library. As they made their way into the room, a diminutive woman of middling years rose from the settee by the hearth.

"Did you find her, Warren?" she asked. "Was she somewhere on the grounds, after all?"

Seeing Grayson and Duncan following in Worthington's wake, a new kind of distress registered on the woman's face, replacing an expression of acute concern.

"This is Captain Duncan Palmer, Julo, the Marquis of Antire," Worthington explained. "It seems he and Grayson have been out together, stirring up one kind of mischief or another."

Duncan nodded in response to Worthington's introduction, though his thoughts were on the woman at his side. A man's indiscretions were easily dismissed, but a woman's were a scourge on her character and reputation. It was Grayson who would bear the brunt of Worthington's fury, Gray who would have to endure any scandal that might ensue. He was sorry for that, but there seemed to be little he could do to shield her now.

"We've been so worried about you, Grayson," her aunt spoke up as Worthington retired to the table of decanters set against the wall. "When we found your bed was empty, we were utterly beside ourselves. With the West End Strangler still at large we were terrified that he'd attacked you in the coach. But when your maid told us you had come home safely, we didn't know what had happened to you. Didn't it occur to you that we'd look in on you when we got home and be frantic when we saw that you were gone? Don't you know how dangerous it is for a woman to be out alone?"

"I wouldn't have let anything happen to her," Duncan spoke up in Gray's defense.

"I'm sure you wouldn't, my lord. But we had no way of knowing that Gray was with you," Julo Worthington chided him. "And where on earth have you been, my dear? Why are you all dressed up like a man?"

For the first time since they had entered the house, Grayson raised her gaze from the floor, steeling herself to accept Julo's censure. When she looked across at the woman who had raised her, who had shown her the only love she had ever known, Gray saw worry and disappointment in Julo's pale gray eyes.

"I'll wager she's been where no woman should ever go," Worthington answered, returning to the group gathered before the fire. "Sit down and tell us, Grayson, just where you've been this evening. I want to know just how much of a scandal you have caused."

It seemed pointless to lie when by morning half of London was bound to have heard tales of this evening's peccadillo. Her chin came up and she met her guardian's eyes. "I convinced Duncan that for a lark he should take me to Evans's Song and Supper Room."

"To Evans's? To Evans's!" her uncle roared. "I suppose that explains your reasons for dressing so indecently."

Grayson met her uncle's withering stare. "I thought that if I dressed like a man no one would recognize me."

"And did you succeed in your deception, or will I be hearing rumors of this escapade tomorrow?"

The defiance abruptly went out of Grayson's face. "I'm afraid I was not nearly as clever as I supposed. Harry was at Evans's, and I'm sure he recognized me."

"Oh, Lord," Julo gasped in alarm.

"Damnation!" Worthington exclaimed.

"Why didn't you tell me?" Duncan demanded, turning to where Grayson sat on the settee beside her aunt. "When did Harry see you?"

"While you were settling our bill, I'm afraid. But it's no wonder he noticed me, after what happened."

"And just what did you do to make yourself so conspicuous, girl?" Worthington cut in. "Why did Harry notice you?"

Grayson drew a shaky breath. "I got into an altercation with one of the other patrons."

"God in heaven, Grayson! Who?"

"It was a drunkard, your grace," Duncan spoke up. "And she—"

Worthington turned on Duncan. "I was addressing my ward, Antire. Let her answer. I'll get to you in a minute.

"Now, who was the man you argued with?"

"I don't know. A man. A drunkard. And I didn't just argue with him. He hit me, and given half a chance, I would have hit him back."

Julo Worthington gasped again, going pale with shock and alarm.

Worthington turned to Palmer with fire in his eyes. "And where were you when all this happened? Why weren't you defending her?"

"It happened too fast for Duncan to do anything," Grayson hastened to explain. "The man stumbled into me, and I suppose I pushed him back. Then he took a swing—"

"Damnation!" Worthington exploded again and drank down a full two inches of his brandy. "You weren't hurt in the altercation, were you, girl?"

"No, sir."

"Thank heaven for that, at least," the duchess put in, reaching across to pat her niece's hand.

"And you're sure that Harry recognized you?"

Grayson nodded.

Her guardian's face went grim. "Then the marriage is off for sure. There's no question of Harry forgiving this."

Without letting more than a moment pass, Worthington turned to Duncan. "Now, Antire, I want an explanation of your part in this affair."

Palmer faced the older man squarely, the knowledge of his complicity in his eyes. "I have no explanation, your grace. I was wrong in taking Gray to Evans's. My behavior was inexcusable. All this is entirely my fault."

"Damn right, it's your fault. By dawn tomorrow her reputation will be in ruins. By ten, the most eligible bachelor in all England will surely have turned tail and run."

Worthington rose from the chair and strode distractedly around the room. It was clear he was distraught at the forthcoming dissolution of Grayson's betrothal, at the destruction of the plans he had made for her future.

"You know, of course, Grayson, that once news of your behavior gets out there will be no hope of making another suitable match."

Without waiting for her reply, Worthington made another circuit of the room, running his hands through his already tousled hair.

At last he came to stand toe to toe with Duncan. "Well, since you accept the full responsibility for what has happened, for taking Grayson to Evans's, for endangering her reputation, for the certain withdrawal of Stinton's suit, you can marry Grayson instead!"

Marry Grayson. The words boomed in Duncan's head. Cold sluiced through his veins.

"Marry her?" He stared at Worthington in disbelief.

"Yes, and by God, Antire, you'll do it soon. You'll do it before this gets around, before her reputation is in tatters. After what I saw in the garden, a speedy wedding seems doubly urgent."

Marriage. Duncan's mouth went dry.

Marriage. The sound of shouting rang in his head. He heard the curses his parents had hurled at each other, the sound of furniture being overturned, the clash of breaking glass.

Panic slithered through him, knotting his belly, making his heart thud hard against his ribs.

Marriage. Duncan knew what marriage was. It was love that had turned to hate. It was passion gone desperately wrong. It was pain and disillusionment and fear. It was hell on earth.

His head went light, and it hurt to breathe. He felt chilled to the marrow of his bones. He did not want to marry Grayson. He didn't want to force her into a life like the one his mother had—arguing, weeping, and ultimately submitting to a man she had surely come to loathe. He didn't want to turn into his father—badgering, bullying, beating a woman he had promised to love.

Yet superimposed on the images of the mayhem at Antire Manor and the travesty his parents' marriage had become were flickers of the moments he'd shared with Grayson in these last weeks: the communication that had flowed between them the night of Lady Monmouth's party, the compassion in her touch the afternoon he'd spoken of his parents' death, the delight they'd taken just tonight in sharing the entertainments at Evans's. They were wondrous moments, precious moments, moments Duncan didn't want besmirched by what would happen when they wed.

"Antire, will you marry her?" Worthington's question exploded in his ears, the concussions shaking him, the words echoing and echoing. Desperation thundered in his blood; fear for the future wrung his insides.

No. No. He could not marry Grayson.

"Duncan, are you all right?" Grayson's voice was frayed, breathy with anxiety and concern.

She cared about him, and Gray mattered to him, too. In an instant their feelings for each other came crystal clear. If Grayson mattered to him, if she meant as much to him as he was beginning to think, he couldn't condemn her to the life his mother had. He couldn't damn Gray to a future with a man like him. He couldn't marry her and watch the tender feelings that had grown between them turn to hatred.

"Antire, will you marry her?"

No. No.

"Antire?"

"Yes."

He should have realized before agreeing to take Grayson to Evans's what would happen if they were caught. Of course he would be expected to right the wrong he'd done her. Of course he would be expected to marry her. His own feelings did not even enter into the matter. The fact that he did not want Grayson as his wife had no bearing on his obligation to accept the responsibility for what he'd done. From the moment they'd left the town house, this moment had been inevitable.

He drew a shaky breath and looked up into Worthington's face. "I'll marry Lady Grayson at any time and place you say."

His capitulation seemed to fill the silent library like the last notes of a requiem.

Then Grayson was on her feet, her face set, angry color in her cheeks. "Now wait just a minute," she demanded. "Am I to have no say in this at all? Am I to be shunted from one suitor to another without an opportunity to express my preferences?"

Julo Worthington reached out to catch her niece's hand. "It's decided, Grayson. Let it be. Perhaps this is what's best for both of you."

There was understanding in her aunt's quiet words, an insight that Grayson did not want to acknowledge, either aloud or to herself.

"Let it be?" she repeated, shaking her head. "No, I can't let it be. I can't allow Duncan to be forced into marrying me when this scandal isn't his fault. I am the one who persuaded him to take me to Evans's. I am the one who pressed him when he refused. I am the one who argued and drew attention to myself. I am the one who was too arrogant to entertain the idea that no good could come from what I'd proposed."

She might have been arguing with three marble statues for all the response she got from any of them.

"This is my fault," she declared passionately. "Let me ride out the scandal. Send me off to the country estate for a month or two. Let me take a tour of the Continent or book passage to America."

She saw something kindle in Duncan's eyes, and she hurried on. "Don't make Duncan pay the price for something I instigated. Don't expect him to shield me with his name for something that's been my doing from the start."

Worthington was obviously reluctant to allude to what he'd seen in the garden while his wife was still in the room, but it was clear he meant to have his way.

"Then you feel nothing for this man, Grayson? Nothing a wife should feel?"

Fierce color flared in Grayson's cheeks as she thought of exactly what Duncan had come to mean to her. He touched her physically with the depth and passion of his kisses, emotionally with something that was deeper and more satisfying than any friendship had ever been, spiritually with an understanding that bound them together in ways she couldn't even begin to explain. Marriage to Duncan would be worlds apart from what marriage to Harry would have been. But was she willing or able to give what marriage to Duncan would demand of her? Could she put her commitment to him above her own ambitions? Did she even want to try?

Her gaze moved to where Duncan sat in the high-backed chair as she sought some clue to his feelings. There was no expression on his face; it was as blank as a new chalk slate.

Uncertainty bubbled through her; indecision gnawed at her insides. Duncan didn't want this, did he? She wasn't sure she wanted it herself. What chance of happiness would she and Duncan have if marriage was forced upon them both?

Gray didn't know what to do. Should she continue to argue with her uncle? Should she accept marriage to Duncan for the solution it was? Could she reject her uncle's ultimatum and strike out on her own?

All at once there were tears spilling down her face—tears for Duncan's sudden coldness, tears for her uncle's disapproval, tears for her aunt's disappointment. They were tears for herself as well, for her confusion and disillusionment, for her thwarted hopes and dreams. She was well aware of what marriage was for those in the privileged classes. It was not visions of romance, not love that came gliding on gossamer wings. Marriage among the privileged classes was an alliance, an agreement, a merger of families and fortunes. And for all that she had lost a duke, she had garnered a marquis.

There was a hand on Grayson's arm and her knees went suddenly weak. Gray sank down beside her aunt, curled like a child into her embrace, sobbing softly into the velvet collar of the older woman's dressing gown.

Above her head, Grayson's future was being decided. The men had taken charge.

"You'll come by tomorrow afternoon so we can discuss the wedding arrangements?" Warren Worthington asked, though the question he posed to Duncan was little less than a command.

"I will make myself available whenever you say," Palmer answered in a voice that was as soft and brittle as the rustle of ancient parchment.

"It should be a relatively small wedding," her guardian went on, "considering the circumstances. But it should be fashionable and well attended enough to stifle any gossip Harry starts."

"I'll agree to whatever you suggest, your grace."

"And it should be soon."

"Perhaps the end of next week?"

"If we can get a dispensation on posting the banns."

Duncan answered as if in perfect accord. "I'll be by tomorrow at two o'clock, your grace, if that's convenient."

Worthington gave a silent nod.

Without another word Palmer rose and left the room, closing the library door behind him. Grayson realized only after he had gone that Duncan had not even paused for the moment it would have taken to bid her a civil good-bye.

* * *

Neither hurricane, typhoon, nor tidal wave could have been more devastating to Captain Duncan Palmer's life than the last hour in the Duke of Fennel's library. As he rested his head against the squabs of the hired cab, Duncan fairly reeled with the abruptness of the change.

The duke had been furious about this evening's escapades, enraged with Grayson for inviting scandal and angry with Duncan for encouraging and aiding her. And rightly so, Palmer supposed. They had acted most irresponsibly. It was true that he had done what he could to dissuade Grayson from going to Evans's. He had even written her a note to break the engagement. But none of that had really mattered once Gray appeared at the town house in her disguise, once she announced she would go to Evans's on her own, once Duncan began to realize how much he wanted to spend the evening with her. In a way he was glad he had gone. Things had been bad enough with him there to protect her. He shuddered to think what might have happened if Grayson had been alone.

As the rented carriage trundled through the waning night, Palmer's thoughts turned to the wedding that was about to be foisted upon him. Her had always known he would have to marry one day. He needed an heir to inherit his title and lands here in England, an heir to oversee the vast riches he and his uncle were amassing through their various business ventures. But never in his wildest dreams had he envisioned marrying anyone like Grayson. He had intended to marry someone who would demand no more of his affections than he was willing to give, someone who would be happy running his household in his frequent absences, someone quiet and obedient. He had intended to marry someone safe.

Grayson had never been safe. From those first moments in the garden, she had challenged him, argued with him, teased him, provoked him. Conversing with her was a mixture of clever repartee, insightful observation, and intelligent discussion. Being with her was an adventure, because she upset his usual perceptions, made him see the world through her eyes. And touching her—oh, God—touching her was like making contact with a bolt of lightning. His skin tingled, his nerves went taut, his heart began to boom inside his chest. When he was with Grayson he was more alive than ever in his life, but he was also out of control.

Still, there was nothing he could do but marry Gray. After he had taken her to Evans's, after she had been recognized, after they had been discovered mauling each other in the garden, what choice did he really have? He had to move ahead from here, in spite of his reservations about committing himself to Gray, in spite of his misgivings about marriage, in spite of the detestable renewal of his ties to England.

When the cab pulled up in front of the town house, Duncan noticed that the lantern on the archway that guarded the front door was still burning brightly, giving evidence that the servants were still abed. After paying his fare and letting himself in, he climbed the stairs to his suite of rooms. Duncan was exhausted, aching, bone-weary. He wanted nothing so much as to sleep away what was left of this horrible night. Tomorrow would be soon enough to consider what marrying Grayson would truly mean. For now all he wanted was oblivion.

He pinched out the candle guttering on the nightstand and began to undress in the dark. He was down to his shirt, his trousers, and his socks when he heard a noise from the direction of the dressing room. Duncan whirled as Ryan Barnes appeared in the doorway, carrying a candle of his own.

"I told you there was no need to wait up," Palmer snapped. "I'm perfectly capable of getting myself to bed."

"I only meant to wait a little while, my lord, but I must have fallen asleep."

Barnes looked as rumpled and irritable as Duncan felt, and small wonder, since the cot in the adjoining dressing room was hardly big enough for a child.

Palmer turned away and continued tugging at his clothes, but when the valet moved to put them away, Duncan stayed him with a gesture. "That will wait for morning. Go get what little sleep you can."

Barnes nodded and turned toward the door, but before he reached it, Duncan stopped him.

"Since you're up, you might as well know that this evening's entertainments have brought me a wife."

"A wife, my lord?" Barnes echoed, turning to face his master. "A wife?"

Feeling as if the events of the evening might lose their sting if he could discuss them with someone else, Duncan continued. "Lady Grayson Ware. I introduced you to her earlier. She came here dressed as a young man, determined that I should take her to Evans's Song and Supper Room."

It seemed to take a moment for Palmer's words to sink in. "That was Lady Grayson Ware all done up in the finest gentleman's haberdashery?"

Duncan grinned in spite of himself at Ryan's choice of words. Gray had indeed looked as if she had been dressed by London's finest tailors: clothes by Poole, hat by Lock, boots by Lobb. Dressed as a man or as a woman, there was no denying Grayson's sense of style.

"Pardon me for asking, my lord, but did you?" Barnes wanted to know.

"Did I what?"

"Take her to Evans's?"

"Damn me, of course I did. That's what started all of this."

Barnes's eyebrows rose in perfect arcs above his black shoe-button eyes. "And what happened there that you had to marry her?"

"I haven't married her yet. The fact is, she's still betrothed to the Duke of Stinton. That small problem has to be resolved before we can take our vows."

Barnes nodded and waited for Duncan to continue.

"I did take her to Evans's, as she asked, and there we had the misfortune to stumble across her fiancé."

"Has he called you out?"

"No, but I suppose I should expect it. Dueling has been outlawed here in England, but that doesn't seem to stop the hotheads from blasting away at each other. Good God! This gets more complicated with every minute that passes. And Stinton is reputed to be a crack shot, if I'm not mistaken."

"But then, my lord, so are you," Barnes commented quietly. "He'd be wise to let this go."

"Indeed. I hope he will."

"But, my lord"—Ryan's mouth was pursed in confusion—"who is forcing you to marry Lady Grayson? Surely you didn't simply offer for her hand."

"We were discovered as we were returning to Worthington Hall. It is Lady Grayson's guardian, the Duke of Fennel, who is demanding I do the honorable thing."

"And will you?"

Duncan paused. "Of course I will. What choice do I have?"

"Then I suppose I should offer you my good wishes." Barnes sounded as reluctant as Palmer felt.

He snorted in disgust. "It will take more than good wishes to make this marriage succeed."

Barnes pulled thoughtfully on his beard, aligning the straggling tufts of his usually immaculate chin whiskers. It was clear that there was something on his mind, something he wanted to ask. Duncan had known Ryan far too long not to recognize the signs.

"Well, what is it?" Palmer asked in irritation. He was thoroughly worn out and wanted nothing more than to crawl into the bed that awaited him.

"I was wondering, my lord," Barnes began with obvious reticence, "what your lady thinks about—your past?"

It was the first time either of them had spoken about his parents' death in years. They had kept their silence as if by mutual vow. Though there had been times when Duncan had wished he could discuss the matter openly with his valet and oldest friend, he had no wish to do so now. He was too unsettled by the responsibilities being thrust upon him, by his conflicting emotions where Grayson was concerned, by the sense that there was something wrong in his life that he didn't understand. He did not want to discuss the death of his parents, but since Ryan had broached the subject at last, there seemed no way to avoid it.

"She thinks I should confront the matter," Palmer answered, recalling the conversation he and Grayson had had over tea the previous day. "She thinks I should return to Antire Manor and see if being there helps me remember what happened. It's her opinion that if I can find a way to make the memories return, I will be able to put the incident behind me."

For a full minute Barnes did not reply. "Is that wise?" he finally asked.

Duncan shrugged. "I don't know. Perhaps. Sometimes I think it would be a tremendous relief to be able to remember what happened, for better or worse."

Barnes went silent again.

"When will you marry Lady Grayson?"

"Some time next week, I suppose."

"And she'll go with us to America when the repairs on the *Citation* are completed?"

Barnes's question brought something into focus, something that had been rattling around in Duncan's head since earlier in the evening. During the discussion in the library, Grayson had mentioned that she could leave the country to escape the scandal, and he had wondered then if her suggestion had been more than mere coincidence. Grayson had been badgering him for weeks to grant her passage to New York. Wouldn't marrying him guarantee the thing she wanted most? Wouldn't he be forced to take her to America if they were husband and wife? The idea set up a glow behind his eyes.

"I suppose she will," Duncan answered distractedly. "But it's late, now. We can talk about this in the morning."

His words were clearly a dismissal, and Barnes made his way toward the door. Pausing with his hand on the knob, he said, "I wish you well in your marriage, my lord."

Duncan didn't acknowledge his words; he didn't even hear Barnes close the door. Lost in thought, Palmer donned his dressing gown and made his way to the table near the windows where a few dark bottles stood. As he poured himself a brandy, his suspicions began to gel.

Grayson had been desperate to escape her marriage to the Duke of Stinton, and by noon tomorrow Harry Torkington would be out of her life. She had all but begged for passage to New York, and where Duncan had refused to take her as a passenger, he would be forced to take her as his wife. Was it possible that Gray had planned all this to win her way?

In his head he reviewed the argument they'd had the previous day. When he had flatly refused to help her reach America, Grayson had suddenly changed her mind about what she wanted. She had demanded only the favor of a night at Evans's to take its place. It was a most peculiar change in priorities, and he'd been struck by that at the time.

Had there been more to the request than he had realized? Had it all been part of some desperate plan? It was a suspicion he didn't want to think about, but he couldn't put it out of his mind. Was it possible that Grayson had deliberately made herself conspicuous in Evans's hall? Had she known that Harry Torkington would be there, ensuring the scandal that would blacken her name? Could Gray have made certain that her absence from her bedroom would be readily discovered?

Then, with everything in place, had she deliberately seduced him by the garden gate, making sure that they were discovered in the most compromising of circumstances? Could all this have been premeditated? Was Gray as devious as that?

No, Duncan told himself, no. Yet his hands were unsteady as he raised the glass of brandy to his lips.

The suspicion spun through his mind, gaining momentum from snatches of remembered conversation, from coincidences that suddenly seemed so much more than that. Had Grayson played him for a fool? Had she deliberately betrayed his trust?

Yet she had argued with her uncle when he proposed the match, flatly refused to marry to save herself from scandal. If this was all part of some elaborate charade she had concocted to win her way, why would she have resisted Worthington's ultimatum?

How good an actress was she, really? Palmer suddenly wanted to know. Could Gray have counterfeited the feelings he had seen in her eyes? Had she deliberately stirred emotions in him that he had never wanted to feel? Had Grayson bartered her body and her reputation for some irrational, half-baked dream of one day being a famous actress? Had she used him coldly, callously, remorselessly, to get what she wanted most? Or was Grayson caught in this trap, too? Was she condemned to spend her life with him?

Confusion mounted to his head in a swirling red haze. His skin was afire with the rage and suspicions searing through his blood. Disillusionment gathered in his throat; fury stole his breath. Had Grayson manipulated him for her own ends? Had she deliberately betrayed him?

Duncan simply didn't know.

In blind frustration he hurled his drink across the room, drawing satisfaction from the unleashed anger, the clash of shattering glass. Where the tumbler had smashed against the paneling, liquid trickled slowly down the wall, dark as blood against the wood. He stared at the spreading stain, realized what he'd done, and suddenly began to tremble.

He had lost control. He had given way to violence, as his father might have done. The realization frightened him, appalled him. He was not the man his father was, he told himself, someone who would let his anger and confusion override his common sense. He wasn't a tyrant given to mercurial moods and rages. He didn't shout and curse and throw things. Duncan Palmer was a rational man. He never lost his temper, never let his passions get the best of him.

Except with Grayson. *Except with Gray.*

Duncan sank into a chair, stunned by the confirmation of something he'd only sensed before.

Grayson threatened everything he was, everything he'd tried so hard to be. She made him feel instead of think; she made him want instead of accept. She had the power to enrage him, confuse him, stir the tempest in his soul. She could rouse laughter, passion, and delight in him. But she could also turn him into a monster, the kind of monster his father had been.

Grayson Ware could tap his darker nature. She alone could ignite the anger and fear that could destroy his world. She was a blight on his life, his nemesis, his destruction. She was his salvation and his hope. She was everything he wanted, everything he could not have.

Duncan dropped his head into his hands, his fingers clenching and unclenching in the heavy strands of hair. What was happening to him? Why was he acting like this? The questions tortured him. What was it about this woman that could make him a stranger to himself?

He sucked in a labored breath, closed his eyes, and tried to think. But the tranquillity he usually enjoyed eluded him. The rationality he brought to any problem seemed useless to him now. He did not understand why everything about Grayson affected him so. He only knew that it did.

He was not sure that Gray had manipulated him into a marriage he did not want. But if she had, he could not comprehend why she would take such a terrible chance. She knew what he was; she knew what he'd done. She knew what demons haunted him, knew what his childhood had been like. Was passage to America worth the risk Gray was preparing to take? Was she as unwillingly caught in this snare as he?

As he sat alone in the quiet room, Duncan only knew that he must protect them both from the emotions she could stir. No good could come of the union Worthington had proposed. He had to find a way to warn Grayson away. He had to find a way to save himself. But how? he wondered. How?

It was dawn before he had reached any conclusions, and he greeted the graying of the light with chilling calm. If Grayson had used him, lied to him, traded shamelessly on his honor, he would learn of it. He was a man not easily duped, and if she had played this game by her own set of rules, he would have no compunction about turning them against her. But if she was innocent of complicity, if she was every bit as much a victim of circumstance as he, Duncan would know that, too. It was only a matter of hours before he would be with Gray again, and then he would know if she was cunning or guileless, a schemer or an innocent, a manipulator or a pawn. He had to prepare himself in either case, and now he knew what he had to do.

Thirteen

"YOU ARE A WHORE, MADAM. A WHORE, A HOYDEN, AND A cheating jade!"

Harry Torkington had arrived on the stroke of ten o'clock, and by then Lady Grayson Ware was fully prepared to receive him. Wearing her most demure dress of ivory satin and lace, with a high ruffled collar, pink satin sash, and narrow sleeves, Gray had been awaiting his arrival in the library, the scene of the previous night's debacle. Harry had stormed in without waiting to be announced and had not even bothered with a greeting. Instead he had launched directly into an assassination of her character that was, Grayson was forced to admit, not totally inaccurate.

"When I saw you last night at Evans's, I could hardly believe my eyes!" he raved at her. "To find my fiancée in a place where no decent woman would ever go, brawling like a common seaman with some drunkard twice her size, and in the company of a man like the Marquis of Antire! I was totally appalled! How could you behave in such a manner? How could you subject me to this kind of ridicule? I simply don't understand what you were thinking of!"

When he paused long enough to draw a breath, Grayson cut in, her voice calm and controlled. "Do you want your ring back, Harry? Are you breaking our engagement?"

It was obvious he had planned to say far more to her before he got around to making that demand. His jaw dropped as if she had stolen his thunder, with two simple, misplaced questions.

"Of course I want it back," he snapped when he had recovered himself. "I want the ring and the rubies as well. You hardly played the part of my fiancée well enough to earn them."

Gray's mouth narrowed and her jaw clenched tight. There was

no call for him to denigrate her ability as an actress. The role of fawning fiancée was one she'd never wanted anyway.

"Do you realize I can sue you for breach of promise?" he went on. "Your dowry wouldn't be nearly so large if I did. And without all that money as a lure, you'll never catch another husband."

"But, Harry," she pointed out imperiously, "it really isn't my promise that was breached."

Harry looked nonplussed. "Y-your uncle's, then," he stammered.

"You had only my uncle's promise. And I know you'd never take the Duke of Fennel on in court. Besides, if you did, all this would come out, and you'd look even more the fool than you do now."

"And you think last evening's escapades won't come out?" he countered. "A dozen men saw you at Evans's last night. Do you think they'll keep this quiet? Do you think they'll hold their tongues? This is the worst society scandal in two years' time. Your reputation's ruined, Grayson. Make no mistake about that. By the middle of next week, not a person of quality anywhere in England will so much as give you the time of day."

Grayson smiled sweetly in response to Harry's tirade, refusing to give him the chance to gloat. "But, Harry, what does all that matter when by the middle of next week I'll be married to Captain Palmer and on my way to America?"

After a few moments of resounding silence, Harry managed to recover himself; he was clearly disappointed by the news. "So Antire's willing to marry you? Well, he's welcome to your hand. Perhaps you'll do quite well together, a murderer and a harlot."

With difficulty, Grayson stifled the urge to slap his face. She did not care what Harry said about her, but she couldn't bear the thought of Duncan being hurt by a revival of the scandal that had surrounded his parents' death. Duncan had suffered enough over what had happened all those years ago, and she would not stand idly by and let those horrible rumors begin again.

Still, she knew better than to defend Palmer to Harry Torkington. It would only make things worse to let him know how much Duncan's well-being meant to her.

"But then," Harry went on, "I suppose I could poke a finger in your pie, couldn't I? I could call Antire out and kill him. That would leave you at a pretty pass, Grayson. Yes, wouldn't it indeed?"

Fear for Duncan prickled at the back of her neck, rose in her head, and spread down her arms. Gray went dizzy and cold at the thought of a duel. Still, she managed to keep her face impassive so Harry would not sense what she was feeling. Her fear would act as a goad, and she didn't want Duncan to face any further consequences of the illicit evening they'd spent together. He was being forced to marry her; surely that was bad enough.

"Shall I challenge him, Grayson? Do you like the idea of two men fighting over you?"

In response Grayson merely shrugged. "You men have your own ways of settling your differences," she managed to answer with far more sangfroid than she felt. "On the other hand, it would certainly feed my vanity, Harry, to think that you consider our broken engagement reason enough to issue a challenge. Go ahead. Do what you want. It's all the same to me."

She could see the thoughts churn behind Torkington's eyes as he weighed the things she'd said. Would she, would society at large, think him a fool if he called Duncan out over the question of Grayson's loyalty? Was she worth risking his life and freedom on the field of honor? How much satisfaction would he gain from shooting down a man like Duncan Palmer? He wasn't really a gentleman, after all, for all that he had been born a marquis.

She knew what decision Harry had reached a full minute before he put it into words.

"Oh, the hell with it," he said on a sigh. "You're hardly worth the risk of being shot at or arrested. And you and Antire deserve each other."

"Why, thank you, Harry," Gray answered sweetly. "It is so kind of you to give us your blessing."

His face clouded with confusion, and she instantly regretted her words. He had totally missed the sarcasm in her tone, and she realized how dangerous it was to toy with him.

"I want the ring," he finally said. "I want the rubies. And I want them now."

Relief washed through her with the knowledge that her unguarded words had not further incited Harry, that in spite of what she'd said, he would not pursue Duncan further. For the first time since she had known him, she blessed Harry's lack of subtlety and wit. Another man might have seen the ploy she was using to keep Duncan well and safe, but Harry never looked beneath the surface. Subtlety was totally lost on him.

"The ring and the rubies are right here on the table," she assured him, "safely returned to their boxes."

Harry had the poor grace to inspect the jewels. Satisfied that she was returning everything he had given her, he gathered up the boxes and moved in the direction of the door.

"May you sleep well in your marriage bed, Lady Grayson." He paused for a parting shot. "But remember, as you do, that you lie couched with a murderer."

She waited until she heard the slam of the front door, until there was the sound of Harry's carriage on the cobblestones in the courtyard, before she took a breath. She had weathered the confrontation with her former fiancé and managed to avert the disaster of a duel.

In spite of what Harry said, she was not afraid of Duncan. Regardless of what had happened in the past, Duncan would never hurt her. She knew what kind of man he truly was. She had staked the rest of her life on it.

There was too much on Duncan Palmer's mind that afternoon for him to give the magnificence of Worthington Hall more than passing notice. As his coach pulled up before the door, as the porter helped him alight, as the footman took his hat, gloves, and walking stick, Palmer's thoughts were occupied by the decisions he had made about his future during his long and sleepless night.

Frowning, he reflected on how Barnes and his cousin Quentin had greeted the news of his forthcoming wedding. His valet had said little more about his marriage this morning, but Quentin's reaction had quite made up for Ryan's silence.

"You're marrying Lady Grayson Ware?" Quentin had gasped as they sat over breakfast in the dining room. "But what of her engagement to the Duke of Stinton? Is he simply going to step aside? And what about her guardian? Surely Fennel won't approve."

"It was the Duke of Fennel who proposed the match," Duncan told his cousin as he pushed what was left of his eggs around on the plate.

"But why?" Quentin wanted to know.

Duncan was reluctant to reveal, for his cousin's benefit, just what it was that had led to the betrothal.

"Fennel realizes that Grayson and I want to be together,"

Duncan lied. "He's afraid that if I leave, if they go ahead with the plans for Grayson's wedding to Stinton, she will follow me to America. And wouldn't that cause a scandal!"

"She's strong-minded, to be sure. Lady Grayson has refused more proposals in the last three years than a bevy of women get in a lifetime."

Duncan made no reply, allowing his cousin to read whatever significance he chose into the sudden change in Grayson's allegiance.

"But when have you and Grayson been together? When have you had time to court her?" Quentin demanded.

"We've been together here and there," the younger Palmer answered noncommittally.

"I had no idea," Quentin dithered, "no idea you were so attracted to her, that you would want to marry her."

"Well, a man does need a wife to beget an heir, and Lady Grayson's certainly a bright and comely woman. A fellow could do far worse."

It was as if something had suddenly come together in Quentin's brain, making his eyes narrow and his face close in.

"An heir," the other man repeated. "An heir. Of course a man as wealthy as you are must think of that. Is Lady Grayson breeding?"

Duncan threw his napkin aside and glared down the table at his cousin. "Let me make this very clear," he answered in his coldest tone. "I've had no truck with Lady Grayson's virtue!"

It was the truth, but it had made Duncan furious to have to defend Grayson Ware's good name when he suspected her need for passage to New York was the reason she'd orchestrated the evening at Evans's in the first place.

Quentin had been more than conciliatory after that, but the damage was already done. Despite Duncan's protests, despite the eventual evidence to the contrary, Palmer knew that once word of Grayson's broken engagement and their imminent marriage got out, most of London would believe she was carrying his child. It was the way society gossip worked, and there was nothing either of them could do to stem the speculation.

Now as he waited in the drawing room at Worthington Hall, he realized that while he'd had "no truck with Lady Grayson's virtue," he fully intended to. His fantasies had been liberally laced with images of her since the morning he had met her in the garden, and one of the decisions he had made the night before was that he was through denying himself.

The thought was still fresh in his mind when Lady Grayson made an appearance a few minutes later, dressed in a gown of creamy ribboned satin. The furls of pale lace that rose against her throat were the perfect foil for the heavy waves of deep red hair that cascaded down her back, and against the folds of luminous fabric, her skin seemed to glow with the warmth of ancient ivory. In spite of himself, Duncan let his gaze glide over the perfection of her features, the flush of dusty pink along her high cheekbones, the moist curves of her lips, the sweep of nutmeg-brown lashes over downcast eyes. Standing in the doorway, she looked innocent and demure, but he had begun to suspect that beneath those maidenly trappings beat a heart far less pure and guileless than he had previously imagined.

Grayson crossed the room with a smile on her lips and gently caught up his hands.

"Oh, Duncan, I'm so glad we have these few minutes alone so I can apologize for what happened last night. I had no idea our little outing would have such dire repercussions. I wouldn't have asked that you take me to Evans's if I'd had any inkling of where it would lead."

Her apology caught Duncan by surprise. It wasn't what he had expected her to say. She actually looked sorry the evening had ended as it had.

"And if, in the light of day," she went on, "you want to rescind the proposal of marriage my uncle extorted from you, I will certainly understand."

He stared at her as if her words weren't making any sense. Was she really offering him an opportunity to recant, or was she continuing to manipulate him? Was Grayson the consummate actress playing a conciliatory role, or was she sincere in offering him his freedom? As usual, Duncan didn't know what to make of her, and his seething frustration grew. Could he walk away scot-free, or was there some other bargain she was ready to make?

Grayson must be having second thoughts about giving up the title of duchess and Harry's fortune in favor of a life on the stage, he told himself. She was probably wondering if she had done the right thing in opting for marriage to a mere marquis and passage to America.

"Has Harry reconsidered, then?" he asked. "Have you managed to mend your fences?"

A frown drew Grayson's high-arched brows together, and there seemed to be distress in the depths of her eyes. "No, Harry hasn't reconsidered. He was here at exactly ten o'clock to demand the return of his ring."

"And did you give it to him?"

She drew a breath. "Of course I did."

"Then you've broken your engagement?"

"Harry broke it," she answered shortly.

"Was he angry?"

"Wouldn't you be angry if it were you?"

Briefly Duncan wondered about the scene Harry must have made. What had he done? What had he said? Grayson seemed reluctant to talk about what had happened, and Palmer was angry with himself for wishing he could have spared Grayson Stinton's unpleasantness.

He frowned and pressed ahead, intent on the plans he'd made the night before. "There's a vacancy on your finger, then?"

"Yes." The word came on a shaky breath. There was uncertainty in her tone.

"So you do have a place to put the ring I bought you just this morning?" As he spoke, he withdrew a jeweler's box from the pocket of his frock coat.

Her eyes widened in astonishment. "After all that happened last night, it never occurred to me that you might actually give me a betrothal ring."

Duncan swept off the lid of the box, and held the contents out for her inspection. On a bed of night-dark satin was an enormous emerald of brilliant green, a huge square-cut stone, flanked by a brace of shimmering diamond baguettes.

Gray stared at it, unmoving.

"Don't you like it, Grayson? I bought an emerald because I thought it matched your eyes."

"Well, I— Yes, it's— This is so totally unexpected."

He removed the ring from the jeweler's box and slipped it on her finger. On hands any smaller than hers, the gems would have been vulgar, overpowering.

"Didn't you think I could afford the kind of jewels Harry had given you? Didn't you think I would want people to know that we're betrothed? I admit that my fortune may pale in comparison to his, but I'm able to buy you a bauble or two. I'm not without resources."

"The ring is lovely, Duncan. Thank you," she managed to reply. "But the size of the jewels you give me or of the fortune you've amassed doesn't really matter to me."

"Doesn't it, Grayson?" he asked, vaguely unsettled by her pretty speech. "Well, perhaps it doesn't matter when there are other things to recommend me."

She looked up from her appraisal of the ring as if trying to discern the reason for his skeptical tone.

He smiled at her. He wet his lips. He knew he mustn't let a few sweet words sway him from the plans he'd made.

"Then, if you like the ring I've given you, are you willing to thank me with a betrothal kiss? It seems we neglected that formality in the confusion here last night."

Gulled by the gift and his teasing words, Gray stepped within the reach of his arms. For an instant she seemed to him like a gillyflower turned toward the sun, all pink and white and delicate. He could see the eagerness and expectancy in her face, the trust and anticipation in her eyes. Something deep inside him curled and turned with the knowledge of what he was going to do to her.

Yet it was necessary to let Grayson know what it would mean to be at the beck and call of his baser urges, to be his wife and bear his name. It was something she would have to accept if she had indeed bartered her body and her pledge for passage to America. Gray had to learn what passion was before she committed herself to a marriage that would surely damn them both.

Resolve blunted the corners of his mouth as he reached for her. His fingers tightened on her shoulders, over the satin and frills of lace, his grip crushing and deliberately harsh. He saw a flicker of surprise and confusion in her eyes as his lips poised over hers, but it did not prevent the kiss he pressed upon her from being all that he'd intended, demanding and blatantly sexual.

A mew of protest rose in her throat as he forced his tongue between the sweet petals of her lips, pushed past the barrier of her teeth, scoured the interior of her mouth. Beneath the onslaught, her softly nubbled tongue retreated, yet Duncan pressed on, letting the taste of her, the scent of her, incite him further.

In spite of the ineffectual pressure of her hands against his ribs, he drew her closer, binding her to him with angry determination. He sensed her resistance and reveled in it, sensed a confusion inside her that mirrored his own. This was what he wanted, he told himself: to frighten her, to warn her away. There would be no peace for either of them if they were forced to wed. Life would be a battle without any hope of surrender, a war without any hope of victory. Duncan knew what marriage was, and he couldn't let a few hours of innocent pleasure compromise whatever happiness either of them might one day achieve.

He had planned his strategy for this afternoon's meeting flawlessly—how he would approach her, how he would calm her fears, how he would attack swiftly and mercilessly when she was least expecting it. Once he let her feel the power of the forces he could bring to bear against her, he would retreat. This was only a quick, fierce skirmish to remind her of his strength, a sharp, bitter taste of the dominion he would have over her if she became his wife.

He felt her struggles lessen and knew it was time to withdraw, but in spite of his most stringent resolves, his blood was beginning to seethe. Wanting rose in him like mercury in a thermometer pushing toward the boiling point. Her nearness, the taste and feel and smell of her, were undermining his plans. The campaign he had laid out so carefully was going awry. Self-preservation made him pull away, but he had committed too much of himself to subduing Gray to regain his equilibrium.

He wanted her, he realized as disillusionment lanced through him, wanted her more than he'd ever wanted anything in his life. Her beauty, her nearness, her uniqueness, sundered his control. The emotional distance he'd tried to maintain had suddenly disappeared. He fought a short fierce battle with his own desires and lost, struggled against his compulsive yearning for the woman in his arms and met with resounding defeat. His head went light, and he could not think. Anger and passion mingled in his veins. Grayson, and only Gray, touched something deep inside him, appeased some turbulent nameless need, and he could not force himself to turn away.

She was soft as eiderdown, and he sank into her. She smelled like a bouquet of flowers, and he breathed deep. Her kiss was like drowning in honey, and he craved her sweetness like a drug. He seemed to be melting inside, his fury and resolve dissolving and seeping away.

Grayson was instantly aware of the change in him. A moment ago there had been a stranger in Duncan's place, a man without Duncan's warmth, a man without Duncan's tenderness. It wasn't the man who had offered her comfort and reassurance the night before, wasn't the man who had agreed to marry her for honor's sake. The stranger had hurt her, bullied her, frightened her. Then *her* Duncan had returned, his hands splayed against her back, his mouth drinking deep of hers.

In that moment, the irresistible current had begun to flow between them, loosing the strange, inexplicable alchemy that made everything between them so wondrously right. Warmth cascaded through her, filling her chest, curling deep into her belly, winding down her arms and legs. It invaded every cell, making her skin tingle and her heart pound.

She stretched deeper into his embrace, giving herself to Duncan in every way she knew: acknowledging the physical desire he could stir in her, admitting the emotional needs Duncan seemed able to both arouse and satisfy. There was such potential in what they had already shared, so many possibilities for a future filled with happiness and real communion. In the past the possibility of marriage had filled Grayson with lurking dread, but with Duncan she was not afraid. She was not afraid of who she was or who she might become. She was not afraid of what Duncan might ask of her, nor did she doubt her ability to give it. As she offered herself to the promise of his lovemaking, gave herself without reserve, she believed with all her heart that what was happening between them was infinitely right, the prelude to something glorious.

Duncan was drawn deeper, hopelessly beguiled by Grayson's growing ardor. Her tongue circled the inner surface of his lips, launching sizzles of excitement through his blood. It sought the depths of his mouth, sending swirls of unleashed desire skimming through his body. His senses wallowed in the wonder of her: in the provocative gardenia scent that clung to her hair and skin, in the delicious feminine warmth of her, in the raw-honey taste of her gently parted lips. His breath throbbed in his throat, rasped in his ears, shuddered in his chest. His hand closed around her breast, seeking the nub of her nipple beneath the layers of satin and lace.

As Gray moaned into his mouth, he swept her in the direction of the velvet settee and pressed her down beneath him. As his body hovered over hers, his hand probed up beneath her clothes, along the silk-stockinged leg that was both filmy and firm against his palm. He passed the frilled garter with its bows and clusters of lace, moved across the velvet softness of the skin at the inside of her thigh. The texture was a revelation, a promise of things to come. Duncan closed his eyes, preparing for fierce and imminent ecstasy.

Aware that they might be disturbed at any time, Grayson fought the potent spell of Duncan's seduction. Then, just when it seemed that she might break free, Duncan's hand made its way through the opening of her underdrawers, reached the apex of her legs, the delicious most feminine part of her. He touched her and stroked her at the very place where her body was aching and vulnerable. Yet instead of his touch easing the pain, it was turning it to a throbbing that made her tremble.

Sensation came like an undertow to drag her down; weakness ran through her. A whimper rose in her throat, and her eyes fell closed as his fingers discovered some exquisitely sensitive place that sent lightning spiraling down her limbs. She drew a long, shuddering, tortured breath, succumbing to the touch that was sending glowing streamers of sensation pulsing through her blood.

Duncan was as oblivious to the world as she, unaware of anything but the woman who writhed in his arms, unaware of anything but his desperate need for union with her.

A dozen yards away there was the creak of the latch on the drawing room door. It had opened no more than a crack when there was the sound of voices just outside.

"Your grace."

The words penetrated Duncan's mind like a lance.

"Your grace."

Oh, God!

"Your grace, if I might have a word with you?"

Duncan felt as if he'd slammed into a wall. There were men in the hallway just outside.

"What is it, William?"

Duncan was only beginning to realize where he was, what they were doing.

Beneath him, Grayson drew a desperate breath.

His hand was up Gray's skirt and her uncle was in the doorway.

"Can't this wait?"

Grayson arched against him.

It didn't seem likely that it would.

"My ward and her new fiancé are awaiting me in the drawing room."

Not nearly as eagerly as his grace might believe.

Grayson gasped again, and her head fell back. She twisted and rose against him. Duncan felt her most intimate flesh constrict and knew exactly what she was experiencing.

"This will only take a moment, your grace."

It had better take longer than that.

Duncan pulled Grayson hard against his body, crushing her face into the curve of his shoulder. She twisted and shuddered against him, riding the crest of a welling sensation he desperately wanted to share. The tremors that shook her shook him, too. The wildness that was running through her blood found an answering wildness in him. It pulled at him, buffeted him, but Duncan knew he dared not succumb when discovery was mere footsteps away.

"Your grace, I need to know what explanation you want me to give the Austrian ambassador for not attending the meeting on Tuesday afternoon."

An explanation? One look at either of them and Worthington wouldn't need an explanation of what was happening here.

Beneath him, Grayson looked as fragile and limp as a fine bisque doll. Her eyes were closed, and she was trembling. Though Duncan could tell by the cadence of her breathing that her crisis had past, he knew how very shaken and vulnerable she must be. Gently he withdrew his hand and smoothed down her tumbled skirts. He stroked her cheek, brushed aside a tendril of her gloriously bright hair.

Grayson looked up at him. Her eyes were huge, dark, and dazed. Her face was luminous, and he wanted to kiss her long and hard, as both a promise and a reward.

Instead Duncan signaled her for silence with a finger across his lips. The scent of her flesh clinging to his made weakness slide down his legs.

"For God's sake, William. Tell him I have a previous engagement." The duke sounded more than a little frustrated.

Duncan was feeling more than a little frustrated himself.

"Tell him I have a meeting with the prime minister, if you feel I must explain."

An explanation. An explanation. Duncan tried to dredge up one of his own. Perhaps he could tell Worthington that Gray had been feeling faint, that he had merely helped her to lie down.

It was a fatuous lie, and Duncan knew it. So, undoubtedly, would the duke. Moving silently, Palmer shifted on the settee until he and Grayson were seated side by side. He curled his arm around Gray's shoulders and drew her into his arms.

"Very well, your grace. I'll write the letter immediately."

"Then there's nothing more?"

No, there was no time for more just now. The questions Palmer could see forming on Grayson's lips would simply have to wait for answers.

"Not that I can think of."

"Well, thank goodness for that."

Thank goodness indeed.

Worthington pushed the door to the drawing room wide. On the settee were Antire and his ward, Palmer's arm around Gray's shoulders, her face buried deep in his cravat. There was tenderness in the scene, but also a blatant familiarity that the duke found most offensive.

"It's a good thing you'll soon be married off, Grayson girl, or you'd surely disgrace us all."

What she'd done hadn't been the least bit disgraceful, Duncan thought defensively. Gray had done nothing but enjoy herself, and he could hardly wait to do the same.

At her uncle's observation, a brilliant cherry-red flush colored Grayson's face. If she'd pinched Queen Victoria's jewels, she couldn't have looked any guiltier.

Duncan pulled her more protectively against his side, and she came willingly, curling against him with a soft, melting intimacy he hoped the duke would neither recognize nor understand.

Palmer took Gray's hand and tried to smile. "It sounds as if you've found someone to waive the banns so that Gray and I can be married as soon as possible."

The duke took his usual seat in the high-backed chair beside the marble fireplace. "As a matter of fact I have. And I've sent a letter to the *Times* to announce that my ward and the Duke of Stinton have called off their betrothal. I thought that should be taken care of as soon as possible."

Duncan nodded, trying to force his brain and mouth to work simultaneously. "A good thought," he agreed. "A good thought."

"And we'll place the engagement announcement, at the end of this week."

"Ah," Duncan offered. "Ah."

He nodded his head. He took a breath. He didn't dare look at Grayson.

"I thought we'd wait for my wife to join us before we discussed the rest of the plans for the wedding," the duke went on, "though I must say I'm pleased that the pastor of St. George's in Hanover Street has agreed to waive the banns."

"Is that where the wedding will take place?"

"Hasn't Grayson told you?"

He and Grayson hadn't had too much need for words in the last few minutes.

"Ah, no. I suppose it is the ring I brought that made her forget to mention it. Show your guardian the betrothal ring, darling," Duncan prodded her.

Obediently Grayson extended her left hand across the low table that separated the settee from her uncle's chair.

As she did, Gray tried to shake off the inexplicable lethargy that had suddenly enveloped her. She felt tingly, content, and warm, shivery, exhausted, and malleable. She wanted to curl up in Duncan's arms and send the rest of the world away. She was in desperate need of a nap.

Gray didn't know what had happened, didn't have any idea what Duncan had done to her. She only knew that she had reveled in the stroke of his fingers against her most private place, had gloried in the fierce sensation that had rushed shimmering through her veins. She had gone viscous, liquid, and hot, melting gloriously under the press of Duncan's hand. He had brought her from helpless need to exquisite relief, from trembling desperation to shattering delight. The feeling lingered still, in the languor that sapped her strength and will, in the unaccustomed sensitivity of her skin, in the faint breathlessness that assailed her. She felt quivery, soft, and satisfied, deliciously tired but wondrously alive.

Across the table Grayson became slowly aware of the expression on her uncle's face. She could see how his eyebrows were drawing together over the bridge of his nose, see how disapproval was tightening the lines around his mouth as he struggled to find something appropriate to say about the ring Duncan had given her.

"Quite an impressive piece of jewelry," Worthington finally murmured. "On a smaller woman's hand that ring would be downright ostentatious."

Gray tried to rouse herself to respond, to defend Duncan's choice of a betrothal gift. But thinking or, more precisely, making sense of what she was going to say was proving very difficult.

"I want people to know I can afford to keep Grayson in her usual style," the younger man answered, with more than a hint of belligerence in his tone. "I want people to know Grayson is losing nothing by marrying me instead of Stinton."

Gray wasn't sure of Duncan's intent in giving her such a ring, but she wasn't prepared to let her guardian slight Duncan in any way.

"Oh, it is exquisite, though, isn't it?" she murmured dreamily, turning the ring to catch the light.

"Oh, yes, the ring is exquisite indeed," her uncle agreed, staring at her as if she'd lost her mind.

Gray made herself reply, forcing enthusiasm into her voice. "Duncan says the emerald matches my eyes. I can't say I've ever seen a ring I like any better than this one."

Duncan was surprised and unexpectedly pleased by her words. He hadn't meant for her to like the ring, hadn't meant for her to respond to his selection in quite this way. But before he had time to question the reasons for Gray's reaction or the depth of her sincerity, Julo Worthington was crossing the room from the doorway.

"Oh, do let me see," she begged, catching Grayson's fingers with the tips of her own. "Why, the ring is lovely, simply lovely. I can't say I've ever seen a more thoughtful or romantic gift."

The Duchess of Fennel fairly beamed at Duncan where he sat with Grayson all but huddled at his side. The trust and happiness he saw in the older woman's face made him acutely uncomfortable. This wasn't the way it was supposed to be. They weren't supposed to like the ring. They weren't supposed to be pleased that he was taking Grayson as his bride. What the devil was wrong with everyone?

And this absurd mixture of foolish pride and dawning chagrin wasn't what he was supposed to be feeling, either. He tried to rouse the anger he had felt the night before, recapture his fury at being manipulated. He tried to remember why it was that he wanted to be free of Gray, what unwelcome things it was that she could make him feel. But with Grayson pressed close to his heart, with wedding plans on everyone's lips, those feelings somehow eluded him. And suddenly Duncan wondered if, when the time came for him to leave, to sail away to America, he would be able to carry out the plans he'd made. Was he going to be able to go away, to leave Grayson disillusioned and humiliated, standing alone at St. George's altar?

Fourteen

"DAMN IT, LEAPHORN! OPEN UP! I KNOW YOU'RE IN THERE!" As Quentin pounded on the door to the smuggler's rented room, other doors along the inn's second-floor balcony opened, and some of the most unsavory people Quentin had ever seen peered out at him.

"Shut up, will you?" a straggly-haired woman demanded. "There's some folks here who needs their sleep."

"What's the ruckus?" a man with bleary, bloodshot eyes wanted to know.

"Shut up or I'll shut you up!" another voice threatened from far across the court.

Though the doors banged shut around him one by one, Quentin did not let up his frenzied knocking. He was desperate to see Leaphorn and didn't know where else to find him.

Finally the rough wooden panel opened, and the smuggler glared out at him.

"What are you doing 'ere? I told you I'd let you know when there was something else I wanted you to do."

"Something's happened," Quentin dithered as he pushed into the room. "Something that might change our plans."

It was not until he was inside that Quentin saw two men seated at the table in the corner. Their backs were turned to him as if they did not want him to learn their identities.

"Now you see, you stupid fop, why I didn't answer. I've guests, and they won't take kindly to your interruption."

Palmer hesitated just inside the door, uncertain as to what he should do. He didn't want to know any more about Leaphorn's mysterious dealings than he already did. It might well be worth his life to remain uninvolved and ignorant.

Leaphorn must have sensed Quentin's confusion, for he took him by the elbow and steered him out the door. "You wait at the foot of the front steps until I've concluded my business 'ere. I'll come and get you when I'm free."

"A man dressed as I am isn't safe in this part of town," Palmer protested. "I'll be fair game for every footpad between here and the river."

"You'll be fair game for a damn-sight more than that if you insist on staying 'ere," Leaphorn threatened through narrowed lips. "Get on with you. This won't take but a few minutes more. You'll be safe enough at the foot of the stairs until I'm finished."

Reluctantly Quentin descended the well-worn steps, then hovered in the shadows of the lower landing. It was anyone's guess if he would be better off here or standing out in the sun where anyone might see him. With his polished boots and walking stick, his immaculately tailored clothes and high silk hat, he was bound to draw attention in a neighborhood like this. The streets were lined with hovels for blocks around.

He lit a cigar to pass the time, wondering after he had, if the scent of expensive tobacco might be as much of an invitation to mischief as his apparel was. As he waited, he looked around, appalled by the filth, the squalor. The place where Leaphorn kept a room had been a coaching inn in days gone by. The establishment had once had stables below and rooms above, accessible from a series of balconies around a central court. Now there were people living where the stables had been, families getting their water from what had been the horse trough pump. Places like this were where the dregs of humanity lived, Quentin thought with a shudder, day laborers so far gone in drink that they no longer labored, harlots who had become crones before their time, men like Leaphorn who had truck with the most unsavory elements in London society.

Quentin wondered why he was here, where he fit into the continuum of rich and poor, honorable and dishonorable. But he knew. Quentin Palmer knew, and he was terrified that someone who mattered might find out. That was why he needed the money. For a time he'd made enough from smuggling to see to his needs, but now he wanted the money from Duncan's estate to buy back his respectability. He needed the insulation from what he had become, the distance from crime and corruption that only fabulous riches could bring. And he meant to have it.

There was the thud of distant footsteps on the balcony above, but Quentin didn't turn to look. Knowing too much was often more of a curse than ignorance. He'd had eight long years to learn that lesson: Never ask why, never ask how. In dealing with men like Leaphorn, he was safer knowing nothing.

Then there were footfalls at his back, and he glanced over his shoulder to see Leaphorn descending the stairs.

"Well, what is it? What the 'ell brought you 'ere in such an 'uff."

Quentin waited until they had returned to Leaphorn's shabby room before answering.

"He's getting married!" Quentin exploded the moment the door was closed behind them.

"Who?"

"My cousin Duncan's getting married!"

The taller man hesitated for an instant. "An' am I being invited to the wedding?"

Leaphorn's question made Quentin furious. "He's getting married. Duncan's getting married. Don't you understand? There could be an heir to his fortune at any time!"

" 'As 'is lovey a bun in the oven, then?"

Quentin shook his head. "He says not."

Leaphorn's eyebrows rose. "An' you asked 'im? Then you're a far braver fellow than I took you for. Your cousin's got more than one surprise up 'is sleeve, now, doesn't 'e? It does no good underestimating 'im."

"That's what I'm afraid of."

"An' when's the wedding to be?"

"In two weeks' time, I'm told."

After a moment Leaphorn shook his head. "Well, then, it won't make no difference to what we're planning. Things are well under way. You'll get 'is money, never fear."

"But aren't we going to do something? Make things happen faster somehow?"

"It's in 'and. It's all in 'and," the taller man muttered by way of reassurance.

"Are you sure?"

Leaphorn's already narrow face narrowed more, his hooked nose growing another inch, his lips closing in upon themselves. "You listen 'ere, Master Quentin. This is my show, and we run it 'ow I say. Me plans 'ave worked well enough for you these eight years past, but if you've a problem with that, you let me know."

The menace in the man's tone was as thick as a November fog.

Quentin shook his head, and he involuntarily retreated half a step. "No, I've no problem, no problem at all."

"Well enough. Be on your way. Do what I tell you an' there's every likelihood that your cousin's lovely bride may well be standing alone at the altar."

As he headed toward the center of Westminster Bridge, toward the spot where he was to meet Hannibal Frasier, Duncan Palmer's head fairly spun with the complications that had befallen him since his return to England. Grayson Ware and his forthcoming wedding were foremost in his thoughts. After two days filled with discussions of wedding invitations, decorations for the church, the reception menu, and the cake, Duncan had finally managed to extricate himself from the turmoil at Worthington Hall. He didn't know how Grayson stood it. But then, perhaps women were better able to deal with minutiae, or perhaps Gray was throwing herself into the preparations because she was getting precisely what she wanted.

Warren Worthington had made very sure there had been no chance for Duncan to be alone with Grayson since the afternoon he had given her the ring. He'd had no chance to accuse her of trapping him into marriage or to gauge her response. But then, he hadn't had another chance to maul her, either.

He frowned abstractedly as he walked. He did not want to think about how responsive Grayson had been that day in the drawing room, nor did he need more proof of how deeply she stirred him. She touched him in ways he did not want to be touched, understood him in ways he did not want her to understand. She seemed to see things in him no other woman had ever seen, accept the parts of him and his past that were totally unacceptable. Did that explain why his need for her seemed to grow with every passing day, why the decision he had made to leave her waiting at the altar seemed less and less appealing?

Sighing, Duncan hooked his elbows over the parapet at the edge of the bridge and stared out across the Thames. As he did, Palmer took note of the traffic on the river below, the wherries scuttling across the water like bugs on a pond, the coal barges lumbering downstream, the halfpenny steamers leaving white wakes across the current.

Surely he'd had enough on his mind, with the repairs to his ship being slowly completed down in Portsmouth, with the memory of his parents' death to haunt him, with his need to unravel Samuel Walford's crooked business dealings, without Grayson and plans for a wedding making everything more difficult. There was also a sense that something was amiss in his life, something with dark implications.

Damnation! That was one more thing preying on his mind, one more thing—

"Your lordship?"

The voice at his shoulder startled Duncan, and he whirled to where the grizzled Scotsman stood beside him dressed in a plain dark coat and trousers, a soft-collared shirt and battered hat. There was no telling how long Frasier had been standing there without Duncan even noticing.

"Why are you scowling so darkly, your lordship, on such a lovely day?"

Duncan ignored the question. "Mr. Frasier, have you news?"

"Aye," Frasier muttered, "but it's not wise to discuss it here on the bridge. The arches in the turrets along the walk catch sound and throw it back, like the whispering gallery in St. Paul's."

Duncan raised his brows in skepticism, but followed the older man as he moved toward the Westminster bank. As they strode along, Duncan remembered that once, when he was a boy, his parents had brought him to Westminster Bridge to see the yearly race between sculls of watermen competing for the coveted coat and badge. He and his parents had cheered themselves hoarse as the teams of oarsmen had rowed their way upstream. They had gone to a fete on a river barge after the race and watched the celebratory fireworks blossom in the darkening sky. It was a memory that made Duncan smile.

When he and Frasier reached the bank, they moved north and east in the direction of Scotland Yard. There were wooden benches at the top of the stairs where the watermen waited for their fares, and they settled themselves comfortably in the sun.

Duncan waited with markedly poor grace while the older man packed and lit his pipe, while he took a crumpled page of illegible notations from the pocket of his jacket.

"Your Mr. Walford is quite a fellow," Frasier began at last. "He was the fourth son of a fine old family, took schooling at Eton, and had an appointment to Oxford before he left for the war. He served with Wellington on the Peninsula, just as your uncle did."

"I know all that," Palmer put in impatiently.

"Well, yes. But you see certain things went on while Walford and your uncle were with Wellington that have ties to their lives today."

Palmer's eyes brightened.

"It seems your uncle and his partner were involved in several of Wellington's more successful campaigns. Both were decorated for their bravery."

"Uncle Farleigh never mentioned that. He never talks about the war, though when I was younger I used to ask him."

Frasier nodded once as if the comment confirmed information he already had. "There are things that occurred during their time with Wellington that neither one of them would be willing to discuss."

"What do you mean?"

"I mean that they were involved in things that neither could take pride in."

A lump seemed to lodge in Duncan's chest as he waited for Frasier to go on.

"It is rumored that during the Battle of La Albuera," the Scotsman continued, "Samuel Walford and your uncle came upon a church that had been heavily damaged in the shelling. It is said that they killed a priest and seized certain priceless religious objects as the spoils of war."

"Religious objects? What religious objects?"

"A jewel-encrusted cross and chalice were taken from the church. Some say it was the sale of those artifacts that provided the money for your uncle and Walford to start the shipping concern so soon after the war."

Duncan's mouth thinned and his eyes went hard. "What you're saying is that my uncle killed a priest and stole from a church to finance his business ventures?"

Frasier inclined his head.

"No! That's preposterous! Both my uncle and Samuel Walford are gentlemen. They wouldn't steal from a church, not even a Papist church! And they'd certainly never kill a priest. They wouldn't do something so dishonorable! Who told you that?"

"I never reveal my sources," the older man answered calmly in spite of Duncan's obvious agitation.

"My uncle wouldn't do that," he insisted.

Frasier shrugged. "Well, your lordship, you know your uncle far better than I do."

In spite of his conciliatory tone, it was clear the man stood by what he had discovered. It did nothing to assuage Duncan's anger.

"No, I don't believe it. My uncle wouldn't kill and steal to further his own ends."

The Scotsman shrugged again and began to fold away the page of notes. "If you doubt the truth of that intelligence, your lordship, then you have no cause to believe the other things I've discovered, either." Frasier's tone was calm, his refusal to continue absolute.

Caught between the shocking revelation and the need to hear what else Frasier had discovered, Duncan felt his frustration grow. His uncle was the most honorable of men. He never cheated in his business dealings, never lied. Yet Farleigh had been willing to blindly accept the business reverses the English branch of the company was experiencing. When Duncan had gone to his uncle with his suspicions about Walford's stewardship, Farleigh Wicker had refused to consider that his partner was doing anything wrong. He had ordered Duncan out of his office. Had his refusal to question Walford's honesty been based on Farleigh's belief that his old friend was above reproach, or on something that had happened between them decades before? If the stories about the theft of the cross and chalice were true, there was a twisted kind of logic behind his uncle's actions.

Unbidden, something Grayson's guardian had said the day Palmer went to Worthington Hall for tea began to nibble at the edge of his memory. "They were quite a persuasive pair," the Duke of Fennel had ventured, referring to Walford and Wicker's attempts to finance their shipping concern. "And they had amassed a fair amount of capital on their own." Even more damning to Palmer's conviction of Farleigh Wicker's innocence was the expression Duncan had seen on Fennel's face. He had looked away as he spoke, as if his comment was some kind of subtle condemnation.

"I would be willing to believe that Walford stole the objects," Duncan hedged.

"Would you, now?"

"And I'd like to know what else you've learned."

There was a gleam in Frasier's eyes, a lift at one corner of his lips. "You refuse to believe me in this, your lordship, but you are willing to accept whatever else I tell you. Is that it?"

Damn the man! Duncan thought. Frasier's arrogance was unspeakable.

"It's possible there is some truth in the claim," Duncan conceded. "Besides, I've paid you handsomely to gather this information. Surely I'm entitled to hear everything you've learned."

Frasier puffed on his pipe, blew two perfect smoke rings that were quickly dissipated by the breeze from the water, and opened the page of notes. As he did, Duncan tried to steel himself for whatever other disillusioning facts the older man might have discovered.

"It seems that during the war," Frasier began again, "Walford had a Spanish mistress. She was a woman of good family who had been sold or abducted into slavery in a brothel. While he was on the Peninsula, Walford set her up in her own pasada and acted as her protector. Six months after La Albuera, she gave birth to Walford's child. Of course by then Walford had returned to England, and his mistress had begun a brothel of her own, presumably with money Samuel gave her.

"They had no contact for many years, not until 1837 when both Walford's former mistress and his daughter turned up here in England. The woman's health had been ruined by the life she'd led, but her daughter was beautiful, canny, and well schooled in the ways of the world. Again, perhaps to stem the scandal she could cause, Walford gave her money. The daughter began an establishment of her own in Bloomsbury, and she has been very successful catering to the more jaded tastes of gentlemen in society."

Suddenly it all made sense. Suddenly Duncan had the connection he'd been seeking.

A slow smile drew at the corners of his lips. "And the daughter's name is Sidney Layton, isn't it?"

The older man's response was everything Duncan had hoped it would be. His mouth popped open, and his eyebrows rose. He laughed deep down in his chest, a laugh that fully acknowledged Duncan's cleverness.

"You've a future in investigation, your lordship," Frasier fairly crowed, clapping Duncan on the back. "You're far brighter than you let on."

Though it was not quite a compliment, Duncan was pleased, both by Frasier's words and by the information he had gleaned. Now he had the tie between Sidney Layton and Samuel Walford he had been seeking. The other items that Hannibal Frasier had to report were either things that Duncan knew or amplifications of what he had learned on his own. The only surprise came when Frasier reported that Walford had been proposed for a knighthood in recognition of his good works in raising money for London's orphanages and his economic service to the Crown. To say the very least, this would be an inconvenient time for Walford's duplicity to be revealed.

In the next few minutes Duncan told the older man about his own investigation.

"And what I need from you now," Palmer went on, "is evidence of Samuel Walford's involvement with Enterprise Manufacturing."

"The public records don't connect him in any way?" Frasier asked.

"Not that I can find."

"Has it occurred to you that our Miss Layton may have proof of his involvement secured in her establishment?"

"Or perhaps it is stowed safely in a vault somewhere in the city."

"If she has things put away in a bank or in a countinghouse, I can have that information to you by noon tomorrow. It will take a few days longer to arrange to see what's there."

"I'm amazed by your inventiveness."

Behind his beard, Frasier's lips narrowed in a cocky smile.

"If what we're looking for is hidden in the brothel, there's nothing I can do. Men like me don't frequent establishments like the one Miss Layton runs."

"We'll see what you can find in the banks and countinghouses before we consider how to proceed from here."

Duncan thought briefly about the interview he'd had with Sidney Layton several days before. "Walford knows I've traced the bogus company to his daughter, so he's bound to be on his guard. And so is she."

"We'll find those papers, your lordship," Frasier assured him. "Never fear."

Duncan nodded in agreement, feeling more optimistic about the prospects of proving Walford's embezzlement than he had since he'd come to London.

When their business was complete, Frasier rose to go. "I'll come by your town house tomorrow afternoon to let you know what I have found."

"And I'll be waiting for your report," Duncan said with a nod. "Once we've proof of the connection between Samuel Walford and Enterprise Manufacturing, I can confront that blackguard and make him pay."

Fifteen

"WHAT THE HELL?"

Duncan stared into the mirror that hung above the washstand in his dressing room, trying to figure out what was the matter with his face. Four long red marks ran from just below his left cheekbone to a point midway down his neck. They looked painful and raw, the skin around them raised and faintly puffy. He lifted one hand to touch them, as if to make sure the marks were really there, and it was then he noticed the same kind of wounds marking the back of his left hand. But the gouges there were deeper, shorter, then the ones on his face. They ran across the sinews, trailing from the base of his fingers toward his wrist. As the left hand was patterned with bloody tracings, so was the right when he raised it to look.

He stared down at the skin on his hands with confusion and dismay. The marks looked as if they had been made by talons of some vicious bird or by the claws of some predatory animal. But how had he come by these bloody scratches? He had been in bed with a headache all night long, since just after dinner the previous day.

"What the hell?" he muttered again, trying to think of how the injuries might have been inflicted. Carefully he considered what he had done since leaving Hannibal Frasier the afternoon before. But even as he reviewed his actions step by step, he could think of nothing that would account for the injuries he had discovered on his face and hands this morning. He had come straight home from Westminster Bridge to the town house on Berkeley Square and had eaten dinner with his cousin. With the beginnings of a headache plaguing him, Duncan had gone directly from the dining room to his bedchamber. By the time he reached his rooms, the headache had become truly incapacitating. Even the effort it took to undress had made him weak and sick, and only the balm of laudanum offered any respite from the pain. To the best of his knowledge, Duncan had not stirred from his bed since then. But if that was truly the case, where had he gotten the scratches?

He was no closer to finding an answer to his query when he heard Ryan Barnes enter the adjoining bedchamber.

"My lord?" the valet called out.

"In here," Duncan answered, turning from the mirror as Ryan entered.

"My lord, I know how fuddled you often are after you've had a headache, so I brought your coffee straightaway—"

Barnes broke off in midsentence when he got a look at Duncan's face. "What's happened to you, my lord? Where did you get those marks?"

"I was hoping you would be able to tell me where I got them."

Barnes came closer, shaking his head. "They look for all the world like scratches."

"I know what they look like," Duncan snapped. "What I want to know is how I got them."

"They weren't on your face when you came home yesterday afternoon?"

"If they were, I wasn't aware of them."

"Nor did I notice them after dinner."

"I'm sure I didn't have them when I went to bed."

"But then where did the marks come from, my lord?" Ryan wanted to know.

"How the hell do I know?" Duncan's uncertainty was congealing deep in his belly, turning to a kind of nameless dread. "And look, there are more of them on the backs of my hands."

Ryan Barnes took one of Duncan's hands in his and studied the marks carefully. "They *do* look like scratches, my lord."

"Yes, I'll grant you that. But how did I come by them? That's what I want to know."

"Well, sir, you went to bed just after dinner last night with one of your headaches. Is it possible that in your distress you scratched yourself?"

"Of course I didn't do this to myself! I wouldn't have any reason to scratch myself in such a manner. In all the years I've been having headaches, I've never done myself harm during one of the attacks. Besides, I dosed myself with laudanum as soon as

I reached my room. Under its influence, I slept right through until this morning."

Ryan's brows drew together thoughtfully. "Are you sure you didn't recover from your headache and go out again last evening?"

"Wouldn't I know if I'd gone out? Wouldn't you know?"

"Well, my lord, since I thought you would have no more need of me last night, I took the evening off. I only went as far as the pub on Curzon Street, but I was there for several hours. Shall I ask the other servants if one of them attended you?"

Duncan shook his head in exasperation. "I didn't go out last night. No other servant attended me."

"Then where did the scratches come from?"

The argument was circular, without a beginning or an end. There seemed to be no answers to the questions Duncan had about the scratches, and the speculation was making him even more uneasy. All questions without logical answers made him uneasy these days. There were more unanswered questions in his life since he had returned to England than he'd ever hoped to contemplate.

"I'd like to bathe as soon as possible," he demanded suddenly, eager to change the subject from things he could not explain. "I'll eat the food you've brought while you get water for my bath."

Ryan nodded and turned to go. "Yes, my lord. I'll see to it immediately."

Alone in the dressing room, Duncan leaned closer to the mirror once more and studied the scratches on his face. Under the effects of the drug, had he indeed scratched his own face and hands? It seemed unlikely, and yet . . .

Slowly he lifted his left hand and placed his fingers over the pattern of marks that marred his cheek. He drew his hand downward to his neck, letting his close-cut nails trail over his face. But as he did, he found it difficult to trace the scratches. The marks were too close together; they had been made by a hand far smaller than his own. He did the same with the scratches on the backs of his hands and found that they did not match the width of his fingers either. He had not scratched himself; Duncan was certain of that. But if he had not made the marks, who had?

Still puzzling over the question, Duncan made his way into the adjacent bedroom and poured himself a cup of coffee. What was going on here? Why couldn't he remember what had happened the night before? Whom had he been with, and why had that person attacked him so viciously?

Searching for a clue, Palmer returned to the dressing room with coffee cup in hand and went to where his belongings were spread out on top of the chest of drawers. There was the usual array of objects: coins, a neatly folded handkerchief, his wallet, his pocket watch and fob, his lucky doubloon, all lying just as he had left them when he emptied his pockets the night before. But then, with a chill of apprehension, he noticed a twisted silver chain snaking out from the fold of his handkerchief. He stared down at the fine linen cloth for a full minute and more before he could bring himself to lift the monogrammed corner. Inside the fold the fabric was stained with tiny spots of blood, as if it had been used to blot some recent injury. And coiled in the center of the handkerchief was something he had never seen before—a woman's moonstone necklace.

Something heavy and cold curled in his middle as Duncan stared down at his discovery. Something vile and ugly fluttered through his veins, turning his face flaming hot and his hands ice cold.

He was certain he had never seen the necklace before, never seen the three broad gold-flecked stones set in filigreed carriages of ancient silver, never seen the fine twisted chain lying swirled inside the handkerchief. He reached out to touch the moonstones, to test the texture of the chain, but something stayed his hand. If the twisted threads of silver and semiprecious stones were an illusion, he did not want proof that he'd imagined it. If the necklace was real, he did not want to contemplate how it had come to be lying on his dresser with these other mundane objects.

Duncan forced himself to act, forced himself to take the necklace in his hand. It was cool, surprisingly heavy, the chain serpentine and shimmery as it lay across his palm. The moonstones glittered in the morning light spilling through the brace of windows on the far side of the room; the chain trickled between his fingers swinging lightly against the back of his hand. To whom did the necklace belong, and how had it come to be in his dressing room?

Shivers seemed to radiate through him at the contact with the metal, shivers of doubt, shivers of fear. The skin on his face seemed to shrink against his bones as he contemplated the object he had found among his belongings. Then, as if the necklace had been dipped in a slowly seeping acid, Duncan flung it away. It clattered to the top of the dresser and lay curled like a question mark on the smooth mahogany surface.

He closed his eyes and tried to quell the sickness surging through him. What was happening to him? How had the necklace come to be in his possession? Why were there suddenly so many things in his life he could not explain?

He looked down at the scratches on the backs of his hands, thought of the advertising card he had found among his belongings nearly a week before. He remembered how that discovery had shaken him.

Was this necklace a token of another crime? Was it connected to the West End Strangler's murders, as the advertising card might well have been? What was the link that connected him to the madman stalking women in London's streets?

What did all this mean? Duncan wondered in a swirl of panic. Had he been at or near the Crown Inn at the time the murder was committed? Who was the gentleman who had been seen with the victim shortly before the crime? Was the murderer from the privileged classes? And why—dear God—why did the murders coincide with the nights when he had been incapacitated with one of his headaches?

The conclusions that formed in his mind were too horrible to contemplate. They turned him sick and cold. They were suspicions based on circumstantial evidence, on things that could not be proved. Besides, it seemed impossible that he could have been a party to the murder of four young women and not remember any part of it.

But you don't remember shooting your father, do you? a voice inside him whispered. *You don't remember anything at all about what happened at Antire Manor the night your parents died.*

Duncan couldn't breathe, couldn't think for the maelstrom of emotions spinning inside him. He shivered as if with an ague, trembled like a glass about to shatter. He tried to suck air into his lungs, tried to sort through his roiling thoughts. The images that had come to him in the Crown Inn returned, so clear he could not banish them, so fierce that they might well have been seared into his brain.

I would know if I were the West End Strangler, wouldn't I? I would know if I were doing this.

For a time Palmer stood frozen in black despair, resisting the possibilities that had suddenly presented themselves, praying that he was wrong about the conclusions he had drawn.

There was the sound of someone entering the adjacent room, and Duncan stepped into the doorway. Barnes was settling the heavy copper tub on the rug before the fire.

"Barnes, I need to know," Duncan began, determined to ask the question before his courage deserted him. "Was there another woman killed last night?"

The valet turned to face his master. There was concern and compassion in his eyes. He nodded very slowly, his face gone grim. "Yes, my lord, there was."

Duncan had quite forgotten about his appointment with Hannibal Frasier until the butler came into the study to announce that the investigator had arrived. It seemed like a year since he and Duncan had sat together on the bank of the Thames and discussed Samuel Walford's connection to Enterprise Manufacturing. It seemed like a century since proving Walford's guilt was what Palmer had been most concerned about. In truth, it had been the previous afternoon.

Duncan turned as his visitor entered the study on the ground floor of the town house, and whatever Frasier had been about to say in greeting died in a sputter on the way to his lips.

"Your lordship," Frasier exclaimed instead, "have you met with some kind of accident?"

"An accident?"

"The marks on your face, your lordship."

The scratches on Duncan's cheek seemed to throb under the investigator's appraisal. He raised his hand to touch his cheek. "Something like that," he murmured.

"Are you all right?" There was far more concern in the older man's tone than Duncan would have expected.

"They're only scratches," Palmer explained.

As Frasier's canny gaze moved over the younger man, a frown drew at the corners of his mustache, puckered the lines between his brows. "You're sure that you're all right?"

Though Duncan nodded, it was clear the older man wasn't convinced by his assurances.

To break the silence lengthening between them, Frasier returned to the reason for his call. "You asked me, your lordship, to seek out the location of certain of Miss Layton's papers."

"Oh, yes. Miss Layton's papers," Palmer said absently. He motioned the Scotsman into a chair before the desk and sank into the one behind it. "Does this mean you've managed to locate them?"

"No, I haven't," Frasier replied. "That is to say, your lordship, if Miss Layton has copies of Enterprise Manufacturing's charter and books, she has not entrusted them to any of the financial or banking institutions here in London."

It was difficult for Duncan to turn his mind to Samuel Walford's embezzlement when other crimes seemed infinitely more important to him now.

"Could the papers be held for safekeeping somewhere else?" Duncan asked, his gaze wandering aimlessly, settling somewhere north of the detective's head.

"It's possible," Frasier conceded. "But my money's on them being hidden somewhere in that fancy house of Miss Layton's. Surely she has a safe or strongbox in which to store the evening's receipts; establishments like hers rarely run on credit. My guess is the papers we're after are in there."

Palmer sighed heavily. "Yes, I suppose you're right."

"Then it seems necessary for one of us to go and see what we can find," Frasier went on. "And, begging your pardon, your lordship, I think that had better be you."

Duncan's attention sharpened at Frasier's words. He blinked once as if to bring the man before him into focus. "Me? Me? I'm paying you for your ability to investigate, am I not?"

"Aye, you've paid me handsomely, I admit. But I was under the impression that you were in a rush to get this settled so you could be off to America. If I was to go poking around at Sidney Layton's place, I'd be spotted quick as a cornstalk in a rose bed."

When Palmer did not respond, the older man continued. "'Course, I could probably find employment in Miss Layton's establishment. Whorehouses do need laborers now and then. But even if I was able to get a job, it might be weeks before I had a chance to get a look at the things in her safe."

"What you're saying, Mr. Frasier," Duncan acknowledged on a long, slow breath, "is that I would fit in with her usual clientele, that I would have a better chance of locating the papers, if indeed she had them hidden there."

"That you would, your lordship. You could go into her establishment without arousing undue suspicion. And if you should happen into her office, if you should chance to riffle through her things, I'd bet money you'd find exactly what you were looking for. And the safe might well be open if she was having a particularly busy evening."

"I see," Duncan mumbled. "Yes, I see."

"Then again, I could do it myself," Frasier offered, sensing Duncan's reticence, "if that's what you really want."

Duncan thought it over. What Frasier said was probably true. He could get the information he was after more efficiently himself than by asking the other man to do it. Though Sidney Layton was aware of who he was, that he was looking into her father's business practices, his presence at her town house need not arouse undue suspicion. Any man alone in London might seek out an evening's pleasures. If that man was a stranger in town, if he was unsure of where else to go, he might well return to a place he was familiar with, a place where he'd already received a warm reception.

It was only that there was so much else on his mind just now: the Strangler's murders, his own terrifying suspicions, Grayson Ware. Oh, God! Where did Grayson fit in to all this? Was Gray in peril every time she was alone with him? This decided the matter definitively: he certainly couldn't marry her.

Forcing his thoughts to the problem at hand, Duncan shook his head. "I'll do it. What you say makes perfect sense. I can get into Sidney Layton's establishment, and I admit I have a better chance of finding the papers than you."

A frown creased Frasier's face again. "You will take care when you go there, won't you? The Layton woman knows who you are and will be on her guard."

"I will be careful," Duncan assured him.

"Well, then, your lordship, what else is it you want of me?"

The detective's question took Duncan by surprise. What other service could Frasier render? If Duncan found the papers connecting Samuel Walford to Enterprise Manufacturing, he would have the proof he needed to confront his uncle's partner. But now, with his knowledge of the theft of the religious relics during the war, with his awareness of his uncle's complicity in raising the funds to start the company, there were more uncomfortable questions to ask than ever before. His meeting with Walford was something Duncan was no longer eagerly anticipating.

Hannibal Frasier had done his job too well, uncovering things that Palmer would have preferred not to know. But in essence Frasier's job was over. He had accomplished everything Duncan had set out for him. Duncan withdrew his wallet from the inside pocket of his jacket and prepared to give the man the remainder of his fee.

Surprisingly, Hannibal Frasier waved the notes away. "Your lordship, if I may speak frankly . . ."

"By all means, Mr. Frasier. I doubt you know how to speak any other way."

The Scotsman's mouth tilted upward at the corners for just an instant before he sobered. "I'm worried about you, your lordship. I've been hearing things about you on the street."

Duncan sat forward in his chair, a shade paler than he had been a moment before. "Hearing things? What things?"

"I've heard that several men have been asking about you."

Cold crept through Duncan, making his lungs ache, turning his blood to ice. A heaviness weighted his legs, dragged on his arms. The police must be on his trail. They must already suspect him of being involved with the Strangler's crimes.

Palmer drew a shaky breath. "Who are the men?"

"I haven't been able to track them down, at least not yet."

"They haven't asked—" Duncan 's face was ashen now. "They haven't asked how I've spent my nights since I've returned to England, have they?"

Frasier's eyes narrowed as if he was confused by Palmer's question, by the intensity of his concern.

"I don't know what they've asked. All I know is that it has something to do with you, with you and Antire Manor."

"Antire Manor?"

"Walford isn't somehow connected to Antire Manor, is he?"

"Antire Manor?" Duncan repeated, then shook his head. "No, as far as I know, Walford has no ties to Antire Manor. He was only there a time or two. I believe the last was when he came to fetch me to London after my parents died. Walford acted as Uncle Farleigh's surrogate then, just as my father acted as surrogate in some of Farleigh's business dealings here in England."

"Then what's going on at Antire Manor? How is it connected to you?"

"I have no connection to Antire Manor; I haven't been there for seventeen years."

"You haven't gone there since you've been back in England?"

"No. For God's sake, no."

"Then you can't be sure that Antire Manor is exactly as you remember it?"

Duncan's face hardened as he replied. "The place has been abandoned since my parents died."

"I'm sorry, your lordship, but I really think you're wrong." The tone of Frasier's voice revealed how reticent he was to offer the contradiction. "If Antire Manor's just another moldering country home, why should there be talk of it here in London?"

"The place has been abandoned! Nothing is going on there."

Frasier was patient but patently unconvinced. "I believe there is, your lordship, and it's somehow tied to you. Give me leave to go to Antire Manor—"

"No."

"Just let me just go and see—"

"No."

"Surely there's no harm in letting me—"

"No."

Duncan felt as if he'd spent the day struggling up from the bottom of a sand pit. Now another load of heavy, clinging sand seemed to have been dumped upon him, and he wasn't sure he had the strength to fight his way free.

Palmer only knew that he couldn't let himself think about Antire Manor or what had happened there. He couldn't let himself think about the death of his parents—especially now.

In spite of the determination in Duncan's voice, the detective continued to argue. "If Antire Manor truly has been empty all these years, why am I hearing about it on the streets? Why do I have the sense that something about the place poses a threat to you?"

The detective's perceptiveness was unnerving, and Duncan resented his intrusion into a decidedly private affair. "If you're hearing about Antire Manor now, it's because I've returned to England. It's because that's where my mother died, because that's where I killed my father! If there's any threat to me about the place, it's to my peace of mind!"

Duncan rose and turned away, staring desperately out into the small sunny garden at the back of the house. There were drifts of gaily colored flowers hemming the perimeter of the tiny yard, the shocking pink and blazing white of honeysuckle, butter yellow dahlias and spiky, vivid-blue delphinium. How could those flowers bloom so brilliantly, he found himself wondering, when his whole world was going black?

He'd worked so hard to put his parents' death behind him, and there were times when Palmer truly believed he'd escaped his past. He couldn't let this wiry Scotsman break into the graves of those long dead. He couldn't chance sending Frasier to Dorset where he might stumble across some damning, long-buried truth that Duncan didn't know himself.

The press of Frasier's hand against his arm was consoling, unexpected. He hadn't heard the man cross the room to where he stood.

"Your lordship." Frasier's gruff voice was surprisingly gentle. "In looking into Walford's affairs I've uncovered a good deal about you and about the death of your parents as well. And there are things that have been bothering me."

Duncan tried to shake him off, but the Scotsman was as persistent as a burr.

"Can you tell me why a dueling pistol was primed and ready to use the night you killed your father? Do you know where you picked it up?"

The question echoed in Duncan's head, but he didn't know how to answer it. It was just one more in the endless stream of questions he would never be able to answer about that night.

"Oh, please," he whispered, closing his eyes. "I really can't remember."

He didn't want to know what he'd done all those years ago in his father's study, just as he didn't want to learn what he'd been doing during his headaches these last weeks in London. Was it all connected somehow, laced together in some intricate pattern he could neither fathom nor escape? He hated the blank spots in his life; he hated the truth he might discover if he probed too deep. Sometimes he hated himself.

Exhaustion sifted over him like heavy snow, thick, silent, muffling the fierce reality of his emotions. He sagged against the window casement, overwhelmed, overcome.

Frasier was still at his elbow, waiting for his answer. And Duncan had no strength to spare for more denials.

"Do what you want. Investigate what you will. In the end I'll pay the price."

Frasier nodded before he turned to go. "This won't cost you, your lordship. You have my word on that."

Duncan's mouth twisted in a bitter smile as the detective took his leave. Who could guess what Frasier might discover, and what it would cost him in the end?

Eavesdropping wasn't polite. It was one of the hard and fast rules of correct behavior both Aunt Julo and Ellison's Finishing School had spent years drumming into Grayson's head. She had learned the rule grudgingly, for while care and concern for others was basic to her nature, so was an insatiable curiosity about the world at large and, more specifically, the people who lived in it.

But even the most rigid stickler for propriety wouldn't have been able to resist the temptation to listen in on a conversation that began with Duncan Palmer saying: "Your Grace, I have come to talk to you about Grayson."

Surely Grayson couldn't resist.

She had been sitting at the elegant Louis XIV desk in the small writing room off the rear of the library, catching up on her social correspondence, when Duncan's voice reached her through the half-open door.

"What is it about Grayson you've come to discuss?" Her guardian sounded irritable, short-tempered. Grayson knew he had been working on the speech he was to give in Parliament at the end of the week and probably resented the interruption.

"I've come to break our engagement. I'm no longer willing to marry Grayson."

At his words, Grayson went perfectly still, hardly breathing, her pen poised in an upstroke above the sheet of creamy vellum stationery.

It seemed as if her uncle was as stunned as she was by Duncan's words, for it took him several moments to respond. "Not marry her? That's preposterous!"

"Nevertheless, that's what I've come here to tell you."

"But the plans for the wedding have all been made. The invitations have all been sent. The announcement of your betrothal was in the newspapers only this morning."

Her uncle made it sound as if those actions made the deed irrevocable.

"In spite of that, I don't intend to marry Grayson on Saturday." Duncan's tone was determined and grim.

"Now, Antire, it's not uncommon for a groom to have second thoughts. Marriage is an enormous step for any man. But Grayson's a winning girl, and she'll make an excellent wife for a man like you." She could almost see her uncle's condescending smile as he tried to soothe her fiancé. "Her fortune alone is recommendation enough—"

"And you've made it very clear that you're more than willing to trade her bounteous assets for an aristocratic husband." Duncan sounded angry.

"No, of course I haven't!"

"But wasn't that what you were doing by marrying her to Harry Torkington? Isn't that what you're trying to do in foisting her off on me?"

"I've turned away more noble suitors than you can possibly imagine."

"From what I hear, it was Grayson who turned most of them away."

Grayson knew her uncle well enough to imagine the flush that must be rising in his cheeks. Outright contradictions made Warren Worthington furious.

"If you weren't interested in her hand, why did you so blatantly compromise her?"

There was a pause before Duncan answered. "Unfortunately for you as her guardian, Grayson is a woman who simply begs to be compromised."

It was Grayson's turn to flush, and it was with the utmost difficulty that she remained in her chair. Begged to be compromised, indeed! She had never led Duncan on; she had only responded to his lead. It was not her fault that from time to time their common understandings had led them to more physical expressions of what they felt. It wasn't her fault that there was something in Duncan's touch that evaporated her will to resist.

To his credit, her uncle seemed every bit as incensed as she. "Nonetheless, you compromised her. You mauled her in the garden—"

"Not without her consent."

"—and for all I know you were mauling her the day I came upon you at Mrs. de Rothschild's estate. And as for having her consent, you are well aware it is up to a gentleman to set the limits of physical expression. Women don't understand the scope of their own passionate natures, and a gentleman always puts a lady's virtue above his own baser needs. Your uncle should have taught you that."

"I did her no real harm."

"You mean she's still a virgin."

"Exactly. And as far as I'm concerned, she'll stay that way."

In the silence she could almost hear her uncle marshaling his forces.

"Now you listen here, you arrogant young pup," he began, any touch of reasonableness gone from his voice. "You've been the cause of enough scandal where Grayson is concerned. You took her to Evans's and risked her safety. You caused the breach in her engagement to a man far more suited to her needs than you. You used her to gratify your own baser urges—"

"Not gratify, surely."

"Damn you, Antire!" Worthington's voice was shaking. "You've done her far more damage than you can possibly know. I don't care why you want to break the engagement. Your reasons are immaterial to me. But either you meet her at the altar on Saturday afternoon or you meet me on the field of honor. I won't have you sully her reputation more than you already have. Grayson is under my protection, and I intend to see that you do right by her, or by God, I'll see you dead!"

At Worthington's pronouncement Grayson drew a harsh, uneven breath. She was furious at the things her uncle and Duncan had said, terrified by the threats her uncle was making. The last thing she wanted was to be fought over like a tart in some saloon. The mere thought of it made her feel dirty, cheap. Nothing would be settled by Duncan and her guardian meeting on the field, by one of them dying to save her good name. She had to intervene.

On knees that quaked, she came to her feet. It was time to make her presence known, time to learn just why Duncan was refusing to marry her. In her mind that question was more crucial than anything else.

"Please, your grace, I have my reasons—"

"To hell with your reasons. To hell with you," Worthington shouted. "I agreed to this match against my better judgment. I agreed to it for Grayson's sake. But I see now what a mistake it was to let someone who has committed patricide within miles of anyone I care about, to let a man without a shred of honor so much as touch the hem of Grayson's gown. But now the damage is done, and all I can do is protect my ward. You will marry Grayson on Saturday. You will treat her with the respect and concern of a dutiful husband. And if I ever hear of you abusing her as your father abused your mother—"

Even from behind the half-closed door, she could almost feel Duncan pale.

"I would never harm Grayson. Never."

Worthington continued as if he had not heard. "If I ever get word that you are abusing Grayson, if I ever hear that you've deliberately made her unhappy—"

There was the rumble of furniture moving, as if one of the men in the adjoining room had abruptly come to his feet. Then came the thud of angry footsteps.

"You be at the church on Saturday, Antire," the duke commanded in his most threatening tone. "And in the meantime you will play the doting fiancé. I will not have Grayson humiliated. I will not have Grayson hurt. You mark me well on this, or you'll be sorry you were ever born."

The only answer Palmer gave was the slamming of the library door.

With the sound, Grayson sank back into her chair, more shaken than she had ever been in her life. So Duncan was refusing to marry her, though he had forgone the chance to back out a few days before. Why had he suddenly changed his mind? What had she done to alienate him? How was she going to face him at the ball her guardians were giving the following evening? Would he even put in an appearance? What would she do if he left her waiting at the altar on Saturday?

Her stomach heaved and her head went light.

I will never eavesdrop again, she vowed to herself, I will never eavesdrop again. But her good intentions for the future could not change the recent past. With the knowledge of what Duncan thought of her fresh in her mind, Gray abruptly threw up in the wastepaper basket.

Sixteen

DUNCAN DIDN'T WANT TO BE HERE, STRIDING UP THE WALK TO Sidney Layton's town house, preparing to search the premises for the papers he so desperately needed to prove his case against Samuel Walford. There was too much on his mind, too many suspicions gnawing at him, to give this evening's enterprise the attention it deserved. He wasn't even sure he should be alone on the streets of London, but he really had no choice about coming here. He needed the information about Enterprise Manufacturing, and he needed it now, before he set sail for America. He couldn't give up his investigation when he was so close to proving Walford's guilt.

He stood before the door for a moment, trying to muster his energies, his concentration. He could get through this, he told himself. He had managed to give a fair accounting of himself during the difficult interview with Grayson's guardian just this afternoon, and he would find a way to gull Sidney Layton, too. All he needed was a few minutes to search her rooms and her office. The papers had to be in the town house somewhere.

No, he didn't want to be here. But he was, and he intended to accomplish everything he'd come to do. He raised the knocker on the door and reluctantly let it fall. The same servant who had admitted him several days before, motioned him inside, then took his walking stick and hat. When he had come to the establishment in the afternoon, the place had been deserted, but now well-dressed men and scantily clad women swarmed through the elegant hall and overpopulated the parlor. As the strains of a familiar song tinkled in the background, a servant came to offer Duncan a drink. As he sipped from the tumbler of whiskey, he took note of the others in the room.

He did not have many acquaintances in England, but among the guests milling around the sitting room or lounging on the velvet settees, he recognized several recent dinner companions and one or two men who had been his hosts. The women he had never seen before, but their attire gave more than a hint of the roles they would play in the bedrooms on the floors above. There was a wide-eyed girl dressed for the schoolroom, an exotic fair-skinned Negress in a diaphanous saffron gown, a tall hard-faced whore wearing a black corset and thigh-high boots. And in their midst was Sidney Layton, her lush breasts overflowing the neckline of her purple satin gown, her heavy dark hair spilling down her back from a matching set of amethyst combs.

Noticing Duncan's arrival, she swatted aside the hand of a young swain, who had been tracing the perimeters of her décolletage, and crossed the room to where Palmer stood.

"My very dear marquis," she greeted him. "I'm delighted that you decided to return. I'm much more accommodating during the evening than I am in the afternoon. Though I admit that for a man like you, I'd have been glad to make concessions."

"Indeed, I hope you will be willing to concede to me tonight. I have need of your company and expertise."

"My expertise, my lord?"

Duncan gave her a shallow smile. "Your establishment comes highly recommended."

"Does it, now? I'm pleased to hear that. We pride ourselves on satisfying our customers."

His smile became more genuine. "That's exactly what I've heard."

"And is your need for satisfaction pressing, or have you a moment to savor the ambience?"

It seemed unwise to be too eager to adjourn to the rooms upstairs, and Duncan shrugged. "I believe I would like the opportunity to finish my drink and to enjoy the music and a bit of conversation before we go to other things."

"And shall we be conversing on the subjects we discussed the other afternoon, or have you something more stimulating in mind?"

"I'd like something a little more stimulating. I want you to help me put all thoughts of business out of my mind."

"Well, then," Sidney murmured as she led Duncan toward one

of the couches at the far end of the room, "let me tell you about my ladies and how they can fulfill your wildest fantasies."

Though he didn't want to be fobbed off on one of the other courtesans, he listened carefully to Sidney Layton's erotic explanations of what her girls could do for him. As she extolled the talents of each of the women in her employ, she saw that Duncan's glass was kept refilled and that his senses were fully engaged. As they sat close together on the secluded settee, her hands ranged over him, stroking the interior of his thigh, the fabric above his nipples, the sensitive lobe of his ear. She paused as she touched the scratches on his cheek.

"Do those hurt, my lord?" she asked him sympathetically.

Her attention to the scratches made them burn. "Not at all," he lied. "They're nothing to be concerned about, nothing at all."

Her actions and the words she continued whispering in his ear made warmth rise in his face, made his breathing accelerate. His encounter with Grayson several days before had left him aching and frustrated, and he responded more than appropriately to the whore's suggestions and her prodding. He could feel the tightening in his loins even before Sidney Layton began to kiss him. Her carmine-colored lips moved over his, moist, hot, and enticing. Her tongue searched out and found the tip of his, teasing it, drawing it into the beckoning hollow of her mouth. Of their own volition, his arms came around her shoulders, dragging her close as his opposite hand began to scale the broadening curve of her thigh.

Sidney Layton was good at what she did, he thought abstractedly, very good, the consummate whore. She knew what all men wanted, gave it without reserve. Her eyes said he was the most desirable man in the room, her kiss hinted at untold delights. The scent of her perfume was sweetly feminine, the movements of her hands provocative yet coy. She knew just how much to give, just how much to withhold, and the desires she sent stirring through his body were far more genuine than he would have liked.

Drawing away at last, Sidney Layton laughed and tossed her hair. "Are you ready to adjourn to more private surroundings, my lord? Is there some woman you would like me to send to you?"

"I want you." His words came out in a rasping tone. "I want you to spend the night with me."

It was obvious that she was pleased by his request, pleased that her enticements had garnered an appropriate response. "But I have a duty to my guests. I must oversee their enjoyment."

"Damn your guests," Duncan whispered, nipping at her ear. "I want you—you and no one else."

She smiled, preened, then turned her face to his. "It will take some time to make arrangements," she hedged, pressing one knee against the juncture of his legs. "Are you sure you're willing to wait?"

"Of course I'm willing to wait. Let me stay in your apartments while you do what you must. I only hope you won't be too long."

Something dark and eager flickered in the depths of her eyes. "I'll have one of my servants escort you, and I'll come as soon as I can."

She kissed him deeply, scouring the interior of his mouth even as she rose to go. "Wait," she whispered as if to quell his eagerness. "Wait."

Because of his reason for coming here, Duncan was more than willing to do just that.

As he watched, she crossed the room and conferred with a liveried servant who was passing refreshments among the guests. The man left the room for a moment to set aside his tray, then came to where Duncan sat.

"If you will follow me, my lord."

Duncan rose and trailed the servant up the wide carpeted stairs to the floor above and down a long dimly lit hallway that led toward the back of the house. They paused outside a door at the very end of the corridor.

"Madam said to tell you she would be joining you shortly," the servant assured Duncan as he swung the door wide. "In the meantime there is whiskey on the table, some opium, a pipe, and a few other things you might enjoy."

A faint prickle of foreboding stirred through Duncan as he stepped into the room, but before the reason for it could register, there was a movement to his left. In that instant an enormous hulking shape loomed out of the shadows, and something came crashing down on him. Duncan staggered and fell to the floor. Before he could manage to right himself, a second blow was dealt and the world went black.

Damn it, she loved him! Somewhere between throwing up in the wastepaper basket and lying sobbing across her bed, Grayson had realized it. She had fallen in love with Duncan Palmer!

An hour before his visit this afternoon that would have been a wonderful revelation, but in the light of what she had overheard in the library, her reaction to the discovery was tinged with anger, irony and hopelessness. The conversation between Duncan and Warren Worthington had turned the pleasant anticipation of her forthcoming wedding to searing disappointment, blinding pain.

Duncan didn't want to marry her, and Grayson had to find out why. When she thought about it, there were several possibilities. It could be that he simply didn't want a wife or that, in spite of his obvious attraction to her, he didn't want a wife with ambitions of her own. The even less acceptable prospect was that he felt he had been trapped into marrying her, believed that the evening at Evans's had been part of an elaborate plan to rid herself of Harry Torkington and substitute Palmer as her groom. She could see how Duncan might think that, especially after she had tried so desperately to persuade him to take her to America. Did he think that marriage was merely another ploy to gain passage across the Atlantic? Was his refusal to marry her based on that? Gray would never sell herself so cheaply. But did Duncan realize how she felt, or would he think the worst of her?

The day he had brought her the ring, the ring whose ostentatiousness was causing so much comment among the dowagers of the ton, she had tried to offer him the chance to recant. Why, if he wanted to break the engagement, hadn't he done it then? Instead he had brushed aside her explanations and apologies, made love to her in a way she had never suspected love could be made, and given her a ring that was a blatant sign of his possession.

It made no sense, especially in the light of what had taken place in the library this afternoon. That conversation had given her no clues to what Duncan was thinking, and it was largely her uncle Warren's fault for denying Palmer a chance to explain. At any rate, she needed to confront Duncan, to hear from his own lips his reasons for refusing to marry her.

It was the need to hear his explanations that had brought her here this evening to wait in a hired carriage parked just down the street from the Antire town house in Berkeley Square. She had dressed for the occasion in her guise as the Honorable Herbert Fortescue, complete with wig and false mustache. There had been two reasons for her disguise. Because she had not wanted to call on Duncan at the town house where her reputation could be further compromised and where the servants could bar her way, she had decided to confront him in some public place, and as a woman, there were many public places she could not go. The other reason was more practical, more frightening: there was a murderer loose on London's streets who preyed on lone women, and Gray had no desire to risk her life for the sake of asking a few questions. As it was, a cold kernel of fear had lodged deep in her chest that had nothing to do with finding out why Duncan had broken off their betrothal. The murderer's presence, and the police's inability to catch the man, had frightened every woman in London. And where females had once felt safe walking alone, the streets were now almost deserted.

Duncan's appearance in front of the Berkeley Square town house saved her from further speculation about the West End Strangler's crimes, and after she had seen Palmer climb into his own crested coach, she instructed her driver to follow it. But before they could pull away from the curb, another hired cab cut them off and a second fell in behind it. As they skirted the perimeter of the deserted square, the carriages gave the impression of being a part of some bizarre parade. Grayson peered out the window, wondering if Duncan was aware that he had picked up an entourage.

The carriages made their way north and east toward Bloomsbury, where Duncan's pulled up before a town house not far from Russell Square. From a little way down the block, she watched him alight, make his way through the gate and up the steps to the front door of a tall stone-fronted town house. It seemed as if he hesitated a moment before he raised the knocker, and when a servant answered the summons, she could see that there were crowds of people in the lighted foyer. Duncan was attending a party of some kind, and though she worried about how she would gain admittance, she felt that this was as likely a place as any to approach him. It seemed unwise to follow him too closely, and as Gray waited, she saw men emerge from both the other carriages and post themselves at either end of the block. Their presence was most peculiar, and she wondered again if Duncan knew he was being followed.

When she deemed enough time had passed to allow her to make her entrance an inconspicuous one, Grayson had her driver pull up at the front of the house. After alighting from the cab and giving the driver instructions, Grayson quickly made her way up the wide stone walk. She was admitted to the party without question and elbowed her way into the parlor. It was a credit to her ability as an actress that she didn't gape at what she saw. The men—gentlemen, judging by the cut of their clothes—were everything they should have been. But the women—oh, Lord, the women—were all half naked! Gray quickly averted her eyes, her gaze coming to rest on the carvings above the fireplace. It took her an instant to realize what was depicted there, and that subject shocked her, too. There were satyrs and nymphs cavorting in a totally lascivious manner!

Grayson melted into the corner of the room nearest the front window, attempting to make herself invisible while she tried to get her bearings. Her gaze moved over the opulent parlor, over the maroon velvet couches and chairs filled with talking, laughing people; over the elegant papier-mâché tables beneath a forest of half-filled glasses; over the huge gilt-framed mirrors that reflected the dishabille of the women and the unbelievable behavior of the men who stood beside them. Not that the women's attire didn't invite that kind of intimacy, but the men were fondling them in public. There were men kissing bare shoulders, kneading scantily clad hips, stroking breasts that bulged above the necklines of shamelessly low-cut gowns. It was shocking, disgusting! Grayson had never seen anything like it.

As she watched, a woman dressed in little more than a lacy nightdress and ruffled satin wrapper guided the man she was with toward the stairs that led up from the hall. He was laughing, feigning reticence, until she paused at the foot of the stairs to plaster herself against his body and press her carmined lips to his. Grayson simply stared at them, seeing the hollows form in their cheeks as their kisses deepened, seeing the way the man's hands moved over the woman, closing over her buttocks, pulling her hips even closer to his. With a toss of her hair, the woman jerked away and sprinted up the stairs, with the man climbing the steps eagerly in her wake. Grayson didn't want to think what would happen next, but in spite of her reticence to think on it, she had a vague idea.

It was then she realized where she was. She had followed Duncan into a place where courtesans stayed, where bawdy women went with men for money! What they did once they went with them, Grayson wasn't totally sure, but she had the feeling that before the night was over she might have a far better idea about it than she had ever wanted to. She had heard about places like this. They were spoken about in whispers by matrons who heartily disapproved. They were called houses of joy, and indeed, everyone *did* seem joyful.

There was no question that she should leave immediately. This was no place for a lady to be. But just as she was considering how she could make a graceful exit, the crowd parted in its inevitable ebb and flow, and she caught a glimpse of Duncan on a couch at the far end of the room. He was kissing the most gloriously beautiful woman Grayson had ever seen.

Anger went off inside Gray like a roman candle. Her hands clenched at her side and she could feel her face get hot. She wanted to storm across the room, tear Duncan out of this woman's arms. She wanted to scratch the woman's eyes out, rip the hair from her head in handfuls. That she was jealous of Duncan Palmer's affections was the second devastating shock of the day. It froze her where she stood, made her want to burst into helpless tears.

Resolutely Grayson controlled herself. But her discovery had made her change her mind about what she was going to do. Whereas before she had been eager to escape the brothel, she was now determined to stay. She wanted to see what Duncan did here, wanted to know what made him choose to spend time with a woman like this when he refused to marry her.

Moving from the shelter of the corner, Grayson accepted a glass of sherry from one of the servants passing among the guests. She sipped from it as she made a circuit of the room, sidling closer and closer to where Duncan sat with the courtesan, hoping to hear a snatch of their conversation. But from her vantage point near the wall, she could see they weren't talking very much. Duncan was kissing the woman as if he never intended to stop, and his hand was halfway up her thigh.

"I want you," Gray heard Duncan whisper as he ended a long and searching kiss. "I want you to spend the night with me."

Grayson heard the tart demur: She had other things to do, other guests to see to. The discussion was heated and brief. Duncan won his way. He would wait in the courtesan's rooms while she discharged her responsibilities. Gray saw one of the servants lead Duncan across the parlor, out to the hall, and up the stairs. She bristled as she watched them, determined not to follow.

But as the evening progressed, the courtesan remained in the parlor. A half-hour passed in which Grayson rebuffed the attentions of several of the half-clad women in the room. An hour dribbled away, and the crowd was beginning to thin. The woman in the revealing purple gown made no attempt to go to Duncan, and Grayson began to wonder where he was.

Her curiosity was like a burr against her skin. Where was he? Why hadn't Duncan returned? Had one of the other women been sent to service him?

Finally she set her empty glass aside and asked directions to the washroom. It was down the hall toward the back of the house. Striding purposefully in the direction one of the servants had indicated, Grayson moved away. Once she was far enough down the hall, she began opening doors to see where they went. There was a small cozy sitting room midway down the hall, a washroom exactly where the servant had said it was, and an office at the back of the house.

Opposite the office was another door, which led to the servants' stairs. She closed it behind her and crept up toward the landing. Her stomach clenched tighter with every step she took. Her hand was slick against the banister. Were the courtesans' rooms on the second floor of the house or on the floor above it? Reaching the top of the first flight of steps, she stole into a carpeted hall illuminated by oil lamps hung at distant intervals. There was no sound from the room opposite the stairs, and Gray moved quickly down the hall. From behind the others she could hear people laughing, talking, gasping, moaning, and because she had no desire to discover what was going on inside, she continued along the passageway. When she reached the front of the house, she faced a second flight of stairs. Was Duncan up there somewhere or in one of the rooms behind her?

She had not recognized his voice, though she had to admit she might well have mistaken it. She had never heard Duncan moaning the way these other people were. The room that lay in silence at the back of the house might be the one where he was waiting. Deciding to look into it before she went on to the floor above, Gray retraced her steps. Stopping before the very last door, she listened for movement or voices inside. There was no hint of occupation.

With fear thrumming in her veins, she reached out and turned the knob. When the door refused to open under her hand, she realized it must be locked. She stood for a moment wondering what to do. Could she force the door without alerting anyone to her unauthorized presence? Was there a way to get the key without committing herself to an evening with one of the women in the parlor below? Then, just as she was about to give up the idea of looking inside, she noticed a key hanging on a nail toward the top of the doorjamb. As she glanced up and down the hall she could see that each of the rooms had a key hanging up in the very same place. Might it be necessary to lock the patrons of the whorehouse in? Were the keys there to enable others to break into the locked rooms on a moment's notice? The reason for the keys made Grayson's blood run cold.

Taking the key from the nail, Gray inserted it in the lock. The noise of the mechanism working seemed to reverberate in her ears. As the tumblers clicked into place, the vibration moved up her arm. She caught her breath and paused to see if anyone had heard the noise, waited to see if anyone would come to check on what she was doing. But in spite of her misgivings, the hallway remained deserted. She turned the knob carefully, afraid of what she might find.

Grayson opened the door a sliver, and then a little more. As she did, she saw Duncan sprawled utterly still and totally alone, bound hand and foot in the center of the bed.

When he heard someone at the door, Duncan had been conscious and struggling to loosen his bonds for several minutes. That he had walked into the trap Sidney Layton had laid for him was patently obvious, and in spite of the fact that the house was still alive with patrons, he knew she must be coming to question him.

It wasn't a prospect Palmer was particularly anticipating. He was still feeling woozy from the blow on his head and would have preferred to have his wits about him when it came to facing Walford's daughter. He had no illusions about what would happen if Walford came instead. If the man had been willing to kill for a few religious artifacts thirty years ago, he would be more than willing to dispose of Palmer rather than risk a scandal now.

Lying perfectly still, Duncan waited, watching the door from beneath his lowered lashes. There was the creak of a floorboard in the hall, the rattle of a key in the lock, and the ornate brass knob moved a half-turn to the left.

The door opened just slightly more than a crack, and he could see a man standing just outside. Against the glow of the light at the end of the hall, his face was hidden in deep shadow, but Palmer could see that the fellow was thin and of middling height. It was not Sidney Layton. It was not Walford. It was not the tall man who had attacked him earlier. Duncan began to hope.

The man pushed the panel open another foot and crept as far as the edge of the rug. From where he lay, Duncan could make out a pale oval face, a reddish mustache, a thatch of cinnamon-colored hair. There was something familiar about the man, but with his head booming like a drum at an infantry parade, Duncan couldn't seem to place him. There was a full lower lip visible beneath the fringe of his red mustache, a rounded chin, and bright green eyes that were watching him most curiously.

Recognition came with a jolt. It stopped the breath in his throat. It sent cold sluicing down his arms, and hot blood rising in his cheeks. It was the very last person in the world he would have expected to see in such surroundings.

"Hay-hun?" he gasped around the red satin scarf someone had shoved in his mouth as a gag. "Hay-hun!"

Silently returning to close the door, Grayson crossed cat-footed to the bed and loosened the knot beside Duncan's ear.

"You damn fool woman!" Duncan began the moment the cloth was out of his mouth. "What the hell are you doing here? What's going on in that head of yours? Aren't you aware of what would happen if someone saw you here? The scandal at Evans's would be mild in comparison! Don't you have any sense of propri—"

Gray shoved the gag back in his mouth, effectively cutting off the blistering string of exclamations and epithets. Was it possible that Duncan wasn't pleased to see her? Had he had himself tied up like this deliberately? She'd read about such behavior, but she would never have suspected that Duncan was the kind of man who was given to this peculiar sexual proclivity. Still, one never knew . . .

"Plaugh!" Duncan spat out the gag and glared at her. "As long as you're here, untie me!"

"Being tied up isn't something you paid for, then?"

The color in Duncan's face went three shades darker. Where the hell did Grayson learn about things like this? he wondered as she leaned across him to free his hand. But Duncan knew. It was amazing the amount of scandalous reading material Gray managed to come across. If he was still going to marry her, the first thing he'd do was censor the books she read.

Then again, maybe he wouldn't.

"Don't you realize what a chance you took by coming here?" he demanded. "If the people who own this place had realized you were a woman, you might well have been drugged, beaten, and sold into white slavery! What on earth made you come to a place like this?"

"You did! I followed you here, Duncan," she told him nose to nose. "That's why I came. I came because I needed to talk to you, because I needed to find out why you broke our engagement. And from the way it looks, it's a damn good thing I showed up!"

Duncan blinked, stunned by what she'd said, stunned by their situation. Her words put everything into perspective, and he realized lecturing her about the chances she'd taken could wait. They were facing dangers far beyond those of Grayson being found in a house of joy, far beyond those of propriety and scandal. There were people here who were willing to kill him, and because Grayson had allied himself with his cause, they'd be willing to kill her, too.

They had to get away. That should be his first priority. Still, he had come here for a purpose, and the instant his ankles were free of their bonds, he rolled off the bed and began going through the dresser.

"Duncan! What are you doing?" Gray demanded. "What on earth are you looking for? I think it's clear we need to get out of here!"

He was pawing through a drawer, answering her without even looking up. "I came here to see if I could find some important business papers, and I don't intend to leave until I've had a chance to search for them."

"You mean you didn't come to—to—you know."

Duncan glanced over his shoulder to where she stood. "No, of course not. I don't need to pay a whore if all I want is a tumble!"

Color suffused his cheeks again when he realized what he'd said.

It exactly matched the crimson shade in hers.

"Oh, I thought . . ." she muttered weakly, sagging onto the edge of the mattress.

Then, glancing up, she turned to him again. "Is it usual in places like this to have mirrors over the beds? What earthly good can they do up there?"

Duncan ignored her and continued his search. Within a few minutes the room was a shambles. There were dresses, corsets, and stockings trailing onto the floor. There was jewelry shimmering across the surface of the dresser. The mirror above it and several picture frames had been ripped from the walls and the back panels had been removed. The mattress had been upended and the sheets swept up like a web over one corner of the headboard.

Palmer stopped in the center of the room, glancing around distractedly. "Where the hell could she have hidden them? The business papers I told you about."

"There's an office just downstairs," Gray offered helpfully.

"Is there? Did you notice a safe? A strongbox?"

She tried to remember, then shook her head. "I don't know. I suppose there could have been."

Snatching her hand, Duncan tugged her toward the door, but Grayson hung back.

"There is also a servants' stairs behind the door across the hall," she offered. "Why don't you let me see if the coast is clear before you go charging out there?"

"How do you know about the office and the stairs?"

"It took me rather a long time to find you."

"Did it?" Duncan couldn't suppress his grin. He'd be willing to wager that Gray had gotten an eyeful tonight. He was stunned that she had followed him, appalled that she had stayed on once she realized what kind of place this was. But he could only thank his lucky stars that Gray had been so eager to have a word with him.

"Right." He nodded, returning to the business at hand. "Go ahead and check the hall."

Grayson did as she was told and an instant later motioned him to follow her down the steps. They crept slowly along the narrow staircase, keeping toward the wall to avoid the creak of floorboards, freezing where they stood if there was a sound from above or below. At the bottom was another door. Grayson went through it first.

The office directly opposite was unlocked and unoccupied. A desk with overflowing cubbyholes stood beside the window in a corner. There was a tall bookcase crammed with what looked like ledgers and an old-fashioned freestanding strongbox with three huge locks.

Duncan cursed when he tried to open it.

Gray stood peering out into the hall, keeping watch as Palmer had told her to do. The crowd had thinned dramatically since she'd gone upstairs, and she knew that didn't help their predicament. She could still hear the piano playing in the parlor, but the babble of voices had dropped to a hum. She stiffened as a couple came into the hall at the foot of the stairs and stood kissing against the banister.

Still she stared with a fascination she could not seem to quell, watching as the man's lips moved over the woman's mouth, watching as his hand dropped to the curve of her half-clad breast. He moved slowly, his motions caressing and tender. He seemed to be kneading the woman's flesh as his tongue plumbed the depths of her mouth.

Quite unexpectedly, Grayson's nipples tightened in response, and her mouth went suddenly dry.

The woman's head fell back as the man pressed kisses along her throat, and Gray noticed the woman's body had begun to move rhythmically against the press of the man's narrow hips.

Gray recognized that rhythm and felt heat coil between her legs. She didn't know what had come over her.

"Grayson?" The sound of Duncan's voice startled her. Color flooded into her cheeks. "Do you have a hairpin, or maybe two?"

"Hum?"

"A hairpin."

He glanced up from the strongbox toward where she stood, and she could see the lamplight setting off the reddish cast to his hair. It limned the strong bones of his face, the curves of his sensual mouth. She couldn't seem to remember a time when Duncan had been more appealing to her.

"A hairpin," he repeated. "Have you got one? I'm going to pick the lock."

"Can you do that?" she asked him.

"Oh, I've a few illicit skills tucked somewhere up my sleeve."

Nodding, she fumbled along the edge of the wig, extracting one hairpin and then another.

"Thanks," he whispered as he turned back to his work.

Out in the hallway things had been progressing at a rapid pace. The woman's breast was now freed from the neckline of her gown, and it lay heavy and pale in the curve of the man's dark hand. His touch against her bared flesh was unhurried, gliding and strangely graceful. What he was doing made the woman smile into his eyes and cup his face in her hands. As they kissed, his thumb traced a path around her nipple, bringing it erect.

Gray's mouth fell open as she watched them, and her chest went tight. What would it feel like to have Duncan touch her in just this way, with his hand on her bare breast, with that look of intense concentration in his eyes? She loved the way it felt when Duncan kissed her as he had that day in the drawing room, that night by the garden gate. Would she have enjoyed it even more if his hands had been on her naked flesh?

From behind her there was the click of an opening lock, but as she stared at the people in the hall, Gray was barely aware of its significance.

Then the man in the hall lowered his head to the woman's breast, taking her nipple between his lips to suckle it. His mouth widened and narrowed as he drew on the tip, slowly, sensually, pleasing the woman in his arms.

Gray's body went liquid from her waist to her knees. She felt hot and weak and dizzy.

The woman arched her back, pressing hard against the banister as a soft moan rose in her throat. The tone was rich and raspy, incredibly articulate. She was almost purring.

The sound set sympathetic vibrations quivering in Grayson's chest. They spread down her arms and legs, trickled deep into her belly. There was a pull, a tightening along the midline of her body. It began between her thighs, clutched in her abdomen, spread to her breasts. Her lungs seemed to be on fire and her head went light. It was like the day Duncan had made her senses sing, when his hands and lips had wreaked such sweet havoc on her body. She didn't know what was happening to her now, didn't know what had happened to her then, but she knew that Duncan could help her understand. If only he would.

She turned to him with fierce color in her cheeks and fire in her eyes. But just then there was another sharp click from the strongbox, and she saw Duncan smile triumphantly.

"Only one more lock to go."

It wasn't quite the response she had hoped he would make, and her disappointment was compounded when she discovered that the couple kissing by the banister had made their way upstairs.

Still, she seemed more able to concentrate on keeping watch than she had been before. Her senses sharpened, and she became aware that the piano was no longer playing. She could hear the clink of empty glasses, as if the servants were collecting them for the night.

The woman in purple crossed her field of vision, headed toward the steps. Panic leaped in Grayson's chest. It would only be a minute or two before she discovered Duncan was gone.

"Hurry!" she whispered toward the man bent over the iron-bound chest. "Hurry, Duncan, hurry. She's on her way upstairs."

Duncan was cursing quietly and steadily as he worked the final lock. He seemed determined to get the papers even if the delay meant disaster for both of them.

There was a thud and a shout from the floor above, and Grayson had no doubt about what the woman in purple had found. In response to the commotion, several servants went racing upstairs after her.

Grayson turned just in time to see Duncan lifting the lid of the strongbox.

"Hurry, Duncan. Please," she whispered from the doorway. "Find the papers you need, and let's get out of here!"

There were footsteps thundering on the stairs, and the door opposite the office burst open with a crash. Then there were servants in the hall, standing so close Grayson could have touched them. Some of the harlots joined the search, and others clustered in the entrance, cutting off their escape.

Across the room Duncan was still riffling through what seemed like reams of paper, tossing sheets of it in the air. If he didn't find what he wanted soon, someone would surely find them.

As it was, Grayson didn't know how they would make their escape—until she realized the window was standing open to let in a breath of evening breeze. Locking the office door behind her, she hurriedly thrust up the sash. Their only hope of getting away was to leap from the window into the tiny yard a dozen feet below.

There was the thump of contact against the office door, and in an instant they could hear a woman shout. "He must have gone in here. Johnny, Johnny, come here and be quick about it!"

As Grayson lifted her legs to dangle them over the sill, there was the sound of more running footsteps and the crash of someone's shoulder battering at the door.

"Duncan!" she exhorted. "Duncan, please!"

He turned to her with papers in hand, then pushed her out the window and leaped over the sill right after her.

The door to the office banged open just as Palmer dropped, and the moment he hit the ground, they were racing across the tiny garden.

"Shoot, damn you! Shoot!" the woman yelled as Grayson and Duncan sprinted toward the carriage house. A bullet slammed into the brick above their heads, and several liveried servants burst into the yard.

Gray and Duncan ran headlong, past the stable and into the mews, along the back of the row of town houses and into the street. They could hear that there were people in pursuit, and they pushed themselves for greater speed. Their footsteps rang on the cobblestones as they skidded around the corner; there was no safety in silence, only in flight. They spent themselves relentlessly, racing through the warm spring evening.

At the next corner, Duncan would have turned south, toward Oxford Street and Mayfair, but Gray seized the sleeve of his jacket and pulled him in the opposite direction.

"Carriage waiting," she gasped, praying that it was. As they rounded the corner, she saw that the horse and driver were exactly where Gray had left them. They dived into the cab as it began to roll, the cabby whipping his horses as if sensing the chaos that had erupted behind them.

It was several minutes before they could catch their breath as they sprawled, hot and sweaty, on the floor of the coach. As soon as she could speak, Gray asked about the papers.

"I think I got what I needed. At least I hope I did. I've been investigating an embezzlement I suspect my uncle's partner of being involved in, and these will surely connect him to the crime."

Gray nodded in partial understanding, still too winded to say much more.

When she didn't reply, he reached across to catch her hand. "I owe you a lot for coming to my rescue tonight. But Grayson, with God as my witness, I had no intention of getting you involved in this."

She hesitated a moment, pushing her own concerns aside. She loved Duncan and she wanted to be sure he was safe. That was more important than anything.

"Is he a dangerous man, your uncle's partner?" she managed to ask.

"I think he'd kill me if he could."

"And is it possible he had you followed?"

"I suppose he might have, at that."

"Then, Duncan, I think you should know there are *two* sets of men following you."

"I really think you owe me an explanation for breaking off our betrothal."

Duncan and Grayson were seated at a table in a genteel little pub on a back street in St. James's Village. He had been all for taking her directly home after their escape from Sidney Layton's town house, but Grayson had insisted that they talk. And after what she'd done to help him tonight, Palmer didn't know how to refuse her.

He dreaded the conversation, though. He hated the lies and half-truths he was going to be forced to tell. He hated what they would do to Gray, hated the way they would make him feel. Still, there was no way to explain about the broken engagement without revealing the suspicions he was beginning to have about himself.

"I could have understood it, Duncan," Gray continued, "if you had withdrawn your offer of marriage the day you came to Worthington Hall with my betrothal ring. I could have accepted it then. My uncle would have made it difficult for you, but the two of us could have convinced him that a marriage between us would be a mistake. I think that in his heart, Uncle Warren only wants what's best for me."

Duncan tried to remember how he had felt the day he gave her the ring. He had been angry, filled with suspicion, frightened by the prospect of spending the rest of his life with her. But he had not been as frightened then as he was right now. He had given her the ring before the last of the West End Strangler's victims had been found, before he had awakened with the unexplained scratches on his face, before he had discovered the mysterious moonstone necklace tucked neatly inside his handkerchief. He had given her the ring before he had begun to wonder if, in another reality, he was killing women in London's streets.

He shuddered at the thought, and Grayson seemed to sense the depth of the turmoil within him.

"Please, Duncan," she whispered. "Can't you tell me what it is that's bothering you? I need to understand."

Oh, God, he thought as he looked away, surely he didn't deserve this kind of concern from her. There was worry in her face, boundless compassion in her eyes. She was making it so difficult to do what he must. He didn't want to hurt her.

But there was fear for Grayson stirring in him, too. It was better to let her think he was a cad than to go ahead and marry her. It would be better to hurt her feelings now than to awaken in his marriage bed and find Gray cold and broken beside him, the victim of a madman.

He tried to remember how he had felt the morning after their sojourn to Evans's, what it was he'd wanted then. He had been coldly furious with her for duping him into marriage. He had been torn between the desire to pay her back for deceiving him and the need to warn her away. He had to use those feelings, those suspicions, as an excuse to save her from herself, to prevent her from making a mistake she might very well die regretting.

He drew a long slow breath, staring down into his tankard of ale, mustering his concentration, every shred of courage he had.

"I'm breaking our engagement because you tricked me, because you planned the evening at Evans's to force me into marrying you." He made his accusation boldly, baldly, knowing it would be easier for both of them if the break was sharp and quick.

He saw her shrink away, saw an expression of reproach in her huge green eyes.

He didn't let her reaction stop him. "I know you had reached the point where you would have done anything to break things off with Harry, where you'd have risked everything you had for passage to America." He raised a hand to forestall any denial she was preparing to make. "It's something I might have done myself if I had been in your place. I can imagine how desperate you must have been. I know how badly you wanted your freedom, your chance to prove yourself as an actress. I understand your ambition, that search for approval that's driving you."

"Damn it, Duncan!" she interrupted, quite obviously furious at his condescension. "You don't know anything at all. I didn't plot against you. I didn't try to trap you into marriage. Please, Duncan, if you don't believe anything else about me, I want you to believe I wouldn't stoop to such vile manipulations. I wouldn't try to force you to marry me, not even to achieve something I want as much as I want to be an actress."

He shook his head, letting his expression reveal his doubt, letting it say he couldn't accept her explanations.

Her voice began to fray as Gray sought words to convince him. "The evening we went to Evans's it never occurred to me that we'd be found out. Harry's arrival at the supper room and my uncle's presence in the garden were as much a surprise to me as they were to you. It never crossed my mind that Uncle Warren might try to force you into marrying me. Besides, I gave you the chance to rescind your proposal. Why didn't you simply take it?"

Duncan smiled coldly. It reflected the way he felt inside. "By the time you gave me the chance to recant, I had already done some scheming of my own. I had decided to pay you back, and that option was no longer open to me."

"What exactly do you mean?"

"I had decided to go along with your uncle's plans and play the fawning fiancé. I meant to do everything your uncle wanted, then leave you waiting at the church."

Grayson could not have looked more stricken, more disillusioned, if he had slapped her. Her lips drew together in a soft, puckered "oh," and her face was the color of chalk. Her expression made him want to call back the words, made him want to take her in his arms and comfort her. But it was imperative that she believe him, and if what he'd said rang true, it was because he really had meant to abandon her.

He could sense her retreat from him, and he was glad of it. He could sense her outrage and her pain. If their relationship was to be severed, Grayson would have to come to hate him, to despise him for what he'd planned to do. She would have to detest him so completely and so thoroughly that there would be no reason for a wedding on Saturday. She had to be the one to call it off, and this was the surest way he knew to force her to do it.

"Is that why you gave me such an enormous ring?"

"You mean you didn't like it?"

"You meant for everyone to be aware of our engagement so that you could humiliate me at the church?"

"Something like that. Yes."

Her face began to crumple, and he could see her skim the edge of tears. Something in his chest contracted, and he buried his face and his misgivings in the depths of his pewter tankard.

"You wouldn't have been the first bride left waiting at St. George's Church," he observed as he glanced up at her over the rim. "There would have been a scandal, to be sure, but it wouldn't have lasted long."

It was as if she hadn't heard, as if nothing he'd said had mattered to her.

"You kissed me," she accused.

"Yes."

"You made love to me that day in the drawing room. You made me feel things I've never felt before, things I never knew were possible."

"Yes."

He remembered that day, too. As angry and confused as he'd been, he had known what she was feeling. He had gloried in his ability to give her pleasure, in her ability to experience it. Her passion had touched him in a way that had nothing to do with anger and manipulation, everything to do with tenderness and caring. It made him want to make love to her in earnest, sweetly, passionately, with all the depth of emotion she could stir in him.

"How could you have done that?" she demanded. "How could you have kissed me, touched me, made love to me as you did and felt nothing in return?"

How indeed? In truth he had felt a great deal for her, far more than he'd ever wanted to feel. But he couldn't think about that now. He couldn't let himself dwell on what she had come to mean to him. He had to remember that what seemed to her like cruelty was really kindness in disguise.

"And if you were so determined to see me humiliated," she went on, "why did you come to Worthington Hall this afternoon? Why did you decide to break the engagement instead of continuing with your plans? Why didn't you go ahead and leave me waiting at the church, make me the laughingstock of London?"

The woman's mind was as sharp as a blade, slashing through his hasty fabrications like a rapier through thin air. And what could he say? He couldn't tell Grayson that he had come to care for her. He couldn't reveal to her the doubts and fears that had been circling through his brain like a flight of bats in the twilight sky. He could not confide to her the terrifying half-formed suspicions that lay like a weight in the pit of his belly. There was no way to speak the truth.

In utter silence she stared at him, looking long and hard. It was as if she could see right through him, as if he'd turned as transparent as glass. But she couldn't read his mind. Gray couldn't know the things that were driving him. She had to take him at his word; there was no other course open to her.

When she finally moved, her hands lifted to the collar of her shirt, one finger dipping inside the circle of fabric to hook a strand of narrow blue ribbon. With a jerk she pulled it free and lifted the loop over her head. As she did he could see the emerald and diamond ring he'd given her hanging at the dip in the length of ribbon. She looked down at it for an instant, then pressed the ribbon and the ring into the palm of his hand.

It was warm from the contact with her skin. It carried the feel and heat and scent of her.

"If it is what you want, Duncan, the betrothal is over between us. You are free to leave for America any time you like." Slowly she rose to stand over him, staring down into his face. "But if you change your mind, I will be at St. George's on Saturday."

Without another word, without a backward glance, Grayson left Duncan at the table and made her way out into the night.

Seventeen

SOMETHING OLD—HER GRANDMOTHER'S GOLD-TIPPED IVORY FAN. Something new—the floor-length veil of gossamer silk and lace. Something borrowed—Julo's magnificent pink pearl necklace that lay framed by the portrait neckline of the luxurious gown. Something blue—the traditional blue ribbon garters that supported her pale petit-point stockings.

"And a penny for your shoe," Julo said, tucking the coin into the toe of one of the ivory kid slippers as Grayson was preparing to put them on.

Gray had upheld all the traditions, had done all the things that superstition decreed would make for a long and happy marriage. Now if only her groom was at the church when she arrived, she and Duncan might have a chance for a life together.

If he was there.

Grayson had seen neither hide nor hair of Duncan since she walked out of the tavern on Thursday night. He had not put in an appearance at the prenuptial party her aunt and uncle had given for a hundred and fifty of their closest friends the previous evening, and in spite of the story she gave that Duncan had been called to Portsmouth on a matter of grave importance, there had been more than a few raised eyebrows. Nor had there been any word from him, not so much as a line scribbled on a card, not so much as a word of reassurance passed on by Quentin the night before. It surprised Gray that her aunt and uncle had accepted her explanations for Duncan's absence with such aplomb. After the confrontation between the two men in the library, she had expected Warren Worthington to react to Palmer's truancy far more strongly than he had.

Going ahead with the wedding was the biggest gamble of

Grayson's life, and she only hoped that when the day was over they would not all be humiliated. They would escape scandal only if Duncan came to the church.

If he came. If.

Stepping before the full-length pier glass in her bedroom, Gray surveyed herself with a critical eye. The gown she wore was like something from a fairy tale. The neck was low and wide, edged by scallops of frothy lace that swirled down the center of the tight-fitting bodice and onto the sweeping skirt. At the bottom, the lacy overskirt blossomed into swoops of ruffles, and tucked into the delicate pattern was the gleam of hundreds of seed pearls. There were clusters of pearls in the gathers of the elbow-length sleeves, and more were sewn along the hem of the tumbling veil. It was the most beautiful dress Grayson had ever worn, and she wanted Duncan to realize she had dressed in it only for him.

Would he be at the church? Would he speak his vows? God, she prayed he would! She loved the man. She wanted to be his wife in every way. There was so much more to this marriage than needing to get to America, and she hoped he understood that.

In the weeks they had been together, in the moments they had shared, she had come to understand Duncan Palmer. She had discovered he was a man of strong convictions, a man with a mind of his own. He would never bow to convention for propriety's sake, and in spite of what he was expected to do, he would never be forced to wed. His admission that he had planned to walk away from the commitment confirmed all that.

But in returning his ring, Gray had given him a choice. For a man like Duncan Palmer, a choice might make this marriage possible. If he came to her today, if he was there at the church, it would only be because he wanted her for his wife, because he cared for her, at least a little. Gray knew she dared not hope for more.

As Grayson stood before the mirror lost in thought, Julo fluttered beside her, adjusting a ruffle here, a fold of fabric there. Her manner set Gray on edge. Did Julo know what she was facing as they prepared to go to the church? Did she have any idea what doubts and fears were swooping through Grayson's mind? In spite of the circumstances of the wedding, her adoptive aunt acted as if this was a marriage where the bride and groom honestly wanted a life together. She had given Gray advice, even spoke to her about the marriage bed. She had explained what Gray should expect and how she would feel as she embarked on her life with Duncan.

Flustered, Grayson pushed the thought away. She couldn't consider those things now, when everything was cloaked in uncertainty. She would think of what Julo had told her once Duncan had spoken his vows. Still, thoughts of being with Duncan strayed through her head, thoughts of his tenderness, his kisses, the passion he had evoked in her. What would married life really be with a man like Duncan as her lover?

There was a discreet knock on the door to Grayson's bedchamber.

"Your grace, Lady Grayson," a young housemaid announced, "the coach is waiting."

Grayson squared her shoulders and clasped her aunt's small hand in hers as they made their way down the stairs.

"Something old, something new, something borrowed, something blue." Gray whispered the old rhyme like a prayer for a happy marriage, like a litany to give her courage when she had never been more frightened and unsure. As she entered the flower-decked coach prepared for the short drive to the church, she only hoped those ancient charms had real power, that they would somehow work their magic for her.

Grayson had been right, Duncan was forced to admit. There *were* people following him. And this morning, just after ten o'clock, a pair of them—only one pair—had arrived at the town house to help him dress for his wedding.

They were the Duke of Fennel's men—sober, tough, and determined. They had come to make certain Duncan showed up at the church, that he didn't disappoint his bride. They watched over him as he bathed, shaved, and dressed for the ceremony, and Palmer was very sure that they would have overseen the process at gunpoint if such a desperate measure had proved necessary.

He'd tried to make his decision about Grayson as he sprawled alone and sleepless in his bed the night before. Did he love Gray? He wasn't sure. Did he want her? There had never been any question about that. Was he going to take her as his wife? That was what had kept him lying awake until the birds had begun to stir.

Who and what he was had made the question nearly impossible to answer. He was the son of a man who had beaten his wife. He was a boy who had murdered his father. He was torn by bitterness and remorse, by emotions so deep, so all-encompassing that he wondered if he would ever be free of them. He had loved his father and he had hated him. He had worshiped his mother and he had pitied her. Those feelings were even more hopelessly tangled and confused after seventeen years of wondering than they had been on the night his parents died. They were twisted by the boy he was then and the man he had become. But at the core of everything he said and did was his desperate need to be free of the past.

If he married Grayson, he would never be free. She would be a tangible tie to England, a constant reminder of the failures in his parents' marriage. She could make the two of them relive the nightmares from his childhood with him and Gray cast in his parents' roles. Would he abuse Grayson as his father had abused his mother? Would he let jealousy and uncertainty override any love he might come to feel for her? Would he turn into the monster his father had become, controlling Grayson's actions by fear of retribution? When Worthington had warned him against abusing Gray, Palmer had denied he ever would. But when he thought about his past, he wasn't sure he should have promised that.

Gray was a strong-minded woman with ambitions of her own. Underlying all his feelings for her was his respect and his desire to see her succeed. But in a marriage forced upon them by convention, would her determination threaten him, driving him to control her by whatever means he could? He didn't want to believe that such a thing could happen, but how could he be sure?

Further from the surface, but perhaps even more important, was his fear of what he might already be—a man who walked the streets preying on defenseless women. A murderer. A madman. The concurrence of the West End Strangler's crimes and the times when he could not explain where he'd been or what he'd done terrified him. He had proved himself capable of killing with his bare hands by choking a man to death in an alley in Limehouse. Was that only one in a series of strangulations? Had his proficiency at murder come from oft-repeated experience? Was it possible that there were things inside him he could neither fathom nor control?

If he married Grayson, how could he protect her? How could he prevent her from falling prey to the Strangler's madness? How could he keep her safe when he might be his father's son in every way?

Yet this was Grayson whom he must refuse, Grayson who to

Worthington looked away, his eyes suspiciously bright. "I waited far too long to tell you. I know that and I'm sorry."

There was so much more for them to say, but that couldn't happen here and now. The music had begun to swell, and the guests were waiting in the church. Gray squared her shoulders and raised her chin. Even if Duncan had not come to make her his bride, at least she would have this.

Warren Worthington took her hand in his and, gently, reassuringly, placed it in the crook of his elbow.

As they stepped into the nave, Grayson's fears returned. Duncan would be at the altar, wouldn't he? Surely her guardian wouldn't have let things go this far if Duncan wasn't waiting.

The guests formed an impenetrable wall of bodies to her right and left, pale faces peering at her from either side of the aisle. All she could see ahead of her was the mosaic of colored light the stained-glass windows cast on the marble floor. All she could hear was the swell of the organ reverberating around them. Everything seemed unreal to her, far less real than if she were a character in a play; in a play she would have known her lines, known what was expected of her, known how all this would end. Living in a world of make-believe was so much easier than facing reality.

Grayson supposed she nodded at people she knew, supposed she smiled, as a happy bride should, but the only thing she could think about was whether Duncan would be standing at the altar. She was three pews from the chancel when she caught a glimpse of his chestnut hair glinting in the sun, and the rush of relief that swept through her was tantamount to a tidal wave. Her mouth was desert-dry and her knees quivered beneath the layers of lacy petticoats. Her face was blazing hot, though inside she was shivering.

Then somehow she was standing next to Duncan, looking up into his sun-darkened face, staring into his clear blue eyes. He looked so solemn standing there, so serious. So condemned. This was what she wanted, wasn't it? This was the man she loved.

Her gaze moved past him to where his cousin stood, weaving slightly, at Duncan's right, then went on to the pair of men who seemed to be stationed at the vestry door. They were not dressed like their fashionable counterparts around the hall, and suddenly Grayson understood. They had brought Duncan here against his will. Without their intervention there would have been no bridegroom to meet her as St. George's today.

The realization was chilling, and her nervousness dropped away and, with it, the illusions she had cherished in her heart. Duncan wasn't here because she had given him a choice; he was here because others had denied it. He wasn't here because he cared for her; they had somehow forced him into this.

No one spoke when the minister asked if there was just cause why they couldn't be lawfully joined together. Neither she nor Duncan answered when he inquired if there was any impediment to their union. They both promised to love, honor, and keep the other in sickness and in health. They agreed to forsake all others for the sake of their love. But the vows were empty, as hollow as Duncan's words ringing through the church, as echoing as the void Gray felt within herself.

"Who giveth this woman to be married to this man?"

"Her guardian, the Duke of Fennel."

Grayson knew without a doubt why Duncan was here. It had been Warren Worthington's doing, his determination to see her wed. In his bid to marry her off, in his determination to avoid a scandal, in his need to control every aspect of her life, he was making Duncan marry her. The words of pride and approval Worthington had said at the head of the aisle were spurious, cheap. They had not been said to express his inner feelings; they had been meant to manipulate her. The urge to weep was overwhelming. She wanted to turn and run. Then fury seized her, molten and hot. Never in her life had Grayson been so hurt, so angry, so humiliated. Never in her life would she forgive her guardian's callousness.

When the minister took her fingers from Worthington's palm and placed them in Palmer's waiting hand, it took an act of will to keep from jerking away. Yet for all that Duncan did not want to marry her, his clasp was firm and warm, oddly reassuring.

She looked up at Duncan again, and he allowed her the slightest of smiles. It was a smile that made the words he was saying all the more painful for her to hear.

"I, Captain Duncan Palmer, Marquis of Antire, take thee Lady Grayson Ware to be my lawfully wedded wife, to have and to hold from this day forward . . ." The words went on and on: "For better or worse . . . to love and to cherish, till death us do part."

Her own replies were no less frigid than his, no less tragic for her to speak. She loved Duncan with all her heart, and yet the vows she spoke might as well have been a curse.

"According to God's holy ordinance"—Grayson felt she might be struck down where she stood as she murmured the words—"and thereto I plight thee my troth."

Then Duncan was placing a circlet of gold on her finger. It was a broad band set with three shimmering diamond baguettes. It was a beautiful ring, far more tasteful and refined than her engagement ring had been. When he gave her that monstrosity it had been his intention to taunt and embarrass her, to blatantly seal his possession of her before he walked away. Her guardian had made certain Duncan would not carry out his plans, but that act made this ceremony even more of a travesty.

But then Grayson became aware that there was another ring in Duncan's hand, another ring sliding onto her finger as if to lock the first in place. It was the emerald and diamond ring she had returned to him in the tavern two nights before.

She stared down at it, caught her breath, then looked up into Duncan's face. An expression of tenderness hovered and settled in the cerulean depths of his eyes.

"With this ring, Grayson, I thee wed."

Confusion hummed in her head. What did he mean? Why had he placed the second ring on her finger? Could it mean that she mattered to him? Was there really a chance for them to make a life together?

She wanted to shout the questions, wanted them to echo around the church. She wanted to demand that Duncan answer them before the clergyman declared them man and wife. But it was too late, the words of declaration were spoken for all to hear and the cleric was beaming at them over the rim of his prayer book.

"You may kiss the bride, my lord," he said.

Duncan's hand came to touch the side of Grayson's jaw, slid like swansdown along the curve of her throat. His kiss was cool and brief, but his tenderness was genuine.

They led the recession up the aisle amid smiles and whispered good wishes. Outside, the waiting people cheered. As they stepped into Duncan's carriage for the ride to Worthington Hall for the reception that would follow, there was a smile on Grayson's lips and a faint insistent flicker of hope for a happy future deep within her heart.

Eighteen

THE CANDLES WERE LIT. A BOTTLE OF CHAMPAGNE WAS CHILLING in an ice-filled monteith. The covers on the bed had been turned neatly aside and the sheets beneath them dusted with rose petals.

The bride was ready to greet her groom. Her bath was completed and taken away. Her hair was brushed to a ruddy sheen. She wore an ivory satin nightdress trimmed with lace that gleamed like gold and alabaster in the halo of muted candlelight. She was beautiful, enticing, and quaking inside.

The reception at Worthington Hall had passed in a blur. There had been food and wine and music and hundreds of people wishing them well. Duncan had carried off the role of doting bridegroom with unimpeachable conviction, and there had been moments when Gray could almost have let herself believe that everything between them was exactly as it should have been. But it was not. Her uncle's men had brought Duncan to the church, and no matter how companionably she and her new husband had talked and laughed, how gracefully they had swirled across the dance floor, how cordially they had acknowledged the toasts to their health and happiness, Gray knew there were things to resolve between them once they were alone.

Her nervousness about being with Duncan in her new bedroom in the town house on Berkeley Square was heightened by the advice her aunt had offered when she had come to Grayson early this morning.

"Men have physical needs," Aunt Julo had begun sagely as she settled herself on the edge of Grayson's bed, "needs that find a warm and deep expression within the bonds of marriage. And women have needs, too, no matter what some claim. When

Duncan comes to your room tonight, he will want many intimate things of you. He may want to touch and kiss your breasts, and you must let him. He may want to caress you in private ways and places that may seem shocking to you at first, but you must submit. He may ask you to touch and caress him, too, and you must do whatever he requires. The things that Duncan will want of you will bring you pleasure, if only you allow yourself to feel it. They will bring satisfaction to you both and make you truly a woman."

That afternoon in the drawing room just a week before, Gray had become stunningly aware of all the marvelous, frightening things that Duncan could make her feel: the sweetness and communion that flowed between them when they kissed, the security and warmth she felt when she was pressed close at his side, the trembling confusion that crowded in her veins when his hands moved over her. She suspected that tonight they would share all of that and more, and though her stomach dipped and quivered at the thought, she was filled with mounting eagerness.

It was the question of his intent in marrying her that plagued her as she awaited his approach. What reason did he have for playing the doting groom if their marriage was something he did not want? Why had he placed the emerald ring on her finger at the end of the ceremony as if he meant it to seal the bond between them? She tried to remember the expression on his face as the pastor had pronounced them man and wife. There had been pride and possessiveness in Duncan's eyes, a flash of defiance, and another emotion she could not name. How did Duncan really feel? What would he say and do when he finally came to her?

As the house went quiet around her, Grayson's heart skipped quick and light inside her chest. She prowled the room as she waited, plucking at the flowers on the nightstand, pulling back the tasseled curtain and staring out into the night, rearranging the gaily patterned ginger jars arrayed across the mantelpiece. She picked up a book and tried to read, pulled a wrapper around her shoulders against the chill. She twirled the bottle of champagne in the bowl of melting ice, smoothed the covers on the bed, and tried the latch on the connecting door to Duncan's room. The clock in the hall pealed out the passing hours, striking one o'clock, one-thirty, two.

About quarter after two there were signs of life in Duncan's room. There was the sound of footsteps, of drawers opening, of muted conversation. A few minutes later she heard Duncan bid his valet good night, heard Barnes move off down the carpeted hall.

Hardly daring to breathe, Grayson waited for Duncan's arrival, waited to hear the rattle of his hand on the latch, waited for the door to open, waited for him to call her to his side. She stood by the window, trembling, listening, hoping. But Duncan didn't come.

The candles around her bedchamber were guttering in their holders; the unopened bottle of champagne was awash in melted ice. The rose petals on the sheets looked limp and bruised, though no one had lain upon them. Then all at once Grayson realized that Duncan was never going to come to her. Her guardian and his men might have been able to ensure Palmer's attendance at the church, might even have made him speak his vows. But they could not force him to consummate a marriage he did not want, no matter how they threatened him.

Disillusionment sucked the strength from Grayson's limbs, brought tears that burned like acid to the corners of her eyes. She sank into a slipper chair beside the hearth, pressing her fingers against her lips in an attempt to quell her rising panic. Gray might well be Duncan's bride, but he was not going to make her his wife. In spite of all that had passed between them, in spite of the understanding she thought they'd shared, Duncan didn't want her.

Yet of her feelings for Duncan there was no doubt. Gray loved him. She wanted him. She needed his sage counsel, his strength, his tenderness. He alone seemed able to see beyond the facade she showed to the world, recognize her doubts and aspirations, her ambitions and liabilities. He had freely offered her an understanding and encouragement she had never known, and his unquestioning acceptance had won her heart. There was such potential in what had already passed between them that she longed for all the wondrous possibilities laid out before them now. But what chance would their marriage have if she allowed Duncan to withdraw from her? What kind of future could they hope for if he denied them union now?

Panic tightened in the back of her throat as Grayson stole toward the door to Duncan's room. Beyond the wide double panels were a man and a life she longed to embrace. How could she hope to achieve happiness in her marriage to Duncan if he staunchly refused to come to her, even on their wedding night?

As things stood now, they could go on as strangers bound

together in the eyes of God and man, never touching, never sharing, never communicating their desires and fears and needs. They could live as husband and wife forever without experiencing the joy she believed they could find together, without fulfilling the promise of their joining.

The thought of living such a life appalled her. It was more disturbing than marriage to Harry Torkington, more distressing than living forever alone. Being wed and remaining apart would bring a loneliness so profound that it could destroy them both, a meaninglessness that would slowly undercut their appreciation of everything around them. It would be hell on earth to know the depth of feeling Duncan was capable of, to love him unequivocally and be denied a communion that would enrich them both. If Gray wanted all that Duncan could give to her, wanted to offer all she could give to him, the only choice she had was to risk her pride and go to him.

The decision froze her where she stood. The realization of what she must do to become Duncan's wife in every way stirred a morass of horrible doubts. Was she brave enough to go to the man who had refused to come to her? Did she want Duncan enough to risk his rejection? What would she do if she went to him and he turned away?

It was the memory of Duncan's lips and hands on her body that firmed her resolve. That his trembling touch and shuddering breath were part of the lovemaking she had already experienced reminded her that Duncan was no more immune to her than she was to him, reminded her that her untutored caresses were every bit as potent as his skillful, far more practiced ones. That his kisses were filled with passion, that his touch against her skin was imbued with ardor and tenderness, helped her to believe that Duncan felt the bond between them, too. He might not love her as she loved him, but he cared for her. She was sure that Duncan cared.

Her hand was shaking as she reached for the doorknob. There was fear on the back of her tongue. But drawing herself up to a regal height, Gray slowly opened the connecting door.

Even in the darkened chamber, she could sense Duncan's presence immediately. There were wafting tendrils of bay rum drifting on the heavy air, the rhythm of his breathing, the faint outline of his body beneath the sheet. His aura beckoned her irresistibly, drawing her slowly toward the bed as if with invisible tethers.

This was the man she wanted more than any man in the world, Gray reminded herself. Duncan Palmer was the man she loved, and now that he was her husband, she had every right to be with him.

Trying to ignore the wild thumping of her heart, Grayson eased herself onto the edge of the high, half-canopied bed. Beside her Duncan lay motionless and silent, as if he was already deeply asleep. As she hovered at his side, her gaze moved over him. His profile was dark against the stark white of the linen pillowcases; his heavy hair was mussed and disarrayed. She could see the faint marks that ranged down across his cheek and was appalled that anyone could hurt him in such a fearsome, wicked way. She traced the lines to the turning of his jaw where the scratches faded and disappeared, let her regard slip over the cords and hollows of his throat. Above the covers his chest and shoulders were bare, the hard muscles delineated by the faint amber light that glimmered through the open door. His arms lay on the top of the sheet, the undulations of muscle and sinew and bone pleasing in their symmetry.

She wanted him. With her heart and her mind, she wanted him. Deep down at the hungering core of her womanhood, she wanted him. And if she wanted him, if she really wanted him, she had to act to make him hers. It was the love she felt for him that gave her the determination to do what she must.

"Duncan." His name slid like satin ribbons through the night. "Duncan."

As she spoke, her hand stroked his jaw, traversed the expanse of vulnerable throat, and came to rest on the dip of hair-roughened skin just above his breastbone.

"Duncan?"

He stirred and turned his head as if newly roused. "Grayson?" His voice was drowsy and deep. "Grayson, what are you doing here?"

She did not answer him with words. There was no need to tell him why she'd come.

Instead she bent to press a warm, evocative kiss against his mouth. She let it say what she would not, let the bittersweet movement of her lips chide him for rejecting her, let the press and retreat of her mouth promise the infinite wonders a man and woman could share. She let it rouse his passions and her own, let it hint at the world of pleasure that lay well within their grasp.

His hands came up to grip her arms, the thrust of his thumbs biting deep as they pushed her away, the pressure of his fingers drawing her close. His hold hurt, but only a little. His actions gave proof of the struggle within him.

She let her tongue dally at the seam of his lips, soothing, prodding, provoking him. His mouth gave beneath her gentle stroke. It softened, widened, providing access to what she craved. She took the half-measure for what it was, a breach in his defenses, an unwilling invitation.

Gray stroked the outline of his lips, savoring the taste and texture that were uniquely Duncan's own. She brushed the moist inviting corners of his mouth, the ridge of his straight white teeth. He opened to her reluctantly, inciting a sweet invasion. She claimed the territory of his mouth as her own, pressing deep with fleeting strokes, exploring with languorous ease. Her tongue feathered over his, taunting, teasing, enticing. His resistance seemed to wilt with every foray she made.

"Grayson. Grayson, no." His hands tightened on her arms as he struggled with himself and her, seeking to deny them both.

Though she heard his murmured protest, Gray pressed on, kissing him until his breathing went sharp and deep, until she felt the muscles knot along her side, until he stirred restlessly beside her.

She gloried in her own response to him, the dizzying sensation of bubbles bursting in her blood. She tingled and she warmed. She fluttered and succumbed. As she did, her hands moved over his smooth bare skin, one skimming the expanse of sculptured flesh, the other raking into his heavy hair. She moved against him as she deepened the kiss, giving herself entirely.

Duncan moaned helplessly, deep in his throat, as his hand came to cup her breast. The weight of it nestled into his open palm. His thumb moved to stroke the tightening tip. Sensation sizzled through her.

Then as if suddenly realizing what he'd done, Duncan tried to pull away. Gray moved with him as he did, not permitting him to relinquish his hold on her, not allowing him the slightest retreat.

With the press of her flesh to his, with the fullness of her breast contoured to his hand, the last of his resistance seemed to sift away. She could feel his fingers move over her of their own accord, closing to claim and savor her. His kiss began to echo hers, his tongue entering the tender tryst. He drew softly on her mouth, his lips clinging, searching, acknowledging the growing need inside them both.

He dragged her down beside him on the bed, pulling her across his body, pressing her back into the enveloping softness of the feather tick. His thigh came to lie across her hips. She could feel the comforting weight of it holding her down, feel the imprint of his arousal pressed hard against her side. Heat spread from the places where their bodies touched, radiating through the adjacent flesh like the glow of a well-banked fire through a chilly room. Until that moment Gray had not fully realized how cold and barren she had felt without him at her side.

She caught her breath as his mouth covered hers again, as his lips brushed and dallied enticingly. They teased her softly parted mouth, hovering and retreating, returning and savoring her as if she were some delicacy he'd begun to crave. His hunger for her was growing. She could sense it in the longer and longer drafts he took of her, in the ravenous way he claimed her mouth, stroking her lips with his tongue, nibbling compulsively, drinking deep.

His hand was on her breast, cradling the fullness in his palm, his thumb stirring relentlessly against the tip. There was the rasp of the satin and lace nightdress against her engorged nipple, the insistent pressure that made her arch into the movements of his hand. She quickened to his touch, shivering. Aching sweetness trembled through her body until she thought she might go mad with the need to feel his hands on her naked flesh.

Then he was tugging at the fasteners of her wrapper and gown, raising her shoulders from the bed. With practiced ease he swept her clothes and the blankets away. They lay naked together on the rumpled sheets, each clearly revealed to the other by the silvery light of the fading moon. That light pearled the pink and cream of her flesh, which gleamed like alabaster alongside the smooth, hard planes of his sun-darkened skin. It highlighted the arching curves and angles of their bodies, cast the hollows in mysterious shadows that begged to be explored.

"You're more beautiful than I ever dreamed," he whispered against her shoulder, as if he felt compelled to reassure her, to offer recompense for what he had tried so hard to deny them both. "Oh, Grayson, you can't know how often I've thought of you like this, how desperately I've wanted you."

Further assurance of her loveliness came in the worshipful

sweep of his caress. It skimmed downward from her throat, across the plain of sensitive skin between her breasts, down the midline of her body to her waist. It flared along the rise of her hip, his thumb tracing her hipbone, moving along the petal-soft skin at the curve of her belly. His fingers brushed the top of her thigh, paused, then returned along a different route, hovering over the cluster of curls at the joining of her legs.

She sighed as he touched her there, the place where she most wanted him to touch her. With the exquisite eloquence of that gentle stroke, delight trickled through Grayson, making her weak. It pooled deep within her chest and seeped slowly down her arms and legs. It gathered at the juncture of her thighs, thickening and warming like honey in the sun. What she felt as she nestled in his arms was so much more potent than mere pleasure, so much more binding than simple desire. It was the melding of wonder and love, the merging of understanding and ecstasy. It was everything she had hoped to find when she had come to Duncan's room, the reward she had hoped to win when she exposed her vulnerability.

Sprawled barely a hand's span apart, they let their fingers flutter and stroke of their own accord. His touch was as soft and tentative as hers, though no less compelling. Her exploration was as gentle as his, though no less complete. She came to know the straining texture of his flesh. He came to learn the moist convolutions of hers. As they moved in tandem, giving and receiving pleasure, the emotions glittering in the depths of their eyes gave proof of all they could not say.

They kissed and Duncan's tongue echoed the movements of his hand. They touched and Gray drew him toward her, welcoming him, willing him to take her completely. Like a hard, heavy wind driven before a storm, the urge for coupling swept over them. It tangled them together as he rolled over her, as she opened soft and moist beneath him. It made them one as he sought delicious solace in her flesh, as he bestowed on her the wondrous favor of himself.

She sighed as he came into her, a sigh of swift dark pain, a sigh of ultimate completion. She closed her eyes and smiled into the night. He was part of her now; they were totally joined, inseparably one. He could no longer deny the bond of sweet possession. She was his. He was hers. They were united in every way.

That joining was all Gray had hoped it would be. It was a breathless wonder that welled between them, the nectar of two lives merging in the dark. It was an answer to the impossibly desperate need that ran so strong in both of them. It was reassurance that his concern and desire for her were everything she had hoped they would be. And it was more.

With unutterable tenderness Duncan moved over her, inside her. The exquisite care he took with her assured her of his deep commitment as words could not. The movements of his body were rhythmic and gentle, filling her with joy, with wild delight. The fervid kisses he pressed upon her mouth were desperate and deep, confirming that he was as lost in bliss as she.

In response to those heated kisses and tender strokes, Gray quivered and trembled, swelled and burst, shattering with a beauty she had never known. Pure heart-stopping pleasure rushed through her to the farthest reaches of her body, invading the substance of every cell. She gave herself to the sensation, reveling in the selflessness of the man who had taken her for his bride and joined his life to hers.

Even lost in the rapture of her own completion, she could tell that Duncan's passion was blossoming, too. She felt him clutch her to him with a fine-edged desperation that verged on frenzy, heard him gasp in the shuddering world of utter release. She let his satisfaction feed her own, let it take her once more into the bright, unfurling world of pleasure and delight, the magnificent sweetness of communion that was selfless and complete.

Then they were drifting together, buffeted by slow lilting waves of ebbing bliss, floating at the soft muted edge of helpless rapture. They kissed, nestled, curled together. They slept as the moon's pale light crept silently away, as the darkness of the waning night retreated, making room for the glory of the bright new dawn.

Nineteen

DUNCAN HOVERED ON THE FRINGES OF SLEEP, FEELING MORE CONtented than he had in months. Beside him Grayson lay drowsing, her shoulders and hips nestled to the curl of his body, her heavy hair streaming back over the pillows to rest beneath his cheek. Smiling to himself, he turned his face into the silken mass, liking the coolness of it against his skin, the sweet gardenia scent that clung to the waving strands.

They had made love again in the dawn, coming together slowly in the pale light of early morning. The faint color in the sky had given Grayson's flesh a dewy glow, turning it a luminous shell pink along the tops of her breasts and thighs, while the rest of her lay cloaked in enticing shadow. The joining had been good—better than good—for both of them, and Duncan was amazed by Gray's uninhibited response to him. She seemed to understand on a level that went beyond words that bestowing pleasure was as vital as receiving it, that loving at its best meant sharing every part of herself.

It was he who had been unable or unwilling to share all of himself as they'd made love, he who had held back when she was as open and as giving as a woman could be. The reasons for his reticence dishonored him, but only a little.

The decision to marry Grayson was one he had come to on his own, in spite of how it must have looked to her. Since the night she had given him back his ring, Duncan had been wrestling with the only options open to him: he could leave for Portsmouth and New York, or he could stay in London and make Grayson his bride. It had been a difficult question to resolve, mitigated by concerns and doubts that Gray could never know. But in the end his feelings for the woman at his side had made it impossible for him to heartlessly abandon her. But pressed as he had been by Fennel's men to attend the ceremony and speak his vows, Duncan had become even more determined not to consummate the marriage, for Grayson's sake. If their union was one in word but not in fact, an annulment, should there be a reason for Gray to want one, would be easier to obtain. It was the only way he knew to protect Gray from what he was, or from what he had begun to fear he might be.

Yet it had been nearly impossible to come to his room last night and prepare for bed, knowing Grayson was waiting on the opposite side of the connecting door, knowing that she must be expecting him. It had been exquisite torture to know that in the eyes of God and society Grayson was his wife and still not have the right to go to her. Neither his grim resolve nor the quantity of brandy he had consumed had been able to ease the lonely ache inside his chest when he knew she was so near at hand.

Once Barnes had left him alone, Duncan had lain staring into the dark, trying to ignore the faint ribbon of amber light that seeped across the floor from the room adjoining his own. He'd closed his eyes and rolled away, trying to put Grayson out of his mind, trying to believe that self-denial was the most noble choice he could have made.

Yet Gray had filled his thoughts; the memory of her beauty was a merciless goad, his desire for her a constant threat to the decision he had made. Was she waiting for him still, he had found himself wondering, sleeping alone in her marriage bed? Had she accepted that he was never going to come to her? Was she confused and hurt by his rejection? Was she angry? Had she cried? Would she hate him for what his doubts and fears were forcing him to do? Could he explain his reasons for rejecting her without revealing the secrets he was forced to keep?

When he heard her open the door between their connecting rooms, he had gone perfectly still, unable to believe that Gray had come, stunned by her boldness and her courage. Didn't she know what she was risking by seeking him out? Wasn't she afraid he would reject her in fact as he had by his inattentiveness? As her feet whispered across the carpeted floor, he had feigned sleep, hoping Gray would leave him in peace, praying she would allow him the sacrifice he was fully prepared to make.

Instead of leaving, she had come to sit beside him on the bed, and wanting had sifted through him like heavy fog. His head had gone light and his mouth dry as he realized that well within his reach was the woman he wanted more than any other woman in the world. How, he had wondered as his heart drummed and fluttered in his ears, could he refuse to make Grayson his wife in every way when she was offering herself so openly?

His muscles had gone tight and hot as she'd spoken his name. His body had begun to ache as she'd trailed her fingers along his throat. He had stirred and murmured her name, knowing it was more dangerous to ignore her than to acknowledge that she'd come. His hands had closed around her arms, and he'd tried to push her away. It was to his eternal damnation that he had lacked the strength to deny them both. She'd bent above him and let her mouth drift over his, teasing, fluttering, soft, and unutterably sweet. He'd closed his eyes and tried to think, tried to deny the delectable promise of her lips.

It was the prod of her seeking tongue that had sent desire flaring through him like a blinding light, skittering along his nerves like an electric charge. His brain had ceased to function and his reason had flown away. In spite of his best resolves, he'd begun to kiss her back. Then his hand had found the swell of her breast and he'd been lost, unwillingly lost, hopelessly lost, unequivocally lost.

In the delicious sensual haze that had enveloped them, Gray was all he had ever dreamed she could be: temptress, virgin, lover, wife. He had treated her with all the care and consideration he could muster, courting her with his kisses, preparing her with his caresses, holding back his need until she was ready to accept him. When she had opened her delicate, untried body to him, when he'd pressed into her yielding flesh, he had felt a completion and delight that had shattered his perceptions of the world.

Even now, in the cool dim light of day, the acceptance he had sensed in her as they made love was beyond his ability to comprehend. He had been reluctant to take her as his bride, had tried to break off their betrothal, had told her he had meant to leave her waiting at the church. He had rejected her as cruelly as any man could, refused to make her his wife in the most intimate of ways. Yet Grayson had still come to him. She had bestowed her passion and sweetness like a gift, offered him a satisfaction and communion he had never hoped to have. She had given all of herself, risking her pride, risking her feelings. He didn't understand the reasons for what she'd done. He didn't understand Grayson herself. Yet deep inside he was glad she'd had the courage to seek him out, glad he'd given her his name, glad he'd made her his wife in every way. She'd lit a fierce flicker of hope and joy deep within his heart, and he vowed to protect her and care for her and cherish her above all else. He closed his eyes and pulled her close, letting the peace of drowsy contentment settle over him like a balm.

From beside him, Grayson heard Duncan's breathing slow and deepen, felt the arm that lay across her waist go heavy and slack. She stared toward the windows where the sky beyond was turning from powder blue to mauve, and she smiled to herself, thinking of the night they'd spent together. She had been right in coming to him, in braving the dangerous darkness of his silent bedchamber. Once Duncan had acknowledged her, once he had surrendered to the passion that existed between them, everything had been sweet, magnificent, right. Gray's face warmed with the memory of what they'd done, of how wonderful it was to be Duncan's wife in every way.

The color was still bright in Grayson's cheeks when she heard footsteps in the hall, an opening door, a breathless gasp. Scrambling into a sitting position, Grayson peered over the contours of Duncan's body and the drape of rumpled sheet toward where Ryan Barnes stood frozen in the doorway of the bedchamber, a heavy covered tray balanced in his hands. The expression on the valet's face was one of shock and outrage.

"Good God!" Barnes finally whispered, scandalized. "I did not expect to find you *here*!"

Gray's chin came up and there was more than a hint of challenge in her tone. "And why wouldn't you expect to find me here?" she whispered back. "Lord Antire is my husband, after all. And this is the morning after our wedding night."

At the sound of their voices, Palmer mumbled and stirred, but did not waken.

Sharp disapproval narrowed Ryan's features as he went on, his manner rife with insolence. "Of course, my lady, you have a perfect right to be anywhere in the house you choose. I only thought a proper bride would be content to wait in her own bed for the attendance of her groom."

Grayson drew a hissing breath, then caught her lower lip between her teeth. On the first morning of her new life, it seemed unwise to make an enemy of her new husband's most trusted servant. Still, Gray was furious at being chastened by a mere valet, even a valet who had been with the Palmer family for years and years. Barnes's comment also indicated that he knew of Duncan's reticence to come to her the night before and heartily approved of the decision his master had made. That his manservant should be privy to Duncan's thoughts when she was not incensed Grayson, threatened her, and made her even angrier than before.

Yet having some inkling of the bond between Duncan and Ryan Barnes, Gray was determined to put a different face on what she felt. In a situation as tenuous as hers, it was not wise to alienate her husband's only confidant.

"Well, I can see why you might be surprised to find me here," she began, forcing herself to smile, "but perhaps it is a circumstance you should come to expect in the days to come."

Hostility flared in Barnes's dark eyes. His disapproval seemed to become more conspicuous, more insidious, more deeply entrenched. "As you say, my lady. It is something I may be *forced* to accept."

In that instant the battle lines were drawn, with Duncan Palmer's loyalty as the prize.

They glared at each other for another moment before Barnes cleared his throat. "My lord," he began in a voice that should have been able to raise the dead. "I have brought you coffee, and I fear it's growing cold."

Blinking in confusion, Duncan pushed up on his elbows. "Oh, good morning, Barnes. It looks like another lovely day."

"Indeed, my lord, it does."

Then suddenly Duncan realized that Grayson was curled in the bed beside him, and he flushed like a schoolboy. It was as if he was embarrassed to have Barnes arrive unannounced in his bedchamber.

The servant seemed to sense his master's uneasiness and take pleasure in it. Still, when he spoke, Barnes's words were no more than they should have been. "Your coffee, my lord?"

Duncan shrugged and made a vague motion in the direction of the desk. "Just put it over there," he answered. "Then you may leave and wait downstairs until I see fit to ring for bathwater."

Barnes did as he was told, and bowed stiffly at the door. "And how long do you think it will be before you'll want your bath?"

Gray was instantly aware of the valet's ploy and the need for control that lay behind the question. In response she smiled and, beneath the cover of the elevated sheet, slid her hand the length of her husband's thigh.

Duncan's response was everything she might have hoped. It was as if a dazzling light had been lit behind his eyes, as if he'd forgotten everything in the room except the woman in bed beside him.

What the valet could not see, he seemed to sense. His body went as stiff as an oaken plank.

"Your bathwater, my lord?" Barnes prodded. "How long before you plan to ring for it?"

Duncan seemed barely aware that Barnes was there. "Oh, it will be quite a while, I think," he answered abstractedly. "It might be quite a while indeed."

"There's a tradesman to see you, sir," one of the footmen announced from the doorway of the study.

"A tradesman?" Quentin Palmer asked, glancing up from the drifts of unpaid bills spread out across the surface of the desk. He had been trying to separate them into two neat piles: those that had to be paid immediately and those that could be put off for another month or two. Had this man come to demand money for some service he had rendered? Quentin wondered in alarm. How was he to explain that his appalling lack of funds prevented him from paying up?

"Yes, sir. It's a tradesman, sir. Someone by the name of John Leaphorn."

Quentin's expression froze. Leaphorn never came to the house. He always sent a message to set up a meeting at a tavern or in his rooms. If Leaphorn had come to see him here, something had to be desperately wrong.

"Please send him to me," Quentin said, trying to keep the rush of panic he was feeling from infecting his voice and manner.

A few moments later the servant returned with Leaphorn trailing in his wake.

"It's good of you to see me, sir," the smuggler began, doffing his hat and adopting a properly servile tone for the waiting footman's benefit.

"I know you wouldn't have come," Quentin murmured, dismissing the servant with a wave of his hand, "unless it was something quite important."

"Indeed it is, sir." Leaphorn inclined his head politely as the door was closed. "Indeed it is."

The instant the door latch clicked in place, Quentin was on his feet. "For God's sake, Leaphorn! What can you mean by coming to the house? Think how it might endanger my position here if our connection should be discovered."

Leaphorn placed long, smudgy hands on the polished-mahogany desk and leaned across it toward where Quentin stood.

"There's a stranger poking around at Antire Manor," he said, without even acknowledging Palmer's concerns. "Do you know who 'e is?"

Quentin drew a breath of what seemed like wintry air. "A stranger at Antire Manor? I haven't any idea who he is. What has he been doing there?"

" 'E's been asking questions, for a start."

"Questions? What kinds of questions?"

"About the property, about the murders years ago."

"About the murder of the marquis and marchioness?"

"Aye. Do you think your cousin sent 'im?"

Quentin shook his head. "I don't know. If he did, Duncan hasn't said a word to me. What does the man look like? Is it someone I might know?"

Leaphorn shrugged. " 'E looks a bit like a brawler, though more from 'is face and body than from 'is clothes. And 'e's bearded, graying, about this tall." The smuggler indicated a height an inch or two below six feet. "An older man, maybe fifty, fifty-five. You haven't seen him about the 'ouse?"

"No," Quentin offered softly as if deep in thought. "Have you talked to the man yourself?"

"Now, what would I want to talk to 'im for? Though some of the other fellows 'ave."

"And what did they have to say about him?"

"That 'e's quiet, soft-spoken. That 'e doesn't miss much."

Quentin's brows came together in a frown. "I don't know why my cousin would send someone down to Dorset to investigate, though if the man is asking about the murders, it's possible Duncan did. I do know he has been going over the books at Wicker and Walford's offices, and he's looked over the records I've been keeping, too."

"There's nothing in your books to make 'im suspicious about Antire Manor, is there?"

"No, no. I've kept my hands out of the till where Duncan's property and investments are concerned. Nor has he said a word about the manor, not once since he's been in England. Do you think he got wind of the smuggling somehow?"

"All I know is that this fellow showed up at Swanage three or four days ago, taking a whole lot more interest in Antire Manor than anyone should."

"And he's asking about the late marquis and marchioness?" Quentin's manner was subdued and grim.

"That's what I've 'eard."

"But that doesn't make any sense."

"Not much in this life does," Leaphorn muttered philosophically.

"Perhaps we shouldn't have interfered with Duncan while he was here in England," Quentin murmured as he began to pace. "Perhaps something we did has made him wonder about Antire Manor."

"And what would that be? There's been nothing in all we've set up that would draw 'is attention to Dorset."

Quentin paused to review everything that had transpired since Duncan had been in England. He had to admit that Leaphorn was right; there was nothing in anything they'd done to link them to Antire Manor.

"But why is this fellow down there asking questions? Could it be something else to do with the smuggling? Could the man be from the magistrate's office? From the treasury?"

"If 'e is from the Crown, why ain't 'e asking about goods 'e wants to buy? Why does 'e care about your cousin's parents, about people who're so long dead?"

Quentin shook his head, terrified by the news of an unexplained visitor at Antire Manor, terrified by what this stranger might uncover, terrified anew by the plans they'd made for Duncan.

"And we've a ship due in two days' time," the smuggler went on. "A shipment come from Spain. If this fellow is on the property then, it won't matter what 'e's found. Dead men tell no tales, and that's what 'e will be."

"You'd kill him, then, without finding out what he wants?"

"We've killed our share of others. Why should we spare this bloke?"

Quentin shrugged, more from the chill in Leaphorn's words than from the indifference he meant to convey.

"Well, I leave the stranger's fate to you. I know you'll do whatever you must. But will his presence change the plans we've laid? Will it make any difference in what's been set up for Duncan?"

It was obvious Leaphorn had considered the question long and hard, and he sagely shook his head. "Nah. Those things are all in place. We'll be ready to act again whenever you give the word."

Quentin didn't like the fact that Duncan's life was in his hands, didn't like the role he'd had to play thus far or what was yet to come. He had never enjoyed responsibility, and the responsibility for such as this made his stomach crawl. Still, he had so much to gain simply by doing what he was told, so much to gain by betraying Duncan. He needed to continue to think about the money to be made, the security and position he would gain. He glanced down at the bills scattered across the desk, and they seemed to firm his resolve. After everything that had happened, what was one killing more or less?

"Do what you must at Antire Manor," he told Leaphorn with a sigh. "I'll set the other things in motion as soon as I see the time is right."

Leaphorn smiled across the desk at the other man. It was a smile that never reached his eyes. "You just do what you've been told, play the role you've played before. In two weeks it will all be over and you'll be enjoying the life of a wealthy man."

"I hope that what you say is true," Quentin said as he came around the desk and escorted the smuggler toward the door. "With a stranger prowling around, I just hope we get away with this."

The coffee had gone stone cold by the time Grayson and Duncan had the chance to sample it, and though it had been no hardship then, Palmer's stomach was rumbling now. After Ryan's peculiar reaction to finding Grayson in his bed, Duncan had decided to head for the kitchen himself rather than risk another encounter between his new wife and his valet. But just as he was passing the study on his way to the kitchen for a bite to eat, the door swung wide to reveal his cousin and a tall, emaciated man preparing to step into the hall.

"Duncan!" Quentin gasped when he saw the younger Palmer slow his stride. "I didn't expect to find you prowling the house today, not with a bride to claim your company."

Duncan shrugged aside his cousin's comment. "Grayson is getting dressed. We're going out later to make some calls."

"Yes, I suppose that's what's expected, since you've decided to forgo a proper honeymoon."

"Just until we reach New York," Duncan corrected him.

Though Quentin seemed disinclined to issue one, Duncan waited in the hall for an introduction to their visitor.

Prodded by the silence, Quentin complied. "This is Mr. Leaphorn, Duncan. He lives near Antire Manor and came to discuss a business matter with me."

"Oh?" Duncan murmured. "A business matter?"

Quentin swallowed hard and then continued. "Yes, Mr. Leaphorn has some—ah—workhorses he thought we might be interested in purchasing for the estate. But I told him we already had more than enough horses for the limited cultivation we're doing there."

To Duncan's practiced eye, the man his cousin had introduced looked like anything but a horse trader. His clothes were rough and none too clean. There were no calluses on his hands, and there was something about the fellow that Duncan didn't trust. If his stables were as unkempt as he was, if he did not work the horses himself, if there was indeed something of the shyster in him, the horseflesh he was offering was not likely to improve their breeding stock. Still, it paid to be polite.

"And how are things at Antire Manor, Mr. Leaphorn?" Duncan asked the stranger.

"Well enough, my lord."

"It's crossed my mind that I should go down and look the place over before I leave for America."

Quentin stared at Duncan as if he'd gone quite mad. "You're going to go down to Antire Manor? But why?"

"It's something Gray suggested," he admitted with a shake of his head. "She seems to think I should."

"Per'aps that wouldn't be such a bad idea, your lordship," Leaphorn broke in, watching the two cousins from beneath sly, half-open eyelids. "It must be nearly a score of years since you've seen the place, and it's changed a bit since then."

"Yes," Duncan answered with a frown. "I suppose it has. It's seventeen years since I've been there. And though I vowed I'd never return, Grayson's made me reconsider."

"It really hasn't changed as much as all that," Quentin put in quickly. "The house and grounds aren't kept up the way they once were, and you wouldn't have a place to stay if you decided on a visit."

"Well, it was only a passing thought," Duncan answered, dismissing the idea with a shrug. "With Gray's affairs to set to rights and the voyage two weeks away, I doubt I'd have an opportunity to visit Antire Manor even if I wanted to."

"Well, then, let me give my best wishes to you and your bride," Leaphorn offered. "Be lots of little Palmers soon enough, what with the beauty I hear you've taken as your wife."

With difficulty Duncan ignored the ribald tone of the comment and extended his hand. "Thank you for your kindness, Mr. Leaphorn. And I'm sorry about not needing any horses."

Quentin nudged Leaphorn in the direction of the tradesmen's door, and Duncan wondered at his cousin's obvious impatience to see the fellow gone. He waited in the hall for Quentin's return, and followed him into the study, closing the door behind them.

"I don't want you doing business with that man," Duncan said, as Quentin settled himself behind the desk. "There's something about him I just don't trust."

"Are you questioning my judgment after all these years?" Quentin snapped, turning on his cousin unexpectedly. "You've never taken an interest in the holdings and property here before, and it seems a little late for you to doubt my stewardship."

It must be a day for unpredictable behavior, Duncan noted before he responded to his cousin's gibes. First there had been the uncomfortable reaction Gray had had to Ryan Barnes, and now Quentin was acting most peculiarly.

Duncan reached across to touch his cousin's arm and felt the muscles jump and flex inside Quentin's sleeve.

"Of course I don't have any quarrel with the way you've handled my affairs these past few years," he assured the other man. "You've looked after my interests here in England more than satisfactorily. But something about that man Leaphorn sets my hackles rising. It's not something I can explain, but humor me in this."

"Rest assured, Duncan, that I do my best with what's been entrusted to me. I look after your interests here in England as if they were my own."

"I know that, Quentin, and I appreciate all you've done."

"Then just let me get on with it, will you? I understand the situation here far better than you do. I won't do business with

Leaphorn if that's what you prefer, but just leave me to the rest of it, if you're as satisfied as you say."

Duncan gave a nod and turned to go, happy to leave his cousin and his prickly mood behind him.

"I won't do any more business with Leaphorn," Quentin repeated almost to himself as Duncan's footsteps echoed down the corridor. "No more business with him at all—once this is over and the Antire fortune is mine."

There was something wrong at Antire Manor, and his lordship, Duncan Palmer, needed to be told. As Hannibal Frasier penned the message he would post from Bournemouth, across the bay, he tried to convey the urgency of the situation at Antire Manor without giving any details of what he'd found. The last thing his employer wanted was to return to the place where his parents had died, and what Frasier said in the note had to persuade him to do just that.

It was certain Palmer would never come to Dorset if he was privy to the rumors that were circulating through the countryside. Hannibal had heard them for the first time from a barmaid at the inn where he was staying. She had assured him that Antire Manor was haunted by the ghosts of the late marquis and marchioness. Frasier didn't believe in ghosts and had all but dismissed the woman's tale, when a respectable quarryman mentioned that people fishing just offshore had seen ghostly apparitions on the lawn. When the innkeeper added that a boy who had strayed too close to the house was found dead at the bottom of the cliff, Frasier had begun to realize that there was more going on at Antire Manor than anyone was prepared to admit.

He was convinced that Duncan needed to come here, to help unravel the mystery surrounding his family home and to restore his lordship's peace of mind. But Frasier wasn't sure what he could say or do to get Duncan into a coach.

Running his tongue along the fringe of his mustache, Hannibal struggled with the note, seeking the suitable words to pique his lordship's curiosity.

Frasier liked the lad—if an arrogant, combative thirty-year-old marquis could be called a lad—and he found himself hoping the questions in Palmer's life could be resolved by the facts he was uncovering here. The day he'd gone to the town house on Berkeley Square, he had seen terrible turmoil in Duncan's eyes.

Right then Frasier had known it was more than Sidney Layton's business dealings and a few unexplained scratches that had put it there. Hannibal had spoken of the things he'd heard on the streets to gauge Duncan's feelings about his family's country home, and when Palmer had paled at the mention of the house in Dorset, Frasier had become even more determined to investigate. Only the mystery surrounding his parents' death could have unsettled his lordship to such a degree, and while Palmer had argued with Hannibal about pursuing the matter at Antire Manor, Frasier had prevailed.

If he was honest with himself, Hannibal had to admit he was curious about the killings, too. Things that didn't make sense always niggled at him, and the inconsistencies in the stories he'd heard about the murder of Jeremy and Johanna Palmer pricked at him like a burr. So he had come to Dorset, come to see what he could learn, and as he'd begun to investigate, he'd found things he hadn't anticipated.

After reading over the lines of tiny script, Frasier signed his name, pleased by the tone of the message.

Your lordship,

There's more here than meets the eye. Come as soon as you can. More information now impossible.

Frasier

Tucking the paper inside of his coat, Hannibal made his way toward the door of his room. He would send the message immediately and be back at Antire Manor by moonrise.

Frasier's timing was impeccable, for there was a smudged half moon peering above the horizon as he approached the ivy-covered walls of Antire Manor. He'd seen the place in daylight more than once, but with a faint mist wafting up from the sea, a pale glimmer of moonlight reflecting in the few unbroken panes of the tower windows and the long shadows cast across the lawn, the place looked spectral enough to account for the locals' stories.

After checking the pistol tucked into the front of his trousers and the knife shoved down his boot, Frasier skirted to the east of the house. He moved noiselessly across the fields and through a windbreak of twisted trees, coming out at the crest of the rocky cliff that undulated behind the mansion. To his right and left headlands sprawled out into the open sea, embracing a tiny protected cove between their rugged, rocky arms. The wind on the cliff was brisk and cool, picking at the material of his rough dark shirt and flattening his trousers against his legs. There was a salt taste to the breeze, the faint balmy scent of the sea in his nostrils, the insistent hiss of waves stroking the beach below. It was a fine night for clandestine exploration, and he fully intended to make use of it.

Off to the east were the lights of a ketch that was running toward the shore, and as he stood watching its steady progress, Frasier realized it was making for the cove. Then from beneath the lip of the cliff, there was a sudden flash of light. It was as if the shield on a lantern had been removed, as if a signal was being sent or answered. Frasier became abruptly aware that he was not alone at Antire Manor, and a random gust of wind confirmed his fears, carrying with it the sound of voices.

Leaving the safety of the shadowy trees, Frasier crept toward the edge of the cliff and sprawled full length between clumps of gorse to peer down onto the beach. It lay like a faint, pale crescent at the edge of the cove, the waves foaming pure and milky white against the round sea-polished stones. Toward the center of the crescent, ten or fifteen men gathered around a lantern that poked its beam into the dark. They seemed to be waiting for the ketch to anchor in the bay, waiting to do their evening's work. Snuggled up at the edge of the beach were a half-dozen boats, and from the scene laid out before him, Frasier knew why these men were here.

For centuries smuggling had been an institution along the Dorset coast, and the deserted manor house and grounds provided the perfect spot to do it unobserved. There was no question that the ghost stories circulating through the town were a boon to the men below; they had probably encouraged or embellished the tales to keep the villagers at a distance.

As Frasier lay watching, a tall, thin man approached the rest, and with a nod of his head and a sweep of his hands gestured the men toward the open boats. There was the clatter of pebbles beneath their boots as they moved across the beach, the grinding of wood against the rocks as they pushed the skiffs into the waves. They pulled against the swells toward where the ketch was anchoring, and as they approached its side, a launch from the ship moved into open water.

While the smugglers were unloading the ketch, the launch approached the beach. As it eddied in the shallows, a portly man climbed over the side and came splashing toward the beach, waving a hand in greeting at the single man who was waiting there. The two talked for several minutes before the tall man passed a sack of money to the newcomer. There must have been honor among these thieves, for he didn't even bother to count it. The smugglers made three more trips before the ketch hoisted sail to go, and as it beat out of the cove, they wrestled chests of contraband toward the base of the cliff.

Having discovered what he had come to learn, Frasier skulked back toward the clump of trees, but before he reached their sheltering darkness a man loomed up before him.

"Seen what ye came ta see, have ye?" he asked as he pointed his pistol at Frasier's chest. "There ain't many who'd brave the ghosts to find out what it is we're doing here."

When Frasier said nothing the man went on. "Not from around here are ye? Ye a revenuer or worse? Ye go on and give me yer pistol, there, and I'll give ye a peek at our business firsthand."

Pulling the gun from the waistband of his trousers, Frasier did what he was told, and when the smuggler had secured the weapon, he nudged Hannibal toward a trail that led to the beach. As they made their winding descent down the face of the cliff, Frasier prepared to make his escape. There was a dagger tucked down his boot, and his captor was blissfully unaware of it.

As stones skittered and rolled beneath his feet on the narrow path, Hannibal slid gracefully sideways and dipped his hand inside the shaft of his leather boot. His captor stumbled on the treacherous bit of trail, and as the man fought to regain his footing, Frasier swiftly turned on him. The knife blade flashed in a dangerous arc, and though the smuggler was hard-pressed to defend himself, he struck sideways with his pistol butt. The stock caught Frasier above the ear. He staggered with the force of the blow. His feet slid out from under him, and the dagger flew out of his hand. He made a wild grab for grass at the edge of the trail, but it came away in his fists. Then he was falling, rolling, bouncing, skittering, down two dozen yards of sloping cliff face.

Frasier landed heavily, skinned and dazed. His head was throbbing, his hands and knees burned from contact with the crumbling stone. The wind was knocked out of him by the force of the fall, and pain pierced his side every time he tried to get it back.

As he lay sprawled on the beach at the base of the cliff, a pair of boots came to stand over him. "What 'ave you found, Engles?" the tall man above the scuffed boots asked. " 'Ave we someone poking about who 'as no business being 'ere?"

"Aye, Leaphorn," Engles answered as he joined them. "I found him creeping along behind the house. No telling how long he's been there, or what he might've seen."

The man called Leaphorn kicked Frasier, landing a blow on his injured side, and though he had no air for it, Hannibal managed to grind out his blackest curse.

" 'Ow much did you see?" he demanded and kicked again.

Pain exploded before Frasier's eyes in a flash of dazzling light. Swirls of darkness came and went as he tried to catch his breath. When his vision finally began to clear, Hannibal became aware that the circle of boots had widened as half a dozen men had come across the beach to investigate. As he lay there, one toe came forward in a well-placed kick. Several others followed it, bruising his shoulder and hip. The men in the circle around him were like a pack of dogs attacking a cornered prey. There was nothing Frasier could say or do to stop them from tormenting him.

"Who sent you 'ere to spy on us?" Leaphorn asked as he squatted down. "Who is it you are working for?"

Curling inward to protect himself, Frasier shook his head and shut his eyes. He'd be damned if he would answer them.

With a curse Leaphorn caught the front of Hannibal's shirt and hauled him roughly to his feet. Frasier staggered twice before he managed to gain his balance. He wove slightly as he stood there, battered and bruised, pain piercing his side, his head thudding like a drum. They dragged him across the shifting stones, pulling him in the same direction the men with the smuggled goods were moving in.

As Frasier's captors hauled him around a cluster of sheltering boulders, Hannibal could see the opening of a cave in the side of the cliff. They shoved him into a passageway that ran a dozen feet into the rock before it opened into a wider chamber. As they pushed him down the tunnel, Frasier could see the place was mined. There were explosives tucked into crannies in the rocks and fuses dangling near the entrance. There was only one reason for such a precaution: The smugglers were prepared to destroy the evidence of their activities if the authorities interfered.

By the light of the half-dozen lanterns and torches placed around the cavern, Frasier tallied the wealth that was hidden there.

There were goods from half the countries in Europe waiting for sale, crates stacked three and four high, ranks of trunks with arching lids, barrels of every size and description.

As the rest of the men finished stacking the goods the ship had brought, they filtered toward the entrance, toward the intruder and his guards. That their mood was hostile was, at best, an understatement.

"Who's he?" one of them demanded.

"We going to kill him?" another asked and seemed eager to do the job himself.

Leaphorn waited until the whole group had gathered around them before making an explanation. "This gentleman was found at the top of the cliff overseeing this evening's work. And 'e's been asking about the manor, too. But 'e's been a little quiet since I asked 'im why 'e's 'ere. 'Ave you any questions you'd like to ask?"

"You a spy from the magistrates?" one of the smugglers wanted to know.

"You the tax collector's man?"

"You want to see the light of dawn," a third threatened in an undertone, "you better tell us what you're doing here."

"You tell us what we want to know and you might live until tomorrow," the leader threatened, then balled his fist and drove it into Frasier's middle.

Hannibal's legs went wobbly, and he sank to the floor of the cave. As if it had been a signal, the others began to come at him. Fists mashed his face and pummeled his ribs. Hands tore at his hair. Feet bashed at his body, striking and retreating, coming to strike again. Through a haze of grunts and moans, of fear and pain, Frasier finally heard the order to stop. Though broken, bleeding, and barely conscious, he felt Leaphorn press the bore of a heavy pistol against his temple, heard the hammer raked back to click in place.

"We've been watching you since you came to Swanage and 'ave been wondering why you're 'ere. You come for the taxes or because you're Antire's man?"

Blinking the sweat and blood out of his eyes, Frasier looked up into the smuggler's face. It was hollow, waxy, cadaverous. There was no mercy in his eyes. He looked as if he'd as soon put a ball in Hannibal's brain as draw another breath.

"Antire's man," Frasier mumbled in defeat. He fully expected the words to be the last he'd ever utter, but the smuggler pulled the gun away.

"Antire's man. And why are you here?"

The truth came freely to Frasier's lips, since his wits were too addled to lie. "I came to see about the matter of Antire's parents."

"What about 'is parents?"

"About the murders."

The smuggler seemed surprised. "Don't Antire know 'ow they died? 'E killed 'is father, didn't 'e?"

Frasier shook his head, though the effort sapped his strength.

The smuggler came slowly to his feet, as if using the pause to think through his captive's answer.

"We going to kill him, Leaphorn?" one of the others interrupted him.

John Leaphorn shook his head. "We'll let 'im live until the matter with Antire is settled. 'E's upset our plans before, and it might be good to 'ave something 'ere to bargain with. Tie this one up at the back of the cave. The guards will take good care of 'im. Once Antire's been dealt with as we've planned, we'll have Quentin kill this one to show 'is gratitude."

There were murmurs, muttered undertones from the men around him. Whether they were expressions of complaint or approval, Frasier could not tell. But in a moment it was evident Leaphorn had prevailed. Two men hauled Frasier toward the back of the cave and trussed him up accordingly.

Leaphorn followed in their wake and watched until the prisoner was secure. Then he knelt at Frasier's side, wanting more information. "Does Antire know what we're doing 'ere?"

Frasier wished Duncan did. "No," he answered truthfully.

"Are you expecting 'im to come 'ere before 'e sails for America?"

Frasier shrugged. He had done his best to entice Duncan to visit Antire Manor, but he was not sure now just how such a trip would end. Was the note Frasier had sent tantamount to signing Palmer's death warrant? Yet if Duncan Palmer never came, there was no hope for Frasier, either.

"I don't know if he'll come." Hannibal gave Leaphorn the truth once more.

"Well, don't you worry none," Leaphorn confided. "As things stand now, 'e's better off 'ere than where 'e is."

Twenty

IF THE FOOTMAN HAD ANNOUNCED THE DEVIL HIMSELF, DUNCAN could not have been more surprised than he was by the news that Samuel Walford was waiting to see him.

Palmer and Grayson had just returned from another round of the visits newly wedded couples were expected to make and had retired to the upstairs parlor where Gray was busy with the task of acknowledging their many wedding gifts.

"Show Mr. Walford into the study and ask him to wait," Duncan instructed. "I'll be with him as soon as I can."

"What do you suppose Walford wants?" Grayson asked, obviously thinking about the night they'd gone to the brothel to find proof of Walford's nefarious business dealings.

Duncan left his chair and came to stand beside her at the desk, his fingers trailing over the curve of her cheek, the pale, petal softness of her throat. "I haven't any idea."

"Are you prepared to talk to him?"

"I suppose that depends on what he's come to say." Duncan's fingers paused in their absentminded caress. "To tell you the truth, I haven't really decided what to do about Samuel Walford's intrigues. My first impulse was to turn him over to the police and let him take his chances in the courts. But that could do irreparable harm to the company, and I'm afraid to risk Uncle Farleigh's reputation and livelihood for the sake of petty revenge."

"Perhaps it would be wise to see why Walford's come before you make a decision. But, Duncan, please be careful," she warned with a squeeze of his hand. "From what I've seen of Walford's methods, he's not a man to be trifled with."

When Palmer reached the study two floors below, Samuel Walford was waiting, his usually florid face pinched and gray.

"It's good of you to see me," Walford greeted Duncan. "I wanted to be certain we had a chance to talk before you left for America."

"Oh?" Duncan responded, offering Walford a seat and settling himself in the chair behind the desk. "I fully intended to pay you a visit before I left. There are several things we must discuss—quite pressing matters, really."

"Yes." The older man sighed. "Yes, I can well imagine what they are."

"Can you?" Duncan's tone was deceptively bland.

"Indeed. I have the distinct impression they involve Enterprise Manufacturing."

The younger man merely raised his brows and waited for Walford to go on.

"I know you found the papers at Sidney Layton's town house that prove exactly what I've done. And I suppose that now, of all times, you are going to set out to ruin me."

"Now that you have been proposed as a Knight of the Order of Bath, you mean?"

"You know about that, too?"

"I find it pays to be well informed."

Walford rose from his chair and paced around the room, his movements spare and jerky. "A knighthood is something I've always wanted, something I've always dreamed about. In a family as illustrious as mine, I've always hoped to achieve some kind of recognition on my own."

"And you believe that what I know will jeopardize it?"

"You mean you don't intend to make this public?" Walford asked as he stopped and stared at the younger man.

"I suppose that depends," Duncan answered. "It depends on how long you've been cheating Uncle Farleigh and what your reasons are. It depends on whether you sent the men who've tried their best to kill me."

Walford's mouth dropped open, and his heavy eyelids rose. "Sent men to kill you? That's absurd!"

"Then who were the men who attacked me in Limehouse, not half a dozen blocks from the Enterprise Manufacturing building?"

"I don't know anything about an attack."

"Don't you? Somehow I find that difficult to believe. And I suppose it wasn't your fault I was hit over the head and trussed up like a Christmas goose at your daughter's brothel, either."

Through narrowed eyes, Duncan watched the older man's response to his accusations. Walford seemed to shrink with each of them, seemed to grow more wizened and white with each allegation of his complicity.

"And I suppose you haven't had me followed, either," Duncan went on, "though the men you hired for the task are most inept."

Walford stared across the desk at the younger man. "I swear to you, I've had no men following you, and I am certainly not responsible for any attempt on your life.

"As for your treatment at my daughter's establishment, that was her doing, not mine. Sidney deals with a far rougher segment of society than you or I do, and I won't answer for her methods. If you'd not already escaped when I arrived, I would have admitted my involvement in Enterprise Manufacturing and sent you on your way."

Duncan was not sure he believed Walford, but for his uncle's sake he wanted to. Farleigh Wicker would not welcome the proof of embezzlement Duncan had found, and the truth would be even harder for his uncle to accept if Walford had been behind the attempt on Duncan's life. But if Walford hadn't planned the attack, who in blazes had? And who were the two shabby men who still clung to Duncan like a second skin?

The possibility that they might be from the police, looking into the West End Strangler's deeds, turned Duncan cold. He had been hoping that there was another explanation for their dogged persistence in following him.

Pushing thoughts of the Strangler to the back of his mind, Duncan eyed the man before him. There were questions from Walford's past that were clamoring for answers, and he wanted explanations now rather than having to confront his uncle later. Perhaps what Walford said would help Duncan gauge the truth in the rest of his claims. Perhaps his explanations would offer more insight into this man's motives and his character.

"I want to know what happened at La Albuera," he told Walford quietly.

The older man went a shade paler than before and resumed his seat before the desk. "You've unearthed all my dirty little secrets, haven't you?"

"I'd like to think I have."

"And you've unearthed a few of Farleigh's, too."

Duncan nodded. "I can't imagine that my uncle was a party to the theft of religious objects, but the facts seem to bear it out."

There was a long pause before Walford spoke, and when he did, there was resignation in his tone. "The theft wasn't his idea," he conceded. "But in the end, Farleigh didn't have much choice about going along with what I'd begun."

"Why don't you tell me what happened?"

Walford drew a ragged breath. "La Albuera had been under fire since just after dawn, and the town was all but razed when we entered it in the afternoon. By then the French were fighting house to house, tenacious in their resistance. They were picking us off from the doorways and the rooftops of the ruined buildings as we approached, and I took refuge in a church to reload my weapons.

"The building must have taken a direct hit from one of the mortars earlier in the day. Most of the roof had come down into the nave, and two walls were all but gone. A priest was there in the rubble and the dust, an old priest who'd been trapped beneath the shattered roof beams. His chest was crushed, and even if I had tried to help him there was nothing I could have done. He was very nearly dead, but with the last of his strength he was clinging to a burlap sack. From the way he fought when I tried to take it from him, I could tell there was something of value inside. But until I wrenched it from his hands, I had no idea what it was the two of us were fighting for."

"What was he trying to protect?" Duncan wanted to know.

"They must have been two of the most precious objects in that whole part of Spain: a silver crucifix encrusted with jewels and a gold and ruby chalice every bit as valuable. He must have known I meant to keep them as my own, for with his dying breath he cursed me, called God's wrath down upon my head."

Even in the cozy study Walford shivered with the memory of the old man's words. "In those days a simple priest's curse couldn't frighten me. After all that we'd been through, nothing did. We were fighting a cursed war in a cursed land. Life was cursed, as were we all. One more blasphemy didn't seem to matter. At least it didn't matter when I saw that my salvation could come from possessing such rare and glorious riches. The crucifix and the chalice were spoils of war, and as a victor in the battle, I had every right to take them."

"And you were bending over the priest with the relics in your hands when Uncle Farleigh came into the church."

Walford nodded. "I was admiring my booty when he stumbled in and became a party to something he never could have condoned. I think he believed I'd killed the priest to get the things, and though the crucifix and chalice represented more money than either of us had ever seen, Farleigh wanted to turn them over to the authorities. I couldn't see why someone else should benefit from what I alone had come upon, and we argued, really argued, for the first time in our lives. Though there was firing all around us, we nearly came to blows. And we might have fought each other, too, if a pair of French grenadiers had not come rushing into the church. They launched themselves at us with hate in their eyes, and your uncle and I were lucky to defend ourselves.

"The struggle was violent and brief," Walford recalled, his voice reluctant, faded with the force of the memories that trapped him now. "I shot the man who came against me, but your uncle was armed only with his infantry saber, and the Frenchman was most skilled in swordsmanship.

"They fought like fiends among the rubble and the smoke. Your uncle's every thrust met with a skillful parry, and the grenadier's attacks were stronger than Farleigh could repulse. He was disarmed at last, backed against one of the pillars in the church. As he prepared to die, he caught sight of me over his adversary's shoulder." Walford shivered again. "Our eyes met and it was as if the air between us sizzled. To my dishonor, I considered abandoning him to his fate, letting the grenadier kill him so I could take the things I'd found and claim them as my own. And Farleigh knew it. He knew that I meant to sell his life for riches. He knew I was prepared to see him die. When I saw that he understood, I had no choice but to prove him wrong. I killed the Frenchman, and because I had saved your uncle's life, Farleigh let me keep the spoils.

"We buried the chalice and crucifix beneath the floorboards of a neighboring stable, and when the campaign was finally over, we went back and dug them up. Farleigh was dishonored by what we'd done. He hated me for making him my accomplice. It pained him that we used the money from selling the objects to start the trading company, but we had no choice if we were to become more than family parasites. We needed the money after the war was over, and with that and what we got from a few forward-looking investors we were able to start an enterprise that promised the kind of life we both wanted for ourselves."

"It's because the money for the trading company came from ill-gotten gains that my uncle refused to consider that you'd been embezzling, wasn't it?" Duncan observed quietly when Walford's words faded away.

"I suppose it was his way of denying the source of the money that gave us our start, of repudiating the dishonor he felt tainted everything we'd done. Now all that remains is to discover what price you'll demand from me for trying to defraud him."

"How much money have you taken out of the company in the last few years?" Duncan asked, secure in the knowledge that he could verify any figure Walford gave.

Walford seemed to know that, too. "Since 1839 I've taken just short of seventy-five thousand pounds."

"And did you take any money prior to 1839?"

The older man shook his head. "It was only when I saw the chance to curry favor in the interest of being granted a knighthood that I began to take the money. Garnering a knighthood is an expensive undertaking. There are donations to be made, entertainments to sponsor, discreet favors to be done. Not every man who is named a knight needs to do such things; many achieve the honor on merit alone. But that's not how it works for someone like me."

"And that's where all the money went?"

Walford stared down at his hands. "Most of it."

Duncan sat back in the tall desk chair, considering what he had learned. There were still dozens of questions left unanswered, but it seemed that Walford had told the truth, about the embezzlement at least. Now it was up to him to dictate terms. But what terms did he want? Would ruining Walford publicly serve any purpose? Might it undermine Wicker and Walford's otherwise sterling reputation? Might it expose Farleigh Wicker to dishonor?

"I want you to sign over your interest in Wicker and Walford to me," Duncan said at last. "I will pay you what it's worth, of course, minus the seventy-five thousand pounds you've already taken. And I want this to be a private transaction. My uncle is never to know of it.

"To keep up appearances, you will remain the nominal head of the London branch, but I will oversee every facet of the business. And let me warn you, if there is so much as a penny unaccounted for, if there is any question of your honesty in the years to come, I will make everything I've learned public knowledge. And damn the consequences. I'll see that you die a disgraced and broken man. There won't be a corner of the earth where you can run to escape my wrath. To doubt me in this, Walford, is to court disaster."

The older man's face was white, but he seemed to be breathing more easily. "If those are your terms, my lord, I have no choice but to accede to them."

Duncan rose and came around the corner of the desk. The interview was over. "I will have my solicitors contact you. I want this settled and the papers signed before I leave England for America."

Walford came to his feet and let Duncan escort him toward the door. "I appreciate your keeping these revelations to yourself, my lord."

"I'm not doing it for you, Walford. Make no mistake. I'm doing it for my uncle and for the business he's worked so hard to found."

"I appreciate it nonetheless," Samuel Walford said as he turned to go.

"And one thing more," Duncan added, halting the older man in the doorway of the study. "I want you to write a letter to the queen declining the honor of a knighthood."

Grayson slipped the string and paper from the parcel that had just been delivered and opened the tiny velvet jeweler's box. Inside on a bed of rich brown satin was the signet ring she had ordered as Duncan's wedding gift. Carved into the carnelian quartz that was set in a broad gold band was the Palmer family shield, crossed swords surrounded by scallop shells. The jeweler had done a marvelous job of matching the caramel-colored stone to the one in Duncan's watch fob, and Grayson was pleased by the craftsman's work. The signet ring was a lovely piece—rich, heavy, masculine, and worthy of the man who was now her husband. She was eager to present it but determined that the time be right. Should she give it to Duncan as they prepared to go to dinner at Worthington Hall? Should she wait for a more intimate moment when there would be time for him to thank her properly?

With a smile tugging at the corners of her lips, she decided on the latter course and made her way to the door of Duncan's bedchamber. Crossing the room, she paused before the bed, thinking of the wondrous magic that happened there. Something inside her quivered, stirring a warm, sweet music through her. A curl of anticipation swelled in her chest at the thought of the brush of Duncan's lips and hands along her flesh. It made her want him here beside her now. She wanted to give him her gift, accept his thanks and whatever else he cared to offer in return. She drew a slow unsteady breath and pushed the thought away. It was daylight, midafternoon. Even if Duncan came to her now, they could hardly—

Of course Aunt Julo hadn't said they couldn't make love in the middle of the day.

A twinkle of devilment turned Gray's smile into a grin, and she began to wonder where Duncan was. But first things first, she told herself sternly. She wanted to put the ring where it would be handy when they did make love, so she folded back the dark green coverlet on Duncan's bed and tucked the box beneath the pillows. Just as she was flipping the covers back in place, the door behind her opened.

Whirling toward it guiltily with hope and anticipation in her eyes, she saw it was Ryan Barnes, not Duncan, who had come into the room. He was carrying a pile of his master's carefully laundered shirts and a pair of gleaming top boots.

"What are you doing there?" Barnes demanded, as he pushed the door closed with a nudge of his hip. "What are you putting into the master's bed?"

It sounded as if he was accusing her of doing something sinister instead of planning a pleasant surprise. Annoyance flared in response to his disapproving tone, but Gray tamped it down as best she could.

"I've bought a gift for Duncan," she answered in what she hoped was a friendly tone. Tugging back the coverlet, Gray withdrew the box to show him.

Ryan deemed it appropriate to cross the room and peer down at the ring she meant to give his master.

"It's my wedding gift to him," Grayson explained. "It wasn't ready before. Do you think he will like it?"

Barnes stared at the ring for a full minute before he replied. "I doubt that even so fine a gift as this will make up for forcing his lordship to marry you."

Grayson reacted as if she'd been slapped, recoiling and gasping in spite of herself. She snapped the cover over the box, and pulled it protectively against her chest. She was determined not to let this horrid little man spoil the pleasure she had taken in selecting the gift for Duncan.

In the space of an instant a dozen angry responses spun through her mind, but Gray deliberately bit each of them back. She didn't want to start another argument with her husband's manservant, no matter how he provoked her.

"I believe it is customary for a bride to give a gift to her groom, no matter what the circumstances. I only hoped that you would approve of what I'd selected, since you know Duncan's tastes far better than I do."

Placated, Barnes seemed to consider the woman before him. Yet as his eyes moved over her, Gray could feel his lingering hostility.

"His lordship's never worn a ring," he told her. "'Course that doesn't mean he won't wear it if you're the one who's given it to him."

It seemed as close to approval as Gray was likely to get, and when he turned away to deposit the shirts and boots in the dressing room, she tucked the box back beneath the pillows. But by the time he returned from the dressing room, Gray had stationed herself in front of the door.

"Mr. Barnes, please," she began, blocking his path. "I would very much appreciate it if there could be a truce between us. I know how close you and Duncan have become over the years, and I really have no desire to come between you. If we could find a way to coexist, it would make things so much easier for Duncan."

His round face narrowed at her words, closing in, going hard. His black eyes glittered like multifaceted jet beads, showing an intensity of distaste she could not fathom. She took a step away from him, angry with herself for backing down.

"Are you asking me to approve of you? Do you want me to say it was right for you to force his lordship into a marriage he never sought, a marriage he clearly didn't want?"

When Grayson couldn't find words to answer, Barnes went on. "No, Lady Grayson, I'll not do that. And once more, I'll forever curse the day you crossed his path. For all your fine breeding and elegant ways you're nothing but a lying jade, using your beauty to entice him, using your tricks to bend him to your will. I won't ever forget the way you worked your wiles on him, and I won't forgive it, either. Now if you will excuse me, I've duties to perform. One of us, at least, is concerned with his lordship's welfare."

Moving around her, Ryan Barnes jerked open the bedroom door. Grayson stood stunned to silence by his words, wishing she'd never confronted him.

"This was a particularly fine year for claret, don't you think?" the Duke of Fennel asked, as he motioned for one of the footmen to refill Duncan's glass.

Palmer dutifully sipped an inch of the ruby liquid and nodded. "I'm not much of a judge on wine," he offered. "I've never developed a taste for it."

"Just give me a good glass of wine," the duke went on, "and let others have their ale and brandy. I suppose it is a taste I came by all those years ago in Spain when the water wasn't fit to drink."

It was the second reference to that particular time and place someone had made in the last few days, and Duncan wondered if an entire generation of Englishmen had been molded by Napoleon's attempted conquest of the Continent. Samuel Walford had been tempered by it, and Duncan's Uncle Farleigh. Besides his taste for wine, what other lasting effects had the wars with Bonaparte had on Warren Worthington? Had they made him the ruthless, opinionated man he was? Had they prepared Worthington to seek out the powerful position he now held in Parliament? Were all the men who had come to manhood in the years of conflict similarly affected?

What had those years done to Duncan's own father? Duncan found himself wondering. Jeremy Palmer had served with Wellington, too. Had the experience changed him? Had it made him more volatile and harsh than he had been before? Had the things he saw in battle changed him as they had these other men? Though Duncan had been born in the years of conflict, he could not remember his father ever being different than he was on the day he died. He had been mercurial and complex, elusive and unpredictable. In an instant his father could change from a charming, laughing companion to a fierce, angry stranger. Had Jeremy's experiences in the war corrupted him, turned him into a man capable of chastising, beating, and finally killing Duncan's mother? Or had those characteristics been genetic, a part of his personality from birth? And more important, had those traits been handed down to Duncan? Had the seed of that cruelty been planted in him, too?

Duncan let his eyes stray to where Grayson was seated on the far side of the table. She was lovely in the light cast by the tall candelabra that stood on either side of the matching Wedgwood centerpiece. She was so vital, so filled with laughter and kindness and spirit. In the last few days his feelings for her had deepened, grown far more compelling than he would have thought possible. Could he make her happy in the years they would have together? Would they find the kind of contentment that had eluded his own parents, or would he hurt and abuse Grayson as his father had his wife? He shuddered with the thought and tried to shut his doubts away. In this intimate setting, with his wife across the table and her guardians at his side, his doubts seemed profoundly inappropriate.

"Duncan?" he heard his wife say in a teasing tone, "Duncan? Have you been woolgathering again?"

"I suppose I have," he admitted sheepishly, glad to be diverted.

"Why don't you show my aunt the gift I gave you?"

As Duncan extended his left hand to his hostess, the striated band of the signet ring flashed brilliantly in the light. It was a lovely gift, unlike anything he had ever owned, and he was pleased by the evident care Grayson had shown in ordering it. From where the box had been hidden, he knew she had meant to wait until bedtime to give him the ring, but late this afternoon her eagerness had gotten the best of her. She had presented it to him when he returned to their rooms, and he had thanked her for it in a most appropriate manner. As a matter of fact, the fervor with which he had thanked her had made them a little late for dinner here at Worthington Hall. The thought made him smile, and when his gaze met his wife's across the table, his smile grew broader still.

As the meal progressed, through cream of asparagus soup, a fish course, of poached turbot with a caper sauce and stewed mushrooms, through the entrée of hearty roast lamb with mint sauce and vegetables, through the puddings and the creams, they discussed the repairs to the *Citation* and the plans for the Atlantic crossing. Julo fussed, saying she did not want to see them go, and in spite of Worthington's brusque questions about sailing and navigation, Duncan sensed his reluctance, too. After dessert, Julo and Grayson adjourned to the salon, leaving the gentlemen in the dining room to enjoy their port. Once they were settled on the settee, Julo ordered that tea be brought to them and began to inquire discreetly about her niece's adjustment to married life.

"Oh, Aunt Julo," Grayson said with a laugh. "Things with Duncan are wonderful, far better than I thought they would ever be."

"You love him, don't you?" her aunt inquired.

"Yes."

"And he loves you?"

Gray shrugged a little self-consciously. "He hasn't said he does."

"He will," Julo assured her sagely. "He will. Just give him time."

"How can you be sure? Duncan was all but dragged to the church. I saw Uncle Warren's men standing guard by the door to prevent his escape. That's not a very promising way to begin a marriage."

Julo reached across to pat Grayson's hand. "Those men told Warren he was already preparing to go to the church when they reached the Antire town house that morning."

"Was he?" Grayson's heart rose with a surge of hope. "Was he really?"

"I have it on the best authority."

"Then, why did he try to break our engagement? Why didn't he . . ."

Grayson bit back the question on the tip of her tongue. Asking her aunt why Duncan hadn't come to her on their wedding night would have revealed more about their intimate relations than Gray wanted anyone to know. Still, she wondered why Duncan hadn't wanted to make her his wife in every way. His enthusiasm for their lovemaking was evident now, but the question of his initial reluctance plagued her.

"Why didn't he what, dear?" Julo asked.

"Why didn't he tell me that?" Grayson answered instead.

Julo shook her head. "Pride, I suppose. These men do have their pride, and Duncan, I suspect, has more than most. How would he have survived this time in England without it?"

It was true. In spite of the scandal in his past and the gossips whispering behind their fans, Duncan had reentered English society with his head held high.

Unaware that she was doing so, Grayson sighed.

"Is there something else on your mind, my dear?"

In those few quiet moments, their tea had arrived, and Gray accepted a cup of the steaming brew before she answered.

"It's not something about Duncan that's bothering me. There's a problem with his valet."

Julo stirred sugar into her cup and set the spoon aside. "His valet?"

"Ryan Barnes. He has been with the Palmer family since before Duncan was born. From what I gather, Barnes was Jeremy Palmer's childhood friend, a crofter who was given a position as Jeremy's valet. When the former marquis was killed, Ryan was the one who took Duncan to his uncle in America, and over the years the two of them have grown very close."

"Well, where's the problem in that?" Julo wanted to know.

Grayson set her teacup aside. "I think Ryan Barnes hates me," she told her aunt. "He wishes I'd never come into Duncan's life."

"What has he done to make you think that?"

"He said some awful things to me just this afternoon: that I forced Duncan to marry me, that I tricked him into it. Since the morning after the wedding I've felt Barnes's hostility. It's as if we're in a tug-of-war with Duncan's loyalty the prize we're both straining so hard to win."

Julo nodded. "Ah, yes, I see."

"Do you? I wish I did."

"Has it occurred to you that this Ryan Barnes is jealous of you? I think he's threatened by your place in Duncan's life and is wary of losing his. After all these years of having Duncan to himself, he probably resents your intrusion."

Gray peered across the rim of her teacup at her aunt. "Do you really think that's it?"

"It seems as clear as day to me."

"But I only want to assume my rightful place as Duncan's wife."

"And become his friend and confidante." Julo took a sip of tea and continued. "Of course the man is threatened. Until the other day he was both those things to Duncan. Your presence has turned both their lives upside down, and this Mr. Barnes is clearly afraid of the change. Once he realizes your marriage hasn't really altered the relationship he and Duncan have, his jealousy should abate."

What Julo said made perfect sense. Grayson knew that Duncan and Ryan Barnes had shared an unusual closeness. Because of the tragedy that marked them both and the years they had spent together in America, they had grown to depend on each other, care for each other. It was not the kind of friendship that generally developed between a man and his valet, but given the circumstances in Duncan's life, Gray could readily understand why it was so. After his parents died, Duncan must have needed security, stability, and she knew she should be grateful that Ryan Barnes had provided it. Surely Ryan had done his part in making Duncan the man he was, and she should be grateful for all he'd done.

Perhaps now that she understood a bit of what Barnes must be feeling, she could curb her own response to him. It did no good to argue with the man. Their disagreements upset them both, and their conflicting loyalties made life difficult for Duncan as well. If she could only manage to hold her tongue, Grayson thought, if she could only manage to keep her temper in check, perhaps a change in Ryan's attitude would come sooner than anyone expected.

"How did you come to be so wise?" Gray asked as she reached across to give Julo a brief warm hug.

"It's the wisdom the years impart, I suppose," the smaller woman said with a laugh. "And I've a passed a goodly number of them on earth and hope for many more."

Julo had just poured them both another cup of tea when Warren and Duncan came into the drawing room. With a single glance at her husband, Gray knew there was something wrong. Perspiration beaded his brow, and his face was the color of chalk. From the way he held his head and the glassiness of his eyes, she recognized the signs of a headache.

Rising immediately, Grayson asked for their carriage to be brought around and murmured their good-byes. In less time than it took the servants to get their wraps, the chaise was waiting at the door. With promises to come by the following day, Grayson hustled Duncan inside and gently took his hand.

"You've got one of your headaches, haven't you?" she asked when they had pulled away. His fingers were so icy in her grasp that she chaffed them against her own.

"I'm sorry to spoil your evening," he apologized. "I never know when this is going to happen, and when it does, there's just no help for it."

"It's all right," she assured him, concern in her tone. "I just want to get you home and do what I can to take care of you."

With exaggerated care, Duncan settled his head against the squabs and closed his eyes. In a voice gone frayed and deep with pain, he murmured an almost inaudible thank-you.

* * *

By the time they reached their rooms in the town house on Berkeley Square, Duncan was the color of ashes. Without taking time even to strip off her bonnet and gloves, Grayson pulled back the covers on the bed and went to help him undress. Instead of welcoming the assistance, he shooed her away, pointing instead in the direction of the nightstand.

"Laudanum," he whispered in an almost frenzied tone. "It's in the top drawer."

Gingerly Grayson took out a sinister-looking dark bottle and a small clear glass. "How much?" she asked, scanning the label for some indication of the dosage.

"Fifty drops," he instructed, struggling out of his shirt. His motions were tense, erratic, and the panic they revealed heightened Grayson's uneasiness.

"Fifty drops?" she echoed. "That seems like far too much. It says here—"

"Damn it, Grayson. Just do as I say. I've been taking laudanum so long I need half again the usual dose or it simply doesn't work."

That information made Grayson more nervous than before, but she quelled her misgivings and did exactly what he asked. The smell of the laudanum was pungent, bitter, the liquid viscous and dark. By the time she had added water from the ewer, Duncan was undressed and sitting huddled on the side of the bed.

He took the glass from her with hands that shook and downed the contents in a single desperate draft.

"Duncan, I don't think it's wise for you to take so much laudanum. The effects can be quite—"

"Don't think, Grayson. And please don't lecture me now. Just stay with me until I sleep. Then all of this will be over."

Swallowing her words of concern, Gray helped him ease back against the pillows, smoothed the covers over his chest, and settled herself beside him. He looked ghastly as he lay there, hollow-cheeked and hollow-eyed, his lips parted ever so slightly, as if even breathing was an effort. As she took his hand, he nestled back and closed his eyes.

"Is it always like this?" she whispered, shaken by what she'd seen.

"Almost every time. I'm sorry if it frightens you," he answered without opening his eyes. "Sometimes it frightens me, too."

Grayson sat with him for a time, stroking his hand until it went lax and limp against her palm, watching the tension seep out of his face. As Duncan drifted into a deeper sleep, she stirred and left the bed, removing her hat and gloves, dimming the lamps, gathering up his scattered clothing. There was comfort in performing the simple tasks. It gave her time to come to grips with what had happened to him, with the torment she had witnessed. The day he had come to tea at Worthington Hall, she had been aware of the onset of one of Duncan's headaches, but from what he had said to her then, she would never have suspected their virulence, their intensity.

She moved once more to the side of the bed, watching Duncan, wondering what more she could do for him. She wanted to hold him, protect him, prevent him from ever knowing such terrible pain again. But for now the laudanum had done its work, and no matter how concerned she was by the dose he had taken, she was glad he had found repose.

Just as she was heading into the dressing room with Duncan's clothes, Ryan Barnes came to the door.

"The servants said you came home from dinner early, that his lordship has one of his headaches."

"I think he's all right now," she answered quietly, echoing Ryan's whispered tones.

"Got his laudanum, did he?"

"I'm only worried that he takes so much. How often do the headaches come?"

Barnes's arched brows narrowed in concern before he answered her. "Not usually so often as they have of late. They've been worse since we've been in England."

"I wonder why," Grayson puzzled.

"His lordship wonders that, too."

Then, as if just noticing the clothes across her arm, Ryan reached out to take them from her. "I'll just go ahead and put his things away."

"No, it's fine. I'll do it myself. Go have the footmen put a layer of straw down in the street to muffle the sound of carriages. I don't want Duncan to be disturbed."

At her refusal of his help, Barnes's face changed. "There's no need to do that. If he's taken his usual dose, he'll sleep like the dead till morning. Now let me see to those things, and you go on off to bed."

Suddenly Grayson felt like a stranger here, rebuffed, dismissed, as if she didn't belong. She wasn't sure if Barnes was trying deliberately to exclude her from helping with Duncan's care, or if Ryan was simply so used to taking charge when his master was ill that her presence simply wasn't required. In either case, she resisted his suggestion. Duncan was her husband, her responsibility. She had promised to care for him in sickness and health, and she intended to do just that.

She took a step backward. "No, I'll take care of his clothes and Duncan, too," she answered stubbornly.

An antagonistic light fired up at the backs of Ryan's eyes, and she was abruptly reminded how her aunt had warned her that the conflict between her and the valet might well be motivated by feelings of jealousy. But Grayson was suddenly feeling jealous, too. What history did these two men have together that made Barnes more able than she to see to Duncan's care? Who was this man to order her about?

"I want straw spread in the street," she told him. "Now, are you willing to see that it gets done or shall I have someone else take care of it?"

She could see the anger and dislike in the valet's face, the flare of rebellion that flashed in his eyes. There was something about Barnes that had made her uneasy from the very start, and now, with Duncan's welfare the issue between them, what she sensed emanating from the valet was very much like hatred.

Involuntarily she retreated another step, and there was a flicker of satisfaction in Barnes's black eyes.

"I'll see about having the straw spread in the street, if that is what you want. But I'm telling you plain as day, it won't make a farthing's worth of difference to him." With a nod of acquiescence that showed anything but, Barnes whirled and made his way down the hall.

Gray closed the bedroom door behind him, feeling both resentful and drained. Was her every brush with Barnes going to turn into a confrontation, a battle of wills? How was she going to put up with his continued insolence? It was out of the question to ask Duncan to fire the valet. The ties were so strong between the two of them that to demand Barnes's dismissal would be to risk alienating her husband. She would have to find a way to coexist with Ryan Barnes. But how on earth would she do that? It was clear Barnes considered her an intrusion into his master's life, just as it was clear that his hostility was based in his jealousy of her position as Duncan's wife. Even understanding that, Grayson had once again provoked the older man, put herself at odds with him. How could she convince Barnes that she had no desire to undermine what he and Duncan shared? How could she make a life with Duncan when his closest confidant hated her?

Wearily she moved into the dressing room to put away Duncan's clothes, then retired to her own room to prepare herself for bed. Leaving the connecting door ajar in case Duncan should call out, Gray removed her gown and underthings without asking for the assistance of her maid. She was too much at odds with Ryan Barnes to suffer the ministrations of another servant, too much at odds with herself to inflict her uncertain temper on someone else.

After slipping into a nightdress and dressing gown, Gray returned to Duncan's room. He was sleeping deeply, just as she had left him. As she watched him, she could feel the seep of deep commitment. Sick or well, sad or happy, weak or strong, he was hers. Her gaze moved over the contours of his face, the heavy brows, the square jaw and chin, the enticing curve of his lips. She loved this man with all her heart.

Lifting the covers on her side of the bed, she eased herself onto the mattress. She moved slowly, carefully, not wanting to disturb him. Duncan did not stir. Gray knew it would be wiser to sleep in her own bed tonight, but she wanted to be with Duncan. The headache that had struck him down had frightened her, and she needed the solace of his nearness to banish those lingering concerns. She needed to be close by in case he wanted her, needed to be sure that his recovery was well on its way.

She moved gratefully into the aura of his warmth, pressed her cheek against the smoothness of his arm, let her fingers drift to the center of his chest. Duncan slept on unaware. And finally Grayson slept, too—protector and protected, guardian and guarded, husband and wife, curled together safe and sound as the night turned slowly into day.

Twenty-one

IT WAS MURKY, DARK, BUT THE FOG WAS LIFTING. SLOWLY, HAZILY Duncan struggled toward the surface of sleep. He was too warm, stifled by the covers piled high on the bed, tickled by something across his cheek and throat. He stirred sluggishly, pushing the weight of the covers aside, brushing at some feathery filaments that teased his skin.

As he did, his hand encountered heavy silken strands of hair, thick, soft, swirling across his chest and shoulders. Along his arm there was an arc of smooth, cool flesh, and gathered in one fist were the folds of some lacy fabric. His perceptions cleared slowly, one sense at a time: the texture of delicate ribbons and lace beneath his fingertips, a flowery scent in the air, the curves and contours of a body along his side. It took a long, unfocused time for the thought to form: There was a woman in his bed. She was a lush, long-limbed woman who smelled like a garden on a sunny day, whose skin had a subtle velvet feel, like the texture of pale, fresh rose petals.

She was sprawled across the sheets beside him, her head tilted back and away in a spill of hair, one arm curled high above her head. Knowing now that she was beside him, Duncan floated for a time in a twilight world at the edge of consciousness.

As he drifted, the woman lay utterly still, her limbs slack, her body heavy and motionless. He stirred again, shifted, opened his eyes. Overhead the drape of the half-tester came into focus, and he could see the three pale rectangular windows that overlooked the mall. He was in the town house at Berkeley Square, in his own bed—in his own bed with a woman.

He turned his head to look at her, his thoughts still too wispy and confused for instantaneous recognition. She was sprawled beside him like a broken doll, limp, lax, lifeless.

Lifeless.

The woman beside him seemed broken, inert. She lay beside him as if she were dead.

Cold ripped through his body. Panic shot through him in a jolt. It cleared his head like a whiff of ammonia, unscrambled his brain like a dousing of icy rain. Duncan came to full consciousness with a jerk, thoughts boiling through his mind, clawing at him, assaulting him. He sucked air into his lungs in an anguished rasp. It was all he could do to keep from pushing the woman away. Instead, he eased toward the edge of the bed, moving slowly and carefully as if his movements might disturb her. Once he was free, he huddled at the edge of the mattress, deliberately turning his back on her, as if he could deny that she was there.

Though the drug-induced dizziness still assailed him, Duncan forced himself to think. His conclusion was inescapable: If the woman behind him was dead, he had killed her.

The realization exploded through Duncan's consciousness, setting off shivers of disgust, tremors of fear. He buried his face in his hands as the doubts that had been plaguing him for weeks began to congeal. If he had murdered the woman in his bed, if he had unknowingly taken her life, his worst suspicions must be true. He must be the man who was strangling women in London's streets. He must be the West End Strangler!

Duncan curled in upon himself as self-loathing rolled through him like a tidal wave. Caught in the torment of his violent headaches, he must have been killing helpless women. He was the one the police were seeking; he was London's madman. Had his return to England set off this aberrant behavior, tapped some sickness deep inside him? But why wasn't he aware of what he'd done? How had he been able to deny his crimes even to himself? He wondered who his latest victim was and how she had found her way to his bedchamber.

It took all his courage to turn to where the woman lay, her face turned half away, her perfect profile pale against the shadows in the room. One arm was thrown high above her head, the other was flung wide, her hand dangling over the edge of the bed. Through her fair translucent skin, he could see the faint tracery of blue veins along her forearm, along the curve of her throat. He could see the splash of russet hair, bright as blood against the pillowcases. Recognition was instantaneous, the agony so strong and harsh he nearly cried out with the pain of it.

Grayson. The realization seared through him with all the force of a lightning bolt. His heart lurched. He went sick and weightless inside. Devastation ripped through him. He was empty, hollow, terrified. Grayson was utterly motionless, perfectly still. She didn't seem to be breathing.

Denial shrieked through him, fierce and strong. *No! God no! I couldn't have murdered Grayson. I could never, ever hurt her*.

With his pulse throbbing at his temples, he reached for her, stroked the rough, heavy silk of her hair, felt it slide cool and soft between his fingertips. He brushed a few stray strands from her cheek, realizing suddenly that her skin was warm. That warmth cracked up his arm. It jarred his heart, stopped the air in his lungs. Afraid to believe the single perception, he dropped his hand to the hollow at the side of her throat. Her pulse rapped out a steady rhythm beneath his icy, quaking fingertips.

Elation rose in his head in dizzying whorls. The ache of relief moved through him. Grayson wasn't dead! He hadn't hurt her. And if he hadn't hurt her, then he wasn't . . .

"Grayson?" His voice seemed untried and quavery in the silent dawn. "Grayson."

His wife made no response.

He bent above her, bracing a hand on either side of her body. "Grayson," he demanded. "Grayson, wake up."

She stirred and turned within the confines of his arms. Her eyes opened. They were heavy with sleep, filled with drowsy confusion.

She reached up to touch his cheek. "Duncan, are you all right? Is your headache gone?"

Her tenderness and concern were too much for him to bear. He didn't deserve her solicitude. He didn't deserve her at all.

Raw emotion burned in his chest and closed his throat. He went trembly and liquid inside. There was no name for what he was feeling, no way to express it at all.

His knuckles grazed the line of her jaw, the sweep of ivory throat. *Oh, Gray. Oh, God, you're safe!*

Looking down, his eyes bored into hers. *I was so afraid I'd hurt you*.

He buried his face in the curve of her shoulder, unwilling to let her see how terrified he'd been. *Oh, love, you mean the world to me.*

He stretched out beside her and gathered her close, moving slowly so as not to frighten her. He needed to feel the warmth of her flesh against him, needed to feel the steady beating of her heart in counterpoint to the erratic thumping of his own. After the tricks his own drugged mind had played on him, he craved physical reassurance with a fury that stunned and frightened him. But he also wanted to show her how much he cared, how much she'd come to mean to him.

"Grayson," he whispered against her throat, not knowing how to express the fullness in his heart, not knowing how to explain his desperate need for solace. "Oh, Grayson."

Her arms tightened around him in answer to his unspoken plea. She stirred, turned into his embrace, offering the haven of her concern, the balm of her infinite tenderness. In response, he wanted to give her every part of himself, offer her proof of everything he felt. He wanted to thank her, tell her of the feelings he was no longer afraid to name.

He closed his eyes and swallowed hard, his fingers flexing and clutching in the tumbled thicket of her hair.

"Grayson," he murmured, against her throat. "Oh, Gray, I love you so."

She drew a breath as if to respond in kind, but Duncan craved so much more than words from her. He wanted his actions to banish the horrifying possibilities that had occupied his mind, the hopeless, helpless dread that had made him question his sanity. He needed to show Grayson how much he cared, to let the sweetness of their lovemaking assuage the anxiety that had been building in his chest. He wanted complete and utter release from the terrible tension coursing through his veins.

His lips claimed hers in a ravishing kiss, in a kiss that was, for all its harsh demand, infinitely sweet and cherishing. As their mouths merged, his hands swept in widening circles across her back, encompassing as much of her as he could in the breadth of his trembling hands. He crushed her fiercely to himself, his palms pressed flat against her skin as if he needed every nerve to be engaged in the act of savoring her. He wanted to worship her, acknowledge her in a way he had never worshiped or acknowledged another woman.

Gray seemed to respond to the intensity of his caress on a level that was unquestioning and instinctual, curling into the arc of his body, tangling her fingers in the fullness of his hair, accepting the proof of his desire for her. As frenzied as Duncan was, she seemed to surround him with reassuring calm. As anguished as his fears had made him, she seemed capable of offering him infinite peace. If he was night, she was dawn. If he was need, she was succor.

Loving her for her perceptiveness, her selfless generosity, Duncan eased Grayson back against the pillows and moved to lie over her. He looked down into her eyes, and felt as if he was coming home, home to someone who truly cared, home to someone who loved him unconditionally. He stroked a thumb across her cheek, furrowed his fingers into her heavy hair.

"I love you." The words seemed to have been torn from deep within his chest. They were so simple, so inadequate. He hurt with the intensity of what he felt, with the intensity of the emotions he had finally dared to name. "I love you, Gray."

She raised her head and touched her lips to his, drawing gently on his mouth, urging him down to her. As he came, he felt her lawn-covered breasts spread against his chest, felt her hips nestle to the shape of him. A low moan rose in his throat. He wanted to make love to her, and Grayson seemed to want that, too.

Then she was struggling to free herself from her nightdress, seeking to make herself available to him. Duncan moved to help her with the task, though he had little patience for the fasteners and bows. Under the frantic motions of his hands, the thin fabric parted with a rending rasp. Somehow the ruined garment was cast aside and Gray lay open before him, offering all of herself.

He moaned as her hands skimmed along his shoulders and his chest, gasped at the burning intensity that was raging through his flesh. His muscles were tight and hot as he rose over her. His body was heavy and engorged with a desire that only Gray could arouse in him. Her legs parted and she drew him into herself, and he sank blindly into the dark, wet heat of her.

Safe in the haven of her body he was welcomed, revered, loved, accepted in a way that went beyond any acceptance he had ever known. The emotion of the moment caught in his throat. He closed his eyes and swallowed hard.

"I love you, Gray."

"And I love you."

As they kissed her hands moved over him, skimming along his quivering arms, scaling his shoulders, teasing his nipples with the insistent brush of her thumbs. Gray completely filled his senses, her taste seeping through him, her tender words circling in his brain, her gardenia scent drugging him with its sweetness. Streamers of sensation unfurled through Duncan, flooding his loins, snaking down his legs. Desire flared, flashing higher, surging with incendiary intensity. It seared through his body and his brain, engulfing all doubts and fears in a burst of excruciating pleasure.

He stroked and kissed her breasts, laving the tips with the insistent flick of his tongue. Gray was so soft, so delectable, so wondrously alive. And she was his.

Duncan's hands moved over her, touching, cherishing, worshiping. She writhed beneath him in joyous anticipation. Her breathing went shallow and fast. Her eyes glowed. Her body shuddered with a delicious delight that matched his own.

He began to move within her. The racking fears had left his emotions flayed raw, and there was no holding back. He wanted to acknowledge, physically and emotionally, all she had come to mean to him.

"Grayson, I love you. Oh, Gray, I love you so." The words were a litany on his lips, a confession, a prayer for absolution, a pledge of everything that was in his heart. "I love you, love you."

"Oh, Duncan, I love you, too."

They had been dancing at the edge of the abyss, and her fervent exclamation sent them swirling into space. The world seemed to drop away beneath them. Their gazes held as they began to fall. He saw her eyes darken as the exquisite sweetness of release swept over her. An instant later that same mindless ecstasy came to take him, too. They were spinning, cresting, drifting. They wafted in the complementing currents of their own surging completion, clung together in the maelstrom of ultimate pleasure.

What they shared physically was infinitely precious, hopelessly transient, unexpected and rare. But in their hearts the knowledge of what this joining meant nestled deep, nurturing the caring and concern that had been growing there. This union was the flowering of a rich, full-blooming love that was lush and sweet and perennial. It was an acknowledgment of the exquisite bond that had grown between them. It was a hint of something even better to come.

They drifted for a while, spent and sated, gloriously one. They were totally fulfilled, possessed of a wondrous serenity and calm that gave lie to the fears that had brought them together. They were all two people in love should be, more complete and content, more secure and whole, than they had ever been before. The words they had spoken had substantiated what they felt, made it tangible and real. They were all a man and wife should ever be, and as dawn turned to the light of full day, they savored that wondrous reality.

Gray's hair seemed to crackle with life as the maid drew a brush through the heavy titian strands. Her skin seemed to glow as if lit from within. Her eyes seemed unusually dark, especially warm. A slow, soft smile curled the corners of her mouth as she thought about why she felt so gloriously beautiful, so wondrously alive. It was because Duncan loved her, because he had admitted his feelings for her at last.

The memory of the way they'd come together in the dawn was so vivid, so crystalline, she could almost feel Duncan's hands sweeping across her skin, almost feel the demanding pressure of his lips against her mouth. She could almost feel the thrust and draw of his body moving inside her, feel herself burst and flourish in response to him. The words he'd whispered soft against her skin echoed in her ears. His voice had been low, ragged, filled with passion. Just the timbre had left her tingling.

"I love you, Grayson," he'd murmured. "I love you so."

With a few simple words Duncan had given her a wondrous gift, the thing she had been fruitlessly seeking all her life. It was the knowledge that she belonged, that for Duncan she was the most important person in the world. For her, his pledge of love had been a benediction, the unconditional assurance that someone really cared for her. For the first time she felt whole, totally secure, utterly complete, and it was Duncan who made her feel that way.

And I love you, too, Duncan, she thought. I love you, and I'll do everything I can to make you happy.

As if he had sensed her thoughts, Duncan appeared in the doorway that connected their rooms, looking every bit as contented as Grayson felt.

"Good morning, love," he greeted her. "I hope you are ready to go down to breakfast. I think I could eat a full dozen eggs with a pound of bacon on the side."

"We're nearly finished here, aren't we, Anna?" she asked her maid.

"Aye, my lady, that we are."

Gray and Duncan made their way down to the dining room and were delighted to find that they had the place entirely to themselves. Quentin had gone out, though to find him abroad at such an early hour surprised them both.

"It must have been something important," Duncan observed as he filled his plate from the dishes of eggs, bacon, kippers, and potatoes kept warming on the sideboard.

"He's probably gone to see his broker," Grayson offered. "I've heard that his gambling losses are substantial. You really should have a word with him, Duncan, before we leave. Gambling has been the ruination of many an otherwise respectable man."

One of the footmen brought in a toast rack and fresh coffee as Duncan took a seat at one end of the long table. "I know, Gray. I'm worried about his excesses, too. His gambling seems out of hand and he is drinking far more than he should."

Grayson settled herself beside her husband. "You're his only kin. There's no one else to talk to him."

"I promise I'll have a word with Quentin before we leave."

Duncan set aside the newspaper at his place and spread the napkin in his lap. "These eggs look marvelous. The cook here is better than the one Uncle Farleigh employs. I wonder if she'd be willing to emigrate."

They ate in silence for a few minutes, and when Duncan was done, he turned to Grayson. "Well, what are your plans for the day?"

"I promised my aunt and uncle that we'd stop by. After leaving so suddenly last night, I think a short visit would be in order. I also thought we might go to the National Gallery. The Royal Academy Show opened a week or two ago, and I've not had a chance to see it."

"You know, New York has art collections, too," he teased her. "We have concerts, operas, and theaters."

"Why, Duncan, do you really?" she asked with a lift of her brows. "I've been meaning to ask you about New York. What's the city like?"

"It's a lot more cosmopolitan than you probably think. It's an old city by American standards, founded by the Dutch in the sixteen hundreds."

"But what's it like now?" she asked impatiently.

"I should think it's like any other city. It has its shops and markets, its elegant neighborhoods and its slums. Uncle Farleigh's house is on Washington Square, though if you don't want to live with him we can look for a place of our own."

"And how far is Washington Square from the theaters?"

"You still intend to pursue a career as an actress, do you?"

Knowing that Duncan loved her made the conversation about her career less difficult, yet Gray dreaded introducing a subject that might take the glow off what promised to be a wonderful day. Still, it was best to have this settled before they reached New York.

Grayson drew a breath and squared her shoulders. "A career on the stage is what I've always wanted, Duncan. I thought you understood how important acting is to me."

As if sensing that she was preparing a full assault to win her way, Duncan reached across to touch her hand. "I *do* know how important acting is to you, Grayson. And if you want a life on the stage, I think you should pursue it."

His ready acquiescence pleased her, relieved many of the doubts she had been harboring. "Oh, Duncan, thank you. I've been so worried about discussing this with you after what you said when I asked for passage."

"Good God! What did you expect me to say? What you wanted to do scared the hell out of me."

"I know," she admitted sheepishly. "It scared the hell out of me, too."

"Well, at least now you'll have the protection of my name, and all the respectability that will give you. And I suppose if Sarah Siddons managed to be a wife and mother as well as the most well-respected actress of her age, it's not too much to expect from you."

"You have very high standards, my lord," she told him tartly.

"Indeed I have. Though I don't believe I've misplaced my trust in your abilities."

Gray flushed crimson at his words. They were both a challenge and a vote of confidence. He had given her a great deal to live up to, and she could do nothing but her best for him.

"Though, tell me, Grayson, if I had objected to your acting, would you have gone ahead with it anyway?"

Grayson paused, knowing she could not lie to him, especially after what had passed between them in the dawn. "Yes," she admitted baldly. "You would have had to find a way to understand."

Duncan gave an acknowledging laugh. "Yes, and I suppose I would have, too. Well, just don't sign on for long tours to the wilds. I want you with me in New York whenever I am there."

Gray knew she would have to make compromises to his career as well. There would be the inevitable voyages to make on company business, and as the wife of a sea captain she would have to accept the separations. Interests of her own would help her do that, and with the matter of their feelings for each other resolved at last, Grayson was certain they would find a way to make accommodations.

"I love you, Duncan," she told him.

"And I love you."

"We'll find a way to make this work."

"Yes, I know we will."

With a pat he drew his hand away from hers and picked up the folded newspaper.

Sipping from her coffee cup, Grayson watched Duncan, thinking how contented she would be sharing breakfast with him for the rest of their lives. She had learned already that Duncan was a very predictable man whose life was set in a carefully prescribed routine. In the morning he bathed and shaved; he dressed for the day. He liked his coffee black and unadulterated by the chicory used so often here in England. He also wanted it piping hot and was not above shouting for another pot if the one on the table fell below what he deemed the appropriate temperature.

He always ate his breakfast first, set his napkin aside, then retreated into the pages of his newspaper. His reactions to the day's events could be gauged by the expressions that crossed his face, by the raising and lowering of his brows, by the thinning of his lips. If some trend in politics, public opinion, or the weather displeased him, he would mutter to himself about the offending article, then glance up, abashed, as if suddenly remembering she was there.

As she poured herself more to drink, Duncan opened the paper to the second page. It crackled as he folded the sheet back and then in half. It was the way he always did it. His predictability made her smile.

But in midfold, Duncan froze, staring at something. His face lost all its color as he scanned one of the stories on the page.

"Duncan—" she began, wondering what had upset him.

Abruptly he came to his feet, his pale eyes haunted, filled with pain.

"Duncan?"

"I'm going out," he told her. "I don't know when I will be back."

"Duncan," she called out as he strode toward the door. "Duncan, what's the matter?"

He was gone before she could demand an answer.

Coming around the end of the table, Grayson picked up the crumpled paper. There were four stories on the sheet. One was about unrest in Ireland, another dealt with the lowering of tariffs. A third was on the steamship *Great Western*'s crossing of the Atlantic in record time. The fourth, complete with an artist's rendering of the object, dealt with a moonstone necklace. It had been found missing from around the neck of the West End Strangler's latest victim.

It was true. Oh, God, it was true. Duncan's feet tapped out a hopeless litany. He had been walking for hours. He didn't know where he was; he didn't know where he'd been. He only knew that the article in this morning's paper had confirmed his worst fears, confirmed that he was the most despicable kind of criminal. He was the West End Strangler.

Just when he had begun to push the suspicions aside, just when he had begun to believe that happiness was within his grasp, the news story in the *Morning Chronicle* had turned his life inside out. It convinced him he was the man the police were seeking, the madman who had been killing women here in London.

The necklace that was missing from around the throat of the Strangler's latest victim, the heavy moonstone necklace that had been depicted in the newspaper just this morning, was hidden in the wooden box tucked beneath his clothes in the dresser at the town house. It linked him irrevocably to the Strangler's last crime, undeniably proving his guilt.

As if his possession of the necklace was not enough to damn him, there were the unexplained scratches on his face, the advertising card that put him in the vicinity of one of the previous attacks, and the murder just outside Grayson's garden on the night he had taken refuge there. It was more than chance that the murders had begun just after his return to London. It was more than chance that each of the crimes had taken place on a night when he was incapacitated by a headache. The conclusion was very clear: In the throes of his violent headaches, in the void of pain and forgetfulness, Duncan had been murdering helpless women.

There was no question that he was capable of the act. He had killed his father when he was little more than a boy. He had strangled an assailant in an alley in Limehouse less than a month ago. He remembered the moment with excruciating clarity. With nothing more than the strength of his hands, he had killed the man. He had tightened his fingers around his attacker's throat until he felt the grinding crack of vertebrae. The memory made his stomach heave, made bile rise in the back of his throat. Weakness swept through him, and he leaned against a building until the worst of the sickness had passed. Though it made him ill to remember, there was no question that he was capable of taking human life.

He had strangled those women, just as he had that man in the Limehouse alleyway. He had attacked frail, frightened women, using his far superior size and strength to subdue them. Had they struggled? Had they screamed? Had they fought to escape him? Surely the last one had. She had left her marks on his face and hands. But he couldn't remember strangling them. He couldn't remember the women at all.

Duncan realized suddenly that he was running, his feet pounding on the pavement, the air rasping in his lungs, the blood thudding in his temples. He dodged around people on the walk—costermongers crying their wares, women doing their shopping, a throng of laughing children watching a juggler on a street corner. He flashed past them, not knowing where he was running to, knowing only what he was running from. Even as he pushed himself for greater speed, he knew there was no escape. The devil he was fleeing resided within himself.

At the end of his endurance, he staggered to his knees. His breath was coming in sobs. His heart was ready to explode through the wall of his chest. He was wet with sweat, shaking and sick. He closed his eyes and listened to the life coursing through his body, wondering why he'd ever been born.

After a time he became aware of his surroundings, of the street noise, of the people stepping around him on the sidewalk. From somewhere near at hand Duncan could smell the faint, dank odor of the river and instinctively made his way in that direction. The Thames was dirty, rank, a far cry from the freshness of the open sea, but there was something about water that always calmed him, cleared his head.

There was a steep alley to his left, and he followed it sharply downhill. When he reached the bottom, he came upon a jumble of shacks clinging to each other and the slope of the muddy riverbank. There was a small dock jutting out into the current, and he made his way to the end of it. The tide was in; the water was high. He found a place against a piling and sank down beside it, listening to the lap of the waves. The sound reminded him of the *Citation*, of the hours and days of peace he had known as he sailed the seas. He knew that because of what he was, of what he'd done, he would never stride those beloved decks again. He would never hear the creak of the masts and the flap of canvas in a high wind, never feel the crisp salt spray against his skin, never know the luxury of the complete and utter freedom sailing gave a man. He mourned the loss, felt a profound sadness for all he would never see or feel or do again.

There was no question about the course he had to follow now. He would have to go to the police and confess his crimes. It was more than possible that Inspector Lawrence at Scotland Yard already suspected him of being the West End Strangler. Hannibal Frasier had said that men were asking about him, and two of them shadowed his every move. Grayson had pointed them out that night they had escaped from Sidney Layton's brothel. There had been two sets of them then, Worthington's men and the two unkempt fellows who followed him still. Perhaps they were detectives gathering proof of what he'd done, waiting to catch him in the act of committing another murder. In his mad dash through London's streets he had lost them temporarily, but he knew they would be back.

But before he turned himself in to the police, he needed to clarify, in his own mind, why he was strangling these women. Duncan closed his eyes and tried to think. His thoughts were sluggish, restless, elusive as smoke, but he forced himself to concentrate. Perhaps the assaults on the women were tied to his parents' death somehow. Had his return to England stirred some darkness in his soul? Had it driven him to re-create the circumstances of his mother's death? He had to understand what had happened to turn him into a killer, had to find some link between present and past.

A vision of Antire Manor rose in his mind, the wild, idyllic Dorset coast, the huge stone house with its crenellated towers, the library where his father and mother had died. It was a place he loved and hated. In his mind he could still hear the sea crashing onto the rocky beach at the base of the cliff, see the reflected silvery light from the water shimmering on the ceilings of the rooms, smell the freshness of the sea and fields. There were some happy memories associated with his parents' visits to the manor. He remembered riding with his father in the early mornings, picnicking along the cliffs, picking bouquets of wildflowers to delight his mother, having her kiss and hug him with gratitude for his often wilted offerings.

But he could also remember his parents' arguments ringing through the halls. He hadn't always understood the words, but even as a child he had recognized the tone of their voices. Those arguments had sent him fleeing. They'd sent him racing along the cliffs until the waves muffled the shouting, the thud of overturned furniture, the crash of breaking glass. He had stayed away until the soothing whisper of the sea calmed him, and by the time he returned to the house, the violence had always abated. Either his parents were in their bedroom with the door securely closed, or they were talking and laughing together as if nothing untoward had passed between them.

Duncan ran a trembling hand through his hair and stared toward the chimney pots and rooftops of Southwark across the Thames.

He closed his eyes and tried to remember. Had his parents been arguing the night they died? Had he run away? If he had stayed, would he have been able to intervene? Would he have been able to save his mother? The questions grabbed at him, twisted deep in his belly. The pain was unendurable. But he needed to know what happened. He needed to understand what had turned him, all these years after the initial crime, into the most despicable of murderers.

What had he seen in the study on that night so long ago that made him capable of ending his father's life? Had his mother's death awakened ferocious, mindless fury? Had his unwilling return to England loosed that murderous rage again? How had he hidden that anger from everyone for all these years? How had he hidden it from himself? It seemed impossible that he could have.

Duncan knew he had a reputation as an extremely even-tempered man. Among his crew he was noted for his fairness. He had often been applauded for his dispassionate approach to business problems. He had never in his life had harsh words with his uncle or Ryan Barnes. Even when his feelings for Grayson sundered his control, made him acknowledge passions deep inside himself, his responses had never hinted at something so vile, so sternly repressed.

His ability to sublimate that terrible pain, that excruciating anger, was incompatible with everything Duncan believed about himself. It had no place as a part of the man he knew himself to be. It was the antithesis of what he felt for Gray.

Until he met Gray, he had been sleepwalking through life, moving through each day by rote. He had never reached out to touch the world, had never let it touch him. He had kept his feelings, his passions, in check, ruthlessly, relentlessly, unknowingly. He had been living half a life and had never missed the fierce reality of the whole.

Oddly enough it was Gray's vulnerability, not her strength, that had breached his defenses. The defiance and uncertainty in her eyes the night she had recited at Lady Monmouth's soirée had made him want to offer her unexpected insights, share with her an unexplored part of himself. Though he had eventually tried to withdraw from her, Grayson had continued to demand the things he had freely given once before. In return she had offered an acceptance he had never thought to know, a love that awed him still. Grayson's determination and perceptiveness had made him open himself to her, and when he gave her all of himself, it was like stepping from the shadows into the sun.

The world had become a brighter place than it had ever been before, the wind more redolent of the scent of spring, the streets more filled with life, the food he ate more flavorful. He was alive, fully alive, for the very first time. The blood coursed more strongly in his veins; the air in his lungs was ripe and invigorating. The thoughts that flew through his mind were clearer, his perceptions sharper, his world wondrous and new. His love for Grayson, even before he gave it that name, had changed him irrevocably. And now as he sat trying to understand the perversity that had invaded his life, he could not reconcile what he felt for Grayson and the world at large with the taking of a life.

Murder was destruction, madness, horror. A killer embraced death. A killer worshiped fear. A killer hated.

Duncan loved.

A sudden quiet came over him, a quiet so absolute that nothing inside him seemed to stir. It was like the lull in the midst of a violent storm, like the eerie silence of being becalmed. He was barely breathing, felt as if his heart was barely beating.

He had not killed those women.

He knew it now as certainly as he knew that he loved Gray.

Relief broke over him, making him tingle. It brought the sting of tears to his eyes, awakened a flutter of hope in his chest. It washed through him in a wave of utter exhaustion. His tense muscles loosened; his head fell back. He drew one long unsteady breath and then another. He could hear the lap of the water against the dock, hear the voices of watermen from the ferries passing up and down the Thames. He became aware of the waning sun warm on his skin, of the glimmer of deep yellow light catching and shimmering on the tops of the waves.

He was not mad. He was not a murderer. He was not the West End Strangler.

For a time, he sat with his mind empty, his body lax. He watched the traffic on the river, the barges and halfpenny steamers. He watched the birds scribing lazy circles in the golden sky, watched three dirty urchins fishing from the end of the dock. Duncan could not have moved, if he had wanted to, could not have formed a coherent thought, if his life had depended on it.

It was twilight before he was able to stir, able to think. He came stiffly to his feet, becoming slowly aware of his skinned knees, his ruined trousers. There were cinders ground into the palms of his hands. He remembered running, falling. But that seemed like a lifetime ago, as if it had happened to someone else. In a way it had.

It was time to go back to the town house, time to try to explain to Grayson where he'd been and why. He could not tell her the truth, of course. There were some things it was wiser for her not to know. But he could reassure her, comfort her. He could make love to her with a depth of feeling and a relish that would surpass even what they'd shared this morning.

As he picked his way up the street that led to the Strand, his mind began to function again. The questions he had been too relieved and exhausted to ask earlier in the day came to plague him as he wended his way back to the town house. There was no doubt that someone had set out to make him believe he was the West End Strangler. The murders had been done to coincide with the nights when he was incapacitated. The advertising card had been planted in his clothes to lead him to the Crown Inn. The moonstone necklace had deliberately been placed among his things. But who could have done such a thing? Who hated him enough to want to make him believe he was a madman? Possibilities slowly began to present themselves.

Samuel Walford hated him. Duncan had sent word shortly after they had landed at Portsmouth that he meant to review Wicker and Walford's books. If Walford had put his plans into motion then, he could have accomplished such a deed. But Walford had no access to the house, no way to know when the headaches struck unless he had hired someone to do his bidding. It was not impossible that Walford could have paid one of the servants to inform him when Duncan was incapacitated, to plant the advertising card and the necklace among his things, even to commit the crimes. Walford was rich enough to pay handsomely for such services. Now that Duncan had spoiled his game, was preparing to take control of the English branch of the company, and had dashed Walford's hopes of a knighthood, the man had even more reason to be vindictive.

Then, too, there was his cousin Quentin. The elder Palmer had full access to the house and had been with Duncan several times when a headache had come upon him. If Duncan was tried for murder and hanged, Quentin would inherit the title and the lands. With the difficulties he was having with his creditors, Quentin would certainly benefit by Duncan's death. But he'd also had control of Duncan's English holdings for several years, and there was no sign of any irregularity in the way he had handled the funds. Had guilt, hatred, and hope of gain driven Quentin to murder? Was Quentin capable of masterminding such a complex plot?

And then there was Ryan Barnes. The valet had total access to Duncan's things and knew precisely when the headaches struck. But even as the thought strayed into Duncan's mind he was dishonored by it. Ryan Barnes was his friend and confidant. Ryan didn't hate him, would never countenance anything to harm him. Duncan rejected the idea utterly.

Duncan didn't know who the West End Strangler was, but he fully intended to find out. With Hannibal Frasier's help, he had tracked down proof of Walford's embezzlement, and he would solve this mystery, too. There was a link between the Strangler and him, if only he could discern what it was. Somehow he would have to elude the police until he discovered what that connection was.

His hopes on that account plummeted as he rounded the corner of Bruton Street into Berkeley Square and saw that the two men who usually followed him were standing in the shadows of the trees in the mall, waiting patiently for his return.

Twenty-two

"MR. BARNES?" GRAYSON'S RETICENCE WAS EVIDENT IN HER voice as she entered her husband's dressing room. "Mr. Barnes, I was hoping you might be able to answer a question or two."

Ryan Barnes turned from the elegant bowfront dresser with a pile of monogrammed handkerchiefs in hand. He had been putting away Duncan's clothes, and it was clear he was not pleased at being interrupted, especially by his master's bride.

"You want me to answer some questions for you, Lady Grayson? Something about your husband's socks, his shirts, his handkerchiefs?"

Grayson's mouth narrowed at the sarcasm in his tone. "I'm concerned about what Duncan was doing yesterday."

"What his lordship was doing? He said he was seeing to business down at the docks. Is there reason for you to doubt him?"

Grayson had given a great deal of thought to approaching her husband's valet, especially in the light of Ryan's recent hostility. But after Duncan's behavior the previous day, the way he'd fled the house, his prolonged absence, his appearance when he'd returned, and the disjointed explanations he'd given her, Gray was too alarmed to let the valet's petty jealousy stand in the way of her discovering what she could.

"Mr. Barnes, you saw the way he looked when he came back to the house. He was battered and bruised, and his clothes were little more than rags. Is it usual for him to be in such a state when all he has been doing is business at the docks?"

"I thought he said he had been helping the hands with some of the crates when one of them got away from him."

"Is it usual for Duncan to help unload the cargo when there are seamen and stevedores to do it?"

"You don't know his lordship very well if you think he'd stand idly by while others did his work."

What Barnes said rang true. Duncan was the kind of man who was fully involved with anything he deemed was his responsibility. But Ryan's explanation didn't put her mind to rest.

"I suppose I'm concerned because he left the house so suddenly, because he was so recently recovered from one of his headaches."

"Well," Barnes conceded as he tucked the handkerchiefs away, "if you'd not seen one of his headaches before, I can understand why it upset you."

"Indeed." Grayson nodded in agreement. "Is he always in such terrible pain? Does he always drug himself so heavily?"

Barnes picked up a silver-handled whisk broom and began to brush a gray flannel jacket laid out across the cot in the dressing room. "The headaches have always been the same."

"They've always been so severe?"

"And every bit as debilitating."

"They started shortly after his parents died, didn't they?"

"Not more than a month or two, I should think."

"Do you think there's any connection between the headaches and his parents' death?"

Barnes shrugged. "I really couldn't say."

"You were there at Antire Manor when the tragedy was discovered, weren't you?"

Barnes stopped his brushing and looked up at her with haunted eyes. "Aye, I was there."

"Can you tell me what happened?"

"Tell you, Lady Grayson? Indeed I can. I was the first of the servants to reach the library, and I'll remember what I saw until my dying day. I was at the foot of the stairs when I heard a noise, and when I reached the upstairs landing the door to the library was standing open. I could see his lordship, Master Duncan, on the floor not a dozen steps inside the room. His father was lying before the desk in a pool of blood, and his mother was sprawled on the settee. It was evident what had happened, just as it was evident that there was nothing to be done for either of his parents. I went right to where Master Duncan lay. His face was pale as parchment and there was a gun clutched in his hand."

"The gun was in his hand, you say?"

"Aye, it was, and the barrel was still hot."

"There's no chance you could have been mistaken?"

Barnes's eyes were dark, and his brows were drawn together in an expression of grief. "No, my lady. None at all."

"I was only hoping . . ." Grayson sighed and shook her head. "I was only hoping that the truth would be less damning than the stories I had heard. The tragedy of his parents' death plagues Duncan so."

Ryan nodded sympathetically. "I wish that things were different, too."

"And what about Lady Johanna? Why were you sure she was dead?"

"It was the way she looked, the angle of her head. As I was trying to rouse Duncan," he went on, "the other servants began to arrive. They went to her, but she was gone. Her neck was broken clean."

"And Duncan's father killed her?"

The distress on Barnes's round face kept Grayson from asking more. He seemed even more unsettled by the memory of Lady Johanna's death than he was by Jeremy Palmer's. "What happened then?"

"After a few moments it seemed as if Master Duncan was coming around. He opened his eyes, was able to stand. We took the gun away from him and led him to his room. He didn't seem to realize where he was or what had happened. It was as if he was in a daze, as if his body was with us in the room but his mind was someplace else. And I know now that's exactly the way it was for him. He doesn't remember any of it, not the killing, not the funeral, not being questioned by the magistrates, not leaving Antire Manor. And I don't blame him for blocking it out. I wish I could have forgotten, too."

"Were you close to Duncan's father and mother?"

Ryan nodded. "To his father. Jeremy and I played together when we were boys. It was Lord Jeremy who asked for me as his valet when my family had always worked the land."

In spite of the years of refinement, Grayson could see a bit of the laborer in Ryan still. It was evident in his compact stature, in the powerful arms and shoulders, in the strength and breadth of his hands. It must have been difficult for a man raised to a life of common labor to learn the finer ways of a gentleman's gentleman. Yet Barnes had succeeded most admirably. The rough edges were all but gone, and in their place was the precise and proper manner of a fine valet.

"And in spite of what he did to your boyhood friend, you've treated Duncan like a son."

Though Ryan didn't move, Grayson sensed he'd somehow retreated from her.

"Not like a son," he corrected her. "Not like a son. I had a son, and that was different."

"You have a son? Has he been here in England all these years?"

"His bones are here. He died not long before the marquis and marchioness."

"I'm sorry. I didn't know. Duncan never mentioned him."

"I doubt that he would remember. Liam was years older than Duncan, and my boy had gone away."

Something in the valet had changed at the mention of his son. His face went stiff and his eyes were flat. That the man was still mourning his son's death was very evident, but there was anger in him, too. It was a fierce, private anger that Grayson didn't understand, and she was reluctant to press him further.

"I did not mean to pry into things that are none of my concern," she apologized. "I only meant to ask you about Duncan and the way he's been behaving."

When Barnes did not reply, she hurried on. "It's just that I don't understand what's bothering Duncan. It seems to be more than just the headaches, yet he refuses to confide in me."

"Men have their secrets," Barnes answered gruffly, "just as women do. He'll tell you what they are if he wants you to know. You must be patient with him until he does."

What Barnes said was true, but Grayson was not satisfied. There was something wrong in Duncan's life, something that went beyond the headaches, something that went beyond their sudden marriage, something that went beyond his eagerness to leave England and his past behind. Every instinct confirmed that belief, and Gray yearned to help Duncan resolve his conflicts. Nor could she deny the conviction that he should be willing to share his secrets. They'd shared so much already, and after all, she was his wife.

* * *

"Did you know there's been another murder?" Quentin Palmer lowered the newspaper and glanced at the stunning red-haired woman seated across the breakfast table.

"Another murder?" Grayson gasped, her eyes going wide with horror and concern.

"It seems the West End Strangler's struck again."

"Who is the victim this time?"

"A barmaid from a tavern over in the St. James's Village. It seems she went into the alley to empty slops, and it was nearly an hour before they missed her."

"Oh, Lord," Gray murmured in genuine distress. "When will all this end? When will the police catch this awful man?"

"When will the police catch whom?" Duncan asked as he made his way into the dining room. He was frowning and his voice was sharp. Quentin knew that Duncan's bathwater had been late in arriving this morning, and his disposition had evidently not improved since Quentin had passed his cousin's room and heard him in the midst of a dustup with Ryan Barnes.

"Grayson was asking when the police would catch the West End Strangler," Quentin answered.

"You mean there's been another murder?" The younger Palmer looked up in alarm as he took his chair at the head of the table.

Quentin watched him resentfully. The head of the table was a position he himself had occupied until his cousin's return, and Quentin could not quite rid himself of the rancor he felt at seeing Duncan usurp his place. But that would be remedied soon enough, the older man consoled himself. Very soon he would have everything he wanted, everything that should be rightfully his.

"And I suppose no one saw the man who killed her," Duncan observed, obviously itching to get his hands on the paper and read the story for himself.

"No, no one saw him. But this time the fellow left a clue to his identity." With a certain smugness, Quentin snapped the crinkling paper wide and began to read the article.

> "At last we have a small indication of the West End Strangler's identity," Police Inspector George Lawrence told this reporter. "Beside the body we found a handkerchief embroidered with the initial P. It is made of the very finest linen cloth with a hand-rolled hem. The quality of the fabric and the

workmanship lead us to believe that our suspicion that the Strangler fancies himself a gentleman is essentially correct."

"What else does he have to say?" Duncan demanded impatiently. "Give the paper here. Let me have a look."

But Quentin smiled, willing to chance his cousin's uncertain temper, at least this once. Clearing his throat, he continued to read.

When asked how the police could be sure that the handkerchief belonged to the West End Strangler, Lawrence replied: "Because of the cleanliness of the handkerchief we are led to believe that it was not in the alley for very long. Then, too, the cloth was found on top of the victim's skirt, not beneath it. We suspect that her killer wiped his hands after the commission of the crime and dropped the handkerchief accidentally. It is not conclusive proof that the Strangler's name begins with P, but it does give us another avenue to explore in the process of our investigation."

"Damn it, Quentin! I said give the paper here," Duncan ordered abruptly.

Both Gray and Quentin looked up in surprise at the heat of Duncan's tone. The set of his mouth and the expression in his eyes brooked no resistance, and Quentin handed over the newspaper.

"Testy this morning, aren't you?" the elder Palmer drawled. "Did you have another of your headaches?"

"As a matter of fact I did," Duncan admitted grudgingly. "Not that a headache has anything to do with my mood or wanting a look at the newspaper."

Still, Quentin was not quite able to let the moment pass. "Then are you concerned about the initial on that handkerchief? I know I haven't been murdering those women, so it can't be my linen the police have found. Can you be worried, Duncan, that the handkerchief's yours?"

Duncan paled and turned on his cousin like one possessed. "Do you think that this is a matter for jests?" he demanded, glaring down the table with glittering eyes. "Do you consider the lives of these women so insignificant that you are able to joke about what's happened to them?"

Quentin retreated as far as the confines of his chair would allow, feeling the carving bite into his back, feeling the heat of Duncan's wrath deep in his chest. "No. Of course it's not a matter for jests. I'm as appalled by the murders as you are."

Duncan seemed calmer but unappeased.

"Though his remark was in the poorest possible taste, Duncan," Grayson broke in with a meaningful glance at the older man, "I'm sure Quentin meant nothing by his comment. To think that either of you could be involved in such a thing is utterly preposterous."

Without so much as acknowledging either Quentin's apology or Grayson's words, Duncan snatched up the paper and strode to the door. As he slammed out of the dining room and stormed up the stairs, Gray and Quentin exchanged worried glances. Neither of them had ever seen Duncan in such a state, and it was only a moment before Grayson rose to follow him.

That Grayson loved his cousin was very clear, Quentin acknowledged as he returned to the eggs that were cooling on his plate. He regretted that. Grayson was as fine a woman as a man could hope to have, and it was a shame that her tender feelings for her husband could only bring her boundless grief in the days to come.

* * *

Duncan was waiting to take Grayson shopping, when the message arrived.

Your lordship,

There's more here than meets the eye. Come as soon as you can. More information now possible.

Frasier

"Damn the man," Palmer muttered, frowning down at the missive, feeling angry and frustrated. Frasier's message was impossibly vague. It said everything and nothing—just, he suspected, as the Scotsman had intended. It demanded that Duncan set out immediately for Antire Manor, implied that there was something sinister going on at the family estate. Had Frasier unearthed new information about the murder of Duncan's parents? Were the Scotsman's short, intriguing sentences referring to something else entirely? Duncan couldn't hazard a guess, and in spite of the investigator's imperative, Palmer wasn't prepared to visit Antire Manor. He had valid reasons for avoiding the place, as Frasier well knew. How could the man demand that he come to

Dorset now? Where did Frasier get the temerity to stir this up when Duncan was so close to leaving England, so close to putting the past behind him?

In spite of his irritation Duncan was also beginning to wish that Frasier was nearer at hand. The clue that had been found beside the Strangler's victim just this morning was a clear indication that the killer's tactics had changed. Whoever was behind the crimes had begun to implicate Palmer as the murderer. Whether the Strangler suspected that Duncan was aware of his ploy or had simply grown bored with the game, the end was coming closer. How long would it be before the Strangler gave the police the irrefutable proof of Duncan's guilt? How many more women would die before this Inspector Lawrence arrived at the town house to make an arrest? Would Palmer have time to prove his innocence, or was it already far too late?

Duncan stared sightlessly at the note, uncertain of how to proceed. Should he confront Samuel Walford? Would it help to question Quentin? Could he ask Barnes to keep an eye on the servants here at the house in the hope of determining whether any of them were in Walford's employ? He trusted Frasier and needed his guidance in this. The Scotsman would take his word that he had not been involved in the murders and would help Duncan find the man who was. He must send a message ordering Frasier back to London. Duncan cursed himself as a fool for not having seen the necessity of doing so sooner.

"Duncan." Grayson was suddenly at his elbow. He had not even heard her come into the room. "Duncan, what's that note?"

He forced himself to smile as he tucked the slip of paper away. "It's nothing, Grayson, nothing. It's just word from Portsmouth that the repairs to the *Citation* are nearly complete."

"Will we be leaving soon? Shall I have the maids begin to pack my things?"

"Are you as eager to go as that?"

She stared up at him, a pucker of concern between her brows. "Aren't you?"

"I wish we'd left England yesterday."

Realizing abruptly what he'd said and how she would likely interpret it, he averted his eyes. "You're not having second thoughts about going with me, are you?"

"No! Oh, Duncan, no," Gray hastened to reassure him. "Where

you are is where I belong. But I think it would do you good to put all of England behind you."

"You've been talking to Ryan, haven't you? He told you how much worse the headaches have been since we've been here."

"He's every bit as worried about you as I am."

It seemed pointless to assure her there was no need for her concern. The headaches were coming more frequently now, just as the Strangler's murders were. He couldn't deny that it would be better for them both if they could simply slip away. He didn't like keeping his troubles from her, but these were things he couldn't confide.

"It's only the thought of leaving Aunt Julo and Uncle Warren that makes me sad," Gray went on as if she sensed he wouldn't say anything more. "It's leaving everyone behind that's so tremendously difficult."

He put his arm around her shoulders, glad he could offer his comfort in this. "You needn't think about that now. It will be some days yet before my ship is ready to sail. We must make the most of the time that's left."

She looked up at him with a grateful smile, though there was a glaze of emotion in her eyes. "Everything will be fine. I promise you."

He could sense the strain beneath her words, but she spoke them most convincingly. She was an actress, a woman most skillful in counterfeiting emotions. But not with him, not anymore. She was afraid to leave the people who mattered most, afraid of what the future might hold for her. He was afraid of those things, too. But Gray wouldn't let that stop her, and he applauded her bravado.

He straightened the brim of her bonnet, tightened the bow beneath her chin. "Let's be on about our errands, then."

They went to a jeweler in Regent Street, to a man who serviced the Crown. Grayson wanted remembrances for those whom she would leave behind, and the gold heart-shaped locket she selected for her aunt was something Julo would always treasure. Warren Worthington was another case entirely. He was difficult, prickly, not given to sentimental gifts. They ordered a silver match safe engraved with his coat of arms. There were a few other small gifts to be selected, too, things for her uncle's servants, for her maid. There were a dozen packages more or less, and they made arrangements for them to be delivered to the town house later that afternoon.

They stopped in the dining room of the Hobbs Hotel for their midday meal, and Grayson, flushed and garrulous after the bottle of wine they had shared, chatted animatedly about the gifts.

"We must have a daguerreotype made for Aunt Julo. And perhaps we can ask her and Uncle Warren to have one taken, too. That way perhaps they won't seem so far away."

But even as he smiled and nodded, Duncan was only half listening to her words. For reasons he could not fathom, the two men who had been following him for weeks were gone, and Duncan found their absence unsettling. Why, when the police had found the Strangler's handkerchief with an initial that matched his own, would they call off the two men who had been watching him? What had ended the surveillance? It made no sense, and things that made no sense always seemed to bother him.

Eventually they finished their meal and rose to go. But as they crossed the hotel lobby and approached the door, something tightened in Duncan's stomach. The hair on the back of his neck had begun to stir, and there was prickling tension between his shoulderblades. There was danger here. Even in these calm, elegant surroundings there was danger, though he had no idea what it was.

As they stepped out onto the sunny street, Duncan looked immediately for the coach. It was waiting at the end of the block, pulled up behind several others. It was farther away than he would have liked, and his heart jumped crazily inside his chest. He didn't understand his apprehension, but he acted on it instinctively, tightening his fingers on Grayson's elbow as he hurried her along.

It was the spray of stone dust falling onto the brim of his hat that alerted Duncan, and he shifted his gaze three stories upward just in time to see a flash of movement behind a krater filled with flowers that was standing at the edge of the hotel roof.

Time seemed suspended as the huge pot teetered, overbalanced, and began to fall. As it hurtled toward them, he noted its classical shape, the fret design around the rim, the brilliant red of the geraniums planted inside. Then with a cry and a shove, he slammed Gray against the wall, shielding her body with his own as the krater whistled past them. It exploded on impact with the walk, shattering, detonating like a bomb, sending a spray of rock and earth against his back. In spite of the pelting, Duncan hovered over Gray until the sound had echoed away, until the dust had begun to settle around them.

He shifted his weight and stood erect, one arm still encircling Grayson's waist. Gray was clinging to his chest as if he'd glued her there. She was trembling, and her eyes were huge. He dragged her even closer into his embrace, and realized only then that he was shaking, too.

As a crowd began to gather, Duncan's gaze swept up to the roof and along the street. There was no sign anywhere that someone had meant to do them harm, yet he was convinced the careening flowerpot had been far from accidental. When he had settled Grayson in the coach and answered the hotel manager's questions, he stared up and down the street once more. Not a soul he recognized was anywhere in sight. None of this made any sense. What was going on? Just what the hell was going on?

Twenty-three

"GRAYSON?" DUNCAN'S VOICE BARELY REACHED HER. IT WAS NO more than a rustle of sound in the silent room, no more than a sigh breathed deep in the soft, pale dawn. "Grayson? Is that you?"

She turned away from the window and looked toward the bed. In the grainy half-light she could just make out the pale oval of Duncan's face, his dark hair splayed against the pillows, the length and breadth of his body beneath the muffling drifts of counterpane.

"Grayson?" The murmur came again.

Her slippers made sibilant whispers on the carpet as she glided toward him. The bed boards creaked as she sat on the edge of the mattress. Reaching across, she stroked his temple, the line of his cheek. His skin was cool to her touch, and from beneath the heavy fringe of lashes, she could see that he was watching her.

"Have you been with me all night?"

She shook her head. "I only came in a few minutes ago. Are you feeling any better?"

"My headache's gone."

She nodded once. "I'm glad. I know it worries you that they've been so much worse since you've been back in England. Perhaps once we leave for America . . ."

He stirred fretfully beside her, as if unwilling to discuss the indispositions that had plagued him these last weeks. She knew he was uncomfortable with the weakness he perceived the headaches to evidence, uncomfortable even with the sympathy she felt for him.

"Come and lie with me," he offered, sliding across the bed and raising the covers to beckon her. "I've missed having you beside me."

"If you'll try to sleep again."

As she spoke, Grayson slid the wrapper down her arms and stretched out in the place he'd made for her. "I wish there was something I could do for you when the headaches come."

"It helps just to know you're here with me. That I'm not alone."

Grayson nestled against his side, her head in the curve of his shoulder, her hand at the base of his throat. The warmth of his body seeped into her. The feel of him, the smell of him, the unspoken comfort of his nearness was like a protective cocoon around her. She settled in, realizing how cold and lonely the night had been without him. This was the way she had always wanted to feel, quiet, at peace, complete. Duncan had given her contentment like a gift, a boon of such wonder, such value, she hardly knew how to thank him.

At the brush of his lips against her brow, a smile curled the corners of her mouth.

"Better?" he whispered into her hair.

"Infinitely," she answered him.

They lay together for a little while, quiet, drifting, dreamy in the hazy light of dawn. She was nearly asleep when he shifted beside her.

"Grayson?"

"Mmmm?"

"I want you to know that I love you, that no matter what happens, I'll always love you."

Something about his reassurance bothered Gray. Perhaps it was the inappropriateness of the sentiment at a time of such tenderness and peace, or perhaps it was his need to reassure her at all that made something shrink inside her.

She came up on one elbow and looked into his face. Even through the deep shadows that lay across his features, she could see the concern in his expression. She could sense the tension in him, a tension that had not been there a moment before, a tension that there was no rational reason for him to feel. There was something about his quiet intensity, something about the way he said the words that frightened her. It spawned a dread deep down in her belly, made her chest go tight.

"I'm glad to hear you say that," she answered, trying to make light of his comment. "I wouldn't have it any other way."

He turned his head, glanced away. "I just wanted you to know."

Duncan knew he would have been wiser to hold his peace, but since the moment he had opened his eyes this morning, from the instant he had noticed Grayson silhouetted against the pale gray light from the window, he'd had a sense that his time with her was coming to an end. Even before the attempt on their lives the previous day, he had felt the darkness rising. There was evil lurking near. Something that could tear them apart was loose and threatening.

For every headache there had been a murder of some hapless woman in London's streets, and he could not believe that today would be the one exception. Somewhere out there in the gray light and the hovering mist a woman had died by the Strangler's hand. Somewhere out there a nameless, faceless madman had laid a vicious trap for him. The initialed handkerchief was the first sign that the tide had turned, that it was no longer enough to make Duncan doubt his sanity. He wondered what crumb of evidence would be found with the body they discovered today, what link that piece of evidence would have to him. It was only a matter of time before the inspector on the case, George Lawrence, would arrive at the town house to take him in. And what could he say to prove his innocence? He couldn't even remember where he'd been on some of the nights when the murders had been committed. He didn't have any evidence to prove that he wasn't involved. Even if Grayson swore that he had been incapacitated when the last two murders had occurred, they would not believe her. She was his wife, and that would invalidate everything she said. It frustrated him to know the danger and have no clue to who the West End Strangler really was.

"Duncan, are you all right?"

Grayson was watching him, her eyes disconcertingly bright, her expression troubled and sharp.

"I'm fine," he answered her, knowing he could not explain the reason for his preoccupation.

He could see the menace of circumstances swirling around him, could feel the weight of others' doubts dragging him down. Though he had tried, he hadn't yet been able to find a way to combat what someone was doing to him. Today, tomorrow, or next week the woman he loved and the life he was coming to cherish would all be swept away, and there was nothing he could think of to prevent it.

That hopelessness made him desperate for a swift and complete denial of all the things that could destroy the life he had come to love, the woman who lay nestled so trustingly at his side. He turned toward her and stared into her face. Her beauty was like a balm, serene, unblemished, untouched. Her concern for him was nurturing, sheltering, unbearably sweet. He needed to draw on the solace of her unquestioning acceptance just one more time. He needed to submerge his doubts and fears in the wonder of making love to her.

She was mere inches away beside him on the pillow, and he leaned across to kiss her lips.

Grayson surged against him in response to even that simple brush of mouths and tongues, needing reassurance of his love in a way that went beyond his quiet words, beyond his obvious care for her. She wanted the comfort of his lips moving over hers, wanted the unquestioning sincerity of his hands on her flesh. She wanted the complete communion she felt when they were one.

With single-minded deliberation she touched him, letting her hands stroke the satiny skin along his shoulders, the slope of his chest, the pebbly texture of his paps. She was too eager for their joining to linger over him, and her thumbs swept on to graze the undulations of his ribs, the flesh along his side. His hipbone flared beneath her fingertips. There was the texture of rock-hard muscle and downy hair on the plain of his abdomen, the thrust of his arousal against her palm as she closed her hand around his straining flesh.

Her body tingled as she touched him. She went hot and tight inside. She sucked in a breath of air against his mouth, shivered with the need that was building in them both. She rolled onto her back and felt his weight move over her. With a shuddering sigh, she drew him home.

"Grayson," he murmured when they were one. "Oh, Grayson."

For as quickly as they'd come together, his movements inside her were slow and sweet. It was like being held and comforted on a plane that surpassed all tenderness, all reassurance. It was like moving in a dream, sensual, gliding, seminal, pure. Sensations spilled through them, pooling in delicious heavy swirls, miring them in delight, dragging them down. Languor and appreciation governed their actions. Perceptions hovered and diffused, altering, changing, transforming, from welling sweetness into intransigent heart-stopping ecstasy. Clinging together they budded and burst, swelled and ebbed, filled and overflowed in a tangible expression of what each felt for the other. And when it was over, when the proving and the affirmation began to ease away, they lay together, heart to heart, as satisfaction and contentment drifted over them.

It was midmorning when Duncan woke, happier and more contented than he had any right to feel. Without disturbing Grayson, he rose and rang for his bath, then completed his ablutions and his breakfast in the adjoining dressing room. He scanned the paper after he shaved, deliberately seeking word of another murder. He was relieved to see no reference to the West End Strangler, no word of new misdeeds. Perhaps the nightmare was over, he thought as he knotted his cravat in place, perhaps the madman haunting both the streets of London and Duncan's life was receding into the past.

He moved to the dresser to collect his things: his wallet and match safe, his handkerchief and his watch. But as he gathered the watch and chain into his hand, his heart lurched with sudden certainty. The heavy crested watch fob at the end of the chain was gone, and with a jolt of incipient terror he knew exactly where it would be found.

The police arrived at two o'clock. Grayson was alone in the drawing room when the butler announced them, two uniformed officers and a small man of middling years dressed in a misshapen jacket and baggy-kneed trousers.

She set her embroidery aside and rose to greet them.

"Lady Antire, I'm Inspector George Lawrence, and these men are Constables Farrell and Brad," the rumpled man offered as he stepped toward the alcove where she had been sitting.

Grayson indicated the cluster of chairs nearest her own. "Please, gentlemen, won't you have a seat? Is there something I can do for you?"

As he accepted her invitation, Lawrence regarded her from beneath impossibly prickly brows. "We came to see your husband and his cousin, actually. It is on a matter of some importance."

"I'm very sorry, but neither of them is at home." Grayson frowned, remembering how unsettled she'd been to awaken in

Duncan's bed and find him gone. She had hoped that the passion they had shared in the early hours would be the prelude to a wonderful day. "Didn't Forbes tell you that?"

"He did," Lawrence admitted, "but I thought you might be able to give me a little information before I have a chance to talk to them."

"A little information? A little information about what?"

There was a prickle of foreboding at the back of Grayson's neck, and she looked more closely at the inspector, trying to discern some hint of his reason for coming here.

He was a sallow-complexioned man, his face smooth-skinned, yet jowly. He had a furry brown mustache and heavy-lidded mercury-gray eyes that for all their sleepy look sparked with quick intelligence. His hair was thinning, long, and none too neat, poking out at the backs of his ears like the quills of a faintly disgruntled porcupine.

"Innocuous things, really. Nothing much."

Grayson was unsettled, not soothed, by his conversational tone. "Innocuous things? Such as . . . ?"

"Oh, well," he answered, adjusting his lapel, "like how long your husband has been in England, and why he has returned after so many years abroad."

The answers to those questions were common knowledge here in London, and Grayson saw no reason to deny the inspector answers. "Duncan's ship was caught in a storm on the Channel toward the end of March and put into Portsmouth for repairs."

"Yes, I see. And when did he come to London?"

"A week or so after they arrived, I think. I didn't meet him until mid-April."

There was no change in his expression, and yet Gray perceived a sharpened interest on Lawrence's part. "And this is only just the end of May. Yours was a whirlwind courtship, is it safe to say?"

Gray felt the color come up in her face. She was not sure if it was censure she heard in his tone, or something else that disturbed her. Still, there were plenty of society gossips who would be more than willing to entertain Inspector Lawrence with the details of her broken engagement to Harry Torkington and her hasty wedding to Duncan Palmer. It seemed unwise to deny him information he could readily discover elsewhere.

"I suppose some people would call it that."

As if sensing her wariness in talking about her husband,

Lawrence changed the subject. "And your husband's cousin, Quentin Palmer, has he been in London since the beginning of April, too?"

"I suppose he has. Quentin enjoys the social opportunities the height of the Season offers him, though he has been away on business now and then. You see, it is he who oversees my husband's holdings here in England."

"And has anything untoward happened to either of them in these last weeks?"

Gray thought about the livid scar on Duncan's leg, the result, he had told her, of an accident at the shipyards, and the scratches on Duncan's face and hands that had only now begun to fade. Then, too, there was the plummeting flowerpot that had nearly brained them both the day before.

"Anything untoward?" she repeated, buying time to frame her response.

She had not thought much about the three unrelated incidents until just now. Why hadn't she realized how unusual it was to have three such violent things happen so close together? On the other hand, Quentin's life had been as placid and calm as a beauty's looking glass.

"Anything unusual?"

"No," she lied, uncertain why she was doing it. "No."

Lawrence stared at her, his eyes gone cold. There was something in their steely depths that made them seem as bleak and unforgiving as a dead man's.

Gray did her best not to squirm under the slide of his icy regard. "Just what is it you are investigating, Inspector Lawrence?"

Before he could answer her, Quentin poked his head around the half-open door. "I say, Grayson, Forbes mentioned that we had visitors."

"Quentin, I'm so pleased that you've come home," Grayson murmured, meaning it unequivocally. "This is Inspector Lawrence, and Constables Brad and Farrell from the Metropolitan Police. They have been waiting to have a talk with you."

Quentin's face sagged like melting wax. "They want to talk to me?"

"Indeed we do," Lawrence answered.

Quentin hovered in the doorway, as if he intended to bolt. "What—whatever for?"

"Just a few questions, if you don't mind, Mr. Palmer,"

Lawrence answered. "We want to have a word with your cousin, too."

Quentin seemed to have taken root at the spot where he was standing. "Why? What is it you want of me? Has this something to do with Antire Manor?"

"Antire Manor?" Lawrence looked confused. "What is Antire Manor?"

"It's the Palmer family estate in Dorset," Gray informed him.

"Where my cousin Duncan killed his father," Quentin added helpfully.

Grayson's glare sliced across the room to her husband's cousin as if she was fully prepared to skewer him where he stood. At the introduction of the subject of the murder of Duncan's parents, her uneasiness swelled, pressing hard at the back of her throat, making it impossible for her to get her breath.

There was no reason for Quentin to make this police inspector privy to something that had happened so long ago. It was a dangerous thing for him to know, dangerous for Duncan, dangerous for her. Even as she scrambled to think of a way to divert Lawrence from what Quentin had revealed, she could see that the policeman's curiosity was aroused, that his mind was already working.

"The present Marquis of Antire killed his father? What an intriguing bit of news. Please, Mr. Palmer, can you tell me what happened?"

"Duncan's parents died nearly a score of years ago," Grayson offered in her husband's defense. "Surely that can have nothing to do with your reasons for coming to see him today."

"His parents both died at Antire Manor, part of the same incident, I presume?"

Quentin moved a few steps farther into the room, obviously relieved that the focus of the police inspector's questions had passed from him. "I was away at school when the tragedy occurred, but Duncan's valet was in the manor house at the time. Perhaps he could tell you more than I."

Barnes was duly sent for, and he arrived in the drawing room a few minutes later uncharacteristically frazzled and out of breath. His small black eyes went huge when Lawrence introduced himself, and though he stood his ground, Grayson could see that Barnes was trembling.

The inspector offered Barnes a chair, which he quickly accepted, and Quentin folded his long form into a settee nearby.

"Now, my good man," Lawrence began, turning his full attention to the valet. "I want you to tell me what happened at Antire Manor the night the marquis's parents died."

Though his voice quavered as he spoke, the account did not vary much from the one Ryan had given Gray only a few days before.

"And the marquis's mother was strangled, you say?" Lawrence murmured, his gray eyes narrowing. "Was her neck broken in the struggle with her husband?"

Ryan shrugged. "It might have been."

"And has anything untoward happened since you and your master have returned to England?"

It was the same thing Lawrence had asked of Gray, only now the inflection was more purposeful, more intense. The inspector's questions were probing, deliberate. He was looking for something, driving at something, but Gray could not fathom what it was.

Barnes looked as unhinged as Grayson felt, though she was pleased to see his lips narrow uncooperatively in the perfect oval between his mustache and beard.

"We can ask these same questions down at the station house, Mr. Barnes, if you prefer," the inspector threatened. "Now has anything untoward happened to your master since he returned to London?"

Lie! Grayson silently prompted Ryan Barnes. *Don't tell him about the accident at the shipyard, the scratches, or the flowerpot. Lie!*

Barnes drew an uneven breath, and Gray sat quivering.

"Well, his lordship's headaches have been much worse."

The tension went out of her so suddenly, Gray's body sagged.

"His headaches?" Lawrence repeated.

"His lordship has had terrible headaches since shortly after his parents died."

"How often has he had these headaches since he's been in London?"

"They don't come regular like," Ryan hedged.

"And what happens when these headaches occur?"

"Duncan doses himself with laudanum and goes to bed,"

Grayson answered, deliberately drawing Lawrence's attention away from Barnes.

"That's what he always does?" Lawrence asked. "Comes home and goes to bed?"

"I can think of a time or two when he didn't make it all the way home," Quentin offered. "That's how he met you, isn't it, Grayson? Hadn't he taken refuge in your uncle's garden because he wasn't able to reach the town house?"

She glared at Quentin where he sat on a nearby settee. He looked like an evil black spider who'd spun his web.

"And when was that, Lady Antire?"

"I told you, I met my husband in April."

"And just where is your uncle's home?"

"Before I married, my guardian was the Duke of Fennel. We lived at Worthington Hall."

"On South Audley Street?"

"Yes."

"Near where the second of the West End Strangler's murders was discovered sometime in the middle of April?"

The realization of why he'd come chilled Grayson to the marrow of her bones. Lawrence was investigating the West End Strangler. But what had brought him here?

She felt suddenly as if Lawrence were thinking aloud, as if she were privy to his thoughts. He was wondering if there might be some connection between the Strangler who was terrorizing London and Duncan Palmer, between the times and dates of the murders and the occurrences of Duncan's headaches.

She looked around at the others in the drawing room. The two tall constables were hanging on Lawrence's every word, totally in league with him, totally prepared to follow where he led. Quentin's face was blank, either from his inability to comprehend Lawrence's accusations or by design. Barnes was pale and shivering.

"I can't remember exactly when the killing outside my guardian's house occurred," she told him coolly. "It could have been around the time I met my husband. I can't be sure."

But Grayson did know; she was very sure. The murder had happened near the corner of their property the night Duncan took refuge in their garden. When the police came to question the family and the servants later in the day, she had not mentioned his presence on the grounds. Her memory of the incident was crystal clear because her omission had been deliberate.

Lawrence turned suddenly to where Barnes was sitting in his chair. "How many headaches has your master had since you've been in London?"

Flustered, Ryan shook his head. "I'm not sure. Half a dozen, I should think."

"And I don't suppose you took note of the dates?"

Ryan was sweating. Huge drops of perspiration were rolling down his face, clustering at the edges of his beard, wilting the stiff, starched collar at his throat.

"No, I— Maybe one or two of them coincided with the nights of the murders. I can hardly say for sure."

As innocuous as they were, the valet's words were damning. Grayson could see the suspicions being confirmed behind Lawrence's lead-gray eyes. Surely Quentin couldn't believe what this man was intimating. Certainly Barnes knew Lawrence's assertions were not true. Yet the evidence against Duncan was piling up, and the strength of it was frightening.

A need to protect Duncan was rising in Gray, a need so strong, so fierce and primitive, she ached with it. She had to say something, do something. Duncan wasn't the West End Strangler. How could these people think he was?

"And did his lordship have one of his headaches just last night?" Lawrence went on.

There was an utter silence in the room. Looks of surprise and doubt were quickly exchanged. Quentin, Barnes, and Gray all knew that Duncan had been incapacitated by a headache the night before.

Quentin answered first, revealing by his words that he had indeed been following the trend of Lawrence's thoughts. "My cousin was taken ill last night, that is true. But since there was no word of a murder in the papers this morning, that proves there's no connection between Duncan's headaches and the Strangler's crimes."

"And I saw my husband safely to bed under the influence of his medicine," Grayson hastened to add.

"And just what time was that, my lady?" the inspector asked.

"Nine o'clock or so, I think."

"And did you stay with him?" the inspector went on.

"What the devil difference does it make where she stayed?"

Quentin broke in, finally seeing fit to defend her. "It's none of your business where she spent the night, and it is improper of you to ask. Do you think someone who has been heavily dosed with laudanum can simply throw off the effects and walk the streets, murdering women wherever he goes?"

"Did you stay with him, Lady Antire?" Lawrence persisted.

"No, I—I slept in my own room most of last night. It is the room adjoining his."

"Was the door between the rooms open or closed?"

"It was closed." Gray gave him the answer reluctantly, sensing that there was some important bit of information Lawrence had not yet seen fit to reveal to them. "I—I didn't want to chance disturbing him as I readied myself for bed. But I did look in on him just about dawn."

"Was he there? Was he sleeping?"

Grayson colored, cursing herself for the blush she could not seem to control. Duncan had certainly not seemed the least bit sleepy when she went into his room at dawn.

"No," she answered, with an even darker flush rising in her cheeks. "No, he wasn't sleeping."

Lawrence was watching her with those mirror-bright eyes, eyes so intense and hot that they seemed able to bore a hole in her.

"Then you can't swear that is where your husband was between nine o'clock and dawn?"

"Does it mean so much that I can't? Is there a reason you are asking me?"

Lawrence rose from his chair and came to stand over her. She raised her gaze to his and felt his condemnation of Duncan in the depths of her soul.

She should have stayed with him. She should have lied. She should have protected Duncan better. As it was, Gray knew the truth before Lawrence spoke the words.

"The body of another of the Strangler's victims was found shortly before daylight today. It was too late to make the morning papers, and until we arrest the murderer, we don't intend to give the newspapers any details. The victim was a chambermaid in a hotel over on Oxford Street, and her neck was broken clean. But we found proof of who the Strangler is clutched in the victim's hand."

Lawrence dug in the pocket of his rumpled jacket and took out a linen handkerchief. On the corner was the letter P. It was the only other clue to the identity of the Strangler that the police had ever found. Grayson watched in frozen fascination as Lawrence folded back the corners of the cloth. She wondered what was inside.

"This seems to make the identity of the killer very clear," Lawrence said into the silence.

As he tipped his hand forward Gray saw what they had found, and her blood ran cold. In the very center of the handkerchief was the crowning proof of her husband's guilt: Lawrence was holding Duncan's watch fob.

Twenty-four

"I WANT YOU TO KNOW THAT I LOVE YOU, THAT NO MATTER WHAT happens, I'll always love you."

The precious sentiment Duncan had whispered as they curled together in the dawn reverberated like a thunderclap in Grayson's ears as she had stared at the crested watch fob. The words had seemed to beat in her veins as she struggled to grasp the significance of this piece of evidence having been found in the hand of the West End Strangler's latest victim. Based on the initialed handkerchief and the fact that some of Duncan's headaches seemed to coincide with the nights of the Strangler's crimes, Lawrence had been accusing her husband, Duncan Palmer, the Marquis of Antire, of being the West End Strangler. It seemed impossible that this accusation could be true, yet with the words Duncan had whispered to her this morning, it seemed that he had been preparing her for just such a revelation.

How Grayson had survived the last minutes of the interview with Inspector Lawrence, she did not know. She had felt as if her tether to reality had slipped, as if every cell in her body was aquiver with shock. She hadn't fainted, and she hadn't cried. But neither had she been able to put two complete thoughts together. She knew that the answers she gave to Lawrence's questions had been largely incoherent, that the denial she tried to voice had been totally incomprehensible, completely inane.

She had expected either Quentin or Ryan Barnes to mount a defense of Duncan's character, to explain that a man of Duncan's sensibilities could never conceive of or carry out such heinous crimes, but both men had remained silent. Whether they believed Duncan was the West End Strangler was impossible to judge, though Gray herself was certain Duncan could not do such vile and violent things. Still, his words continued to haunt her: "I want you to know that I love you, that no matter what happens I'll always love you."

As she stood in the center of the room where she and Duncan had made such tender, passionate love just hours before, Gray tried to think of some other reason for him to tell her what he had. Knowing how important his love and approval had become to her, was he simply offering reassurance? Had it been his appreciation that she was with him when he awoke that made him say the words? Or had he known that the police were closing in, that discovery of his identity as the Strangler was inevitable and imminent?

Though their acquaintance had been short, Grayson believed she knew Duncan well. She knew his foibles and his strengths, his doubts and his abilities. She suspected he had revealed as much of himself to her as he had ever revealed to anyone. He had shown her his tenderness and his vulnerability, his kindness and his love. She had always felt safe with him, at Evans's, alone on the streets, in the privacy of their bedchamber. He could never have hidden this other self from her at moments of total intimacy. No matter what Lawrence said, no matter what the evidence seemed to prove, no matter what Duncan's own words seemed to imply, he was not the West End Strangler. In the absence of other champions, it was up to her to prove his innocence.

Lawrence had wanted to search the house, but Grayson had refused to allow it. Why should she help the police make a case against her husband? Wasn't the information she'd already given them damning enough? Lawrence's need to obtain the legal-search papers would buy Duncan time. But time for what? Time to find a way to prove his innocence? Time to find witnesses to testify to his whereabouts on the nights in question? Time to make good his escape?

Amid a string of muttered imprecations and promises to return, Lawrence had gone, leaving the two young constables to guard the door. It made Gray worry about what would happen when Duncan concluded his business and returned to the house. Would he blithely walk into the trap Lawrence had laid? What would Duncan say when the police arrested him?

As she paced around the room she and Duncan had shared, Grayson realized that if there was evidence secreted in the house that could be used against Duncan, she had to find it before

Lawrence did. Diligently she began to look through Duncan's things. She searched the desk in one corner of the bedroom, removing everything from the drawers, leafing through what seemed like reams of papers. There were documents pertaining to various business ventures Duncan and his uncle were involved in, the ship's log for the *Citation*, and the papers Duncan had taken from Sidney Layton's establishment, all neatly bound together. There were pens and inks, blank sheets of vellum and foolscap, a button from a jacket, a needle and thread. Nothing in the desk seemed to have the least bit of bearing on the charges the police inspector had made.

She pored through the drawers in the nightstand and commode, opened the secret compartment in the claw-footed table that held decanters of liquor. She looked under the silver tray on which they stood and uncorked each of the tall dark bottles. She turned back the edges of the rugs, felt under the mattress, crawled beneath the bed and risked life and limb to search the top of the satin-swagged half-tester high above it.

Satisfied that there was nothing in the bedchamber, Grayson made her way into the dressing room. She opened the doors of the armoire and systematically went through Duncan's clothes, the pockets on every jacket, waistcoat, and pair of trousers, the hatband and crown of every hat. The drawers of the bowfront dresser were Grayson's next goal, and though it would have been so much easier to dump everything onto the floor, she pawed through each one of them carefully, not wanting Inspector Lawrence to know she'd searched them first.

In the second drawer from the bottom, beneath a pile of carefully folded underdrawers and cravats, she found a wooden box. Holding it as gingerly as one might a lighted bomb, Grayson made her way to the small cot in the corner of the room. She sank down gratefully, her knees gone weak, and held the box in the very center of her lap. There could be any of a number of things inside, she told herself—a cache of fine cigars, a useless gift someone might have given Duncan, a surprise he had gotten for her, a collection of cuff buttons and shirt studs. Still, the fact that the box had been stashed beneath piles of Duncan's clothes worried her. Had he placed it there deliberately, or was it something he had put away and forgotten?

With trembling hands she worked the latch. If Duncan was

intent on hiding something, wouldn't he have made sure the box was locked? She drew a long, slow breath and opened the lid.

There were newspaper clippings inside. As she began to spread them on the cot beside her, she could see that every one of them dealt with the West End Strangler's crimes. There was a piece from the *Morning Chronicle* on the shop girl who had died, another from the *Illustrated London News* outlining the investigation of the same incident. A long piece from a very recent issue of the *Weekly Dispatch* outlined the West End Strangler's crimes from beginning to end, complete with details so clear and grisly that the story made Grayson gag. Another clipping from the *Times* dealt with the murder of the woman who had died just days before their wedding. Folded into that article was another that described and pictured a heavy moonstone necklace purported to be missing from around this victim's neck. There were other articles about the Strangler in there, too, all neatly folded and faintly dog-eared, as if Duncan had read them more than once. Finally, in the very bottom of the box, she found a crude advertising card from a place known as the Crown Inn, and a carefully folded handkerchief.

As Grayson peeled back the layers of cloth, she could see dots of something that looked like blood staining the folds of the linen handkerchief. There was something heavy inside, though it seemed like the weight of a feather when compared to the weight in her chest. As she pulled the last layer of cloth away, her breathing stopped, her heart fluttered like a wild thing inside her. The room spun as if she had been caught in a whirlwind, and she was forced to lower her head until the bout of dizziness passed.

Finally she straightened and stared down at the necklace in her lap. It had a heavy silver chain, three carriages worked in an elaborate design, and three large glimmering moonstones that winked at her like ovals of golden mist. She did not have to make a comparison to the newspaper illustration to know that the necklace she had found among Duncan's things exactly matched the one that had been stolen from one of the Strangler's victims.

I want you to know that I love you, that no matter what happens I'll always love you. No matter what happens. No matter what happens!

The words eddied in her head. All at once there was no question about what Duncan had meant, no question about it at all.

She felt a cry rising in her, pressing up from her diaphragm with the force of a fist, driving the air from her lungs, tearing mercilessly at the back of her throat. She clapped both hands over her mouth to muffle the sound, the primal scream born of fierce and unbearable pain. She curled in upon herself at the edge of the cot, trying to stifle the sobs of agony raging through her. She rocked helplessly, instinctively, with her hands still over her lips to hold back the keening.

Tears poured down her cheeks, pooling against her knuckles, streaming down her arms. She could not see for the flood in her eyes, could not hear for the blood pounding in her ears. The grief that tore through her rent the substance of every cell. Her skin seemed aflame, yet she was shivering. Her stomach heaved, though she had never felt so empty. The whimpers that escaped around her clutching hands were like the cries of some desperate, tormented animal. Betrayal loomed like an abyss at the edge of her world.

Duncan! Duncan, why? Why?

She sensed his presence in the room with a tremor that began at the base of her spine. It moved from an instinctual awareness to a conscious one, like rising from the depths of a horrible dream. Yet the reality of seeing her husband standing in the doorway of the dressing room was worse than a vision from any nightmare. She tried to blink the apparition away. She tried to stare at it so long and so hard that it would wink like the light from a distant star and fade away.

The faint half-step Duncan took in her direction seemed to convince her that the vision was real. She lowered her hands from her mouth and fumbled in her lap. She gripped the necklace in the handkerchief and hurled it at him. It hit the floor and skittered away to land in a lump at his feet. He looked down at the tangible accusation she'd flung at him, then up at her. There was no question that he could read the loathing in Grayson's eyes.

His skin seemed to shrink against the bones of his face, exaggerating their harshness, their strength. His fists clenched and unclenched at his sides as he stood all but frozen just inside the doorway. Finally he stepped around the wad of silver and cloth on the wide pine floorboards and came at her.

Panic exploded at the base of Grayson's skull. She fumbled toward her feet and tried to stand, but before she could push aside the box and the clutter of newspaper clippings in her lap, Duncan reached her. He fell to his knees beside the cot, grabbing her roughly to hold her there.

"No! No!" she gasped and tried to pull away.

He bound her to him instead, clamping her to his chest, tightening his arms around her so she could hardly breathe. She twisted against him desperately, fighting for her life. She arched her back and pushed away. She used her knees to jab at him. He caught her even more tightly to himself, bending her back, forcing her down on the cot with his bulk sprawled over her.

"Murderer!" she panted as she fought. "Murderer!"

He was everywhere, his thighs pinning her legs, his hand gathering her wrists behind her back, his fingers tangling in her hair to control her movements with the threat of pain.

She went still beneath him, mustering her strength to scream. He must have felt her in-drawn breath, for just as she opened her mouth to shriek for help, his lips came over hers. Her throat worked against the pressure of his mouth, but he absorbed the desperation of the sound. Still, her muffled scream seemed to shudder through them both, shaking them, weakening them. As the terrible effort she'd made to cry out died away, Grayson crumpled. With a volley of shivers she went limp, and the shout for help became a noiseless sob.

Duncan released her wrists, though the pressure of his arms around her did not lessen. But Gray had passed beyond the point where she could maintain her struggles, and she clung to him instead, burrowing against his chest as if she sought comfort rather than escape. She cried noisily, quivering and open-mouthed, pushed beyond fear by unadulterated grief. Her fingers clenched and tore at the back of his coat; her head battered his shoulder. The wetness of her tears came against his throat and jaw. She quaked against his ribs, consumed by the agony of what he was, of what he had been doing.

"Wh-wh-why? Wh-wh-why?" she sputtered when she could finally breathe. "Wh-what makes you do such h-horrid things? Are y-you going to k-k-kill me, t-too?"

Duncan went still beside her, his muscles taut as cables, his breathing repressed and flat. "Do you really think I could hurt you, Grayson?" he whispered into her hair.

"No."

The denial came from somewhere deep inside her, an instinct so basic and primitive that it hurdled the doubts and fears of her conscious mind and came unbidden to her lips.

Then she was crying again, shuddering, rending, gulping

sounds of confusion and distress. He held her as she wept, held her as he had not been able to hold her moments before. His arms curled protectively around her as he shifted onto the cot. His hands moved across her back, kneading her shoulders, massaging her spine. She sobbed against the collar of his shirt, further dampening his cravat, tangled her fingers around his woolen lapels as if she willed him closer. His arms enfolded her so tightly it seemed as if he would never let her go, as if they would stay forever as they were, entwined for all eternity.

At length Grayson quieted and looked into his face. "Did you kill those women in the street? Are you the West End Strangler?"

There was pain in the depths of his translucent eyes, a disappointment so fierce and strong it hurt even to look at him. It was as if a light shone out of the brilliant blue, a fire of agonizing hurt and self-loathing.

Grayson could not breathe as she waited for his answer. She sensed he would not lie to her now, not when the emotion in him was so strong. Was he going to deny that he had killed the women, or was he going to confess? Was he going to admit to something so abhorrent that it was consuming him alive, or was he going to swear that he was innocent?

"Did you kill them, Duncan?" she demanded when she would no longer bear the silence.

"No."

His denial was a single word, a single syllable, a single fragile thread of sound. It was so infinitesimally small a refutation for a wealth of terrible wrongs.

He watched her, his eyes no less haunted and intense than they had been a moment before. His expression left her quaking inside.

"Do you believe me, Grayson?"

The whole of their love, their marriage, their world, hung on how she answered him. There had been no explanations to convince her of his innocence, no pleas to win her to his way. There was only this question, only her answer to decide the fate for both of them.

"Grayson, do you believe me?"

His question was like a test, an inquisition. It was a probing of her most basic beliefs about what kind of a man he was, about her love and trust for him. It was the moment that would decide if she would live or die, the moment that would decide if there was any hope in the world for either of them.

For every instant she hesitated, she could see the bleakness in him grow. If he was a killer, would what she thought matter to him? If he was a madman capable of taking life so callously, would he even care what she felt? Everything seemed to indicate that he was exactly what Lawrence claimed. The evidence proved his guilt. His own words and actions damned him. Yet there was something in his face, in the depths of his sky-blue eyes, that left her wondering if all the proof against him was wrong.

"Yes." She was as shaken by hearing herself say the word as by knowing how much she meant it, against all odds. "Yes, I do believe you."

He made an inarticulate sound deep in his throat and bound her to him. His mouth came over hers, desperate and fierce. His wild frustration flowed into her, and she could feel him trembling.

She opened herself to him, softening her lips beneath the press of his, accepting the thrust of his tongue, clasping him around the shoulders to offer him the haven of her body. If she truly loved this man, she had no choice but to stand by him against the world.

He clung to her, seeking the unconditional acceptance he had given her, demanding the unconditional love he had been seeking all his life. Grayson abruptly understood just what they were to each other: the perfect acknowledgment of all the truths the world chose to deny, the ultimate covenant to love and believe when no one else did. How her reticence a few moments before must have hurt him. How betrayed Duncan must have felt by the doubts she had voiced. A need to offer solace rose in her, a need to assuage the hurt she had caused.

She drew him deeper into her kiss, answered his need for succor with a willingness to prove her love for him. Her hands moved over the folds of his clothes, working the knot of his damp cravat, tearing the studs from the front of his shirt so she could touch the warmth of his skin.

One of his hands cupped the fullness of her breast as the other dispensed with the encumbrance of her underdrawers. He probed the ripeness of her femininity as she worked the fasteners at the front of his trousers. With a helpless groan, he came into her, accepting the haven she offered him, glorying in the welcome of her pliant body. He pressed deep and deeper still in response to the urging of her hands. She bent and arched, twined her legs around his back, gave herself to him without reserve.

"I want you to know that I love you, that no matter what happens I'll always love you." They were the words he had spoken as they had lain together earlier in the day. As she said them, Grayson instinctively understood that the reason he had whispered them in the dawn was not to reassure her, not as a prelude to the devastating events of the day, but because they were the words Duncan himself needed desperately to hear.

He rose above her on trembling arms, looked down at her with his heart in his eyes. He knew she meant the pledge with every fiber of her being, knew she had come to understand just what the words of complete commitment meant to him.

"I love you, Gray," he murmured. "I'll love you as I do today until my bones have turned to dust."

She pulled him hard against her heart as tears rose in her eyes. They shimmered on her cheeks and spilled into her hair, shining like shards of shattered jewels. They were tears of love and trust and deep communion, infinitely more precious than jewels. They were proof of her fierce commitment when all the world had turned away. As she and Duncan reconfirmed the precious pledge between them, his body moved inside her, touching the very essence of herself, tapping a well of sweet emotion that was at the very heart of her.

Clasped in the ultimate embrace, her love swelled and broke around him, bathing Duncan in a security and joy unlike any he had ever known. The knowledge that Grayson believed in him when all the world was black, that Gray loved him in spite of everything, brought resounding peace in the midst of exquisite physical turmoil and sundered the last of his reserve.

Delight spilled through them like a shimmering cascade. The love between them overflowed the bounds of their own bodies to engulf the other in a reaffirmation that rocked their world. Love swelled and swirled around them, flooding them in a light and intensity that bound them closer together than ever before. It pledged them—mind, body, heart, and will—to every essence of the other. It made them completely one.

At last the tumult ebbed, and as if forged in a crucible of fear and doubt and pain, their love was stronger, purer, sweeter, than either had ever thought it could be. They lay twined together in a cluster of spent passion and renewed dreams, in a sphere that denied the troubles of their world in favor of a reborn faith in their ability to face whatever came.

They stirred slowly to rearrange their clothes, to creep back toward the reality that beckoned them. Duncan was the first to speak. Sprawled on the floor beside the cot with his head in Grayson's lap, he murmured the words that would burst the faint protective bubble that had far too briefly surrounded them.

"I don't know how to explain what's happened these last weeks. I'm not the West End Strangler, but someone has been trying to make me believe I am."

Grayson sat up a little straighter on the cot and looked down into his eyes. "Whatever do you mean?"

"The fact that the murders occurred on nights when I had a headache is more than chance. Someone planned them to implicate me and planted clues for me to find." He went on to explain about the advertising card, about the scratches on his hands and face, about how the moonstone necklace had come to be in his possession. "I believe the Strangler meant to drive me mad, to convince me that I was killing these women, though I have no memory of doing it."

"Just the way you can't remember killing your father?" Grayson asked, thinking aloud.

Duncan nodded. "I think the real Strangler meant to drive me to confess to the police, to accept the responsibility for the crimes and take the punishment without questioning the circumstances. And whoever is killing these women nearly succeeded."

"Did he?" A new fear was rising in her chest, a fear that went far beyond the police inspector's accusations.

"When I found the moonstone necklace had been stolen from one of the victims, I was ready to confess. I was terrified of what I must be. I was determined to save the unprotected women of London from what I'd become. I thought the Strangler's murders were somehow tied to my parents, to their death at Antire Manor. I think I *was* a little mad the day I discovered the drawing of the necklace in the newspaper. I don't know where I went or what I did."

"That was the day you left the house so suddenly."

When Duncan nodded in affirmation, Grayson went on. "But what made you realize that you were not the Strangler?"

"You did."

"Me?"

He caught her hand and brought it to his lips, pressing a kiss into her open palm. "I knew that, loving you the way I do, I couldn't be doing other women harm. A madman may be obsessed, but he cannot love."

Gray was silent for a moment as she weighed what he had said, as she basked in the unadulterated glow in his eyes. "But who is doing this to you? Who is trying to get you hanged as a murderer?"

"It must be someone close, someone who has something to gain by my death."

"Quentin?"

"A possibility. But Samuel Walford has reason to hate me, too."

"But he has no access to the house."

"That would be easy enough to arrange. Servants aren't incorruptible, you know.

"It was after I realized that I wasn't committing the crimes that the clues began to appear to implicate me as the killer, the handkerchief and now the watch fob. When I noticed the fob was gone this morning, I knew there must have been another murder, that the watch fob would be found at the scene of the crime. It was, wasn't it?"

Grayson nodded. "So that is why you stayed away. But, Duncan, considering the danger, why have you returned? How did you get into the house without the constables arresting you?"

"I came across the roofs and through a window upstairs. I need money, the contents of that box, and a change of clothes if I am going to elude the police until I find a way to prove my innocence. And if I'm going to gather those things, I'd better be about it."

He came to his feet beside the cot and began to throw things into the small valise he took from the bottom of the armoire.

"And because you hoped to find some clue to who is doing this in the newspapers, you saved the clippings about the crimes."

"It's my only hope of discovering who the killer really is. At least it is my only hope until I recall from Antire Manor the investigator I've been employing."

"An investigator?" Gray repeated. "Who is he, and why is he down there?"

"His name is Hannibal Frasier, and he's at Antire Manor looking into my parents' death. It's a wild hare of his I saw fit to indulge," Duncan answered, "once he'd finished looking into Walford's affairs."

"What about the men who have been following you? Wouldn't they know you haven't been a party to the murders?"

"The men from the police?"

"Are they from the police? Somehow I don't think they are."

Duncan paused with a half-folded shirt in his hands. "What do you mean?"

"I don't think Inspector Lawrence has been having you followed. He wasn't sure if the watch fob belonged to you or to Quentin, and that leads me to believe that you weren't a suspect in the Strangler's crimes until this afternoon."

"Then who the hell are the men who have been following me?"

Before Grayson could answer him there was the sound of someone entering the room beyond. Grayson leaped to her feet and came face to face with Ryan Barnes in the dressing room doorway. As he looked past Grayson to where Duncan stood, his eyebrows levered upward in surprise.

"That Inspector Lawrence is below," he informed them, "and he wants to search the house. I told him, my lady, that you were lying down and that he needed your permission. He waved some paper and said he had the right to search whether you agreed or not. Forbes is holding him off downstairs, though I can't say how successfully or for how long."

For a flicker of heartbeats there was no sound in the dressing room; then abruptly Duncan was giving orders.

"Grayson, go downstairs and keep the good inspector occupied. Ryan, take all the cash from the strongbox in the library, a pistol, powder, and some balls. Bring the two-bore Manton pistol and the derringer if you can. I'll finish my business here and leave the way I came."

As he spoke, Grayson flew toward Duncan, not away. He gave her a quick, hard hug and fiery kiss before he sent her off to do his bidding.

"Grayson," his voice halted her in the doorway. "I'll send word as soon as I can. And please try not to worry."

There were tears in her eyes as she turned away, as fear and hope for Duncan's safety took control of her thoughts and actions. She would give Duncan the time he needed to escape, and she prayed that when she saw him next, this nightmare would be over.

Twenty-five

DUNCAN WAS SAFELY OUT OF THE HOUSE WHEN GEORGE LAWrence finally got around to searching it. Grayson had kept the inspector occupied in the drawing room for nearly twenty minutes as she suffered an attack of vapors that did credit to her ability as an actress. Arriving to greet him with tear-mottled face, unkempt clothes, and tousled hair, she must have seemed half mad with grief and shock. Being a gentleman at heart, Lawrence had let her detain him with her weeping and her questions far longer than was wise. Only after Ryan Barnes appeared at the drawing room door to give her a silent nod, had Gray quieted at last.

The search the police conducted was thorough. They poked into every nook and cranny of the town house from the cellar to the roof, but they found nothing that would help them prove their case. The box of newspaper clippings and the necklace were gone.

"Rest assured that the police will find your husband, madam," Lawrence assured her as Gray and Quentin saw the inspector and his men to the door. "The marquis is the West End Strangler, and we mean to see justice done. We have alerted the authorities in Portsmouth to watch Antire's ship, and there are men at every railroad station. Two constables will be waiting here, in case his lordship decides to return. If you hear from him, *Lady Antire*, if you have any contact with him at all, you must urge him to surrender. If we have to take him by force, your husband may well be hurt."

Alone with Quentin in the foyer once the police inspector was gone, Grayson sagged into a side chair, breathing as if she'd run the distance from Plymouth to Newcastle. Quentin dropped to his knees beside her chair, taking up her hand.

"He didn't do it, did he?" Duncan's cousin asked. "I can't imagine that he did."

Grayson pulled her hands away and glared at him. "You would know that, wouldn't you," she accused, "since it is surely you who implicated him."

Quentin couldn't have looked more stunned or hurt if she'd drawn a pistol and shot him. "Me? For God's sake, Grayson, what are you talking about?"

"You knew every time he had a headache. You had access to his things. You have everything to gain should something happen to Duncan."

Dark, fierce emotions passed over Quentin's face like storm clouds driven by the wind. His mouth went tight; his murky eyes went hard. There was self-loathing in his face and something else Gray could not discern.

"It's true that I have everything to gain should Duncan die, but I wouldn't want the Palmer name blackened by such a fowl, detestable thing. A scandal of this magnitude would surely reflect on me."

The selfishness Quentin had unwittingly revealed made a certain kind of sense. He was a man caught up in who he was, too tied to what the Antire title meant to let something like a public accusation of madness and murder tarnish the family reputation. The circumstances of Duncan's parents' death had already besmirched the title, and another incident would put the whole of the Palmer line beyond the pale. As it was, Quentin had complete control of the family lands and fortunes while Duncan was in America, and he would maintain his stewardship in any case. No matter how the caretaker role might chafe him, Quentin would not do anything to devalue a thing he coveted. Greed and envy might lead him to hope for Duncan's demise, but this kind of scheming was beyond him. Or at least Gray thought it was.

"Besides, Grayson, could I possibly be the man killing women in London's streets? You don't think I could do that, do you? Strangulation is so—distasteful."

It was possible Quentin could have someone acting for him, Grayson reasoned. But where would Quentin meet such a disreputable sort of man, and how could he pay him? The price for murder must be very high.

Grayson had reached no conclusion when the clap of the knocker sounded. Forbes answered the door, and though she had only seen the man a time or two, Gray recognized Samuel Walford instantly.

"I have an appointment this evening with his lordship," Walford announced as he stepped into the entrance hall and drew off his gloves.

Behind him Grayson could see that the sky was darkening, that the streetlights were being lit. It surprised her that it had grown so late.

"Duncan is not at home," Grayson informed him as she came to her feet. "Is there something I can do for you?"

Walford seemed taken aback. "Lady Antire," he acknowledged, recovering himself, "I don't know that we've ever been properly introduced. I am Samuel Walford, a partner in your husband's trading company."

"I know exactly who you are, Mr. Walford. What I want to know is why you're here."

The antagonism in her tone must have confused him. For a moment he simply stared at her. "Why, I came to give some business papers to your husband. He and I recently made certain arrangements, and tonight we were to conclude our transaction."

"What arrangements?" Gray wanted to know.

He seemed reluctant to answer her, especially here in the hall where anyone might hear the nature of his business. But Grayson stood her ground, offering no alternative.

"I was to sign over my shares of Wicker and Walford to him," he told her. "It is an arrangement we made a week or two ago."

Grayson was stunned by the nature of the business Walford had come here to transact. Surely this gave the man another reason to hate Duncan, another reason to plan his downfall. From what Grayson knew of Walford, he was clever enough to have planned the scheme to implicate Duncan and ruthless enough to be behind the Strangler's crimes. Walford's daughter had seemed willing enough to kill both Duncan and her the night they went to search the brothel. Surely Walford had been in league with Sidney Layton, and Gray had no illusions about the meager extent of his goodwill.

When Grayson said nothing in answer to his words, Walford continued. "Are you expecting his lordship home soon? I would be willing to wait."

"He's being sought by the police," Quentin burst out, in spite of the quelling glance Grayson slanted in his direction, "in the matter of the West End Strangler."

A flicker of surprise crossed Walford's heavy face and was followed by a twitch of satisfaction. "Is he? Is he really? Let him who is without guilt cast the first stone, hum?"

Grayson took exception to hearing the biblical quote from Walford's tongue, and was preparing to dress him down for his impertinence when the knocker banged again.

This time when Forbes answered the door it was Warren Worthington who stood on the steps.

"Grayson, for the love of God!" he exclaimed as he burst into the foyer. "I just heard about what the police think Duncan has done. I was at a meeting where the police commissioner was asked to bring the committee up to date on the progress of the investigation into the West End Strangler's crimes. I could hardly believe my ears when Duncan's name was mentioned as the chief suspect in the murders. It isn't true, is it, Grayson? Isn't this some kind of a mistake?"

Wearily Grayson ushered her uncle and the other men upstairs to the drawing room. She didn't know what to say to any of them. Was the real Strangler with her now? she wondered. She looked long and hard at Quentin, tried to probe the guile and hatred that shone in Walford's eyes. She turned to her guardian, seated beside her, and knew an overwhelming desire to curl up in his lap and let him deal with this afternoon's developments.

Briefly Grayson related, for her uncle's benefit, what had happened with the police and Inspector Lawrence. Though propriety dictated that Walford should have taken his leave when Worthington arrived, he remained, listening avidly to her explanations. She wondered if he'd stayed to gloat.

"You believe Duncan is innocent of the crimes, do you, Grayson?" her uncle asked when she had finished. "In spite of the affair with his parents, in spite of the evidence to the contrary, you believe he's blameless?"

Resentment stirred in Grayson at the questions her guardian put to her, yet she sensed he would take her word if she assured him of Duncan's innocence. It was testimony to his trust in her judgment that he would believe her when there was so much she could not reveal to him in the presence of these other men.

"I know the kind of man Duncan is," she answered softly. "I

know he could never hurt anyone deliberately, especially after what happened when he was a boy."

"There seems to be only one course open to us, then," Worthington concluded. "We must find Duncan as quickly as we can and get him out of the country. Quentin, you'll do what you can to help me find him, won't you? Samuel, can I count on your help, too?"

No! Oh, no! Grayson's mind whirled with what her uncle was proposing. He meant to send the two men who might well be behind the murders, who had reason to want Duncan dead, out to look for him. But before she could find words to dissuade him, Worthington was organizing the search. Stunned to silence, she listened as he suggested where they might look, and only belatedly noticed that Ryan Barnes was standing in the drawing room doorway. She acknowledged him with a gesture.

"Your grace," he said when Worthington looked up. "If you would give me permission to go out looking, too, it might ease my mind a little. I've been with his lordship for so many years, it is hard for me to sit idly by and wait for word of him."

Grayson made the introductions between her guardian and Duncan's valet, and Worthington seemed pleased by the offer of Ryan's help. One by one Warren Worthington dispatched the men to various parts of the city and then, before he took his leave, clasped Grayson's hand tightly in his own. It was the moment when she might have revealed her suspicions about Walford and Quentin to her uncle, but some instinct kept her silent.

"Grayson, I'm sorry for this. Sorrier than you know. I wouldn't want anything to blight the happiness you've found with Antire, and I'll do everything in my power to see that nothing does."

"Then you believe Duncan is innocent, in spite of what the police think?" Tears rose in her eyes as she spoke, seeking in her uncle a kind of reassurance she had been unable to ask from anyone else.

Worthington drew Grayson into his arms and held her close. He held her gently, cherishingly, as he had never held her before. His hands moved over her tousled hair, across her bowed back. He patted her, cosseted her, wordlessly offering the bulwark of his comfort when she needed it most. Tears seeped between her lowered lashes and spilled down her cheeks as she clung to him, a woman willing momentarily to lay down burdens that had grown too heavy for her to bear, a child who needed his help and comfort.

"I believe that Antire is a man of character and strength," Worthington answered her. "I believe that he loves you and that, because he loves you, he would never do anything to hurt you. Duncan could never commit such heinous crimes."

Worthington made it all sound so simple, reduced the hurtful and confusing events of the day to their most elemental parts. She had doubted Duncan more than he; she had thought, however briefly, that her husband was guilty of the murders. She loved her guardian for having faith in Duncan when she had not. For the wisdom behind his beliefs, for his uncompromising loyalty to the people he cared most about, she loved him.

Warren Worthington was a brash, opinionated, stubborn man. He was determined to do what he believed was right for the people he claimed as his own. In that light, Grayson realized that what she had perceived as domination, as scorn or distaste for her own headstrong behavior, was a mark of profound affection. It had been Warren Worthington's way of protecting her. Why had it taken her so long to realize that?

"I love you, Uncle Warren," she whispered against the collar of his shirt. "I don't know how to thank you for coming here, for knowing how much I needed you."

His hand grazed her tumbled hair. "I love you, too, my girl. I love you, too. And as for thanking me, there's no need. We're family. You can always come to me."

The room wavered and swam before her tear-filled eyes. Family, she thought, family. During all the years of growing up Gray had never felt part of a family, nor was it a need she had ever really acknowledged. Yet she felt part of a family now. Finally, belatedly, she had found the connection that made her whole. With Duncan, and with her aunt and uncle, too, Gray had found the place where she belonged, the ultimate acceptance that always had eluded her. The affection that had never been expressed was there for Grayson now. She nestled into her uncle's shoulder, accepting the haven he offered her, homing to his reassurance and his strength.

They clung together for a moment more, and then Warren Worthington eased her back into her chair.

"Now, Grayson," he began, glancing at his hands as if to hide the shimmer in his own dark eyes, "will you be all right here alone while we're out looking for your husband? Would you like for me to send for Julo to sit with you while we're gone?"

"Does Aunt Julo know about what's happened?"

"No, I came right here from the meeting. The news of the police's suspicions hasn't been leaked to the newspapers, so she'd have no way to learn of it."

"Then I think I'm better off alone. Aunt Julo would be every bit as anxious and upset as I am."

"I don't suppose that would help, then, would it?" Worthington agreed.

"You'll let me know as soon as there's word of Duncan, won't you?" Again there was the need to tell her uncle everything, and again something held her back.

"Of course, my girl, of course. We'll find Duncan a way out of this, never fear."

He hugged her again before he turned to go. "Courage, Grayson," he murmured as he stood over her. "Courage."

When he was gone, Grayson's head sagged against the chair back, and she closed her eyes. "Courage," she whispered to herself, knowing her uncle's word of encouragement was the most appropriate one he could have offered her. It took immeasurable bravery to wait, and wait was all she could do.

It was a risk, Duncan told himself as he ambled along the sidewalk at the Charles Street end of Berkeley Square, but a calculated risk. If the police outside the town house should recognize him and give chase, he was as good as caught, as good as dancing on the end of a rope. But the two men who had been shadowing him for days were outside the house, too, comfortably ensconced in a battered one-horse chaise on the opposite side of the mall.

It was evening, Duncan reassured himself as he paused at the end of the block, and the light was none too good. The constables standing guard outside the town house did not know him by sight, as the other men would. If he kept to the shadows on the far side of the square, he might draw the attention of the men he wanted to attract and go unnoticed by those he hoped to elude. That was the way his plan was supposed to work—if indeed it worked at all.

With a clammy hand he felt for the pistol tucked into his trousers, then for the derringer in the pocket of his coat. There was a knife in his boot, and he smiled to himself at the memory of how

Barnes had arrived in his rooms with nearly three hundred pounds in small bills and this small but effective arsenal. He owed Ryan for his loyalty in this, for not revealing his presence in the town house when most servants would have put their own safety above their master's. His father had chosen well all those years ago, and if he got out of this alive, Duncan meant to reward his valet most handsomely.

Not fifty feet ahead of him, the chaise was standing at the curb. Inside the curve of the collapsible top, Palmer could see the glowing tip of one man's cigar, the faint darker outline of two burly bodies. Duncan paused to light a cigar of his own, hoping the flare of the match would draw their attention, hoping it would induce the men to follow him. He let the flame flicker at the tip of the cheroot a few seconds longer than was necessary, then cast the match into the street and moved back the way he had come. With difficulty he kept his eyes to the front, kept his pace to a steady walk. Anticipation crawled up his back as he waited for some indication that the men in the carriage were following him. The constables on the far side of the mall had shown no sign of interest, and Duncan whispered quiet thanks to whatever forces governed such fortuitous things. Then, from behind him, came the creak of a carriage brake being released, the grate of an iron wheel rim against the pavement, the leisurely clop of a horse's hooves.

He strolled to the southeasternmost corner of the square, turned left and left again into the part of Bruton Lane which had once been the Lansdowne Passage and had followed the course of Tyburn Creek. The street was narrow, and Duncan increased his pace, leading his unsuspecting pursuers toward the blind alley he had decided would serve his purposes.

As he approached it on his right, he realized it was not too late to give up this chancy plan. Perhaps he could convince the police of his innocence in the matter of the murders in some other way. Perhaps he could ask them to question the men who had been following him, convince them to ask these two about where he had been on the nights of the Strangler's crimes. They would do that, he supposed, if they believed he was not the West End Strangler, if they took his word that someone had been shadowing him during his stay in London, if they could find the men once Duncan had been arrested. *If* . . .

He had never been afraid to gamble, but Palmer knew the odds were against him in hoping the police would detain the men. The city of London was in a hanging mood, and it would not matter to either the constabulary or to the populace at large if they hanged an innocent man. Everyone wanted retribution for the Strangler's grisly crimes, and in a situation like this one, it never offended anyone's sensibilities if the wrong man paid the price. Duncan had to take the initiative in proving his innocence before some overzealous constable recognized and arrested him. There really was no other choice.

He crossed the narrow street and stepped into the mouth of the alley. The opening between the buildings was a slash of deeper dark in the settling blue-gray twilight, and the buildings closed like a tunnel around him. As he moved away from the street, déjà vu swept over him. Though it was worlds different in cleanliness and location, this reminded him of another alleyway, of another pair of men. A sick dread rose in his throat. He did not want to have to kill again.

With the memory, other suspicions began to stir. Was there some connection between the men in the alley in Limehouse and the men who were following him now? How long had he been under surveillance? Had his attackers been following him, too? When Grayson had made him aware of his pursuers, Duncan had assumed the men were from the police, that their persistent presence had something to do with the Strangler's crimes. Now he knew he'd been wrong. But if these men were not from the police, who was having him followed? Why were they on his trail?

As the carriage pulled to a stop at the mouth of the lane, Duncan knew the answers to his questions were no more than seconds away. He could just barely make out the two figures who alighted from the vehicle, but he saw that each had drawn what he presumed was a pistol. Duncan's heart thudded as he pulled his own guns free and pressed back against the high brick wall on his left. His palms were wet, and there was the metallic taste of fear on the back of his tongue. He restrained himself from drawing a calming breath, afraid that even the sound of breathing might alert the men to his exact location.

After a murmured conversation, the two began to advance. They moved carefully, stealthily. Their footsteps were muffled by the porous earth on the alley floor; their eyes swept from left to right as they approached the place where Duncan stood hidden in the deeper darkness of a shadow cast by an overhanging roof. Palmer shrank against the wall as they came abreast of him. The pattern of the brickwork seemed to imprint itself through the back of his coat and shirt.

The men moved past him by one step, then two. When they were several yards beyond him, Duncan stepped toward the center of the passage and cleared his throat.

The two men whirled at the sound, raising their pistols.

"Don't even think about firing if you mean to see tomorrow's sunrise," Duncan threatened. "I've a two-shot pistol in my right hand and a derringer in my left."

The men froze where they stood, neither willing to challenge Duncan.

"Drop your weapons, if you please. There are a few questions I want answered."

The man on the right immediately complied with Duncan's demand. His pistol thudded to the earth. The other swung the barrel of his gun in the direction of Duncan's hazy silhouette. There was a burst of light and a roar of sound. As the ball plowed into the brickwork a foot from Palmer's head, the alley was filled by a second bark of noise and flame. Duncan had pulled the trigger of his own gun, and the man on the left crumpled to the earth. As the reverberation of the shots echoed away, a string of livid curses issue from the fallen man's mouth, indicating that the wound he had received was not a fatal one.

Duncan raked back the hammer on the second chamber of the pistol, still facing the men. "Now," he said, with far more sangfroid than he felt, "about the questions I want answered. Who has had you follow me?"

There was an instant of silence before the uninjured man spoke. "John Leaphorn it was," he said.

"John Leaphorn?"

Duncan struggled to place the name, then realized suddenly that Leaphorn was the man who had been with Quentin that morning in the study. Duncan's stomach lurched with the realization that his cousin must be behind the Strangler's crimes. Quentin would inherit the Antire fortune and his title if Duncan died. He would have complete access to the town house, to the land, to all of his holdings. Palmer's mind sped on. It would have been easy enough for his cousin to commit the crimes on the nights when Duncan was incapacitated. Yet the murder of innocent women seemed at odds with Quentin's delicate sensibilities.

"Were you ordered to do more than follow me?" Duncan

demanded, thinking of the first attempt on his life, in Limehouse, and the second one, outside the Hobbs Hotel.

"We were to kill you when we had the chance," the injured man answered him. "And I wish now we'd succeeded."

Duncan had no time to ask the wastrels more, for there was the sound of running footsteps at the end of the lane. The two constables who had been guarding the town house skidded to a stop at the opening to the alley.

Duncan waited until the policemen reached them before he reversed his grip on both the pistols and offered the butts to one of the officers. "I am Duncan Palmer, Marquis of Antire," he introduced himself. "I am the man you have been ordered to arrest for the West End Strangler's crimes. I surrender myself to you and ask that you take these men into custody as well. They are my alibi and can prove I was home in bed on the nights when the last three women were killed."

Grayson sat huddled on the couch in the butler's office to the left of the town house door. She had been as skittish as a stray cat since her Uncle Warren, Samuel Walford, Quentin, and Ryan Barnes had gone out to look for Duncan. Though she had tried, she had not been able to sit and wait for news in either the drawing room or in the privacy of her bedchamber. She wasn't sure what she hoped would happen if any of the men found her husband, but she knew that by being here, she would be the first to learn of Duncan's whereabouts. That waiting seemed so useless angered Gray. Surely there was something else she could do. But try as she might, she couldn't think of anything to help Duncan's cause.

The men had been gone for the best part of three hours, and she didn't know when she could expect word from them. That the police must be looking for Duncan, too, worried her no small bit. Nor was she sanguine about the fact that both Quentin and Samuel Walford were, at least to her mind, suspects in the Strangler's crimes. What would happen if the man who had been strangling women in the London streets found Duncan first? Would he be in danger? Would the real Strangler turn Duncan in to the police and make good his own escape? The questions went around in Grayson's head as she castigated herself for not interfering with the search when she had the chance.

Her recriminations were cut short by the sound of the front door opening. Grayson was instantly on her feet, moving toward the foyer.

"Did you find him?" she demanded as she stepped into the hall. "Is Duncan safe?"

The answer she received was nothing more than a single nod. "He wants you to come with me. I have a carriage waiting."

"Now?" A flicker of wariness moved through Gray. "He wants me to come with you now?"

Thee was a flash of gold in the palm of his hand. "He said to show you this so you'd know that you can trust me."

Grayson recognized the piece of gold immediately. It was the Spanish doubloon Duncan always carried for luck. Her gaze rose from the coin to the glowing intensity of the man's dark eyes.

"He said to come immediately. He said not to bring anything with you, not even your cloak or reticule. No one must know you're gone."

Grayson glanced around. The hallway was deserted, the servants obviously occupied in other parts of the house. With an acknowledging nod of her head, she allowed him to see her through the door. There was a shabby closed coach at the base of the steps. The two constables who had been standing guard on the sidewalk were inexplicably gone. Gray breathed a sigh of relief.

"Where are we going?" she whispered as she climbed into the carriage and settled herself against the cushions.

"You'll see," the man answered as he closed the door behind them. "You'll see."

Twenty-six

My Lord,

He has taken your lady to Antire Manor, and I believe she is in danger. I have gone after them myself. You must follow as soon as you are able.

Barnes

Duncan stood in the foyer of the town house, staring down at the note his valet had left for him. Who had taken Grayson to Antire Manor? Quentin? The Strangler? Were they one and the same? And why had he taken her to Antire Manor, of all places? Palmer read the note again, hoping for enlightenment. In Ryan's hastily scribbled words there was no clue to what was going on.

"Forbes!" Duncan bellowed, then waited for the butler to make an appearance from somewhere belowstairs. "Forbes!"

The man came rushing toward him from down the hall, breathless and only half dressed.

"What the hell is going on?" Duncan demanded, poking the paper into the butler's hands.

It took Forbes only an instant to read the note. "We discovered Lady Grayson was missing about ten o'clock, when the Duke of Fennel returned to the house."

"What was Fennel doing here?"

"He organized a search for you. He wanted to help you leave the country before the police could arrest you for the Strangler's crimes."

Bless Forbes for knowing just what was going on.

"Fennel?"

"Yes, my lord. He was most distressed to find that the police suspected you—"

"Fennel believes I am innocent?" Duncan was incredulous.

"You are innocent, aren't you, my lord? There are those among the servants who—"

"Yes, I'm innocent, and I've just returned from clearing my name."

"That's wonderful news, your lordship!" Forbes fairly crowed. "May I offer my congratulations? I told the others you wouldn't be doing anything so—"

"I want to know where Grayson is," Duncan broke in.

"Oh, I don't know, my lord," the butler was forced to admit. "She disappeared without a trace. Nor have any of the others returned, as far as I know."

"Others?"

"Master Quentin, Mr. Walford, Barnes. Though Barnes must have been here if he left you a note—"

"Walford? Samuel Walford? What was he doing here?"

"He said he had an appointment with you this evening. But when his grace arrived, he pressed Mr. Walford into service in the search for you."

"God Almighty!" Walford had been here, Walford who was the only other person Duncan could think of who might be behind the Strangler's crimes.

Whether Grayson was with Quentin or Walford really didn't matter. In either case, she was in danger. Ryan had been right to follow them. But how had Barnes known where they were going? Was he right in believing that Gray and her abductor had headed for Antire Manor? Duncan had to take the chance that somehow Barnes had learned where Gray was being taken.

He closed his eyes and tried to think. It was nearly one o'clock in the morning. There wouldn't be a train to Bournemouth, the station nearest Antire Manor, until sometime the next day. That left no choice about what he must do.

"I want the fastest horse we own saddled and waiting at the door in ten minutes' time," he instructed the butler. "I want some food and something to drink put into saddlebags so I can take it with me. Send a message to the Duke of Fennel saying that I've been cleared of the charges against me and I'm going to find Lady Grayson."

"Shall I tell him where you've gone?" the butler shouted as Duncan sprinted up the stairs to change his clothes.

"Not even if you're horsewhipped," he shouted back, his voice echoing eerily down the swirl of stairs.

Fennel would send a regiment of dragoons to Antire Manor if he had any idea Grayson was there, and the thought of what that would mean scared Duncan nearly as much as what he himself was going to do.

No matter how he'd fought it, no matter how desperately he had tried to avoid his childhood home, he knew now that he was fated to return. From the moment he set foot on English soil, from the moment his ship foundered in the storm, it had been inevitable that he return to Antire Manor. Who or what he would find when he reached the house where his parents had died, Palmer did not know. But Gray was more important than his fears. She was more important to him than anything. If he had to go to Antire Manor, if he had to confront his past to save her life, he would do it. His love for Grayson would give him courage to face whatever came.

Antire Manor had not changed. It was Duncan Palmer who was different, Duncan who no longer looked upon the place as he had when he was a boy. He had lived in the manor house for nearly fourteen years. He knew every inch of the tall crenellated towers where he had played for hours on end, every one of the rooms, from the scarred stone walls of the fourteenth-century dungeon to the broad oak beams of the Norman trussed attic. He remembered exactly which of the floorboards squeaked, where the secret panel was hidden behind the woodwork in the drawing room, that it was not wise to carry on a conversation in the gallery at the back of the hall unless you wanted everyone below to hear it. He recalled the sound of the waves washing up on the beach, the smell of the grass grown tall in the adjacent fields, and the tang of salt in the air he breathed.

In another life, in another circumstance, he might have enjoyed the sense of coming home, the welcome of profoundly familiar surroundings. But instead of being gripped by the eager anticipation of returning to a place he'd once loved, he was battered by images from his nightmares, assailed by the confusion and guilt that had flayed him half his life. How often had he awakened weak and trembling after dreaming about this house, about his parents, about their death? How could he put aside the terror of those jumbled visions and return to the place he had hoped never to see again?

The road that led to the manor lay just ahead. From the crest of the rise just east of the property, Duncan could see the peaks of the towers at the corners of the house, a sweep of dark slate rooftop shimmering slightly in the damp, the shape of the mullioned windows set in the high gray walls. The fog rising from the sea obscured any changes the years might have wrought in the house, but it did not obscure the reality of what had happened here. It did not ease the sense of foreboding that had been building in Duncan's chest since he had set out from London the night before.

He had ridden all night and much of the day, obsessed and driven by questions that had no answers: questions about the reason for Grayson's abduction, questions about the West End Strangler's identity. Though he had considered numerous possibilities, he was no closer to knowing whom he would find at Antire Manor than he had been the evening before.

It helped to know that Ryan Barnes was here somewhere, presumably keeping watch over Grayson's safety. Duncan had hoped to enlist Hannibal Frasier's aid in confronting Grayson's abductor, the man who, in all probability, had been killing women in London's streets. But when he had stopped at the inn at Swanage, he was told that Frasier went out one evening and never returned. As Palmer talked to the landlord, the contents of the message he had received from Frasier had run through his head, and Duncan hoped it was not his refusal to come to Antire Manor that had put the man in jeopardy. Still, he could not let himself worry about Frasier now. The Scotsman was as careful and canny as anyone he'd ever met, more than capable of taking care of himself.

It was Grayson who was Duncan's first concern. Was she somewhere in the house that lay before him in the shelter of the cove? Was she terrified, hurt, or dead? A flurry of shudders racked him at the thought of what she might be suffering for having loved and protected him.

Straightening in the saddle, he nudged the exhausted gelding down the slope. He had changed mounts several times in the course of the journey, but he had ridden hard, and this horse was about done in. As he neared the opening in the dry stone wall that had been laid up along the perimeters of the property, he considered how he should approach the house. Perhaps it would be wiser to turn the gelding out to graze and cross the rest of the distance on foot. That would give him an opportunity to skulk through the grounds, peer in the windows if he could. Yet Grayson's abduction had been like a gauntlet thrown on the ground, a direct challenge to who and what he was. Somehow it seemed cowardly and wrong not to answer that challenge directly.

The muscles in his forearm tightened as he started to turn the horse into the drive, yet as much as he needed to plod ahead something stayed his hand. He halted at the end of the overgrown lane, his heart thundering in his ears, his lungs laboring to draw in each successive breath. White-hot panic sped through his body like a flush of acid. There was a conflagration in his chest, and his head had begun to ache. His face was hot, yet the mist was cold against his skin, licking tendrils of primal fear caressing his quaking flesh.

The fog swelling across the fields to his right and left, shrouding the tangled clumps of trees and gorse that loomed beside the road, was like something from a nightmare. At the end of the drive he could see the hulking shape of the manor house, the dark, blank shine of windows, the shadows lurking just beyond the half-open door. That open door seemed to beckon to him, while the forbidding blackness beyond it warned him away.

He knew with every fiber of his being that Grayson was in that house. He knew just as certainly that she was in desperate need of him. Yet he was frozen where he sat astride his mount, unable to loosen his grip on the reins, unable to urge the horse forward. His breath was coming in desperate little pants, and the muscles of his body were rigid with fear.

He gritted his teeth and tried to move. He could not. He straightened in the saddle and tried to muster his courage. It refused to come. Frustration raged through him at his own impotence. His vision began to blur and he swiped angrily at his eyes.

What kind of a man was he, anyway? Grayson needed him, damn it! He knew there was bravery huddled inside him somewhere. He had proved its existence countless times before. He was being held back by something that had happened years ago, not fear of what awaited him at the end of the drive.

He urged the horse forward with a reflexive little kick, moving through the yawning gate and into the lane. The bushes at the sides of the road were a tangle of filmy gray and black, as if unquiet spirits were caught and held in their stark thorny branches. The air was very still, and through the unearthly quiet around him,

Duncan could hear the persistent rush of the waves murmuring breathless warnings. The house loomed nearer than before, intimidating him, taunting him. They moved a little closer.

From nowhere two men appeared, one catching the bridle of his horse, the other leveling a pistol at Duncan's chest. For an instant Palmer could not believe what he was seeing and stared at them in stunned surprise.

"Leaphorn said there'd be another one coming," one of them acknowledged in an undertone.

"He was right, as usual, I s'pose."

"All right, you," the first man ordered, addressing Duncan. "Dismount."

During the brief exchange, Duncan had slipped his right foot from the stirrup, and he kicked ferociously at the man holding the gun as he pulled back on his horse's reins. The gelding reared slightly, but with the help of his companion, the brigand managed to avoid both Duncan's kick and the horse's hooves. He made a grab for the center of Palmer's shirt and hauled him halfway out of the saddle. The horse shied sharply to the left, upsetting Duncan's balance, and an instant later he landed with a jolt in the center of the driveway. The man swung his pistol, catching Duncan with a ringing blow above his ear. Pain exploded through Palmer's head like an incendiary bomb, and the world shimmered light and dark. It took a few seconds for his vision to clear, and when it did, the pistol was a hand's breadth from his nose.

"Get up," the ruffian ordered. "You're coming with us."

Duncan struggled to his feet. His knees were unsteady, whether from the length of the ride he'd made or from the force of the rap on his head he could not say. He wavered slightly as the man poked the muzzle of the gun into his back. They relieved him of the pistol tucked in his waistband and the derringer in his pocket, then drove him through the gorse and across the fields to the west of the house. It didn't take long for Duncan to realize where they were headed. The broadest path down to the beach lay off this way.

As they reached the crest of the cliff, Duncan could see that there were signs of activity in the cove. Several boats were drawn up at the edge of the water. Broken boxes and crates were scattered across the rocky beach, and a few men were milling near the mouth of the cave where Palmer had played when he was a boy.

Smugglers. That was what Frasier had discovered here at Antire Manor. He had discovered smugglers, not some damning, long-buried truth about the death of Duncan's parents. In spite of the danger he was in, Palmer knew a moment of profound relief.

The men tied his horse at the crest of the hill, and the three of them picked their way down the path, which seemed wider and more worn than it had been in Palmer's childhood. They made their way across the clattering fog-slicked stones toward the opening in the side of the cliff. In response to a prod from the gun, Duncan made his way inside the cave.

At the end of the entry tunnel, the light of a full dozen torches blossomed, illuminating the broad main chamber of the cavern. As they entered, two men rose from where they had been seated and came toward the little throng. One of the men was Leaphorn, whom Duncan had met that morning at the town house. The other was Quentin Palmer.

"So you did come after all," Leaphorn observed. "Your cousin didn't think you would, not even after the message your lackey sent. Or was it that London got too 'ot for you?"

"Where's Grayson?" Duncan demanded, ignoring the provocation in Leaphorn's tone.

"Grayson?" Quentin asked from where he stood a half-step behind the other man.

"I know you brought her here."

"Not me, cuz. Not me. She may be here with the other fellow. I hear tell they came in a carriage just after dawn."

"Who?"

"Blamed if I know. They've kept to the house, so we've left them alone."

Duncan scanned the cave. There was no sign of Grayson anywhere. During the long hours of the ride from London, Duncan had more or less decided it was Quentin who had abducted Grayson, Quentin who was behind the Strangler's crimes. When the two men who had been trailing him these last weeks, the men who finally cleared his name with the Metropolitan Police, had said they were Leaphorn's men, Duncan had even more reason to believe that Quentin was involved in the murders and the plot to blame the Strangler's crimes on him. Now Quentin was denying that he had abducted Grayson, and Duncan was inclined to believe him. But if Quentin had not taken Grayson from the town house, who had? Walford? But why would Walford bring Grayson to Antire Manor?

"Then why are you here?" Palmer wanted to know.

"I came to tell Leaphorn the marvelous news," Quentin said, "that you are the West End Strangler, that the courts are going to do what we weren't quite able to pull off."

"But I'm not the West End Strangler."

"You're not? Well, it hardly matters, if the police still think you are."

"No, my name's been cleared, and it's Leaphorn's men who gave me my alibi. They knew exactly where I was on the night of each of the Strangler's murders."

As Quentin stared in disbelief, a good deal of what had happened since he'd been in London began to come clear to Duncan. "The attempt on my life in Limehouse was your doing, Quentin, wasn't it?"

"No, it was mine," Leaphorn interjected, "and it cost me two good men. And I arranged for the falling flowerpot outside the 'obbs 'otel. You're a damned 'ard man to kill, your lordship, but I think your luck's run out. Your cousin is too bloody squeamish to 'ave 'ad a 'and in all of that, but 'e'll make 'is bones before the dawn, or 'e'll be lying in the ground beside you.

"Tie 'is lordship up," Leaphorn ordered.

The men who had brought Duncan to the cave pushed him toward one of the smaller chambers in the back, and as they drew closer, Duncan could see there was another man imprisoned there, bound hand and foot. Beneath the grime and an unruly growth of beard, he recognized Hannibal Frasier.

It was hard to say which of them was more surprised, Frasier at seeing Palmer a prisoner, too, or Duncan himself at finding Frasier still alive.

"Your lordship!" the investigator gasped.

"Mr. Frasier," Duncan acknowledged.

Hannibal continued to gape for a moment, then lowered his gaze in chagrin. "It's a shame my message wasn't more specific about the danger here at Antire Manor, or you might not have ridden into this."

"A small miscalculation on your part, to be sure."

"And a fatal one, I'm afraid."

Duncan stood still as one of the men bound his hands. It seemed useless to struggle when there was a pistol pointed directly at his chest. The man threw him to the floor and bound his feet, kicking Duncan twice in the ribs for good measure before he left.

"They've quite an operation going here," Frasier commented conversationally as Duncan struggled to suck in air. "There are merchants who come here to pick out goods like this was a proper warehouse on the London docks. The smugglers are expecting a ship in sometime tonight, and I'll warrant they've decided to wait till they've unloaded it to kill us both. It'll give them time to dispose of our bodies properly."

"Then we'll have to think of some way out of this before they finish, won't we?"

In spite of their predicament, Frasier grinned. "I knew you'd be a good one to have beside me if things went wrong. Have you something in mind, then?"

Duncan shifted slightly so Frasier could see the handle of the knife tucked down his boot, and the other man's grin broadened even more beneath the fringe of his overgrown mustache.

"I've nothing in mind," Palmer answered for the benefit of anyone who might be within earshot. "But if we want to live to see the dawn, we're going to have to find some way out of here."

As they waited, Duncan told Frasier what had transpired during the last few weeks in London. He confirmed that there had indeed been a connection between Antire Manor and the things Frasier had heard about him in London. He explained why he was so unsettled by the news that there were men asking questions about him.

"And you thought they were the police?"

Duncan nodded and continued. Explaining about his fears of guilt in the Strangler's murders was one of the hardest things he'd ever done. It revealed too much about the workings of his mind, about the guilt and anguish he had carried with him from the time his parents died, about the memories that stubbornly refused to return.

"And coming back to the manor hasn't jogged some memory loose?"

Duncan shook his head. "Gray was right about so much else when it came to my feelings about my parents' death, but she was totally wrong about the memories coming back. I doubt I'll ever know what happened."

"And you think she's up at the house?"

"I'm sure of it."

"But with whom? Who abducted her?"

"Walford," Duncan answered. "It has to be Walford."

The conversation came to an abrupt end as the men in the main part of the cave began to stir. They moved in the direction of the entry tunnel, gathering up grappling hooks and cargo nets as they went.

"Looks like the ship is coming in," Frasier observed.

"Then this is the only chance we're going to get."

As the men flooded toward the mouth of the cave like an outgoing tide, Frasier began to shift his upper body toward Duncan's legs. It took what seemed like a very long time for his numbed fingers to grip the handle of the knife, and once he had it in his grasp they moved so they were back to back. Frasier sliced the skin of Duncan's wrists twice before he was able to slide the blade between the loops of rope, and the sawing motions made his shoulders rock against Duncan's back as he worked the blade through the heavy coils. Eventually Palmer's bonds began to fray, and once he was free, it took a few more precious minutes to cut the ropes at his ankles and release the Scotsman from his bonds.

Duncan was stiff and sore from the hour or two that he'd been bound, but Frasier, who had been kept tied as a prisoner for nearly a week, seemed totally incapable of movement. With low curses rumbling in his throat the older man gradually forced himself to his knees.

"Go ahead; get out of here," he mumbled to Duncan as he struggled to make his atrophied muscles respond. "I'll catch up with you as soon as I can."

So sure were the smugglers of their captives' inability to escape that they had not even bothered to post a guard, and under the cover of the piles of barrels and boxes Duncan crept toward the entrance to the cave. He halted less than a dozen yards from the passage to the beach, squatting in the shadow of a pile of crates. To show himself outside while the smugglers were about their work would be to invite recapture, but he was not sure just when a better opportunity to escape might present itself. While he was deciding what to do, Frasier came scuttling up beside him.

"You all right?" Duncan whispered, his back against the wooden box and his eyes on the mouth of the cave.

"Better," the Scotsman muttered grimly. "You planning to wait for someone to carry you out in a shroud, or are we going now?"

Duncan shook his head, wishing he'd come across a pistol as he scrambled through the cave. "There are noises just outside. I think the smugglers are returning."

There were scrapes of wood against rock and the sound of footsteps coming from the tunnel. Duncan and Frasier shrank back into the shadows just in time. As they did, a pair of smugglers dragged another crate into the chamber, groaning under its weight. They were followed by a score of other men, moving in twos and threes, hefting burdens that must have weighed as much as they did. The flow of men was continuous for the best part of an hour as they lugged their booty toward the back of the cave.

An inconspicuous exit was impossible now, and Duncan and Frasier could only wait where they were hidden, hoping that the men were so preoccupied with their ill-gotten gains that they wouldn't think to check the prisoners. Finally Leaphorn returned to the main chamber of the cave with Quentin at his heels, and the men began to gather around their leader.

"A good night's work," they heard Leaphorn say. "Let's get these goods stowed well away before we tend to the matter of our visitors."

From where they were hidden, Duncan and Hannibal could see the eagerness on the faces of Leaphorn's men. That they were no strangers to killing was obvious, and most of them enjoyed it. Still, they did as their leader had bidden them, and a few more minutes of activity ensued before the men began to filter toward the chamber where the prisoners had been held.

"Now," Frasier breathed, watching them. "Now."

Duncan completely concurred and sprinted toward the mouth of the cave. But as Frasier came behind him, the Scotsman snatched one of the torches from its sconce on the wall.

A moment later a curse filled the echoing cavern, as if the disappearance of the prisoners had just been discovered. Though both Duncan and Hannibal were at the head of the tunnel when the shout came, pursuit seemed imminent. Glancing over his shoulder to gauge their chances, Palmer saw Frasier waving the torch he'd grabbed from side to side. He was swinging it in an arc from wall to wall, and Duncan wondered if the Scotsman had lost his mind. Then sparks burst from the ceiling and the sides of the passage, spraying like fireworks around them as they ran.

As they burst out onto the beach, Frasier cast the torch aside. "The entrance of the cave is mined," he explained in a pant. "Those bastards are going to be blown to kingdom come!"

Duncan skidded to a halt halfway down the beach. "Quentin's in there!" he shouted at Frasier's retreating form.

The Scotsman turned back and grabbed Duncan's arm. "What the bloody hell do you care? He was going to see you dead!"

"He's my cousin!" Duncan tried to tell him as Frasier dragged him farther and farther from the entrance to the cave.

Then, behind them, the passage lit up as if the gates of hell were opening, a blinding orange and white flare that lit the beach brighter than noon. It was as if the sun had collided with the earth, bursting, blazing out from the side of the cliff. The concussion from the explosion knocked them flat, dashing their bodies against the stones, grinding their faces into the rocks. The sound of the blast rolled over them like the report of a thousand cannons, battering their ears with unbearable noise and pressure. It echoed through them, pounded through their chests, making them dizzy and sick. The ground beneath them shook, and the waves in the cove recoiled from the beach. Debris pelted them, thudding painfully onto their backs and legs. A sharp rock sliced a furrow behind Duncan's ear, and there was suddenly hot blood welling down his neck and jaw.

Another growling roar began, and Duncan looked back through the swirling dust in time to see the cliff above the cave begin to shudder and dissolve. It was as if the earth had given a slow, lazy shrug. There was a slight lifting of the rock face, then a droop that seemed to go on and on. The stiffness went out of the surface of the cliff as it began to crumble. It shifted, paused, and sagged, sending runners of tumbling stones skittering past the spot where he and Frasier lay. The wave of rocks ran over them, across their boot soles, and up their legs. But they were too far from the cliff for the stones to do much damage. By the time the rock slide reached them, its energy was spent and dissipated, and the debris did the two men no real harm.

Through the thickening whirls of powder and mist, Duncan looked back toward the tall towers at the corners of the house that were all he could see as he lay flat on the beach. Even though it stood well back from the cliff, it seemed to ripple briefly, then settle back, like a cat shifting in its sleep.

Slowly the quiet began to descend. It was a silence thick with smoke and dust, broken only by an occasional resettling of the rocks as they nestled into their new surroundings. The waves returned to the shore, slapping at it at first as if to chastise it for upsetting the ceaseless rhythm of the sea. Then the water's regular shushing beat returned, the beat that had been going on here in the cove since time immemorial.

With gradual movements Duncan and Frasier began to stir, testing their bodies for injuries they might have unknowingly sustained. They were in better shape than they had any right to expect after what they'd been through—capture and escape, an explosion that had surely killed a score of men. The cut on Duncan's head was still bleeding freely, the blood soaking into the collar of his shirt. Frasier had a wicked-looking scrape along one cheek, and his hands were raw from contact with the stones. They sat up facing each other, still breathing hard. Frasier gave a resonant cough in response to the dust, and Duncan wiped his streaming eyes on the back of his hand.

"Well, you see. We are alive," Frasier snuffed, saying the words as if that outcome had never been in doubt.

"Yes, indeed," Duncan agreed and pressed his handkerchief to the spot behind his ear.

"Somewhat the worse for wear, but alive." There was a chuckle rumbling deep in Frasier's chest. It was a profoundly reassuring sound.

Duncan nodded, tucked his boots under him, and came to his feet, extending his hand for the older man to grasp. Frasier was unsteady, but gradually got his bearings.

"What are we going to do now?"

At Frasier's question, Duncan turned and looked back at the house. There was a glow in two of the windows that overlooked the beach. He knew exactly which room it was. The light was on in his father's study.

The older man followed the younger man's gaze. "You're going after her, aren't you?"

Duncan nodded. "Of course."

"You're going to try to rescue her without a weapon of any kind."

"Walford doesn't want Grayson; he wants me. I'm going to get her out of there, and then I'm going to kill that son of a bitch."

Frasier didn't doubt for a moment that Palmer meant to do exactly as he said. He had overheard enough about the way his lordship had dispatched two of Leaphorn's toughest men in the alleyway in Limehouse to know what Palmer was capable of.

Still, it was foolhardy to go against the odds. Walford was doubtless armed to the teeth. He might even have others with him.

"I'll come with—" he began, but Duncan cut him short.

"This is my fight, Frasier, all mine. I intend to see it through. It's my wife he abducted, my name he tried to sully, my life he tried to end."

Duncan started toward the base of the cliff, but the Scotsman caught his arm. "Your lordship—"

"Go and bring back some men from the town, and make one of them the undertaker."

"I doubt they'll come," the older man warned. "They think Antire Manor is haunted."

"Haunted! Well, haunted or not, they'll come. After the noise of that explosion, a score of them are probably on the road already."

Palmer spun on his heel and strode up the beach, across the expanse of broken stones, through the drifting dust, toward the house where his parents had died. Duncan knew exactly what his mission was now. He was going to save the woman he loved. And to do that, he would have to face his past.

A boom louder than any thunder she had ever heard jerked Grayson awake, and as she opened her eyes, the room around her seemed to shift. It was as if the whole building had shrugged, as if it were settling a little deeper into the earth. The brass chandelier above her swung to and fro, casting wavering patterns across the walls. Plaster from the ceiling fell in a flutter around her. It flaked onto her lap and dusted into her hair. It was only when she moved to brush it away that Gray remembered she was tied to her chair.

Another roar—less hollow, more rumbling, and of longer duration—came on the heels of the first. Again the house shuddered. The furniture twitched on the carpet as if each piece were possessed by spirits of its own. More plaster rained down, and a portrait leaped from the wall, the frame splintering as the painting landed with a crash. The tea set on the desk before her chattered with the vibration, and one of the cups danced toward the edge and tumbled to the floor. Grayson fought against the ropes that bound her to the chair, the ones that held her hands immobile, the ones that encircled her chest. She was wild to protect herself from the mayhem all around her, wild to learn what was causing the disturbance.

"What is it? What's happening?" she demanded of the man silhouetted against the darkness of the window that looked out onto the cove. For a full minute he refused to answer, refused even to acknowledge her presence in the room. Beyond him she could see what looked like smoke spiraling past the window glass. There was the smell of dust in the wind.

"Damn it, answer me. Tell me what's going on."

He turned slowly, almost reluctantly. "He's coming. He's coming, just as I said he would."

Across the space of the study, their gazes locked, hers filled with disbelief and naked fear, his as calm as if he were announcing the arrival of some old friend instead of a man he meant to kill. He didn't look like any madman she had ever imagined, and yet she knew that for the best part of two months' time he had been killing women in London's streets.

He had treated her to a graphic recounting of each death: how the housemaid had been easiest to kill, a gentle, innocent girl who had no idea what was about to happen to her; how the shop girl had fought like a lioness; how the barmaid had bitten his hand. Grayson shuddered with the memory of the entertainment he had provided for her. He had told her how each of the murders had occurred, how he had driven Duncan to think he was guilty of the crimes, how he had begun to leave clues behind when it became evident that Duncan could not be convinced he was the West End Strangler, could not be forced to go to the police. What he had not told her was why he had set out to implicate her husband.

With precise, unhurried movements Ryan Barnes came toward where Grayson sat. He paused to retrieve the teacup that had fallen to the floor, clucking his tongue over the stain the contents had left in the carpet and mopping up the mess with one of the napkins from the tea tray.

"Would you like a cup of tea?" he asked. "I think what's left in the pot is still warm. You were sleeping when I brought it up, and I didn't want to disturb you."

His solicitousness made Gray quiver inside, especially when she knew Barnes meant to kill both her and Duncan when her husband arrived. Ryan had told her exactly how he would go about that, too—how she would be found strangled on the couch, just as the former marchioness has been. He had assured her it would be a relatively painless death. He'd had a great deal of practice strangling women of late, and he bragged that he had become unusually proficient. Then he would make it appear that Duncan had died by his own hand, by a pistol ball fired into his brain. He planned to make Duncan write a note, of course. It would be a confession of his crimes against the women of London and an explanation that he could no longer live with what he'd done. Grayson shivered at the prospect of what Barnes meant to do. She prayed that Duncan would not come, that his determination to avoid Antire Manor would keep him away. She only wished she believed it would.

"I'm sorry, Lady Grayson. You didn't answer me. Would you care for a cup of tea?"

Gray drew a shaky breath and moistened her lips. "No, thank you, Barnes. No tea right now."

She thought then that he would turn away. Instead he came toward her, reaching out a hand as if to touch her face. Instinctively she shrank away, noticing how broad his palms were, how thick his wrists, how his forearms swelled beneath the flowing sleeves of his shirt. Barnes was not a tall man, not a big man, but his shoulders were wide for his height, and he was wiry and strong. There was power in that build, and Grayson was afraid of it.

In spite of her resistance, his fingers cupped her jaw and his thumb stroked the curve of her cheek. "You have plaster dust all over you," he chided her, brushing a few of the crumbs away. "You don't want his lordship to be seeing you at less than your best, now, do you?"

"No, I wouldn't want that," Grayson readily agreed. "Why don't you untie me so that I can freshen up my clothes and hair?"

He chuckled deep in his throat and shook his head. "No. No, that would never do. You'll have to accept what help I can give."

He took a handkerchief out of his pocket and dabbed at her face, dusting her as if she were a vase or a piece of furniture.

"Ryan," she began in her most confidential tone, "why don't you tell me what made you do all this, why you killed those women back in London, and why you tried to implicate Duncan in the crimes."

He chuckled again and continued with his work. "That explanation will have to wait till his lordship comes. I'll answer your questions then. He'll be here shortly, never fear."

Grayson was afraid that Barnes was right. After the note he had left, Duncan would have no choice about coming to Antire Manor. He would come to try to rescue her and be caught in Ryan's trap.

A pistol had been loaded and primed in preparation for Duncan's arrival, and it lay now just beyond her reach, an inch or two from the edge of the desk. She turned her head to look at it, wishing she could find a way to loosen her bonds, wondering if there was something she could do to warn Duncan away. It seemed the best she could do was offer a diversion.

"Barnes, will you tell me something?"

"I'll tell you if I can."

"How did you know which nights to kill the women? How did you know when Duncan was going to have a headache?"

"Well, he was often already home in bed when I set out."

"But that wasn't always the case, was it?" Grayson pressed him. "The murder of the housemaid on South Audley Street occurred the night Duncan spent in my uncle's garden."

"It was quite simple to predict when he would have a headache, really."

"Oh? How?"

"The headaches always come when the marquis drinks red wine."

Gray stared up at him.

Barnes nodded in affirmation. "I noticed the pattern soon after he turned eighteen, when he began to stay in the dining room after dinner and have port with the rest of the gentlemen. Every time he stayed with them, he was stricken with a headache."

Grayson sat stunned by what the valet had revealed. Was it possible that something as simple as a glass of wine could bring on the horrible headaches? Her thoughts drifted to the day Duncan had come to tea at Worthington Hall, the first time she'd seen him stricken. They had been talking about his parents, and he had become upset. She had given him a glass of claret herself. She shuddered with the memory, knowing now what she had inadvertently done. Had there been news of a murder in the papers the following day? Grayson couldn't quite remember.

As she sat submitting to Barnes's gentle ministrations, she realized just how long and how viciously Barnes had been manipulating Duncan. He had used Duncan's sensitivity to red wine to undermine his health. He had done everything in his power to make Duncan believe he was a murderer.

Though the valet had not admitted it outright, it was clear to

Grayson now that it was Barnes who had killed the former marquis and in all probability the marchioness as well. Gray shuddered again. Somehow Barnes had killed Duncan's parents and arranged the evidence so Duncan would be forced to accept the blame for his father's death. The things Duncan had been unable to remember about the night of the crime had only added to the constable's suspicions and to Duncan's frustration, guilt, and shame. He had been forced to live through the terrible aftermath of his parents' death, to believe he was guilty of a crime he had not committed, to grow to manhood filled with the most damaging kind of disillusionment and self-doubt. He had been forced to leave the country of his birth under a cloud of speculation, to make a life for himself halfway around the world with an uncle he hardly knew. It was a credit to Duncan's strength of character that he had risen above his past; despite whatever efforts Barnes might have made to undermine his faith in himself, Duncan had prevailed.

But why did Barnes hate Duncan so? Why had Barnes killed Jeremy and Johanna Palmer when the former marquis had been his friend and benefactor? Why was he so determined to see Duncan dead and discredited?

There was something diabolical about the precise little man who stood patiently dabbing the plaster dust from her face, and Grayson trembled helplessly under his hands. He terrified Gray with the obsequious ways that masked the fiend within. He infuriated her, now that she realized his concern and possessiveness of Duncan had hidden his horrible machinations.

Hatred bubbled through her. The need to protect Duncan rose in her, stronger than ever before. If Barnes succeeded in killing them both, Duncan would be remembered as a madman capable of murdering his father, capable of strangling helpless women. Gray would not have her husband remembered that way. She would find a way to save Duncan from what Barnes had planned. She would find a way to save herself.

Angrily she turned away. "Leave me alone, you bastard. Duncan won't come here, so it doesn't matter how I look. He won't come to Antire Manor, not even for me. He hates this place, and if he knew what you had done, he would hate you, too."

Barnes retreated a step and cocked his head to one side as if examining his handiwork. "Oh, he'll come, Lady Grayson. His love for you is stronger than his fear of Antire Manor. He'll come. He's already on his way. All we have to do is wait."

Twenty-seven

AFTER WHAT HAD HAPPENED ON THE BEACH, DUNCAN HADN'T expected the fear would still be with him. Yet it was, heavy in his chest, sour in his throat. As he stood in the shadow of a stand of trees near the west end of the house, he tried to catch his breath after the slow, difficult climb up the face of the mangled cliff. What was left of the path had crumbled away beneath his feet, and he had been forced to scramble over mounds of shifting debris to reach his goal. Now he stared up at the light filtering through the windows of his father's study, wondering what he would find when he reached the room. Was Grayson still alive? Was Walford waiting for him? Would the room look the same as it always had, comfortable and faintly disarrayed, as if his father had left it only minutes before? What would it feel like to return there, to the place where he had done murder so long ago? With a shudder he forced the thought away.

The fog had cleared, and the three-quarter moon cast a pale silver light across the rear of the mansion. He could see the reflection of the moon shining on the bits of glass still clinging to the frames of the broken windows. He could see the hollow where the rear door of the house was set into the wall, the shallow steps that led up to the opening. There was something naggingly familiar about the view, as if he'd stood and watched the house from this vantage point more than once. He couldn't quite remember when.

As he waited, trying to muster the courage to approach the door, lights seemed to shimmer in some of the other windows. An inviting glow came from the dining room, as if people were gathering there for dinner. A gleam of light and movement appeared in the drawing room on the opposite end of the house, as if someone were standing in the window looking out across the cove. He blinked once and the lights were gone, except for the ones that beat out into the night from his father's study.

"It must have been the moon," he muttered to himself as a shiver fluttered the length of his spine.

He knew that the time had come to go into the house. He drew an unsteady breath and crept forward, stealing noiselessly across the lawn. His feet whispered on the high, wind-blasted grass, and from far away he could hear the roar of the breakers as they crashed against the beach. The air licked against his throat, blew cold against his cheeks. He could taste the dryness of the dust still slowly settling around him.

As he came nearer, he seemed to enter the aura of the house, the spell it had always cast over him. There was the familiar sense of coming home, something he'd experienced over and over when he was a boy. Yet the fresh fear of approaching it now ignited a flame in his belly.

From nowhere there were voices in his head, voices shouting, loud and angry.

". . . should have known better than to stop in a deserted barn with one of the grooms."

It was his father's voice.

"And what should I have done instead? My God, would you have preferred that I ride out alone? Would you rather I had come home in the pouring rain, chancing pneumonia or worse?"

"Damn it, Johanna!" his father bellowed. "I'd prefer you not ride out with Sean at all. He's a bonny lad, and Irish, too. Couldn't you have chosen one of the other grooms?"

"And what does Sean's being bonny and Irish have to do with it?" His mother's tone was shrill.

"You know how the Irish are—"

There was the sound of shattering glass, as if something had been hurled across the room.

"Come right out and say it, then, Jeremy. I'm tired of your insinuations. What is it you're accusing me of?"

A wave of dizziness swept over Duncan, and he staggered to a stop a dozen yards from the manor house door. He fought the urge to flee, an impulse so strong and so instinctive that his muscles trembled with the effort it took to stay where he was. His pulse was thrumming in his ears. His skin had gone clammy inside his clothes. What the hell was happening to him?

He forced himself forward, taking one step and then another. Grayson was in the house, and somehow he had to get to her. He had nearly reached the entrance to the house when another sound filled his head.

It was a crack, as sharp as the snap of a bullwhip, like a bottle rocket detonating. He recognized the sound: It was the report of one of his father's dueling pistols.

Duncan dove into the grass, flattening himself on the ground. He lay there, panting, trying to make some sense of his own jumbled thoughts. He had not expected Walford to fire on him as he approached the house. He had thought that his uncle's partner would prefer a face-to-face confrontation after all that had passed between them. He raised his head and looked toward where the light spilled out the window of his father's study. There was no sign of movement beyond the glass, and the window, in spite of its several broken panes, was tightly closed. Confusion assailed him as he sprawled on the grass, his heart thumping madly against the earth. If the shot had not come from the window, just where was Walford waiting for him?

With an effort he came to his knees and forced himself to stand. The door was a dozen steps away, and he drove himself toward the opening. He wedged himself against the wall and reached out to release the latch. The panel swung inward with a long, slow creak that echoed down the corridor. He peered into the darkness, his hands damp with the knowledge of what he had to do. For an eternity he waited—watching, listening, wondering. As far as he could tell, there was nothing between him and the foot of the stairs. He sprinted inside, staying close to the wall.

As he reached the newel post a scream ripped through the air.

Grayson! Oh, God, Grayson . . .

It was his mother's voice he heard—loud, shrill, filled with unspeakable horror. Chills rippled through his body, raising gooseflesh everywhere. The hair on the back of his neck stirred in a primitive reaction to the sound.

"Mother?" His own voice rang in Duncan's ears. It broke and cracked in the middle of the word. There were more sounds from above. "Mother," he cried out again, "are you all right?"

There was a thud from the floor above, another echoing scream that seemed to be cut short, abbreviated somehow. There was the sound of a scuffle from the top of the stairs, another thud, the sound of feet, a moan and a curse. He had to fight the urge to turn and run, run as he had his whole life long from the evidence of his parents' arguing. But this was different from anything he'd heard before, and it filled him with a fear and revulsion so fierce and vast that he did not know how he could possibly go on.

Duncan rounded the ornate newel post, his muscles quivering with the conflicting need to flee and the need to fly up the stairs. Dangerous. It was dangerous to move too fast. Walford would be waiting for him.

Controlling his haste, he stayed near the inner edge of the steps, letting the overhang protect him from above. Sweat ran in his eyes. He wiped it away. He was breathing as if he'd run a hundred miles. His head was pounding. He'd never been so terrified. Yet the impulse to rush up the steps was so strong in him that he had to clench his fists to hold the urge in check.

He reached the landing and made the turn. A floorboard squeaked beneath his boots, and he threw himself back against the wall. He could see the light from his father's study spilling in an uneven rectangle onto the carpeted floor. From the dim illumination of the window at the opposite end of the hall, it was evident no one was lying in wait for him there. Along the corridor the rest of the doors were closed.

Walford was in the study. He had to be. Walford was waiting for him there, just as Duncan had suspected. He drew the knife from his boot and began to climb: one step, two . . .

He could not get his breath.

Then he was standing at the top of the stairs. The door to the study was just ahead. Grayson was in there. Grayson, the woman he loved, and with her was the man he had come to kill. He ordered his feet to move, but they had taken root.

He moistened his lips and concentrated. He slid his left foot forward, followed it with his right. He did that two more times and extended his hand to push the door a little wider. He stepped inside the room.

His mother's body was sprawled on the tapestried settee, her head tilted to one side and her thick dark hair flowing toward the floor. One pale hand lay against her chest like a wilting flower, and her other arm, still swaying slightly, hung over the edge of the seat. In spite of the faint movement, Duncan knew she was dead.

A cry pushed its way through his chest toward the back of his throat, but as he swept his gaze away from where his mother lay, he saw his father crumpled beside the desk. The cry died to silence on his lips. He could not see his father's face, but there was a wet, dark stain spreading from where he lay. It dyed the colors of the scattered flower pattern on the Turkish rug the same rich burgundy as the background. The realization dawned slowly that the stain on the floor was blood.

He came two steps farther into the room, his attention focused on his father's body as he tried to grapple with the reality of what he was seeing. Horror rose in him, driving like a fist into his midsection. Panic spun through his brain.

Then all at once he became aware of a presence to his left. There was someone looming there, a small man. From the corner of his eye, Duncan saw a blur of movement. Some heavy object crashed against his temple, and excruciating pain tore across his senses. Blackness blossomed before his eyes. His knees began to give—

"Duncan! Duncan!" Grayson's anguished cry dragged him back from the edge of the abyss. With difficulty he blinked the past away and focused on where Gray sat on the far side of his father's desk. Her face was ashen, her green eyes huge. There were ropes binding her to the chair. There was a man standing just behind her, with a pistol to her head. It was the man from the vision. It was Ryan Barnes.

Duncan's stomach dipped like a ship sliding into a trough between two waves. His mouth went dry. A shiver shook him. He understood what was happening at a level miles lower than conscious thought. He looked at Ryan. He looked at Gray. It was as if he were staring up at them from the bottom of a thousand-foot-deep shaft. Everything around him was hollow and dark.

He could not think. He could not move. The shock of what he was seeing, of what he'd seen, annihilated his ability to function. The knife dropped from his nerveless fingers, hitting the floor with a hollow thud.

He tried to blink the scene away. It would not go. What had been here before was a memory. He knew that now. Could this possibly be reality?

Gray was staring back at him with terror in her eyes. She wanted him to act, to do something. He could feel her anguish from across the room. He couldn't draw a breath. He couldn't seem to move.

"Surprised to see me here, are you?" Ryan's voiced jerked Duncan back to reality like a dog at the end of its leash.

He drew a breath and wet his lips. "A little."

Barnes laughed as if Duncan had made a joke.

Palmer's brain was beginning to work, slowly, painfully, unkinking like some rusty archaic machine. It was not Walford who had been killing the women in London in the guise of the West End Strangler. It was not Walford who had cast the blame on him. It was not Walford who had abducted Grayson. It was Ryan Barnes, his valet, his oldest friend and confidant. It was Ryan Barnes who had murdered both of Duncan's parents.

Shock was consumed by wrath blazing through him as if all the fires of hell had been unleashed. Fury erupted through him, spewing through his veins. His vision hazed with red, and he burst across the room in the direction of the desk.

It was the sound of the pistol being cocked that checked him in midstride. The barrel was tight against Grayson's temple, pressing so deep into her skin it would doubtless leave a bruise.

Grayson gave a breathless sob, but neither of the men looked down at her.

"You know now, don't you?" Ryan asked.

"Yes, I know. I know what you did then, and I know what you've been doing since we've been in London."

"I thought if you came here you'd remember. I'm surprised it didn't happen long ago."

"You let me live all these years thinking I had killed him, didn't you? You let me wonder and hurt and hate myself."

"What choice did I have? They wouldn't have hanged a boy like you for protecting his mam from his father's abuse. And you couldn't remember, could you? That was the beauty of it all. I knocked the memory clear out of your head."

There was a pause. Duncan wet his lips. "My father . . . did he hit her? Did he hurt her, ever?" Duncan suddenly wanted to know.

"He said he didn't, but who can say? You remember how they argued."

"So you blackened my father's name along with my own."

"I didn't mean to." There was honest regret in Ryan's face. "Your father was my best friend until the day he died."

What Ryan was saying made no sense. "My father was your best friend, and yet you killed him? Why, for God's sake, why?"

The valet shifted the barrel of his gun from Grayson's temple to a point at the apex of Duncan's chest. He could feel his skin contract over the point where the ball would lodge.

"Sit down in the wing chair. A man should have all his questions answered before his time to die."

Palmer moved backward until his calves made contact with the skirt of the chair. It was exactly where he remembered it. He felt for the tapestried arms and lowered himself into the seat.

Barnes came toward him, shifting toward Palmer's right. There was the jab of the barrel against his temple, cold metal against warm flesh. At the feel of the gun against his skin a leap of feral joy rushed through Duncan's veins. Gray was out of imminent danger. Barnes was well within reach. That had been his first priority, and he had readily accomplished it.

Across the room he could see how frightened Grayson was. She was white to the lips, and from the quiver of the lace on the bodice of her gown, he could see how fast her heart was beating.

Palmer himself was strangely calm. Now that his fury had dissipated, now that he'd learned the truth, he was possessed of a strange detachment. Like a rock high on the beach, standing alone at low tide, Duncan found that his memories had washed over and beyond him. He was numb but alert. He could listen and not assimilate, he could focus on the present and push the past aside. He was an expert at ignoring the past; he had been doing it half his life.

"Do you remember my son?" Barnes demanded in his ear.

"Your son?"

"My son, Liam."

Duncan forced his brain to work, tried to dredge up the memory of Ryan's son. It was hazy and indistinct. "Isn't he a dozen years older than I am?"

"He would have been if he'd lived."

"You never talked about him, and he was gone from the estate most of the time when I was growing up."

"Your father sent him away. Did you know that? He sent Liam away because they said he'd beaten and raped a girl, some grubby scullery maid."

"My father wouldn't have sent your son away unless he was sure the charges were true."

"I pleaded with him not to send the boy away. I begged him. I raised Liam myself after his mother died, and that made him kind of wild."

In the back of his mind Duncan did remember Liam. He'd been a bounder, a troublemaker. Liam had terrorized the younger children around the manor and many of the maids. Now that Ryan had reminded him, Duncan vaguely recalled that he'd been glad when his father sent Liam away.

"Do you know how Liam died?" Ryan Barnes went on. "Do you know what happened to him in the end?"

Duncan shook his head and felt the gun barrel scrape against his skin.

"They hanged him. They hanged him for strangling a girl in a town outside of Bath. When word came through of what had happened, I confronted your father. It was his fault, his fault, because he had sent my son away. I came to him in this very room. He was sitting behind the desk. He sat right there and watched me cry." There was a quaver in Ryan's voice, an upward slide in the tone as if his control was slipping away.

Duncan glanced sideways at Ryan's face. There were memories and madness in his eyes.

"He told me how sorry he was, Lord Jeremy did, how difficult the decision to send Liam away had been for him. The whole time he was talking, I stood there crying. I knew he couldn't see the gun in my hand, at least not until I raised it toward him.

"He got up from the chair and came around the desk. He said I didn't want to shoot him. He told me he'd see that the boy got a decent burial. As if that would have been enough. Your father raised his hand and told me to give him the gun. He said I was crazed with grief, that I'd regret it if I hurt him. But I didn't regret it, not then. Not afterward, either. He killed my boy, just as if he'd strung him up himself."

"My mother heard the shot and came to see what had happened, didn't she?" Duncan asked as the shrouded images that had assailed him began to clear.

"I was sorry about what I had to do to her. She'd always been kind to me, to Liam. But she knew what I'd done. She knew I'd killed your father.

"Then I heard you come into the house, heard you call to her. I heard you, and I knew I had to hurry. I dragged her to the settee, and put her down. You were coming up the stairs, so I hid behind the door. It was then it came to me what I must do. I had to make them believe that you had killed your father. I had to make you think it, too. It was the only chance I had."

"So you hit me," Duncan murmured, "and placed the gun in my hand."

"And when the others began to gather, it was easy enough to make them believe exactly what I wanted them to. They had heard your parents arguing earlier in the evening. They knew how violent those arguments were. They'd cleaned up the aftermath often enough."

"How did you explain the fact that I was unconscious on the floor?"

"The constable explained it for me. He said your father must have pushed against you as he fell, and that you hit your head somehow. It was a simple explanation, really. I couldn't have come up with a better one."

"But why did you stay with me? Why did you agree to accompany me to my uncle's in America?"

"I was afraid that someday you'd remember what you'd seen. That I'd be called to account. And I wanted to get away. I wanted to go as far away from here as I could go. When Mr. Walford offered me the opportunity to travel with you, I jumped at it. I stayed with you from fear and because I had no place else to go. I stayed because I wanted to find a way to end all this with you."

Everything was falling into place. Ryan's recitation was nearly at an end. There was only one more thing to ask.

"And was making me think I was the West End Strangler your way to end this? Why did you wait so long?"

Palmer could hear Ryan draw an uneven breath, felt the valet's exhalation brush past his ear. "You were under your uncle Farleigh's protection in America. He didn't let me near you more than he could help. He thought he could make you remember what happened by keeping us apart, but it didn't work. You came to me more often than he knew, with questions about what had happened, with your guilt and grief."

"And instead of helping me remember, you reinforced everything you wanted me to believe."

Ryan nodded. "Then you were away at school and going out on your uncle's ships. It seemed impossible to me that the memories of that night would never return, but you seemed as eager to block them out as I was for you to forget them. Still, I couldn't take the chance that one day everything would come back to you."

"And when we put into Portsmouth for repairs, the time was finally right."

"It was like a sign. I'd been planning my revenge for years. I knew exactly what I had to do. I wanted to see you hanged for killing a woman, just as Liam was. I wanted to destroy you, make you think you were mad. And now it's happened. Now everyone thinks you are the West End Strangler. They have all the proof they need."

Duncan paused before he spoke, glancing across to where Grayson sat. How could he let her know what he was about to do? How could he warn her and make certain she wasn't hurt? Gray looked utterly terrified.

"The police have cleared my name."

"No."

"They know I'm not the Strangler."

The muzzle of the gun bit hard into his temple, and Barnes's voice began to fray. "But you're going to write a complete confession before you die. You're going to say you did it."

A dozen heartbeats passed before Duncan spoke.

"No, Ryan. I'm not."

As he said the words, Duncan threw all his weight on the right arm of the chair. It wobbled and went over sideways, knocking Ryan down. Duncan let the momentum carry him onto the smaller man, let his heavier body pin his valet to the floor. But before Palmer could completely subdue him, Barnes scrambled away. Duncan lunged at him, closing his fingers around the wrist that held the gun, forcing the barrel upward, away from their thrashing bodies. They rolled across the floor, locked in mortal combat. They crashed into a table, knocked over another chair.

They floundered toward the desk as Duncan struggled to find a disabling hold. Barnes was far stronger than he looked. He twisted his gun hand out of Duncan's grip and slammed it down in an arc that ended in a hard clout behind Palmer's ear. The blow made a galaxy of stars swirl past Duncan's eyes, and the cut from earlier in the evening began to bleed.

Palmer heard Grayson scream his name just as the gun came down again. Blindly he reached out to catch Ryan's arm, snagging the fabric of his sleeve. The gun lowered an inch or two, and he heard Grayson shout again. With a whipcord movement, Duncan forced Barnes back the opposite way, toward the center of the room. Freeing his other hand, Palmer tried to rip the gun from Ryan's fingers, but the valet's grip was as tight as a vise around the stock.

From the corner of his eye, Duncan caught a movement in the doorway as a dozen pairs of boots came crowding into the room.

"Cease and desist in the name of the Crown," someone shouted, and both men froze where they were, sprawled in the center of the floor.

Duncan looked up to see a uniformed constable heading the throng. Beside him stood Hannibal Frasier, wearing a grin that reached the tips of his side whiskers. Slowly Duncan and Barnes untangled themselves and came to their feet. In the face of a full dozen weapons, there was little else they could do.

"That one there's his lordship Duncan Palmer," Frasier announced with a jab of his finger. "And this one here—"

"Is London's West End Strangler," Duncan finished for him.

Barnes stood trembling in the center of the room, the pistol drooping at his side.

The constable came a step closer to where Ryan stood, though the officer kept a good distance between them still. "I arrest you in the name of the Crown for the crime of murder," he announced. "Please surrender your weapon."

With the situation well in hand, Duncan turned his head to where Grayson sat. She was slumped in the chair, weak with relief, breathing more easily, he'd wager, than she had in several days.

He was beginning to turn to go to her when he caught the shadow of a movement to his right. He snapped around and reached out instinctively just as Ryan raised the gun. It came up in a blur of dark and light, the polished barrel shimmering. Duncan made a snatch for Ryan's hand and missed, then watched with a terrible, tearing helplessness as the valet shoved the muzzle of the pistol into the depths of his own mouth.

"No!" Duncan cried, as the sound of the shot exploded in the silent room.

He closed his eyes so he would not have to watch the body fall, so he would not have to acknowledge what Barnes had done. Yet Duncan knew. Rather than face his crimes, Barnes had chosen to end his life.

Sickness swept through him as he realized that, only a moment before, Ryan had been alive. Now there was nothing left of him.

Duncan swayed and someone steadied him. Then Grayson was at his side. Her hand was on his arm. Her fingers were stroking his face, his hair, the side of his neck.

"Come with me, Duncan. Come with me, please."

He nodded, too numb to resist. He didn't care where she was taking him. He didn't care about anything at all.

The way parted. They left the study and moved slowly down the stairs. He felt at least a hundred years old, stunned, exhausted, aching in every bone and sinew. He had been born in this house and had almost died here. He had been condemned and exonerated within these walls. He had been scorned and hated and comforted. Everything this house had been to him, it was no more. Everything he knew about himself had abruptly changed. He could hardly take it in.

They made it as far as the steps outside the rear door, and sank down together on the well-worn stone. The night was cold around them. The world was edging toward dawn.

Instinctively Duncan turned to her and felt Gray pull him close. She wrapped her arms around his shoulders and turned his face into her hair. He closed his eyes and clung to her, not feeling, not thinking, not wanting to. They sat like that for a long, long time.

Frasier came to drape blankets around their shoulders, left glasses of brandy beside them on the steps. They never acknowledged his presence, never looked up, never stopped holding and touching and holding.

The wind feathered the grass at the crest of the cliff. The trees around them began to stir. Birdsong pierced the quiet, the raucous crow of the gulls, the lilting call of the lark. The night faded. The sky grayed. The breakers crashed far below them on the deserted, rocky beach. More time passed, an instant or an eternity.

Finally Duncan drew a long, slow breath and raised his head. "Are you all right?" he asked her.

Gray nodded once. "Are you?"

"I don't know," he answered with a shaky laugh. "My life's all turned around, and I'm not sure I know what to make of all that's happened."

"You mean about Ryan and your parents."

He shifted away from her, looking out across the cove. The faint line that separated sky from water was not visible at such an early hour of the day. It lay far in the distance, lost in a hazy blur. It frustrated him somehow not to know where heaven ended and earth began.

"For years I lived with my disgrace, with the belief that I had killed my father, that my mother had died with his hands around her throat. I believed that my parents' love for each other was a sham, that their love for me was little more.

"I've depended on Quentin for many years, and now he's paid for his plots against me with his life. Everything in my world has changed in a single night, and I don't know what I should think or feel or believe."

Duncan shook his head before he went on. "And all my life I thought Ryan Barnes was my friend. I trusted him, depended on him. . . ."

Duncan's throat worked convulsively as if he fought to keep any further admissions inside himself.

"And you loved him?" Gray suggested.

He wouldn't look at her. He wouldn't answer, couldn't answer.

"You did love him, didn't you?"

From the strain around his mouth, the shine in his eyes, Gray could guess at the terrible ambivalence that was tearing Duncan apart.

"Now that I know the truth," he finally said, "just what is it I'm supposed to feel? Ryan killed my parents. He did his best to destroy me. He worked at it every day of my life for seventeen years."

"But he didn't succeed."

"No." The word sounded tentative, as if Duncan wasn't quite sure how well he'd survived.

"What do you think you should feel?"

"I should hate him. I should be glad he is dead. I should want to dance on his grave."

"But you don't."

"No." Duncan rubbed his palms together until the friction might well have set tinder ablaze.

"Duncan, tell me what you feel."

"I hate how my parents died. It was so useless, so horrible, so wasteful. I'm sorry Quentin's dead, even though he did betray me." He turned to her with shame in his face. "And I mourn for Ryan, too. I didn't want him to kill himself. I tried to stop him."

"I know you did. You did everything you could." She laid a hand against his knee, offering reassurance.

"I'm so angry with him. I feel like a fool. I let myself be used, manipulated."

As difficult as it was, Grayson kept silent.

"I used to talk to him about how I felt, about what I thought. I listened to his advice, gave credence to what he said. And all of it was lies."

"Was it?"

"It was based on a lie, the most basic of all lies: the lie that I had killed my father."

"Then there was no truth in anything Ryan said. You never reaped any benefit from all the years you spent with him. He never gave you any reason for feeling all the things you feel now that he's dead."

"Well, I . . ."

She reached across to take one of his hands. His palm was hot against her own. "Ryan was a man obsessed by dark, sinister emotions that you and I will never understand. He was mad, eaten alive by his need for revenge. He sowed vengeance and reaped disaster. But in between, Duncan, is it possible there were some moments of good? Isn't it possible that in all the years you thought he was your friend, he gave you some reason to feel the emotions you're feeling now?"

He sat silent for a very long time, staring out at the horizon as if whatever he saw in the shifting mist might help him understand. She followed his gaze toward the point where the sky and the water met. He stared at it as if it were the end of the earth, as if he were willing himself into that plane of shifting nothingness. He looked so tortured sitting there, so weary, so desperately vulnerable.

But as they watched the horizon, the line became less hazy, more distinct. The water was flat, calm, the color of molten lead. Above it the mist was lifting. A sliver of glowing orange sun seeped above the sea, turning the soft pale violet sky far off to the east warm and faintly pink. The brightness cast a glimmer of apricot across the waves, tinted the expanse above it with mauve and gold.

Gray came to her feet beside her husband and dropped the blanket to the ground. Still holding Duncan's hand in hers, she pulled him up to stand beside her. "Will you walk with me?"

In silence they moved away from the house with all its dark associations, with all its hurtful memories. They approached the crest of the cliff, across the dew-wet grass that had begun to sparkle and shimmer in the waxing light. They moved toward the spear of land that jutted out into the open sea, and the freshness rose around them, crisp and sweet.

When they reached the end of the headland, Gray knew it was time to speak.

"The night is over, Duncan," she offered softly. "It's time to embrace the dawn. What you believed you were once is behind you now. What happened then is over. Today can be a new beginning for both of us, if only you can bring yourself to forget the past and go on from here."

Duncan stood at the end of the promontory, still looking out to sea. "Is it really as simple as that, Grayson? Is it really as easy as turning away?"

With a stroke of her hand against his jaw she turned his face to hers. "It is as easy or as difficult as you choose to make it for yourself. But whatever you decide, Duncan, remember that I'm here with you, that no matter what course you choose, I'll always love you."

He raised a hand to smooth her hair, let the backs of his fingers trail down her cheek, traced his thumb along the silken curve of her throat. She shivered at his touch, at the feel of his hands on her skin, at the love and fear that lay banked in the depths of his eyes.

Then deep inside him some resistance seemed to crumble away. She could feel it in the tremor that racked his limbs. She could see it in the fleeting pain and sudden peace that seemed to settle over his features. A slow, thin smile lifted the corners of his mouth, and his eyes caught the life from the gleaming sky, turning as bright and clear as crystal rain, as fierce and blue as summer skies. The warmth of the sunrise touched gold to the bones of his face, shading the wedge of his high cheekbones, brushing the square of his chin, highlighting the plain above his brows. In his face, serenity came to replace the turmoil, belief came to banish the disillusionment.

He drew her close against his chest, and together they turned to stare out at the ripening color in the sky. The wind rose around them, cool and brisk, whisking away the sadness, the remnants of his doubts, the last impediments to Duncan's acceptance of himself.

"Oh, Gray," he whispered as he drew her closer still. "I love you. I love you with all my heart."

The day came to life around them. The night was gone. The future lay before them, fierce and bright and beckoning.

Author's Note

Sometimes a writer gets an idea for a story that just won't let go. It haunts you; it pesters you until you reach a point where you just can't ignore it any longer. For me *Midnight Lace* was that kind of a story. Duncan and Grayson have been with me in one form or another since 1981. They've been sitting patiently in my office, waiting for their chance to appear on the glowing green screen, waiting for me to mature enough as a writer to tackle the complexity of their tale. I didn't know until fairly recently who the West End Strangler was. But once he revealed himself to me, I felt I had to accept the challenge of trying something new.

Midnight Lace is a bit of a departure for me because, unlike my other books, this one does not rely on historical incidents to drive the plot. I have tried, however, to infuse this book with all the texture and rich detail usually found in what I write. I hope I have succeeded.

The early years of Victoria's reign are not as well documented as the later ones and hence are somewhat more difficult to depict in a work of historical fiction. It was a period of sweeping changes, caught, not only in time but in attitudes, between the regimented but somewhat open age of the Regency and the excessive but straightlaced later Victorian Age. I feel I would never have been able to capture the feeling of London in 1844 without the splendid work by John W. Dodds, *The Age of Paradox: A Biography of England 1841–1851*. A deliciously readable volume, it deals with everything from the way the streets of London looked and smelled to the social injustices and political issues of the day. Two other books—*Victorian London* by Priscilla Metcalf and Elizabeth Burton's work, *The Pageant of Early*

Victorian England—were also of help to me in re-creating another time and place far distant from our own.

Reading historical fiction is as close as we can come, in this day and age, to traveling in time. With any luck at all I have had the opportunity to transport you, for a few hours at least, to an era that is gone and to adventures and romance of which most of us can only dream.

Elizabeth Kary
Box 30026
St. Louis, Missouri 63119
December 1989